Javier Sierra lives in Spain, where he is a celebrated radio and television presenter, and one of the most outstanding authors on the Spanish literary scene. He is the author of *The Secret Supper*.

Praise for Javier Sierra:

'*The Secret Supper*, which has sold more than 500,000 copies in Europe, is set to rival *The Da Vinci Code* for conspiracy theories about one of the most famous figures in art history' *Sunday Telegraph*

'Another religious conspiracy thriller – *The Secret Supper* looks set to sweep the world' *Guardian*

'Javier Sierra, unlike Dan Brown, is familiar with the Catholic Church and does not calumniate its institutions . . . *The Secret Supper* asks more of its reader than *The Da Vinci Code* does' *Tablet*

'[*The Secret Supper*] differs [from Dan Brown] in featuring not present-day investigators, but a monkish sleuth in Italy in 1497. Agostino Leyre, a Dominican inquisitor, is sent to Milan to look into rumours of a heretical movement whose initiates may include the Duke of Milan and Da Vinci, working on *The Last Supper* . . . the passages on art are provocative and absorbing' *Sunday Times*

'*The Lady in Blue* is the haunting and evocative tale of the triumph of modern spirit and science over a 400-year-old conspiracy. Javier Sierra's groundbreaking historical research opens our eyes to a world we thought we knew, and revisits, in a surprising way, the devastating clash between Catholic Europe and the far more ancient world of the American Southwest' Katherine Neville, bestselling author of *The Eight* and *The Magic Circle*

Also by Javier Sierra

The Secret Supper

JAVIER SIERRA

The Lady in Blue

LONDON • SYDNEY • NEW YORK • TORONTO

First published in Great Britain by Simon & Schuster UK Ltd, 2007
This edition published by Pocket Books UK, 2008
An imprint of Simon & Schuster UK Ltd
A CBS COMPANY

Translated by James Graham

1 3 5 7 9 10 8 6 4 2

Simon & Schuster UK Ltd
Africa House
64-78 Kingsway
London WC2B 6AH

www.simonsays.co.uk

Simon & Schuster Australia
Sydney

A CIP catalogue record for this book is available from the British Library

ISBN 978-1-84739-235-0

Printed and bound in Great Britain by
Cox & Wyman, Reading, Berkshire

To the nuns at
the Concepción de Ágreda monastery,
in memory of that providential encounter
on April 14, 1991

And to Carol Sabick and J. J. Benítez,
opportune "instruments" of the Programmer

Le hasard, c'est peut-être le pseudonyme de Dieu, quant il ne veut pas signer.

[Chance is perhaps the pseudonym of God when he does not wish to sign his work.]

—Théophile Gautier, *La Croix de Berny*

Bilocation, *n.*, the fact or power of being in two places at the same time.

—*The Compact Edition of the Oxford English Dictionary*

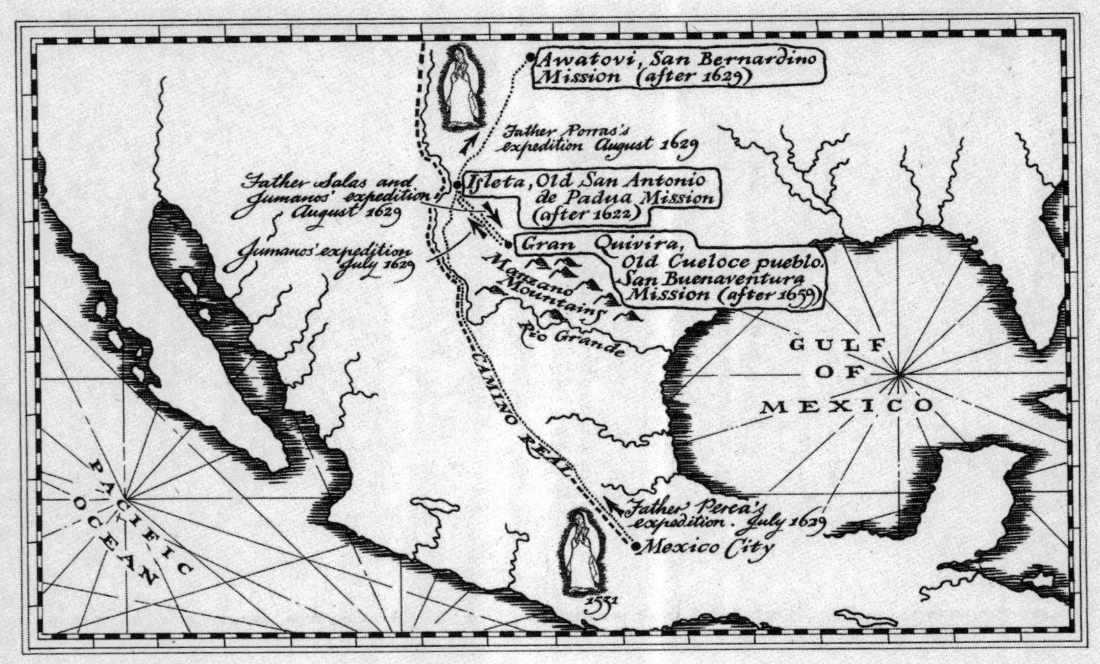
Awatovi, San Bernardino Mission (after 1629)
Father Porras's expedition August 1629
Father Salas and Jumanos' expedition August 1629
Isleta, Old San Antonio de Padua Mission (after 1622)
Jumanos' expedition July 1629
Gran Quivira, Old Cueloce pueblo. San Buenaventura Mission (after 1659)
Manzano Mountains
Rio Grande
CAMINO REAL
GULF OF MEXICO
Father Perea's expedition. July 1629
Mexico City
1531
PACIFIC OCEAN

BAY OF BISCAY
FRANCE
Carrión de los Condes
Moncayo Mountain
Ágreda
Laguna de Cameros
Sierra de Cameros
Madrid
MEDITERRANEAN SEA

ONE

VENICE, ITALY
SPRING 1991

Treading with a light step, Father Giuseppe Baldi left the Piazza San Marco at sunset.

As was his custom, he walked along the canal to the Riva degli Schiavoni, where he took the first vaporetto headed to San Giorgio Maggiore. The island that appeared on every postcard of Venice was once upon a time the property of his religious order, and the old priest always regarded it with nostalgia. Time had brought many changes. *Omnia mutantur.* Everything was subject to change these days. Even a faith with two thousand years of history behind it.

Baldi consulted his wristwatch, undid the last button of his habit, and, while scanning the boat for a seat close to the window, took the opportunity to clean the lenses of his tiny, wire-rimmed glasses. "*Pater noster qui es in caelis* . . . ," he murmured in Latin.

With his glasses on, the Benedictine watched as the city of four hundred bridges stretched out before him, tinged a deep orange.

". . . *sanctificetur nomen tuum* . . ."

Without interrupting his prayer, the priest admired the evening as he glanced discreetly to either side.

"Everything as it should be," he thought to himself.

The vaporetto, the familiar water bus used by Venetians to get from place to place, was almost empty at this hour. Only a few Japanese and three scholarship students whom Baldi recognized as being from the Giorgio Cini Foundation seemed interested in the ride.

"Why am I still doing this?" he asked himself. "Why am I still watching the other six-o'clock passengers out of the corners of my eyes, as if I was going to find that one of them was carrying a journalist's camera? Haven't I already spent enough years holed up on this island, far from them?"

Fourteen minutes later, the water bus dropped him off on an ugly concrete dock. A gust of cold air burst in as he opened the cabin door, and everyone braced against the night air. No one paid any attention as he disembarked.

In his heart of hearts, Baldi cherished his undisturbed life on the island. When he arrived at his cell, he would wash, change his shoes, eat dinner with the community, and then bury himself in reading or correcting exams. He had followed that daily ritual since he had arrived at the abbey nineteen years before. Nineteen years of peace and tranquillity, certainly. But he was always on guard, waiting for a call, a letter, or an unannounced visit. That was his punishment. The kind of load that is never lifted from one's shoulders.

Baldi restrained himself from giving in to his obsession.

Was there a more agreeable life than the one his studies afforded him? He knew the answer was no. His various duties as professor of pre-polyphony at the Benedetto Marcello Conservatory allowed him the peace of mind that had always eluded him as a young man. His students were hardworking. They attended his lectures with moderate enthusiasm and listened as he explained the music of the first millennium, spicing his lectures with interesting anecdotes. In short, they respected him. The faculty admired him as well, even though he sometimes missed classes because he was absorbed in his research.

And yet, such a stress-free environment never managed to distract him from his other pursuits. They were so "confidential" and long-standing that he had rarely even mentioned them to anyone.

Baldi had come to San Giorgio in 1972, exiled for crimes owing to music. The Cini Foundation offered him more than he would have dared to request from his superior: one of the best libraries in Europe; a convention center that on more than one occasion had hosted UNESCO conferences; and two scholarly institutions dedicated to Venetian music and ethnomusicology that so intoxicated him. To a certain extent, it was logical that the Benedictines had made the effort to create that paradise of musicology at San Giorgio. Who if not the brothers of the Order of Saint Benedict would busy themselves with such devotion to that ancient art? Was it not Saint Benedict himself who, once he had established the rules for his order in the sixth century, went on to create the fundamentals of modern musical science?

Baldi had studied the subject thoroughly. He was the first, for example, to appreciate that Saint Benedict's decree, which required all members of his order to attend eight religious services a day, was based entirely on music. A fascinating secret. In fact, the prayers that he and his brothers recited daily were inspired by the "modes" still employed in the composition of melodies. Baldi proved that matins (the prayers said at two in the morning during wintertime) corresponded to the note do, and lauds, recited at dawn, corresponded to re. The offices of the first, the third, and the sixth hours, performed at six, nine, and twelve noon, corresponded to mi, fa, and sol. And the hour of strongest light, none, at three in the afternoon, corresponded to la, while the prayers recited at dusk, during the setting of the sun, corresponded to ti.

That was the class that had made him famous among his students. "Notes and hours are related!" he would boom from his podium. "To pray and to compose are parallel activities! Music is the true language of God!"

And yet Baldi the old soldier had still other discoveries hidden in his study. His thesis was astounding. He believed, for example, that the ancients not only knew harmony and applied it, via mathematics, to music, but that harmony was capable of provoking altered states of consciousness that permitted priests and initiates in the classical world to gain access to "superior" realms of reality. He defended his idea over the course of decades, doing battle with those who asserted that such sensations of spiritual elevation were always brought about by means of hallucinatory drugs, sacred mushrooms, or other psychotropic substances.

"And how exactly did they 'use' music?" Baldi would ask rhetorically, becoming more animated. He admitted that for the wise men of history it was enough to develop a mental "wavelength" adequate for the reception of information from "far away." It was said that in this state, those adept in magic could reawaken any moment in the past, no matter how remote. Put another way, according to Baldi, music modulated the frequency of our brain waves, stimulating centers of perception capable of navigating through time.

But these techniques, he explained with great resignation, had been lost.

While many questioned Baldi's outlandish ideas, even the fiercest polemics had in no way soured his jovial and friendly outlook. His silver hair, athletic deportment, and honest face gave him the look of an irresistible conqueror. No one seriously believed he was seventy-five years old. In fact, had it not been for his vow of chastity, Baldi would have broken the hearts of many of his female students.

That day, serenely unaware of the events that were about to unfold, Baldi smiled as he entered the Benedictine residence, walking at his usual lively pace. He hardly even noticed Brother Roberto waiting for him in the doorway, looking as if he had something urgent to tell him.

TWO

GRAN QUIVIRA, NEW MEXICO
362 YEARS EARLIER

Sakmo fell to his knees, a prisoner of fear. His muscular frame crumpled to the ground as shadows took possession of his soul. No matter how much he opened his eyes or rubbed them, the young warrior could not discern so much as a single strand of light. An indescribable vision had blinded him. Now he was left in darkness, alone at the cleft in the rock sacred to his tribe. The intimate terror that had dimmed his sight had also left him unable to raise a shout. Never in all his nights of keeping watch over the village had he confronted anything like it.

Feeling his way along the ground, not daring to turn away from the brilliant light that only now ceased blinding him, Sakmo tried to escape from the mouth of the Canyon of the Serpent. He should never have come near it. The narrow opening between rocks that led to the crest of the hill was cursed. His people all knew this. The five generations of shamans, witch doctors, and medicine men buried there had stated that this was the only place for miles around where one could commune with the ancestral spirits. It was indeed a fearful place. Why had he let himself be led there? What had possessed him to be lured toward the passage, a half circle in the Rock of the Initiates, if he knew of its dangers? And besides, the rock lay well beyond the area where he was keeping watch.

It was still three hours before dawn. Then they would relieve him of his post, or find him dead. Sakmo remained tense, breathing hard, his senses sharp and a flood of questions surging through his brain.

What sort of light is capable of knocking a Jumano warrior down with a single blow? A bolt of lightning? Could one of its sparks hide itself in the rock and then attack a man? And what next? Would it go on to devour him?

The sentinel was unable to wrestle his thoughts under control. Then, in the middle of his awkward escape, he noticed that the meadow had become completely silent. Not a good omen, he said to himself, and his mind entered the dangerous terrain of irrationality. Would the light pursue him? The memory, still fresh in his mind, jolted him. The fire that had left him cowering in the dark looked as if it issued from the jaws of a monster. A trickster fox who could level the meadow with a single breath. That was how his tribe's prophecies spoke of the end of the world: their universe would instantly perish in flames; a brilliant flash of light preceding the destruction of all forms of life. The catastrophic collapse of the Fourth World.

If what had taken place in the narrow passage was a signal of the end, nothing and no one could stop it.

Was it useless to run and sound the alarm?

And how could he, blinded as he was?

Sakmo was bewildered to find himself entertaining such cowardly thoughts. It took him a minute to understand what had happened, for the intruder was unlike anything he had ever experienced. The dazzling light that had seared his eyes had broken forth from the gap in the rocks without warning. What action could he take against such an enemy? Could another warrior in the village stop it? Perhaps it was better that his wife, his daughter, Ankti, and his people, would all die before they awakened. And what would become of him?

"Ankti," he whispered.

In the shadows, drowning in utter silence, the warrior spun around to face the rock he had left behind him. If he was going to die, he reflected in a fraction of a second, he would do it like a man. On his feet, looking straight at his executioner. Perhaps someone in the future would remember him as the first sacrifice to the Monster of the End of Time.

Sakmo was completely unprepared for what happened next.

A brief phrase, enunciated slowly, broke the vast silence of the meadow. The voice was friendly and gentle, and called him by name.

"Are you all right, Sakmo?"

The question, perfectly phrased in Tanoan, froze him where he stood. Disconcerted, he frowned, while his hand moved instinctively toward the obsidian hatchet on his belt.

Sakmo had been trained by his father, the great Walpi, head of the tribal settlement of Cueloce, as a protector of the living. Not of the dead.

"Sakmo!"

This time the voice reproved him with greater force.

Thoughts of his brave father made him grit his teeth and prepare to defend his life with the sharp edge of his blade. Be it of this world or another, no light with the power of speech would finish him off without leaving some trace of itself on the red earth.

"Sakmo . . ."

As he listened to the sound of that voice for the third time, his hatchet traced a circle of defense in the air around him. His eyes were still closed. "Good-bye, Ankti," he murmured. Whoever or whatever was calling out to him was already at hand. Sakmo could feel its breath and its unbearable heat. His weapon trembling in his left hand, the sentinel lifted his face proudly and awaited the inevitable. Opening his reddened eyes, directing his gaze toward the darkness of the sky, he sensed a silhouette, large as a totem, looming above him. A dire thought crossed his mind: it was a woman! A cursed female spirit was about to put an end to his life.

Years before, in that very spot beside the Cueloce well, his father had prepared to die in battle.

THREE

LOS ANGELES, CALIFORNIA
SPRING 1991

"This dream keeps recurring?"

Dr. Meyers leaned toward the couch where her patient was reclining, to observe her expression. Jennifer Narody, plagued by a persistent anxiety complex, had been having therapy sessions at Meyers's plush office in the heart of the financial district for only two days. Linda Meyers was disconcerted: her patient appeared to be a thirty-four-year-old woman of sound mind, a sports fan with no family history of mental illness. In short, she was a well-balanced, financially secure, attractive individual. She had never been married; she was not in a long-term relationship, nor did it seem that she needed to be; and she got on well with her parents. Judging from appearances, she was a woman without serious problems.

"Yes. I had the same dream two times in three days," Jennifer said in a barely audible voice. She avoided the inquisitive stare of her psychiatrist by tossing her long mane of brown hair off her shoulders."It's not a nightmare, you know? But every time I lie down to sleep, I think it's going to start all over again. And that's getting to me."

"When was the last time you had it?"

"This morning! That's why I asked to see you so early. I can still see it . . ."

"Are you taking the medication I prescribed?"

"Of course, but Valium has no effect on me. What I can't understand, Doctor, is why the image of that glowing woman still obsesses me. You know what I mean? I see her everywhere. I need to get her out of my head!"

"Have you dreamed of her at other times?"

"Yes."

"Okay, but you shouldn't worry." As she tried to calm her patient, she quickly scribbled something on her notepad. "We'll find a way to get the better of this recurring dream. Are you afraid?"

"Yes, Doctor. And worried."

"Tell me, have you experienced any recent traumatic incident, such as a traffic accident or the loss of a loved one? Something that could have provoked a bout of depression or a fit of anxiety?"

Jennifer closed her eyes. She took a deep breath and slowly let it out, concentrating in her search for the right answer.

"Well, I returned from a long stay in Europe a few weeks ago. As soon as I got back to Los Angeles, I started having the dreams again. And this time they were so vivid and so insistent that I had no doubt I was seeing her again. At first I thought it had to do with the shift in time zones, or the change in surroundings."

"Then the dreams returned? You mean you experienced similar things in the past?"

"I told you, Doctor. Years ago I had dreams about the Indians and this mysterious lady bathed in blue light. But I have no idea why!"

"Tell me, Jennifer, what part of Europe did you visit?"

"Rome."

"The Rome of Caesar and the Popes, of pasta and Frascati wine?"

"Yes, have you ever been there?"

"No, but I'd love to go someday."

"Really?"

"Absolutely, but my husband is Argentinian. His family comes from Galicia in northern Spain, so every time we travel to Europe we end up staying in La Coruña, where his grandparents live."

"You never flew over to Italy? It's so close."

"No." Linda Meyers laughed. "I spend the whole time trying to speak Spanish to his family."

Jennifer seemed suddenly melancholy, as though her mind was elsewhere.

"It's too bad," she finally ventured. "Rome is such a great city. The piazzas and markets, the narrow, winding streets, the steaming cappuccinos and dolce farniente."

Meyers took note of the sudden change in her patient's mood, and waited a moment before formulating her next question. Sometimes a memory or a landscape serves to open a breach in a patient's subconscious. Perhaps in some recent experience that her patient had in Rome she could find the key that would shed light on her case. And so, with exquisite tact, she decided to move down that unexpected road.

"Did anything happen in Rome that you want to talk about, Jennifer?"

"What do you mean?"

The liquid green eyes of her patient became wary.

"I have no idea," the doctor responded. "You tell me. Repetitive dreams are sometimes born of small obsessions, or unfinished business, all the worries that our brain tries to overcome by whatever means at its disposal."

"There were many things like that in Rome, Doctor. I left a good deal of unfinished business behind in Italy."

"Tell me about it."

This time Jennifer sought out her psychiatrist's dark eyes. The evident sincerity of her features, set in a wide ebony face crowned with soft frizzy hair elegantly pulled back, had given Jennifer confidence from the first time they met. Simply by looking at Dr. Meyers without saying a word, she was able to let her therapist know that this was going to be a long story.

"Take your time, Jennifer," Dr. Meyers said, smiling. "I love Italy."

FOUR

VENICE

"Good evening, Father."

As he passed through the gates of the abbey, San Giorgio's porter greeted Baldi with one of his officious smiles. Fair warning.

"I left the mail in your cell," Brother Roberto announced with a flourish. "You're in luck. Three big envelopes."

"Nothing else?"

"Isn't that enough, Father? The ones you're always waiting for. You know, from the saints."

Baldi raised his brows in mild disapproval at Brother Roberto's unhealthy curiosity, and then hurried toward the stairs without a word. "The ones you're always waiting for." The old musicologist hesitated between steps. ". . . from the saints."

"Hold on!" shouted the round-faced young monk, a cherub out of a Rubens painting. He was waving a piece of paper in the air. "They called you today, too, not once but twice."

"Who?" Baldi yelled down from the landing. He was in a hurry.

"They didn't leave a name. But there was a meeting. In Rome."

"Then they'll call again."

Baldi had already forgotten about the calls by the time he got to his room. He was happy to find his mail exactly where Brother Roberto had said he left it. Of all his mail, three packages stood out: two from Rome, and a third from an industrial city in the north of Spain. They had been sent by "Saint Matthew," "Saint John," and "Saint Mark." In fact, they were exactly the type of mail he was waiting for. The letters from the "saints."

Those missives were the only connection to his previous life, a life no one at San Giorgio knew anything about. They arrived irregularly, rarely in groups of two, but never before had there been three at once. Realizing that his three colleagues had all felt the need to write him at the same time, he passed suddenly from happiness into a state of alarm.

But there was another, more urgent reason to be startled. It was a sepia envelope bearing the unmistakable seal of the Secretariat of State of His Holiness the Pope. It had been stamped and dated two days before in Vatican City, and was postmarked Special Delivery. Baldi set aside the mail from the "saints" and focused on that one small envelope.

"And this?" he said under his breath. The two calls from Rome began to haunt him.

Fearing the worst, Baldi ran his fingers over the envelope before opening it. When he at last slit it open, a letter on thick, official stationery fell into his hands.

"Dear Saint Luke," he read. "You must immediately cease all aspects of your investigation. The Holy Father's scientific advisers request your presence in Rome so as to clarify the details of your latest indiscretion. Do not delay your visit beyond this Sunday. Contact the secretary of the Congregation for the Doctrine of the Faith, or in his absence, the Institute for External Affairs. They will give you more details." It was signed, incredibly, "Cardinal Zsidiv."

He could barely breathe. It was Thursday, and they wanted to see him in Rome before Sunday!

But there was something even worse than the extreme rush. Unless his memory failed him—and it was usually reliable—this was just the second time in nineteen years that they had rebuked him for an "indiscretion." He had paid for the first with his exile to this island in Venice. What price would he pay for the second?

FIVE

GRAN QUIVIRA, NEW MEXICO
SPRING 1629

Sakmo decided to attack.

But before the warrior could face his assailant and split open its head with his hatchet, a second flash of light arrived. His eyes barely had time to register the tall, mysterious silhouette that was now gazing at him when a gust of wind, as hard as a piece of dry wood, knocked him backward to the ground.

"Sakmo," the voice repeated.

His end was near. He could feel it now. Life would slip away from him in the time it took a breath to escape his body.

What would become of his family?

And his tribe?

What awaited him on the other shore of life?

The valley was once again overflowing with a mysterious, almost tangible clarity. The warrior, meanwhile, lay on the ground while the light fell all around him. The nearby houses of Cueloce, all of stone, the Cemetery of the Ancestors, the great kiva in whose underground recesses his people held their ceremonies, even the banks of the three lakes remained bathed in a blue glow. A humming noise, a thousand times louder than a multitude of locusts, was ringing in his ears, plunging him into despair. Was this what they call death?

The tremendous humming filled everything, even his body, with its pulse.

Seconds later, his hunter's strength failing him, he lost all awareness that his enemy was close by, as darkness took hold of his mind.

And, then, silence.

When the young warrior came to, his face was covered with scratches, and he had no idea how much time had passed. His head throbbed. His hatchet lay a short distance away, but he did not have the strength to crawl over to recover it.

"Dear Sakmo . . ."

The voice that had terrified him thundered from above once again. It seemed as if it came from everywhere.

"Why did you run away from me?"

Disoriented, the son of Walpi took care not to respond. Still lying facedown on the ground, he summoned his courage to decide on a course of action. His small stone knife, the same one he used to skin animals, was fastened to his belt.

A warrior's instincts ran though his veins once again.

"I have made a long voyage to be with you," the voice said, more hesitant with each word. "You have nothing to fear. I will not harm you."

The voice of the spirit was serene, sincere. It spoke the same dialect as he did. And it did so directly, with no sense of haste. Sakmo noticed that the locusts were no longer humming and the light itself had become softer, allowing him to open his eyes gradually and once again take hold of his fate.

At first they appeared to be spots, and then blurry outlines, and finally, after a few moments, Sakmo was able to distinguish a thin line of red ants traveling beneath his face.

He could see again.

It was then, once he had turned over, that he saw his enemy's face clearly for the first time.

"By all my ancestors . . . ," he muttered.

Floating above him, a few inches away, was the form of a woman, just as he had intuited. The figure seemed almost like a wood carving, and yet, a living being, with large, clear eyes. He had never seen skin so white. She was holding her hands apart; her fingers were smooth and delicate. And her clothes were the most unusual he had ever seen. What particularly struck his attention was the vivid blue cloak that covered her dark hair, and the thick rope around her waist, which held her garments securely. The woman smiled, as if taking pity on him.

"Do you know what day it is?"

The question only confused Sakmo. The spirit had spoken without moving her lips. He remained silent.

"The year of Our Lord sixteen hundred and twenty-nine. It has taken me a long time to find you, Sakmo. Now you will help me."

"Help you . . . ? "

Sakmo touched his belt, felt for his knife, and slowly pulled it out of its sheath, concealing it with his arm. The woman whose skin exuded light seemed to radiate gentleness. He no longer had any doubt: Sakmo was face-to-face with the Blue Spirit of the Plains. His father had spoken to him about her once.

"Is this the end of the world?"

The woman, without moving her lips, became even more resplendent when she heard the sentinel's question.

"Not yet, my son. I have come to announce something to the people of your village. But someone like you was needed. Do you understand? There is very little time, Sakmo, before the arrival of the true God. You must prepare your people. Only you can keep blood from being shed."

"Are you going to kill me?" he asked, grasping his knife.

"No."

"Why have you chosen me?"

"Because of your sign, Sakmo."

"My sign?"

"Look at your arm."

Until that moment, the young Jumano warrior had not thought anything of the dark red mark on the inside of his left forearm. It was the size of a serpent's bite, but in fact it resembled a rose.

"It is the sign of those who can see."

The woman leaned over near the Indian, extending her hand

until it gently brushed the top of his shaved head. A shiver went through him. His arms dropped to his sides and his fingers relaxed. The stone knife fell to the ground.

"Do not attack me," she continued. "I have something to give you. Something only your grandchildren will understand, in no less than three hundred years."

"Three hundred years?"

"Almost four thousand moons." She nodded in agreement. "And you will protect it."

"What is it?"

"Soon, when we see each other again, I will give it to you."

And with those words, darkness fell once more over the plains.

SIX

MADRID, SPAIN
SPRING 1991

"And where might we be headed today?"

This was by no means a casual question for Txema Jiménez, who was well versed in his friend's eccentricities. Just to be on the safe side, he took out his all-weather jacket and loaded it with rolls of film. His stocky silhouette, the figure of a man who ate well and rarely exercised, became even larger whenever he threw on his "equipment." In regard to the new arrival, which is what he told himself as soon as he saw his colleague Carlos Albert walking over to him, he was not going to play that game again. The week before in Seville, while he was trying to find a filter for his telephoto lens in a remote part of the Santa Cruz quarter, Carlos had wandered off and left him stranded. He had never before worked with someone quite so high-strung, who lost touch with reality whenever he stumbled upon something that intrigued him.

The camera bag, a used knapsack Txema had taken with him on countless adventures, was at his feet, packed and ready to go. This time he made sure he had batteries for the flash and a decent supply of film.

When he was within a few paces of Txema, Carlos smiled broadly, answering his friend's question with one of his own.

"Ready for a new mystery?"

Txema nodded. "I have everything," he said, gesturing toward his bag and his jacket. "No giving me the slip so easily this time. Your little stunt in Seville won't happen again."

"Let's go, then. It isn't as if you missed anything earthshaking. Besides, the jeweler was adamant about no photographs. That was just a tall story about how he had driven a hundred fifty miles in half an hour, after his car had been enveloped by a big cloud on top of the Castillo de las Guardas."

"An abduction?"

Carlos nodded. "If he had seen your camera, he never would have opened his mouth! You have no idea how they are, the people in that town!"

"Yeah, sure," Txema grumbled. "And our next destination?"

"Our assignment today is the hunt for the Holy Shroud, pal." Carlos checked the route while he took long sips from his second coffee of the morning, which the machine in the lunchroom had just dropped into his hand.

"The Holy Shroud? Since when are you interested in relics? Weren't you the one who said they're for old ladies?"

Carlos made no reply.

"I think that sort of thing is best left to graduate students."

It's strange, Carlos Albert thought. He had been asking himself the same questions for the past two months. Why did he suddenly feel such an overwhelming attraction to the religious, if he was not? Although he was an avowed agnostic, the shadow of devotion continued to pursue him since his return from his last trip to Italy. At first he had refused to take it seriously: once or twice he came across a card with the image of the Virgin of Guadalupe, just like the ones he saw on his grandmother's night table, except that now it was between pages of a book he happened to open. That was enough for him to revisit the days when he still had faith. At other times, it was Schubert's "Ave Maria" playing in the background at work, or the painter Murillo's *Immaculada* on a postage stamp. Were they signs of some sort? Should he be concerned that the only things that caught his attention were news items about religion?

Carlos was certainly unusual. At twenty-three, shortly after finishing his studies, a youthful religious crisis had left him permanently estranged from the Catholicism of Communion and Sunday Mass. Like any conflict worthy of being taken seriously, his had evolved over a period of time. And then it burst out into the open one day when he nearly lost his life in a motorcycle accident. When his shiny chrome BMW K75 ran head-on, at fifty-five miles per hour, into a taxi that had run a red light, he knew that his life would never be the same. Everything was suddenly dark and empty. He was unconscious for fifteen hours, and when he came to in the intensive care unit, he failed to remember a single thing that had happened. Nothing. For the first time in his life, Carlos felt cheated. He seemed disgusted by the fact that he was still alive. Angry at everything and everyone. Later, at home with his parents, he explained it like this: when your life is over, there is no light, no angel plucking a harp, no paradise full of loved ones. They had misled him. For the fifteen hours that he was dead, he encountered nothing but darkness. Emptiness. Cold. A vast, empty space in which he had been trapped.

That had been almost a decade ago. He had spent six months learning to walk again, and by the time he had completed the final stage of his rehabilitation, a profound and permanent change had come over him. It was no secret that after the accident Carlos began to look at life from a very curious angle. He started to take a serious interest in borderline experiences, in psychic phenomena. He believed that a substantial part of what are called religious phenomena resulted from mental experiences that are poorly understood, mirages that one day science would be able to explain.

Yet even with his increasingly mechanical outlook on reality, he felt that one thing, however odd, was absolutely certain: life attracts life, as he put it. And no longer wanting to be separated from it, he began to make a collection of other people's existences. His job was the perfect alibi. As a journalist he let himself absorb the air other people breathed, the things they dreamed or did. And his joining the staff at the monthly magazine set him free in a way he would never have imagined. *Mysteries* was a rigorous publication that kept its ears and eyes open, a journal that for years had been gathering evidence of experiences that bordered on the supernatural. Scientists with pretensions to explaining everything would write for the magazine from time to time, as would theologians who explained that only blind faith could mitigate the suffering in our society. And among the various theories, the editor of *Mysteries* was content to publish Carlos's skeptical reports from the field.

After he returned from Italy, the reporter got to know an elderly professor of mathematics, a retired inventor, who assured Carlos that he had discovered how the universe works. During the interview, the professor explained that the reality we are living is merely part of a vast, invisible precision mechanism in which every action provokes a reaction. "Nothing happens by chance," he told Carlos. "And if at any point some mysteriously linked events befall you, as if something or someone had orchestrated them on your behalf, don't hesitate for a moment: study them! Should you manage to figure out their ultimate cause, you will have discovered the true God, whatever that may be. You'll realize that God is actually a species of supercomputer, a Programmer, and not the ancient bearded gentleman of your imagination. That day, moreover, you will have found the reason for your existence. What else could you possibly ask for?"

As strange as it seems, it made sense to Carlos.

In fact, that morning, an hour before his meeting with Txema, something of the sort had happened to him. A succession of innocuous events, suggestions to change the direction of the magazine, had caught his attention.

It started like this: Shortly before arriving for work, Carlos found a curious gold medal on the street. Someone had lost it, and by chance its chain had ended up wrapped around one of the journalist's shoes. When he took the trouble to bend over and disentangle it from his shoelaces, he was surprised to see Christ's profile engraved on one side. An unmistakable image, which he knew well: the face of the dead Savior as it had been imprinted on a piece of fabric, awaiting his resurrection. Someone had lost it a few steps from the magazine's front door, but who?

There was no name engraved on the medal, no date or anything else that would allow its owner to be identified. Carlos put it in his briefcase, but when he sat down at his desk minutes later and began looking over the daily teletypes, he became absolutely certain that his discovery had not been the result of chance. "A Second Shroud of Turin Found in Village in the Sierra de Cameros," ran one of the headlines.

The Holy Shroud?

The face on the medal had been inspired by exactly that image.

No. This was not mere chance.

Carlos gave serious thought to what the old mathematician had said. Was he going to let an opportunity to catch God slip through his fingers?

Little did he imagine how far his instinct would carry him this time.

"And so?" Txema asked again. He was disguised as a war correspondent as he stood directly in front of the writer, his hands on his stomach. "Where exactly are we headed?"

"North. To Logroño. Familiar with the Cameros Mountains?"

"Cameros?" The photographer's eyebrows arched in playful incredulity. "At this time of year?"

Txema glanced worriedly out the window. A cloudy front, as dark as a bad omen, was moving in to drop its deluge on Madrid, bringing with it a cold, needle-thin rain. Then, in a somber tone, he went on.

"I suppose you listened to the radio? The weather report sounds scary . . ."

None of it seemed to matter to Carlos as he picked up his small travel bag of essentials and headed behind his coworker down the stairs and out to the parking lot.

"I have a hunch that today we're going to find a really big story."

Txema was in no mood. "First of all, are you aware that your car needs chains, just like everyone else's, if we intend to go higher than three thousand feet? Your car's not exactly a four-by-four."

The writer opened the trunk of the SEAT Ibiza and without saying a word, threw his things in. He liked his car. He'd crossed half of Europe in it, and it had never let him down. Why would it do so now on account of a little snow?

"Stop worrying," he said at last. "You have a day with no set plans. Make the most of it."

The magazine's director let them escape like that from time to time. He knew the two men always turned up in the office with a lively story under their hats. One of those articles that softened the polemics, abounding in rabbis, Sufi masters, and cabalists overflowing with divine truth. But would they find anything worthwhile in the obscure sacristy of some remote village?

"Aren't you bringing chains?" Txema insisted.

Carlos looked at him out of the corner of his eye.

"What's the matter? You don't trust me? Do you really believe we'll be brought to a halt by a snowstorm in the middle of April?"

"You said it," Txema grunted. The corpulent photographer from Bilbao was little given to joking around. When he groaned, he sounded like a wounded bear. "I know you pretty well, Carlos. We could be stranded on the top of some mountain searching for a hokey relic as we die of frostbite, stuck outdoors at two in the morning, all because we refused to put chains on the wheels!"

"I know what you think," Carlos said in a mocking voice. "In your opinion, this is a waste of time, right?"

Txema didn't respond.

"Okay," Carlos said quietly as he turned the key in the ignition. "Now let me tell you my plan."

SEVEN

VENICE

Giuseppe Baldi was so angry that his eyes were starting to tear.

"*Un'altra volta lo stesso errore* . . . ," he whispered as he fought his emotions. "The same mistake I made before. . . . How could I have been such a simpleton?"

Irritated, he stashed the letter in his robe. He should have known that the interview he gave two months ago to a writer at a well-known Spanish magazine would come back to haunt him. Other than talking to a journalist from outside Italy, had he done anything else that the Vatican would consider an indiscretion?

The memory was still fresh in the old musicologist's mind: a young foreigner, who must have been about thirty, accompanied by a photographer whose Italian was limited to a few words, turned up at the abbey on the pretext of interviewing Baldi about the unusual pastoral activity he undertook each Wednesday. This alibi, which Baldi would discover only later, served the reporter well, for Baldi gave him permission to record the conversation. As it turned out, his work with those believed to be possessed by the devil had acquired a certain notoriety in the news media, and there were more than a few magazines that asked him for statements or interviews. The Devil was very fashionable in Italy in 1991.

The Benedictine had approached the subject guardedly. Aware that the majority of his "possessed" were no more than people with a mental illness or, in the best of cases, hysterical people in need of compassion, he attempted to use his sermons as a useful way to underscore the healing power of faith.

In fact, the magazines *Gente Mese* and *Oggi* had lavished so much publicity on him in the week before the Spaniards paid him a visit, and there had been such a great response in the media to his book *The Catechism of Satan*, that it did not strike him as strange that some foreign journal had taken an interest in his exorcisms. And, clearly, a touch of vanity had led him to accept the interview.

Baldi realized only later that the reporter had very little interest in his work as an "exorcist." This journalist was different from the others. Little by little, almost without trying, his interlocutor slowly inched toward the subject that Baldi himself had mistakenly let out into the open in 1972 and which turned him, over the course of a few nearly forgotten days, into a great celebrity throughout Italy. No sooner had his interviewer broached the subject than Baldi felt strangely uneasy.

"His latest indiscretion." What else could it be?

Nineteen years had gone by since his name had appeared in headlines, following his revelation that he had spent more than a decade laboring over a device that obtained images and sounds from the past. The musicologist had stated that this wide-ranging project, in which he worked alongside a team of twelve physicists from around the world, had been approved by the Holy See. In fact, the *Domenica del Corriere* was the first to print its version of "the time machine." According to the paper, Baldi's group had already proved capable of recovering lost musical works such as Quintus Ennius's *Thyestes*, composed sometime around 169 BC, as well as an exact transcription of Christ's last words on the cross.

Those revelations, which Baldi had imagined were long buried in newspaper archives, shocked a lot of people, and even though the exclusive had long before exploded like gunpowder among the media's news agencies, the reality of this journalist dredging up Chronovision and confronting him about it left Baldi dazed.

"Chronovision!" Baldi gasped. "What the devil?"

He balled his fists just thinking about it. He was certain he had not given the slightest bit of relevant information to those journalists. In fact, he remembered showing them the door at the mere mention of the subject.

But then, why?

No matter how he tried, Baldi could not explain the cause of his latest "indiscretion." Had he made the obvious error of speaking to the reporter about the "four evangelists"? Or perhaps about his latest and very surprising advances in Chronovision? No. He was sure of it. His indiscretion in 1972 had taught him an unforgettable lesson. At that time, the writer from *Corriere*, one Vincenzo Maddaloni, had decided to mix the priest's statements with fabrications as extraordinary as a supposed photograph of Jesus that neither he nor his team had ever seen, but which the journalist had dug up from God knows where. In 1972 his machine could recapture distinguishable sounds from the past, but the images left a good deal to be desired.

Had the second journalist now made exaggerated claims as well? And in what terms?

"A curse on them all!" Baldi raged. "*Maledizione!*"

As if his life depended on it, the Benedictine took off his glasses, rubbed his eyes vigorously, and splashed his face in his cell's tiny sink. "How stupid of me!" he murmured. "I should have thought of it before."

Baldi hid the three envelopes in the one desk drawer that he could lock and hurried down to the abbey entrance. Once there, he walked quietly past the large table without disturbing Brother Robert's absorption in his favorite television show. He turned and moved in the shadows toward the building's only mahogany door. He needed a telephone and at that hour the abbey's office, which afforded a small measure of privacy, was empty. He mustered his courage and walked inside.

"*Pronto*. May I speak with Father Corso?" he mumbled after dialing a number in Rome.

"Luigi Corso? One moment, please," replied the man on the other end.

Baldi held his breath. A minute later, a familiar voice came on the line.

"Hello. Who is it?"

"Matthew," Baldi groaned, his voice at half the normal volume. "It's me."

"Luke! What are you calling for at this hour?"

"Something happened. I received a letter from Cardinal Zsidiv, blaming me for some indiscretion. And this afternoon Rome has called twice asking for me . . ."

"Zsidiv? Are you sure?"

"Positive."

"And what indiscretion did he accuse you of?"

"Do you remember the Spanish journalist I told you about? The one who came with a photographer who fired off pictures nonstop?"

"Of course. The one who tried to draw you out about Chronovision, no?"

"The same. It's the only thing I can think of. He must have published something that irritated the Holy Father's advisers."

"In which case," Corso said emphatically, "the letter refers to your indiscretion, not ours. *Capito?*"

His tone had stiffened. The professor of music felt himself reproved. He knew he was calling Corso without the permission of the project coordinator.

"I concede the point, Corso." Baldi didn't argue. "My indiscretion . . . The bad news is that they want me to appear in the Vatican to state my case, before Sunday. And as you know, it would be extremely unpleasant for me if they canceled our project."

"I think Zsidiv would be opposed to that."

"Nevertheless, if they decide to open a dossier on me I fear that the project could suffer a new setback. Nobody in Rome is really aware of the deep implications of our investigation; all our reports have been sent in code, and I feel certain you could continue with the project, even if you no longer keep me informed of what's happening. It would be dangerous for you to do so."

Corso, or rather Saint Matthew, was silent.

"You heard what I said?"

"I heard, Luke. But it is very late in the day for what you propose," the man on the other end said in an irritated voice.

"What do you mean?"

"Some goon who works at the Holy Office got in touch with me last night. He gave me all the latest news about what they plan to do. He advised me that our discoveries are now out of our hands. The Vatican needs our latest research. Their idea is to apply it to Church projects. Seemingly, we have no choice in the matter."

Father Baldi was crushed.

"IEA called you? From the Congregation for the Doctrine of the Faith?" He spoke just above a whisper.

The IEA, or Institute for External Affairs, was the Vatican "agency" that acted as the liaison between the secret police protecting the Pope and the old Sant'Uffizio, or Holy Office, now known as the Congregation for the Doctrine of the Faith. Its tentacles extended in all directions. If Luigi Corso had given in, Baldi knew the battle was lost.

"In that case, Brother, it is very late . . ."

The Benedictine leaned on his elbows, cupping the receiver in his left hand.

"My God!" he groaned. "Is there nothing we can do?"

"Come to Rome, Luke," said Father Corso, trying to lift his colleague's spirits. "Resolve the issue personally. Furthermore, if you want some good advice, never speak about the project in public again. Remember what happened the first time you let your tongue loose: Pius the Twelfth classified Chronovision as *riservatissima*, top secret, and even though Pope John later loosened the gag, things have never been the same for us."

"I will bear it in mind," Baldi agreed. "And thanks. Obviously I have yet to open the envelope you sent me. What does it contain?"

"My last report. In it I detail how we refined our method for accessing the past. Last week Dottore Alberto discovered the missing frequencies that will enable us to break the three-century barrier. Do you recall?"

"I remember. You already told me a good deal about the work of this Doctor Alberto. How did it turn out . . . ? "

"An incredible success, Luke. Incredible."

EIGHT

SIERRA DE CAMEROS, SPAIN

Over the course of the next five hours, Carlos and Txema drove out from Madrid to the foothills of the Cameros Mountains, without paying much attention to the traffic or the rain that was slowly turning into snow. The Rioja wine country lay before them, its rugged peaks looming over gentle valleys, its enigmas shrouded. Carlos made use of the time on the road to tell his photographer the strange story of finding the medal, and how it had stirred memories of everything he knew about the Holy Shroud. The time he had spent working at a Catholic magazine in Madrid had not been wasted.

"The worst was in 1988, when a team of scientists dated Christ's supposed burial sheet between the thirteenth and fourteenth centuries," he told Txema. "You cannot imagine the stir that announcement caused! Carbon-fourteen dating left no doubts: the Holy Shroud was a fake."

Txema observed him without commenting.

"I remember how the editor searched desperately for arguments to convince his readers that the scientific diagnosis must be wrong. And one of them was that, way before the fourteenth century, there were copies of the Shroud of Turin circulating with this image on it. So, how could anyone have copied something that had yet to be created? If there were earlier copies, it was because the original must be much older than all of them. Logical, no?"

Before they stopped to refuel, the photographer had already figured out what was preoccupying his friend. "Sudden inspiration," the "incredible coincidence" of finding the medal on the same morning as the news of the Holy Shroud in the Cameros. . . . But something, nevertheless, had yet to make sense to him. A few minutes before they drove into the heart of Rioja, Txema broke his silence for the first time.

"Can you please tell me why you've abandoned your other investigations for nonsense like this?" he asked. "Searching for copies—copies!—of a relic. And the truth is, I can't swallow all that stuff about the medal."

Txema had managed to wipe the smile off his friend's face.

"What are you referring to?"

"You know . . . Ever since I met you, you've tried to avoid news of religion, spiritual subjects, mystical themes. You simply left that sort of thing to others. So why now?"

Carlos stared straight ahead at the road, his lips drawn.

"I have no idea."

"Well, what about your work on the teleportations?" Txema was warming to his task. "Remember those dudes you took me to see, the ones who said that they drove into a heavy cloud and then reappeared who knows how many miles farther away? Not the guy in Seville, who I missed, but those guys in Salamanca. And the night we spent in Alicante, going back and forth on Highway 340, trying to let something 'teleport' our car? Or that priest in Venice a few months ago who suggested there were people capable of traveling into the past, hundreds of miles from where he started, enabling him to watch any historical event he wanted to? It took you a while to wring that out of him!"

"Those are all very different things, Txema," Carlos chided him, drawing his words out slowly.

"Perhaps. But any one of them is more interesting than searching for phony shrouds!"

Carlos grimaced. In fact, he had spent a good deal of time avoiding that other investigation: for the last several months he had been busy interviewing witnesses who were convinced they had undergone "teleportations." People who spoke about how, while traveling across a rarely visited region, something had happened to change their plans. In most cases a cloud bank suddenly appeared, but in some of the accounts that "something" was nothing more than a chill, or a burst of light like the flash of a camera. And then right away everything changed: the highway, the landscape, their itinerary. Everything, down to the smallest detail.

In less than a year he had located some twenty people who told him the same story. He spoke with airline pilots, priests, travel agents, truck drivers, and even the ex-husband of a famous singer. He went so far as to establish a set of rules that, according to him, governed the behavior of those incidents. Carlos knew this was the surest route out of his crisis: if, in the process of a close encounter with the supernatural, he was able to encapsulate it inside a rational, scientific vision, he would perhaps come face-to-face with that evasive Programmer. Perhaps he could even interview him someday, or so he told himself.

But the journalist had badly estimated his powers. The investigation quickly got out of hand. The funds set aside by the magazine dried up, and his work came to a dead end.

Deeply frustrated, he felt he had failed. And Txema knew it.

"If you were so enthusiastic about teleportation, why did you drop it?"

Carlos looked at him out of the corner of his eye and decelerated, downshifting into third. He answered reluctantly.

"I'll tell you if you then let it drop. The blame lies with two historical incidents. I thought I had something important within reach: two references, both very old, to incidents similar to the ones I was researching. But when I started to dig for information, I came up with nothing, not a shred of proof. I was chasing after meaningless urban legends, so I let it go. Does that satisfy you?"

"Like hell! You never told me anything about it. What were those two incidents that defeated you?"

"They did not defeat me!" Carlos insisted. "The first was a Spanish soldier who lived in the sixteenth century. Legend has it that while he was stationed in Manila, he traveled, in the blink of an eye, to the Plaza Mayor in Mexico City—"

"When did this occur?"

"The date is one of the few things I could find out: October 25, 1593."

Txema shifted in his seat. The boy really did have a prodigious memory for names, dates, and places.

"Can you imagine: the infantryman crossed eight thousand miles over land and sea in a matter of seconds, was planted at the other end of the world, and never told a single soul how he did it."

"And the second case?"

"That was even more spectacular: only forty years after the 'flight' of the soldier, a Spanish nun named María Jesús de Ágreda was interrogated by the Inquisition as a result of her repeated visits to New Mexico. They accused her of having Christianized various tribes of natives in the area of the Rio Grande, flying mysteriously from Spain to America. The really amazing thing is that she never left her monastery."

"She went back and forth to America whenever she wanted? As if she were walking over a bridge in the air?" Txema asked incredulously.

"So it seems. This simple nun in a cloister was able to control this capacity to 'fly,' while evading the charge of witchcraft by the Holy Inquisition."

"Did you manage to track her down?"

"Neither her nor the soldier." His voice was resigned. "In the case of the nun, I found her name, but no place or monastery where I could start to look. As for the soldier, I knew the dates when he went to the Philippines and when he returned, as well as the date of his voyage, but didn't have a clue about his name, or any document from that era recording his feat. In fact, I left the subject at a standstill. If you remember, in my last article I cited those two incidents without giving them much importance. I then filed everything away and decided to dedicate myself to other things."

"To religion, from what I can see," Txema said, laughing under his breath.

"Not only."

"Right; you also published the piece on the priest in Venice."

"Ah, yes. Right again. I mentioned that strange machine that, according to him, enabled him to recover images from the past. What was it called? The Chronovisor! That was a dead end, too."

"No doubt."

The Ibiza's diesel engine was straining uphill with increasing difficulty. As the photographer had foreseen, the countryside was growing steadily steeper and the road to the town of Laguna de Cameros, where the copy of the Holy Shroud was being kept, narrower and more winding. The temperature had dropped below freezing. The grapevines were no longer visible beneath the snow. Even worse, the tiny shortwave radio that was clamped onto the dashboard had gone dead. Txema had been a radio fanatic for years, and had taken it with him on every trip. The mere suggestion of traveling "unplugged" was enough to make him insufferable. To which end, he got out of the car on several occasions to redirect the antenna so he could make contact with whoever was out there.

"Nothing," he said, surrendering at last. "Not even somebody else's static. It's dead."

"Things could be much worse. With a bit of luck, we'll sleep in Logroño tonight. We can get the radio repaired there."

"How far do we have to go before we get to this shroud of yours?"

"An hour, maybe more."

"If only we could teleport ourselves."

It was Txema's first stab at humor during their trip.

NINE

LOS ANGELES

"Have you ever heard of the Stendhal syndrome?"

Dr. Meyers's question surprised Jennifer Narody, who responded in the negative with a shake of her head. They were taking a break from the therapeutic session, sipping from two oversized coffee cups as they shared an animated conversation. Linda Meyers's office encouraged people to talk. Its big picture windows looked down on the bustling city, where traffic was winding its way down Broadway, as well as the imposing stone façade of the Hall of Justice and the City Hall's immaculate tower, where workers were constantly scurrying about. But inside Dr. Meyers's room, everything was hushed, peaceful. The office of Los Angeles's most prestigious and unconventional psychiatrist imparted a strange sensation of power, of mastery over time, as if all the activity around it was something foreign from the condition of those who peered down from that privileged vantage point. The room they were sitting in was decorated with sculptures and vibrantly colored canvases from Africa. Meyers was proud of her ancestry, and, in fact, the entire office emanated the palpable allure of the African continent. As did the imported coffee.

"The Stendhal syndrome?"

Jennifer took a sip.

"It describes a common psychological condition that tourists who visit Europe, above all Italy, can suffer."

Meyers smiled broadly. It seemed that she had waited until that moment to make a small confession.

"Stop looking at me like that!" she told Jennifer with a laugh. "Stendhal is not a dangerous virus! This is, in reality, a very common illness, easy to treat. It takes its name from the nineteenth-century French writer who, after spending an entire day passing among the marvels of the city of Florence, began to suffer palpitations, vertigo, fainting spells, and even hallucinations. It seems that his condition was caused by an overdose of beauty. Not everyone can handle the excess of history and art that the Italian streets exude!"

"Wherever are you going with this, Doctor?" Jennifer looked amused.

"Well, you started having these dreams immediately after your return from Rome. That mysterious lady who appears to the Indians really resembles an Italian Madonna, and I was asking myself if—"

"If I have a similar kind of strong reaction to the beauties of Rome? Come on, Doctor! You can't be serious! For two years I lived in the middle of the Via Augusta, near the Vatican. I had plenty of time to get used to the many attractions of the city: its ancient archways, its bridges over the Tiber, its churches, basilicas, convents, statues, obelisks, frescos. Believe me, none of that impressed me by the time I decided to leave."

"Do you know something? I envy you, Jennifer," the doctor said as she took another sip of her coffee. "So tell me, why did you decide to live in Rome for an extended period?"

"I needed to get away for a while."

"An unhappy romance?"

"No, nothing of the sort! I never had trouble like that with men." She was more relaxed now. "The fault was, as always, my work. Although I am prohibited from talking about it."

"You're prohibited from talking about what?" Dr. Meyers placed her cup down on a ceramic platter adorned with zebras. "What are you trying to tell me?"

"Look, I warned you. My work is complicated, and, furthermore, I took an oath of confidentiality when I worked for the military. Most of what I did is off limits to civilians."

"So you were in the military?"

The perplexed look on the psychiatrist's face made Jennifer smile.

It was the same face her mother made when she found out, and the priest she confessed to as well. Perhaps that was why Jennifer had avoided mentioning the fact when she filled out the doctor's forms with her personal data. She simply described herself as an artist, without giving any revealing details. And that was basically how she felt since her return from Italy. She had made plans to obtain a small studio where she could paint and eventually exhibit her work.

"Not exactly the military. I worked with the Department of Defense on a project that, in the end, affected me more than I had realized. You know how those things are, Doctor: they made me sign an agreement not to reveal any details about my activities. 'High treason,' as they put it."

"No secrets are given away when you respond to my questions." Dr. Meyers's face bore a determined expression now. "I, too, have a confidentiality agreement with my patients. Nothing you say ever leaves this room."

"Maybe I should forget about resolving all this business concerning my dreams."

"Let me be the judge of that, don't you think? And now, please explain to me why your work made it necessary for you to return to America."

TEN

ROME

At the same hour and over six thousand miles from Los Angeles, the Eternal City was experiencing its usual early-evening traffic jam. The first warm days of springtime had already arrived, and each new day extended its hours of light.

Giuseppe Baldi was oblivious to it all. He had caught the train to Rome at the Santa Lucia station, and now, six hours later, was walking across Saint Peter's Square at full speed, not bothering to enjoy Rome's priceless evening spectacle.

Baldi's plan was simple. No one would suspect that there, in the shadow of the imposing Egyptian obelisk that Domenico Fontana had installed in the heart of Vatican City, he was about to violate the first and most important protocol of the "four evangelists," or "the saints," as the porter at San Giorgio liked to call them.

The rule of that elite team of scientists was unequivocal: never, under any circumstances, were two "evangelists"—that is to say, the persons in charge of one of the four constituent groups in the program—to meet without the additional presence of the coordinator, "Saint John," one of the Vatican's scientific advisers, or a representative from the special committee constituted for that purpose. The rule was an attempt to ensure loyalty to the project and to prevent splinter groups from forming.

But to hold no meetings under any circumstances?

To Baldi, a scrupulous lover of order, this imminent "sin" did not seem to be eating at his conscience. His need to meet with Father Luigi Corso had become much stronger than the iron discipline of the Vatican. He felt they still had time. He could straighten out certain things with the First Evangelist before making his appearance at the hearing to which he had been urgently summoned. Baldi was certain that Saint Matthew had in his possession privileged information about Chronovision; facts that, for whatever reason, no one had wanted to share with him after his encounter with the Spanish journalist, and which perhaps would help him to leave the disciplinary hearing without a scratch.

As he strolled past Bernini's colonnade, his mind became agitated: why was it, from one day to the next, that the Sant'Uffizio had become so interested in the investigations by Father Corso and the team in Rome that it had decided to bring them to a halt? What had Saint Matthew discovered in his laboratories that was provoking such a sudden shift in authority?

On the train that brought him to Rome, Baldi tried to figure out the answers by rereading Saint Matthew's latest report. He could not find the source of the conflict there, nor in the letters from Saint Mark and Saint John. When those texts were placed in the mail, neither Father Corso nor the other evangelists could have suspected that the project was about to be hijacked by the IEA.

All of which was forcing him to violate the rule forbidding meetings.

Threading his way through the stands selling postcards, soft drinks, ice cream, and commemorative coins as he headed directly toward the obelisk, Baldi remained vigilant. Nothing should come in the way of his meeting with Saint Matthew. He had carefully prepared each detail: even the telegram to Corso indicating the day and the hour had been written in an exquisitely detailed code.

"Take it easy," he said to himself again. "Everything will turn out fine."

One thing was obvious: he was nervous, very much so. He was beginning to think, and not without reason, that the letter he had received from the secretary of state calling him to Rome, and the interruption of Corso's work, could be the first salvos in a witch hunt involving the evangelists. Mere paranoia? If so, it was unavoidable. As he stood only a few steps from the obelisk, a chill scurried up his spine. This was the place he had chosen for the meeting and this was the time he had set. Nothing could go wrong.

Or could it?

Had Saint Matthew received his telegram? And, most important, did he understand it? Would he also be disposed to violate the project's primary rule? There was even a worse possibility: would Corso denounce him in an attempt to ingratiate himself with Chronovision's new overseers?

Saint Luke carefully slowed his pace as he drew closer to the spot. He decided to remain in the shade of one of the colonnades surrounding the obelisk while he waited. Corso should be along any minute.

He swallowed hard.

At each passing second, new uncertainties assaulted him. Would he recognize Saint Matthew after so many years? Could he be one of the priests hurrying across Saint Peter's Square at this hour, en route to the basilica?

Impatient, he glanced at his watch: 6:30. "This is it," he mused. "Just a matter of minutes."

The Benedictine surveyed the various individuals who passed through the open space around the obelisk. Four long-faced Swiss Guards were decked out in their dazzling period uniforms, their wooden lances sheathed in silver. They kept watch at the Arch of the Bells, the principal access to the Vatican. "Ah, the faithful *sampietrini*," mused Baldi, referring to them by their common nickname, "who never once surrendered a Pope . . ."

He also detected the carabinieri as they made their way among the tourists, and even distracted himself watching a group of foreign students admiring Bernini's colonnade and the imposing height of the obelisk.

But there was not even a trace of Saint Matthew.

"Damned Roman traffic!" he cursed under his breath.

It was a ridiculous situation: he had come all the way from Venice and arrived punctually for his meeting, while his colleague, coming from a neighborhood in the heart of Rome, was going to arrive late.

Corso was also a writer. Had the saint sailed to heaven while seated at his typewriter?

By 6:43, Baldi was still at his spot, anxiously looking about.

The wait was beginning to feel unbearable.

"If meeting with me at this hour was impossible, he should have said so," he grumbled.

For Saint Luke, lateness was worse than a mortal sin. He pardoned no one: neither conservatory students nor his monastic brethren, much less his friends. He believed God sent each of us into the world with a chronometer that counted out our time of life, and thus it was an insult to the All Powerful to squander that time in waiting.

"If the bastards in the secret service had intercepted my telegram . . . they would have already apprehended me," he consoled himself by considering the worst case. "There must be some other reason why he's late."

His relief lasted as long as it took for him to take in a deep breath.

At 6:55 sharp, the Third Evangelist could no longer resist, and sped off hurriedly, looking straight ahead and directing his footsteps toward one of the square's exits. He crossed the Via de Porta Angelica and headed toward the Galeria Savelli, the large gift store, which was just about to close. Inside was a public phone, discreetly placed at the rear. It was just what Baldi needed to put his doubts to rest. It would only take a minute, the time required to dig out a token and telephone the First Evangelist.

"May I please speak with Father Corso?"

The voice that always answered at that number asked him to wait. It was a man's voice, the voice of someone soured on life. The call was transferred to another extension. Someone answered very quickly.

"Hello. Who is it?" asked a surly voice that Baldi failed to recognize.

"Ah. You aren't Father Corso. They must have made a mistake."

"No, they didn't make a mistake. Father Corso . . ." The speaker hesitated. "Father Corso cannot come to the phone now. Who are you?"

"A friend."

Baldi decided to try his luck and put the plainspoken man on the other end of the line on the spot.

"Do you know if he went out?"

"No, he's right here. But who is this?" the surly voice asked a second time.

The Venetian was a little disturbed. It was very unusual, this insistence upon identifying oneself.

"And you? Who are you? And why won't you let Father Corso come to the phone?"

"I told you, he can't right now."

"Very well, then. I'll call back later," Baldi barked. He was angry now.

"You want to leave a message?"

"Just tell him"—and here Baldi paused, considering his words—"tell him the Third Evangelist called."

"The Third Evangel—"

Saint Luke slammed down the receiver and walked straight out of the store without waiting for the pay phone to return his unused lira. He needed fresh air to clear his head. "What a cretin!"

Baldi soon realized, however, that something was out of place. For Corso to meet with him at 6:30 at the foot of the obelisk in front of Saint Peter's, he would have had to leave his residence a good while earlier. And not only did they not just say, "He went out," but a strange person insisted on stating that Corso was unavailable, while trying devilishly hard to find out who Baldi was. Was Corso sick? Being held hostage? And if so, by whom?

More paranoia?

Or was it simply another indication that, as he feared, the hunt had already gotten under way in earnest?

Baldi's head was about to explode.

There was no other choice: for the sake of his own mental health he had to resolve the issue in person, right away. Standing in the middle of the street, he opened the small briefcase he carried with him and rifled through everything as if he'd just been robbed, finally pulling out a bundle of letters held together by a rubber band. Saint Matthew's address was printed on the envelope that contained his final report:

S. Matteo
Via dei Sediari 10
Roma

Baldi approached a carabiniere.

"Sediari? That's not so far," the carabiniere told him.

"Can I get there on foot?"

"It'll take you over half an hour, but you can do it." The officer was smiling broadly. "Stay on the Via della Conciliazione to the end, turn right, and continue on straight until you hit Ponte Vittorio Emanuele. Cross the bridge, and head down the avenue almost to the end. When you get to the Corso del Rinascimento, it's close by on the left.

"Perfect. Thanks."

His stroll took Father Baldi forty-three minutes. He stopped twice along the way, just to be sure he was headed in the right direction, passing through a Rome steeped in serene splendor, from the Piazza Navona's fountains, which were already illuminated at that hour, to the aroma of fresh pasta escaping from the trattorias.

He could not understand Saint Matthew's silence. He was beginning to fear the worst: the Institute for External Affairs must have had a hand in this. And if they weren't responsible, then had Corso missed his meeting on account of those damned vows of obedience? That, at least, would explain why he was reluctant to answer the phone.

Baldi's questions would soon be answered.

ELEVEN

SIERRA DE CAMEROS

The visit to the Holy Shroud of Laguna de Cameros was a complete disaster. The town, always deserted that time of year, welcomed Txema Jiménez and Carlos Albert with absolute indifference. Certainly no one who lived there was aware that the town's name had appeared that very morning in the newspapers, in a report from a major news agency. What importance could any such thing have in that lost corner of the world? The only noteworthy news was that a heavy snowfall had begun in the middle of April and spring was still refusing to show its face. So, naturally, the area around the Leza River was deserted, and the only sign of life the strangers saw was smoke spiraling out of four or five chimneys on its way to a leaden sky.

The journalists had the good fortune to find the parish priest, by the name of Félix Arrondo, right away. They met him as he was coming out of the Church of the Assumption, a rustic stone edifice perched on the highest promontory in town, and soon became acquainted. Father Félix was a robust fellow somewhere around fifty, cordial, good-natured, with a beret pulled down to his ears, and a wonderful sense of humor. As there was no reason to wait, he quickly acceded to his visitors' request. "So you want to see the relic? But of course, gentlemen! Although I have no idea where the newspapers got the idea that we just discovered it," he snorted as he grew more comfortable around the two men. "I have lived in this area for twenty years, and I learned about the existence of the shroud the very first day I arrived. It so happens we never used to show it, and

Holy Week this year was the first time we put it on display. Everybody will have a chance to see it now, definitely. It is a beautiful cloth."

The journalists regarded him warily. They were about to discover that their long hours of travel, on curving mountain roads under bad driving conditions, had all been in vain: the chest that housed the shroud, which was swathed in red velvet, bore the exact same date as the copy of the relic.

"Seventeen ninety," the curate pronounced proudly, after dredging the box out of an old armoire in the sacristy. "How does it look to you? Not so bad, eh? From the eighteenth century!"

The world was piling up on top of Carlos.

It was painfully clear to him now that they had driven three hundred miles in one stretch for nothing. The fabric, adorned with the profile of a man on a cross, was of much more recent provenance than the supposed copy of the Shroud of Turin made in the fourteenth century. And no matter how many photographs Txema took, they were still going home to Madrid empty-handed. Furthermore, because of their haste, they had left without snow chains, and the storm had buried the highways under a heavy and, by this hour, frozen white mantle. From the church tower it was the only color to be seen in the surrounding landscape.

"And the snow will be falling all afternoon," Father Félix prophesied. There was a worried expression on his face as he carefully went about folding the cloth. "You'll have to stay overnight. Tomorrow, once the ice melts, you can continue on your way."

And that is exactly what happened.

Father Félix found a modest refuge for the two men in one of the houses in town, and that night they dined on garlic soup and country sausage. When they grew tired of talking and sampling the robust wine from the nearby vineyards, their hostess, an old crone of some eighty-five years who lived alone but who never stopped bustling about, led them to their sleeping quarters. There, curled up in a freezing room with walls of coarse stone, they slept on straw mattresses. Carlos stretched out, his hand holding the medal that had gotten him into this trouble.

"Still believe in your sudden inspirations, pal?"

Hidden beneath the blankets on the other side of the room, the photographer was laughing at him. The blankets were pulled up to his ears, and his cheeks were flush with the warmth of the evening meal and its hearty soup.

"To hell with you, Txema!"

TWELVE

LOS ANGELES

The session that got under way that morning in Dr. Meyers's office lasted until lunchtime. Her patient's unusual intensity forced the doctor to look at her schedule to see if she could find another opening for her later that day. She could only find one at seven PM. The doctor was not accustomed to seeing a patient in the evening, when she would normally be going over her notes to prepare for the following day's sessions, but Jennifer Narody had seemed anxious to unburden herself more fully.

She showed up at the doctor's office in an unusually talkative mood. The setting sun, which the doctor could see from her desk, was spectacular this evening, bathing the sculptures of wood and ivory that lined her African sitting room in gold and ochre tones. Her patient thanked her for making this exception, grateful at the chance to finally open up to someone. It was the first time in a long while that she felt able to do so.

This young woman, with her dark green eyes and a gaze that suggested fragility, had lived a turbulent inner existence that few others knew anything about. Her life had been marked by emotions that isolated her from the world and helped to forge her unique character.

Jennifer Narody had been born in Washington, D.C. Her parents, an evangelical pastor of German ancestry and a Mexican from the border states who was the granddaughter of a Navajo shaman from Arizona, gave Jennifer a normal upbringing from infancy to the age of sixteen. When she reached that age and was beginning to think about which university to attend, her problems surfaced for the first time: she began having premonitions about friends at school or family members. Premonitions that were accurate and precise, and which she never learned how to control. Many times she knew about domestic accidents, fights, or intimate dramas among close friends before they occurred. She "saw" them whenever she closed her eyes or took a nap. At first she had no qualms about communicating her visions to those who were involved, but as her predictions came true time and again, she began to have the reputation of being a witch. Her friends began to reject her, stopped inviting her to parties or to join them at the movies. And little by little her personality became taciturn and solitary. Plans for attending a university soon became less important as Jennifer concentrated on searching for answers to what she was going through. Without success.

Things changed for the worse on the day her high school mathematics teacher, Clive Brown, was killed. Brown had been her favorite. An Irishman with copper-colored hair and exquisite manners, he always came to class in a bow tie and a striped shirt. He was a strict man but he was also kind. The night before final exams, Jennifer had a terrible nightmare: she watched as her professor's blue tie was torn off his neck by a blunt object. Wherever it was happening was very dark. The space looked something like a deserted parking lot, with a basketball court close by. It was too dark to make out any details except for her professor's tie coming undone and flying away, and then a broad-shouldered man, with thinning hair, appeared. He stepped toward her professor and walloped him in the stomach. She watched in terror as he fell to his knees, convulsed in pain, and then, without the slightest warning, was shot in the back of his neck. Brown had no time to see the weapon. That was when Jennifer's dream ended.

That dream vision terrified her. She was unsure if there was enough time to contact her teacher. The next day, after she had finished her math exam, she waited for Brown to collect the materials and then joined him en route to the faculty lounge. Maggie Seymour, the guidance counselor, was there and listened in on the conversation, although neither of the two teachers paid too much attention to her dream. "You had a nightmare," they said. "Exams sometimes play games with your head."

When Clive Brown's body was found the next day, hanging in the parking lot of a supermarket near his house in Alexandria, Mrs. Seymour gave the details of the student's dream to the Washington police. Everything matched what Jennifer Narody had seen: the shot from behind to the small of the neck, the out-of-place bow tie, and even the unlit basketball court.

Since that incident, Jennifer Narody's life had taken a very different course.

For reasons that never became clear, her statement to the police found its way into the office of the nearby army base at Fort Meade. And in September 1984, Liam Stubbelbine, a colonel in military intelligence, recruited Jennifer to participate in a secret program that was, as he said, "of great importance to national security." The project, code name Stargate, was an espionage operation that attempted to use persons gifted with clairvoyance in military maneuvers or in antiterrorist activities. The term "clairvoyance" was rejected in favor of the euphemism more in keeping with the times: "remote viewing."

Fort Meade had received a generous budget allocation for the development of the project, and some of its efforts were concentrated on searching for subjects with intriguing "psychic potential." Such as Jennifer. And so, over the course of six years, they submitted her to all kinds of tests to examine her extrasensory abilities. It was thanks to those very abilities that the police were able to identify Clive Brown's killer.

But that success turned out to be a sentence for her as well. Now Jennifer Narody could never again escape the shadow of the National Security Agency and the Department of Defense. She finished her training as a lieutenant. But the feeling that she was being watched by her own government had a debilitating effect, and she found herself in a deep depression that soon led to a series of strange dreams in which a mysterious "lady of blue light" appeared in a place she had never heard of before.

Peculiar dreams. As if in some way her mind was capable of traveling outside of time in order to be present at remote events that always began at a specific time and geographic location.

THIRTEEN

GRAN QUIVIRA

When the three stars in Orion's belt, which the Indians called Hotomkam, were shining directly over the village, the great Walpi, chief of the Clouds, called the leaders of his group together for a secret meeting in the kiva. Never before had a meeting inside the huge circular room, whose floor was dug deep in the earth and whose wooden roof was supported by the "four columns on which the earth rests," claimed such a large audience.

Before descending into the central, deepest part of the enclosed space, the participants took one last look toward the horizon, in the direction of the Canyon of the Serpent. They had heard rumors of what had happened there. Now, Walpi had called them together so that he could explain what he knew and ask for their help.

At the established hour, the ten chiefs of the tribe sat down in the sand in the innermost part of the kiva. Their leader was ready to speak to them. His demeanor was serious and his bearing did justice as never before to the name his mother had given him at birth, for Walpi means mountain. The old warrior indeed resembled a towering totem, and the lines on his face seemed deeper than usual, like the furrows of that fearful canyon.

"The world is changing very quickly, brothers," he said in a hoarse whisper once the door to the kiva had been closed overhead.

His men nodded in unison. The familiar smell of the enclosed kiva had given way to an air of dense expectation.

"Today marks thirty winters since we received the first sign of that change," he went on. "It was another day of Hotomkam, just like today, when the men of fire entered the plains surrounding our village. Today there are but few of us left who witnessed the horror of which they were capable."

Walpi lifted one of his trembling arms toward the round opening in the roof, through which it was possible to see the three pulsing lights in Orion's belt.

"Those men with pale skin, who brought with them arms that spit out sounds like thunder, who wore protection like the shells of turtles that made them immune to our arrows, brought great suffering to our proud village. They set our fields on fire, slaughtered our animals, took our women hostage, and poisoned our wells by casting the bodies of the dead into them."

The old warrior cleared his throat.

The memory of those cruel days overwhelmed the men congregated there. The tale of their forefathers' sporadic encounters with an expedition of Spanish explorers still incited terror in the Indian lands. The great Walpi himself had fought them, and was one of the few who had withstood the gaze of Juan de Oñate—the Clouds hesitated even to say his name—and the only one to survive his summons. As it turned out, Walpi's ability to convince Oñate that there was no gold in the lands of the Cloud tribe not only won peace for his people, but earned him his current place of leadership.

Nevertheless, fear that the Spaniards might return had never left his mind.

"Killers! The strangers murdered our brothers with their magic!" one of the men gathered for the meeting shouted from the other side of the great bonfire.

"We lost three battles in three winters," another said quietly. "How could it have happened?"

Walpi looked the young warriors in the eye. None of them had ever seen the silver breastplates of the invaders. None of them had ever felt the visceral fear that washed over a warrior the first time he saw the Spaniard's horses. They had never experienced the stench of unbridled terror, but that could change at any moment.

The old warrior stared into the kiva's fire as he pondered his next words.

"You should know that the foreigners are about to return."

No one spoke.

"Last night," he went on, "the sign that I have feared for so long appeared again. I no longer have any doubt that the end of our world is near. And I want you to get your families ready."

Murmurs spread through the warriors.

"Will Juan de Oñate return?"

The great Walpi shook his head.

"Tell us what sign has convinced our chief of these things."

Nikvaya, who was counted among the wisest of the warriors, had stood up while posing his question, his eyes tinged with alarm. He knew that the weapons in his possession were useless against the strangers. His father had died from a bullet fired from a Spaniard's harquebus when Nikvaya was only a year old. Walpi, who had seen the warrior die, now turned to face the man's son.

"Sakmo, my youngest, the father of my only grandchild, met someone in the Canyon of the Serpent, close to the cemetery. It was a 'mother of the corn,' a Chóchmingure. She came down out of the sky enveloped in a blue light to make this terrible announcement: that the white-skinned strangers will soon arrive in our lands, bringing with them a new god."

"The spirits will stand in their way!" shouted another warrior who was standing in the deepest part of the kiva.

"No, my son. It is too late now. Our spirits have spent many years telling us about this arrival. We must see to it that this change does not spill the blood of our families."

"Can we trust Sakmo?"

The leader fixed a severe expression on the warrior, who stood a few feet away.

"He is blood of my blood, Nikvaya. He has inherited my ability to see into the world of the spirits. Furthermore, I have not yet told you that his encounter coincided with a mysterious presentiment I had before nightfall." The warrior paused to take a breath, and then continued. "I prayed before our guardian kachina, in this very place, when I heard a voice speaking to me from inside myself, a voice as clear as the song of the blackbird."

"What kind of voice?" asked one of the tribal chiefs, an Indian of slight build whose eye had been burned in a sandstorm.

"The voice foretold that our village would be visited by a great spirit, a presence from far away that not only those with the gift would see, but all those present on the night of Hotomkam. And it has happened! My son has seen it!"

"Did the spirit say why it came?" the man asked.

"No," Walpi replied, as his hand made rapid, violent movements through the sand at his feet. "That is why I have called you together. As chief of the Clouds I am required to do everything possible to communicate with the spirit. It is my duty to receive its message and inform the community of the fate that awaits us."

"You have called us, Master, so that we might invoke this spirit?" All eyes were on Nikvaya as he asked this last question.

"That is so, my son. Hotomkam will shine above us for the next eight days. We have just enough time to prepare the ritual and to wait for the blue spirit to manifest itself."

"The last man who conducted such a contact ceremony was Pavati, the warrior who preceded our leader. And he died doing so. To invoke a being like that can cost you your life."

The warning came from the very deepest part of the kiva. Another old warrior, the only one whose age and experience were on a par with Walpi's, got to his feet and approached the center of the kiva.

"I know that story well, Zeno," Walpi replied. "And I have no fear of dying. Do you?"

Zeno, too, had nothing left to lose. Moving closer to the crackling fire in the center of the kiva, he raised his voice.

"The spirits leave us no choice. I will help you in this undertaking."

FOURTEEN

ROME

When Father Baldi, or Saint Luke, turned the corner of Via dei Sediari, he became extremely cautious. Sediari is one of the narrow streets near Agrippa's Pantheon, which is nearly always full of visitors and tourists. And despite the fact that no one had ever seen him there, he wanted to be sure he passed unnoticed. His conversation with the surly voice had filled him with doubts.

Thirty seconds later, Baldi was poised across the street from his goal. Building number 10 was a solid structure of gray stone, with wooden cornices, tiny windows, and a large front door that led into a gloomy courtyard. At first glance it was difficult to say whether this was a substantial apartment building, a student dormitory, or the residence of a religious order. Especially if one took into account the two Fiats, belonging to the Roman police, that were blocking the large entranceway.

Father Baldi's face darkened. Police?

"Well, at least it isn't the black Citroën the secret service is so fond of," he muttered in relief. "They could be here for any number of things."

Saint Luke tried to remain calm. Once he had gathered his wits, he crossed the street and, taking a shortcut between the police cars, arrived at the building's front door. A quick glance was enough for him to see a small corridor window from which there issued a thin stream of light. "Santa Gemma Residence" announced the plaque on the wall.

"*Buona sera* . . . Very busy around here! Did something happen?"

Father Baldi, looking as innocent as possible, had cleared his throat before formulating his question. He stuck his head into the porter's office, whereupon he discovered a middle-aged man, his head topped with a few strands of blond hair, his face deeply lined, dressed in the brown habit of the Franciscans. The friar was killing time by listening to a dilapidated old transistor radio.

"Yes . . . ," he answered after lowering the volume. "If by that you mean the police, this evening one of the residents went to the trouble of killing himself. Looks like he threw himself into the courtyard from the fourth floor."

The Third Evangelist identified the man from his voice. He was none other than the man soured on life who had answered the phone whenever he called Saint Matthew. He would never have imagined him to look like this.

"A suicide?" Baldi was distressed. "Santa Madonna. And when did that happen?"

"About five o'clock this evening," the porter answered defensively. "They were just talking about it on the news."

"And you . . . you saw it?"

"Well, I heard a loud noise," the friar said with a smile that revealed rotting teeth. When I looked into the courtyard, I saw him with his head split open, in the middle of a pool of blood. I think he must have died on impact."

"God rest his soul," Baldi said, crossing himself. "Is there any way you can tell me who it was?"

"Naturally, Father: it was Luigi Corso. A professor and writer—brilliant man. Did you know him?"

Baldi turned pale.

"We are . . . we were old friends."

Baldi ran his hand over his silver hair, as if that gesture would in some way help him to think.

"Are you sure that Father Corso committed suicide?"

The porter was silent. His dark eyes, almost diabolical, looked Baldi over from head to toe as he tried to make sense of this suggestion from a man he had never before laid eyes on. He was reasonably certain that Corso was alone in his room when he leaped out into the open space above the courtyard. His last visitor had left more than a quarter of an hour earlier. Yes, he believed it was a suicide.

"Listen," he said in conclusion, "the police are upstairs in his room trying to reconstruct what happened. You can ask them yourself if you like. They arrived over an hour ago and have been going through his things ever since. They asked me to reroute any calls that come in for Father Corso to them. I can call them right now—"

"That won't be necessary." Baldi cut him off. "I just wondered. So they're rerouting his calls?"

"Just routine, so they said."

"Of course."

"Father," the porter leaned over toward Baldi with a certain solemnity. "You ought to know if suicide is a mortal sin."

"In principle, yes."

"In which case, do you believe God will save Father Corso's soul?"

Baldi was caught unprepared.

"God alone knows, my son."

Baldi made an awkward farewell and spun around, pushing his glasses against the ridge of his nose. He retraced his steps down the street, overwhelmed by the news. If someone at that moment had punched him in the stomach, he would have felt nothing. The First Evangelist had died over an hour before their planned meeting, and, to make matters worse, with him went Baldi's only base of support in Rome before the tribunal. Or almost. The departed "saint" was his only friend in Chronovision. He certainly had no faith in Saint John. Furthermore, Corso's death had come about just when someone in the Vatican had decided to close the door on the project. Someone who perhaps knew how much Baldi and Corso esteemed each other.

Or was that just his paranoia?

FIFTEEN

SIERRA DE CAMEROS

The following day, April 14, dawned with intermittent clouds and sun.

It was ten minutes to ten in the morning. Carlos's field book, a cork-covered notebook where he scribbled down information from the trip, held the day's itinerary. He and Txema had left Laguna de Cameros behind, intending to return to Madrid as quickly as possible. With a solid breakfast and their hostess's strong coffee in their bellies, they had everything they needed to make their exit from that labyrinth of secondary roads and small towns. Or so they thought.

Carlos and Txema realized something had gone wrong an hour after they started on their way. This time they blamed the cloudy conditions. Father Félix had warned them. He knew that when the low-lying clouds covered the crests of the Cameros, it would be difficult for them to find their way in the valleys below. As if that weren't enough, the narrow asphalt strip they were driving on was still covered in ice. Going faster than twenty miles an hour in such conditions was a reckless act. With all that, Carlos found himself obliged to pull the car over and open the hood to let the motor cool down while he gave a few swift kicks to all four tires, to dislodge the sheets of ice.

"What happened to your sudden inspirations today?"

Txema had calmly rolled down his window before spitting out his question. The mischievous smile had yet to leave his face since the night before. He would never have predicted that they'd be forced to spend the night in a town of less than a hundred inhabitants, with no hotel, no restaurant, and a bar that was open only in the summer, or that they'd end up sleeping in the private house of a local octogenarian. And at that hour he seemed amused that while they were stopped in the middle of a deserted roadway with his words bouncing off the nearby cliffs, their situation was far from resolved.

"Stop nagging me! Luck is like the weather: it changes suddenly, for better or worse."

Another kick rocked the car.

"Probably for worse today."

Carlos did not answer.

What was he going to say? That he had been mistaken? That his decision to travel there had been the fruit of an irrational impulse, far from professional? Was he going to give that pleasure to Txema so he could continue to laugh at his expense for the rest of the trip?

No way.

A clearing in the mist ahead allowed them to distinguish the outline of a highway sign. It was as if it had secretly come closer to greet the two men and lend them a hand. It stood there, a mere two hundred feet from where they stopped, indicating that there was an intersection ahead, one impossible to discern until this moment. It felt like an apparition, but it was real.

"What if . . . ?"

The photographer never finished his sentence.

Carlos jumped behind the wheel and drove the car slowly forward with the heat pumping at full blast, until he was able to read the words on the sign through the windshield. It revealed the mere minimum, along with an arrow: "Carretera N-122. Tarazona." The journalist turned left and headed down the road that opened before him, gunning the engine with joy.

Moments later, he was able to see through the fog a second time. A fleeting vision, but enough for his brain to process the content of another sign. This one was almost buried beneath the snow, jammed unevenly into the road's shoulder, but with its head supported proudly on aluminum poles. The single word on the sign electrified the journalist: six large, black letters that turned out to be very familiar to him.

"Did you see that?"

His sudden stop tore through the ice on the road and thrust Txema forward.

"Are you crazy?" he shouted. "What are you doing?"

"Did you see it or not?" Carlos asked again, his pulse quickening.

"What? The highway sign?"

"Yes, did you read it?"

The photographer cursed as he undid his seat belt and felt around inside his camera bag, to make sure nothing had been damaged. "Sure I read it: Ágreda."

"Good Lord!" Carlos shook his head, incredulous. "It meant nothing to you? That name doesn't sound the least bit familiar?"

Txema looked lost in the woods.

"Jesus, it's the nun's name!"

Txema's round, unshaven face was incredulous.

"The nun who traveled to America whenever she liked?" he said, almost whispering.

"Exactly."

"Calm down, will you? You're going to get us killed. And keep your hands on the wheel. Shit! It's just a coincidence."

"Coincidence? What a joke! You don't get it, do you?" Carlos's eyes were opened wide, and he paid no attention to anything other than his companion's reactions. "How could I have been so stupid? In the seventeenth century and earlier, many famous people were known by their place of birth . . . in the case of María Jésus de Ágreda, that 'de Ágreda' could be her last name, or the town where she was born."

"Hell's bells!" Txema roared at him. "It's cold. You made a full stop right in the middle of the highway. Do whatever you like, Carlos. Let's turn off the road and drive into the village. Question anyone you like, but get this car out of here!"

"Why didn't I think of it before?"

Txema gave him a serious look. His friend was acting like a drunk.

"This can't be mere chance, it just can't be. Do you know how many villages there are in Spain?"

The photographer doubted he should take the question seriously.

"Do you know?" Carlos insisted.

Txema rummaged around in the glove compartment for the map of the country's highways they always took with them, and leafed through the list of towns by geographical regions at the back of the book.

"I found it!" His finger stopped at the bottom of one of the pages. "There are 35,618."

"You see? One possibility in thirty-five thousand isn't chance. What do you say now?"

"I say let's get the hell off this highway, dammit!"

SIXTEEN

LOS ANGELES

"Tell me, Jennifer, did you ever try to find out if those dreams were real?"

Dr. Meyers had been silent for a long while, listening closely to every detail of her patient's dreams. Jennifer related each of them so vividly that the doctor found it difficult to classify them as simple delirium.

"I don't understand."

"Simple. Did you ever think, once you had awakened, that what you saw in your dream was a memory? That you had really been there, among the Indians?"

"Come on, Doctor," Jennifer protested. "You're not going to tell me you believe in reincarnation? I have some American Indians in my family tree, but I've never read anything about them, or their rituals, or—"

"That's not what I meant. Have you ever tried to differentiate between dream and reality?"

The psychiatrist's tenacity intimidated her patient.

"You know what? Even when I was very little I was able to remember everything I dreamed at night."

"Go on."

"Before I went off to college I told my mother everything. I explained to her that it was like the feeling of flying, or climbing over a wall. Or even like singing underwater. My grandmother, who lived on the outskirts of Mexico City for many years, near the

Sanctuary of the Virgin of Guadalupe, gave me the nickname the Great Dreamer."

"The Great Dreamer?"

Jennifer nodded, pursing her lips in a gently mocking expression.

"My grandmother was the one who taught me to distinguish between the world of dreams and the real world. Thanks to her, I know now that all those scenes of New Mexico were only a dream. They have to be!"

Dr. Meyers rested her chin pensively in her hand. The thick, insulated glass windows of her office muffled the sound of a police siren.

"Tell me about your grandmother," she said as the last reflections of the strobing light disappeared from the windows.

"Her name was Ankti, which in the Indian language means 'dance.' All the women in my family were given that name, at least until I made my appearance in this world on the other side of the border, in the United States, and they named me Jennifer."

"What comes to mind about her?"

"I saw very little of my grandmother, except for the one summer my parents let me stay with her while they went to Europe on vacation. And every day I was there she took me to the basilica of the Virgin of Guadalupe. She told me the story a thousand times. And you know the strangest thing? She taught me to think of the Virgin as a woman surrounded by a blue light, a woman who shone, who every so often appeared in the Mexico of our ancestors."

"She seems like the woman in your dreams?"

"Exactly the same. My grandmother told me the story of her appearance. Did you ever hear it?"

Dr. Meyers shook her head.

"It's a lovely story. Juan Diego, who came from the same people as my grandmother, had several encounters with a mysterious woman bathed in a blue light, on a hill known as Tepeyac. The woman told him that a basilica should be built on that very spot as a way of honoring her. The Spanish who ruled Mexico at that time paid no attention to him. The Archbishop of Mexico City demanded that Juan Diego bring him some proof, and Diego, out of desperation, communicated the Spaniard's demands to the mysterious blue woman herself."

"And what happened?"

"This part of the story was my grandmother's favorite," Jennifer said with a smile. "In her fourth apparition, the blue lady gave him something as proof: she asked him to carry roses to the bishop. Now, roses were uncommon in that part of the world, and it wasn't the time of the year when they flowered. But the Indian, obedient to her request, carried the flowers in his poncho and laid them down at the entrance to the Archbishop's palace. The Virgin had left the roses in some bushes near where she had appeared."

Jennifer took a breath before she went on.

"When the Archbishop let him in and Juan Diego opened his poncho, do you know what happened? The flowers had disappeared! The Spaniard fell to his knees marveling at the phenomenon: instead of the flowers, engraved on his humble poncho was a mysterious effigy of the Lady in Blue."

"A portrait of her?"

Jennifer nodded.

"I saw the cotton fabric, the poncho, every day that summer. In fact, if I close my eyes and concentrate, I can still re-create it in mind. It stays with me."

"This is interesting, Jennifer." The doctor's dark eyes were flickering as she spoke. "Do you feel that someone is always with you?"

Her patient had no idea how to respond.

"Let me rephrase it. This may sound harsh, so please try not to misinterpret me. Were you, at any time either in your civilian life or during your work for the military, diagnosed with some type of psychiatric illness?"

"Well, as you can imagine, before becoming a part of the remote-vision project, they gave me all kinds of medical tests."

"And?"

"Nothing, Doctor. They found nothing wrong with me."

Linda Meyers scribbled something into her notebook, and then took a breath.

"Fine, Jennifer. Before I write a prescription for an anxiety medication to regulate your dreams, let me explain what I think is happening to you."

The Great Dreamer shifted her position on the sofa.

"Among the many sleep disorders that have been cataloged, there's one that is especially rare, affecting less than one percent of the population. They call it somnimnesia, which is a Latin word that comes from *somnium*, sleep, and *mnesia*, memory. In short, it is a question of the difficulty that certain subjects have in distinguishing their dreams from their actual memories."

"But I already told you that my grandmother taught me to—"

"Let me finish, please," the psychiatrist broke in. "At first, many of my colleagues believed this to be a variant of schizophrenia. Just imagine: 'false' memories but seemingly very real, fabricated by the mind. Some patients thought they knew how to drive or to swim because they dreamed that they had done it, and owing to these false memories, they ran the risk of drowning or having a car crash in real life. I have to know if this is true in your case. I have to find the origin of these oneiric experiences. We have to discover what is causing them: why they are so coherent and why their internal structure is so solid. You understand, right?"

Jennifer nodded.

"So you will search for the origin of your dreams?"

"Yes, of course . . ." She didn't know how to answer.

"Take your time. And find out if your mother, her grandmother, or anyone in your family had this type of experience. Should you find anything, let me know. As long as your dreams aren't the source of other problems, I will resist prescribing pharmacological treatment."

SEVENTEEN

GRAN QUIVIRA

Everything followed the course foreseen by the great Walpi. For eight days, the ten men who governed the Cloud tribe remained in the kiva, apart from the others while they practiced the ritual of contact. Two times each day, their wives drew close to the tiny opening in the roof of the building, and without looking inside, they lowered baskets of boiled corn, cactus, agave leaves with its sweet pulp intact, and water.

Neither the women nor the members of the other tribes knew the nature of the ceremony being performed inside. Each group of Cueloces had its own rituals, its ancestral ways of communicating with the spirits, which remained a well-kept secret. All that was known was that the fermented substances prepared in the kiva enabled them to make contact with the Great Spirit.

Inside the kiva there was always a fire. Night and day, Walpi and his men stayed in the shadows, chewing on the leaves of plants and beating their drums, which were made using buffalo intestines. As the days passed, the atmosphere inside the kiva became more and more intense. Only the old leader kept track of the days as they sped by, taking care to perform the ritual tasks in the hours of silence: during the long waits in between rituals, the men slept, adorned one another with new tattoos, and cleaned the masks handed down by their ancestors. These were fearful heads, with sharp teeth and big, bulging eyes, sometimes crowned with feathers and other times with spikes, meant to be an imitation of the faces of their spiritual protectors. And they tightened the heads on their drums, or prayed before the sipapu, a small hole dug in the center of the kiva, which the Indians believed allowed them to communicate with the spirits from the other world.

But all those activities were only a prelude to their true work: dreaming. Once they had ingested the sacred plants and the soup made from fermented yucca, which they had been preparing since the first day they went into isolation, their minds were ready for the search for the blue spirit. The great Walpi was anxious to make contact.

And at first, as might be expected, nothing happened.

It was as if the great spirit who was to come had not yet heard their invocations.

Outside the kiva during the night, four men were posted to guard the tribe's privacy. They were the *kéketl*, or small falcons, young men who, while they had yet to be initiated in the secrets of the adult world, were fully trained as warriors. Sakmo, as the most skillful warrior in the tribe, was in charge of their fighting skills. He was still greatly affected by what he had lived through a few days before.

He instructed the *kéketl* that during a ceremony like this, no one save a benign spirit could approach the kiva. If anyone transgressed this rule, and did not respond to their sacred warning gestures, they would put him to death, tearing his body into four equal parts and burying them outside the village, each piece as far from the other as possible.

No one would dare to profane the kiva of the Clouds.

The eighth night, when Hotomkam shone more brightly than ever, something began to move in the sacred enclosure of the Jumanos. Walpi's face was bathed in sweat when he looked out from beneath his blanket. He looked bewildered. The kiva was asleep. That night's ceremony had left everyone exhausted, except for the head of the tribe. Suddenly he jumped up and rushed out of the kiva telling the *kéketl* to remain on guard. Looking back to be certain no one was following him, he disappeared into the brush.

He behaved as if possessed, as if he were following the steps of someone who could guide him through the darkness. As if, at last, the geometric signs that had been tattooed on his chest when he was a young man as a form of protection were now fulfilling their task.

Someone or something had made contact with him.

In the moments before his flight, an extraordinary blue light had descended around the half-moon-shaped passage in the rock that stood near the Cemetery of the Ancestors. This time Sakmo did not witness it; no one in Cueloce had noticed its presence. If anyone had been able to observe the scene from close by, he would have been struck by a certain complicity between that glow and the ancient warrior. While the pulsing light flickered deep in the canyon, the old man was drawn toward it, running like an antelope.

At the same time, a hush descended on the nearby fields.

The remarkable silence that had so impressed Sakmo now began to spread around the outskirts of the village. And with it, the oceans of grass that surrounded the mountain ceased moving. The grasshoppers stopped chirping. Even the unmistakable gurgle of the waters at Fox's Spring, which the old man leaped across as if it were no wider than a breath of air, quieted their monotonous song and grew still.

The leader noticed none of these prodigies. His five senses had taken leave of this world in order to concentrate on the other.

"Mother!" he yelled. "At last!"

The old warrior had found her.

At first he was only able to see the glowing light. But as his eyes adjusted, he was able to perceive the outlines of a beautiful young woman, her pale face giving off rays of light, who stood just a few feet away from him. "Protective spirits," he said quietly. The woman radiated light in all four directions, partially illuminating the ground where the great Walpi stood. She was dressed in a long white tunic, with a celestial blue cape that descended from her shoulders to just above the ground.

As the great Walpi approached her, the young woman smiled.

"You have called for me, and I have come. What is it you want?"

The woman did not move her lips, nor did she make any gesture with her hands. Nevertheless, her words were as clear and transparent as those Sakmo had heard just nine nights before.

"Mother, I want to ask you something . . ."

The apparition nodded. The great warrior paused before continuing.

"Why did you let yourself be seen by my son and not by me? Have you lost confidence in the one who has guarded the secret of your visits all this time? I have always kept silent about our encounters, I have instructed my people about the next coming of the white people, and you—"

"It is no longer necessary to maintain our silence," she said, interrupting him. "The moment I spoke about so often has arrived. You have completed your task. In a short time, your son will take your place."

"Sakmo? He still has much to learn!" the old warrior protested.

"I need someone like him. He has the sign engraved on his skin. Like you. He is the only one in your family who inherited your gift. And now he will inherit your mission."

"What will happen to our village?"

"God will guide it."

"God? What God?"

The lady did not respond. Instead, she let something fall to the ground. A rough cross of wood, which the Indian looked at incredulously.

The warrior knew well what was going to happen next: the blue light would grow in intensity as a harsh buzzing sound, like the squealing of countless rats, would fill his ears until he collapsed on the ground. It always happened that way.

But this time, the "blue spirit" had one last instruction to give him.

EIGHTEEN

ÁGREDA, SPAIN

Carlos took three deep breaths to steel himself before starting the car again. In response to Txema's pleas, he had steered the car onto the shoulder, while he took a moment to get over the shock his discovery had caused. "Ágreda," he repeated like a zombie. "Ágreda." It turned out to be difficult for him to accept the existence of a town whose name was spelled identically to that of the "last name" of a nun, evidence of whose existence he was unable to produce when he was on her trail, and which he now castigated himself for not finding before this latest incident. "Just one town in Spain among 35,618 listed localities," he said with hindsight. "I should have checked it out!"

"Hidden treasure reveals itself only to those who know what it contains," Txema mumbled, sounding like an ancient Chinese sage. Carlos could never tell when Txema was making fun of him.

"What do you mean?"

"That perhaps when you began your work on teleportations, you weren't at all prepared to understand what they were about."

"What sort of cheap philosophy is that?" Carlos protested.

"Think what you like. I know that you're an unbeliever, but I'm convinced that we all have our own destiny. And that sometimes the force of that destiny pushes us violently, like a hurricane."

The photographer's words struck Carlos as odd and strangely serious, as if they had been pronounced by some long forgotten oracle and not Txema. Carlos had never heard his friend talk like that—in reality, he even doubted Txema was capable of letting his mind entertain such thoughts—but his words had nevertheless stirred something inside him. Right then and there, once he had left the frozen shoulder of Route N-122 behind, he knew he had no choice in the matter. He had to drop the fatuous hunt for holy shrouds, switch the order of priorities in his list of pending assignments, and do a little fieldwork in the small town named Ágreda. When he felt the cool touch of the little medal with the "holy face" against his skin, he smiled. Who knew, he thought, if this most unlikely round of events would revitalize his stalled investigation into teleportations?

The growls from the car's engine dragged him back to reality. He closed the notepad and replaced it inside his coat, then told Txema to put away the highway map. Training his sight on the asphalt once more, he headed down the one street leading into the center of town.

Ágreda turned out to be a real discovery: located at the foot of Moncayo (an impressive mass of mountain over 7,590 feet tall that stared at them defiantly from between passing clouds), the layout of the town was a vivid reflection of the scars it had collected over the course of its history. Christians, Jews, and Muslims had shared its streets and marketplaces until well into the fifteenth century. The setting for royal weddings, the waters from its river, the Queiles, were venerated by Roman smithies, who forged their most durable weapons in it. It was of course a while before the two men learned all this.

That morning, the streets of Ágreda were as damp and devoid of people as those of Laguna de Cameros. The windshields of the cars parked on either side of the Avenida de Madrid were caked with a thick coating of ice, and the town's roughly three thousand inhabitants had taken refuge from the cold inside the thick stone walls of their houses.

"Where are you thinking of going?" Txema inquired gently. His companion was still shaken by their incredible geographic blunder.

"To the main church, where else? If once upon a time a nun had the power of bilocation, the ability to be in two places at the same time, and flew over to America God knows how, the priest ought to know about it."

The small Ibiza snaked swiftly down the town's deserted streets. Ágreda turned out to be larger than it appeared from the highway. Fortunately, the church they were looking for soon came into view; it sat right next to a building that appeared to be the city hall, which stood on the west side of a great rectangular plaza. Carlos drove past the church slowly, parking the car a short distance from its main entrance.

"Closed!" Txema blurted out as his breath enveloped him in a little cloud of fog.

"Maybe another church is open. . . . Look over there."

Looming immediately behind them, next to a four-story building, was the unmistakable silhouette of another baroque bell tower. They slowly crossed the plaza to knock on its magnificent door.

"Also shut tight." The photographer sighed a second time. "No one's around, and it's colder than hell."

"Pretty strange, eh? Even the bars are closed."

"Nothing unusual for the north. Today is Sunday, and with a temperature like this, I'd be at home, too. Maybe we'll have luck at noon, when they ring the bells for the main Mass."

Txema's hint was enough to kick the journalist into high gear.

"Noontime? We're not going to hang around here at a standstill till then!"

"Sounds good to me." The photographer was already quickening his pace toward the heat. "Let's get back in the car."

Once inside, with the heater going full blast and the windshield wipers scattering ever-fewer chunks of ice, Txema mumbled, "Probably nothing would have come of it."

"Probably," Carlos replied laconically. "But you wouldn't deny that a lot of random events led us to this town."

"And those kinds of random events really exasperate you, right?"

"Did I ever tell you about that old professor of mathematics who believed that chance was one of God's disguises?"

"A few hundred times! For two weeks you talked about nothing else!" Txema laughed. "What I fail to understand is why you put so much effort into resisting situations in life that, maybe, just maybe, are arranged in advance, no matter by whom, and are out of your hands. Is it because you're still hoping to 'catch' God behind one of your random events?"

Carlos gripped the wheel of the car as hard as he could, trying to stay in the middle of the narrow street and not brush against one of the unevenly parked cars. One lousy sheet of ice could send them skidding into the cars on either side.

"What kind of question is that!" he said at last. "To agree to what you're saying is the same as accepting that, to at least some degree, someone exists who has traced the blueprints of our lives. And from there to accepting God's existence is but a single step."

"So why not go ahead and believe it then?" the photographer pressed on.

"Because it's my impression that God is the formula people apply to everything beyond their understanding. Belief in God gets us out of the hard work of thinking."

"And what if after all your hard work you conclude that he exists?"

Carlos was silent and stopped the car, putting the engine in neutral.

"So what now?" the photographer asked.

"This is the wrong road," he said just above a whisper.

Txema was concerned. Something was wrong.

"Are we really lost?"

"No, I don't think so."

When Carlos's limbs had regained their feeling, he drove the car toward the road sign that announced Ágreda's city limits. As they had passed the sign, he noticed across the narrow road a stone building that sat next to a small bell tower. He made a show of shutting off the car and undoing his seat belt. A quick glance was enough for Txema to realize they were no longer on Route N-122. This was a badly paved road, full of holes and barely wide enough for one car to pass, much less two.

The photographer watched his friend without knowing where he was headed.

Once out of the car, Carlos slammed the door shut and walked toward the building. "You could use some fresh air," Txema advised from the car, observing his friend's hesitant steps.

"Here it is! Over here!" he heard Carlos shout out of nowhere.

The photographer's heart was racing. He grabbed the bag of cameras from underneath his seat, and jumped out of the car.

"What's going on?"

"Look!"

Txema was shaking in the cold while his companion, who was exhaling puffs of air like a dragon in a cave, was enthusiastically gesturing toward the building behind him. Or, to be more precise, at a kind of moat that lay between the highway and the building, at the very bottom of which they could see a pair of oak doorways with an unusual escutcheon carved in stone over one; and the other, set apart, with a quatrefoil blocked off by thick iron crossbars.

"What is it you want me to see?"

"Down there."

Txema looked down a second time into the moat scooped out of the earth. A statue, rendered in stone, of a nun, her arms spread and a cross in one hand, jumped out at him, as if it had just appeared.

"This is a monastery! You see? What better place to ask about a nun?"

"Sure . . . of course," Txema said under his breath. He was losing confidence in his friend. "Are we going down?"

The two men descended the steep, snow-covered ramp that led to the flat stretch of land in the center of the clearing, and then stood in front of the wooden doors. They soon realized that the building was much larger than they had thought. In fact, it looked a bit like a fortress. Its façade was dotted with tiny wooden windows and a primitive depiction of Christ on the way to Calvary, which time had darkened with soot.

"You're right. It must be a monastery," Txema said just loud enough for Carlos to hear.

But Carlos was no longer listening. He was on his knees in front of the cement pedestal on which the statue stood. He was writing in his notebook, copying down the inscription carved into the base of the statue.

"See?" he said when he was done. "Read the engraving yourself."

Txema directed his attention to the foot of the statue, where he read:

To the Venerable Madre Ágreda,
with reverent pride.
From your townspeople.

"So you think it refers to your nun?"

His question was clearly a trap.

"Who else?"

"You know what?" he said as he held his camera. "Forget everything I said earlier about destiny. We need to remain cold-blooded now."

Carlos nodded, without saying a word.

"You yourself explained to me that it was customary to give the name of the town to the outstanding personages born there. It would be a highly unlikely occurrence if this nun were the exact person you were looking for. . . . A highly unlikely occurrence," he said emphatically.

"Just one more."

Carlos looked at the photographer out of the corner of his eye. Txema was not about to let up.

"And furthermore, if it is a question of the nun who so tried your patience when you were working on teleportations, we will soon know one way or the other. But if this is a different lady, do me a favor: let's forget about this and hightail it back to Madrid, without a word to anyone. Agreed?"

"Agreed."

Carlos got to his feet, and with an energetic stride walked over to the door nearest him and tried it. It was open.

"Go in!" Txema encouraged him.

Once he had crossed the threshold and his eyes adjusted to the darkness, his first suspicions were confirmed. They were standing in a small waiting area whose walls were adorned with heavy blocks of wood on which religious scenes had been carved in relief. A carousel, through which a person inside could speak to someone in the waiting area, built into the wall on the right, left no doubt: this was a monastery.

A small table draped with a crocheted cotton tablecloth, on top of which were deposited slowly yellowing religious pamphlets; a small bell and an ancient light switch screwed into some tiles on the wall at eye level; the unmistakable wooden cylinder that connected the cloister to the exterior world: these were the sum total of the antechamber's decorations.

"Are you going to call them?" Txema asked him quietly. The silence all around him and the cold inside the unheated waiting room had taken their toll.

"Of course."

Carlos pressed his finger down on the buzzer. A piercing whine reverberated throughout the building.

A few seconds later, a door creaked on its hinges somewhere on the other side of that wooden carousel. Someone was walking toward them.

"Hail Mary, full of grace," said the voice that broke the silence. Its echo bounced around the waiting area.

"Conceived without sin, Sister," Carlos said doubtfully in the standard reply.

"How can I help you?"

Their invisible respondent interrogated him with extraordinary gentleness. For a moment, Carlos considered the possibility of throwing together an innocent story that would justify their visit while concealing what was already beginning to be an astounding series of events, but instead he offered a small part of the truth.

"You see, Sister, we are journalists on assignment from Madrid, writing a story on the holy objects that parishes in the Cameros have in their possession. The snowfall and the bad road conditions have deposited us here at your doorstep. What we'd like to know is if a certain nun named María Jesús de Ágreda lived here. She took her vows in the seventeenth century, and we were wondering if you have any record of her. A few weeks ago I mentioned her by chance in one of my articles without knowing if—"

A poke in the ribs from the photographer left the phrase unfinished.

"Why wouldn't we have heard about her! She founded our order!"

Txema and Carlos exchanged mute looks of astonishment. The nun, unaware of their reactions, went on:

"If you're here, it is because she led you here. Of that you can be certain," she said, and a pleasant little laugh passed through the wooden cylinder. "She is famous as a miracle worker, and certainly something about you must have interested her. With all that is happening right now, the Venerable María must have wanted you for some important purpose. She can be very persuasive!"

"Can be?" Carlos asked, in an alarmed tone.

"Very well, she was very persuasive," the nun conceded.

"And what did you mean when you said that she had 'led us,' Sister?"

"Nothing, nothing at all." The nun was laughing. "There's a key in the carousel. Take it and open the small door on the right. Walk all the way down the hallway to the end. When you get there you'll be standing in front of a glass door with a key in it; go inside and light the stove. I will send one of the sisters to assist you straightaway."

The orders, delivered with such sweetness, were so precise they had no choice but to obey. In fact, before they even had a chance to think about it, the carousel had spun around, revealing a small key secured to a yellow key chain. It was their passport into the monastery.

NINETEEN

ROME

At exactly 8:30 PM, Father Baldi returned to Saint Peter's Square. He felt reasonably secure in those environs. A taxi left him on the corner where Borgo Pio meets Porta Angelica, in front of one of the Vatican's busiest "service entrances," used with great frequency by those who work inside the papal state. By that hour, most of them had already left their offices.

After giving it some thought, Baldi decided to play tough.

He understood that this was his one opportunity to avoid returning to Venice empty-handed. The unfortunate death of Saint Matthew had left him in a compromised position, which he needed to clear up at the earliest possible moment. And right there, inside God's fortress, he sensed that a few answers awaited him.

Without giving it further thought, Baldi plunged into the stream of employees, hurried past the Swiss Guards' sentry boxes, and entered the labyrinth of buildings en route to the Vatican's Secretariat of State. The Secretariat's façade, which stretched the entire length of that short block, was covered with gray wooden shutters and black iron grates. The building had recently undergone a restoration, and its copper plaque etched with a tiara and Peter's keys to the kingdom gleamed brightly in the glare of the streetlights.

The interior of the building was another matter: hallways the color of lead and thin plywood doors with the names of cardinals and other members of the Curia taped on, serving to indicate that their status at any moment was merely superficial. The building was practically empty.

"How may I help you?"

A round-faced nun, dressed in a dark blue habit and crocheted head scarf, approached him from behind a large desk.

"I would like to see His Eminence Stanislaw Zsidiv."

"Do you have an appointment?"

"No, but his Eminence knows me very well. Tell him that Father Giuseppe Baldi is here to see him from Venice. It is urgent, and furthermore," he said as he waved the letter he had received from Zsidiv two days before, "I know he will be pleased to see me."

The nun barely wasted a second before pushing the appropriate keys on her switchboard and conveying the message to the party at the other end of the line. After a perfunctory "Very well, he'll see you," which Baldi accepted with satisfaction, the nun guided him through the corridors leading to the Polish cardinal's office.

"Here we are," she said as she stood in front of yet another unremarkable doorway. "You may enter without knocking."

No sooner had he crossed the office's threshold than Baldi's attention was caught by the fact that from his windows Zsidiv could see the lighted dome of Saint Peter's, as well as a good number of the one hundred and forty statues in Bernini's colonnade. His survey of the room ended with a set of splendid Renaissance tapestries, overflowing with pagan symbolism, which hung in well-lighted splendor in one corner of the room.

"Giuseppe! My God! How many years has it been!"

Zsidiv was a man of medium height. He was dressed in the red-trimmed robe of his rank, but his face was that of a clean-shaven Polish woodcutter who had about him all the warmth of a grave, while his blue eyes, hidden behind the thick lenses of his glasses, carefully scrutinized everything around him. The Cardinal rose from his black leather armchair and with a few imperious strides crossed the barely five feet separating him from his guest. Baldi took in the room's odor, a peculiar mixture of expensive cologne and the Vatican's cleaning service.

Baldi bent down on one knee, kissed the Cardinal's ring and the cross around his neck, and the two men embraced. He took the seat directly in front of Zsidiv's desk, straightened his priest's robe, and cast a quick glance over the files and envelopes that lay spread out between the Cardinal and himself. The truth was they had no need of introductions. His Eminence and the Benedictine had known each other for years, since they were seminarians together in Florence. They had shared an interest in pre-polyphony, as well as the most noble ideals of their lives. It had been Zsidiv, born in Cracow and a personal friend of the Pope, who introduced Baldi to the organizers of Chronovision in the 1950s, when the project was just getting off the ground.

He later learned that Zsidiv was "Saint John," the project coordinator, who was in charge of overseeing the team's activities and making sure the Chronovision project remained solely a Vatican affair. Although there was no need for secrets between the two men, they existed nonetheless.

"A stroke of luck that you came to see me, Giuseppe," the Cardinal said. Zsidiv lowered his voice. "I had no idea how I was going to bring you up to date with what happened to Saint Matthew, our Father Corso, earlier this evening."

"That is precisely what I wanted to speak to you about."

"Indeed?" The Cardinal was surprised. His subordinate maintained a tone of absolute obedience. "You already know what happened?"

"I found out an hour ago. I saw the police cars in front of his house."

"You went by his house?" Zsidiv's expression changed. Baldi's action was a clear violation of the rules and regulations governing the Four Evangelists.

"Well, I could say that your letter was in some way responsible for that. As well as the curt order to come to Rome to give an explanation for what happened with the Spanish journalist. That is what the request was about, no?"

"I'm afraid so, Giuseppe. Once again."

"But I swear to you that I never—"

The Cardinal brought him to a swift halt.

"No excuses!" he said, and then leaning across his desk, lowered his voice. "The walls have ears."

Zsidiv leaned back in his chair, and his voice returned to normal. Baldi knew what had just happened. Even if he was Chronovision's coordinator, and a personal ally, the Cardinal played an important role among the guardians of orthodoxy. His part was that of a double agent. Difficult. Ambiguous. Which was why Baldi never completely trusted him.

"I am not the one who demanded your presence here," he went on. "Your hangmen await at the Congregation for the Doctrine of the Faith. The Sant'Uffizio. But you know what? None of that is important anymore, my friend. With the death of the First Evangelist, many changes are in the offing. The Pope is preoccupied by Chronovision. I fear that it will be taken out of our hands and they will uncover things better left buried. Do you follow?"

Gripping the arms of his chair, Zsidiv raised himself above the papers lying between them.

"The worst thing about this whole incident," he continued, "is that we still have no idea if his death was accidental or provoked. The police are busy putting their report together, and the autopsy has to wait until later tonight. Even so . . ." Zsidiv wrung his hands. He thought for a moment. "What bothers me most is that he was conversant with certain subjects related to Chronovision, of which you know nothing, and that now may have leaked outside our circle."

Baldi's face revealed his confusion.

"Someone erased all the files from his computer. A technician from the Holy See has already taken a close look at the hard drive, and he says it was reformatted twenty minutes before Saint Matthew died. Someone copied everything to another disk. We have, shall we say, solid reason to believe that documentation of great value has disappeared from his work space."

"What kind of documentation?"

"Historical papers, but also handwritten notes covering all his experiments."

Zsidiv changed his tone when he saw the look of incredulity on Baldi's face.

"We have placed you in quarantine. Is that clear? We cannot run the risk that this information gets out to the press, much less anything about Saint Matthew, or that you might accidentally give away our project."

"Do you have any suspects, Your Eminence?"

"I am considering several candidates. The minions at the Congregation for the Doctrine of the Faith salivate over this subject. As you already know, Paul the Sixth, in the spirit of reform, stripped them of their responsibilities, and now they follow any project that sounds like heresy in hot pursuit. They tried to bury Chronovision from the moment they heard of its existence, and your statements to the press suited their purposes perfectly. Although I remain in the dark as to how far they may have gone."

"My statements? I never—"

Zsidiv leaned over his desk and fished around for a copy of the Spanish magazine *Mysteries*, which he placed on top of a pile of papers.

"You can understand the title in Spanish, no?"

Baldi flipped the magazine open to the centerfold and read the headline of the story that ran over his photo: "A Time Machine That Takes Photographs of the Past."

"But Your Eminence, do you think I—?"

Zsidiv interrupted him before he could finish.

"That problem is no longer relevant, as I told you. The most pressing matter is to get our hands on whoever stole Saint Matthew's archives. We have to prevent another scandal."

Father Baldi nodded.

"What I fear, Giuseppe, is that this is the work of our allies. But in the present state of our diplomatic relations, even insinuating the possibility is out of the question."

"Allies? Which allies?" The priest's face showed that he had never heard of Chronovision's having allies outside the reach of the Vatican.

"This is something else the evangelists have avoided letting you know. But since we urgently need to recover the lost documents, I am obliged to bring you back into our confidence."

The Cardinal peered out over the top of his glasses.

"I hope I'm not making a mistake in trusting you again."

The words were spoken in utmost seriousness. Baldi merely nodded his head. He sat there, riveted to his chair, waiting for the man on the other side of the desk to explain what had been hidden from him over the last several months.

TWENTY

VENICE BEACH, CALIFORNIA

Jennifer lit a cigarette as she drove back to her house, her emotions running in circles after her session with Dr. Meyers. She thought that the warm breeze off the Pacific, and a long stroll ending in a champagne cocktail at the Sidewalk Cafe, would help her clarify her thinking.

But she was wrong. As straightforward as she had tried to be with Dr. Meyers, there were things she could not tell her. How was she going to convey the assignment she had been working on those few weeks in Italy, a maximum security project, participating in tests in which she ingested hypnotic substances? And how could she get a clean bill of health from the doctor if she refused to reveal certain information classified as "secret" under the national security protocol? On the other hand, were all her dreams closely linked to her grandmother? Was it just chance that the woman who appeared there so resembled the Lady of Guadalupe she had remembered that afternoon?

The truth was that those persistent dreams had ended up divorcing her from the project. They were clouding her mind, they told her. And now she really did feel as if she were moving around in a fog.

The first time she had consulted a doctor was in Rome, after a clinical report issued at Fort Meade attempted to disqualify her participation: "The patient suffers from a strange variant of epilepsy known as ecstatic epilepsy or Dostoyevsky's epilepsy. She should undergo a period of observation and use special safeguards during her work for INSCOM, the Intelligence and Security Command."

What sort of scientific jargon was that?

Jennifer parked her Toyota in the resident parking area and walked to her house. Ever since she was a child, her parents had brought her here during the summer to enjoy the beach and to spend time with her cousins. Which was why, when she had left Washington with the intention never to return, she had been allowed to transform the house into her own place. It was an old wooden structure, the kind that creaks every time you take a step. She could still smell the blueberry pies her mother made each summer in the old stove.

Before entering, she nostalgically contemplated its whitewashed façade. The house was a trove of memories. Once inside, she got out an old carton where she had stored her knickknacks, photographs, and souvenirs from her trips. It was all still there, even the thing that she had just remembered. Jennifer smiled. Why hadn't she thought of it before? She recalled her conversation with the Italian doctor who had "deciphered" the diagnosis of her condition that had been given at Fort Meade. She had made notes on their conversation so that she could reflect on the doctor's opinions later, when she had sufficient peace of mind. That little notebook had been sitting right where she'd left it inside the carton.

As she went through her notes, she could hear the reed-thin voice of Dr. Buonviso. What a charmer. She smiled as she recalled his amusing English with its Italian accent, and it was as though she were back in the cafeteria of Ospedale Generale di Zona "Cristo Re," where they had had their conversation a little over a year ago.

"The illness you are asking me about is extremely unusual," he had told her.

"So I hear, Doctor," she replied. "Is there anything else you can tell me about it?"

"Well . . . someone who suffers from Dostoyevsky's epilepsy generally has extremely vivid dreams or visions. First comes a blinding light, which precedes a rapid reduction in the patient's attention to any surrounding stimuli. The body is then, in the great majority of cases, immobile, as rigid as a board, and finally the patient submerges himself in extremely detailed hallucinations that flow into a state of well-being. Afterward the patient experiences absolute physical exhaustion."

"I am familiar with the symptoms. . . . Can the condition be treated?"

"In reality, we are at a loss for a treatment. Bear in mind that there are only a dozen documented cases in the whole world."

"So few?"

"As I said, this is an extremely rare disease. Combing through the historical records, I find that some specialists have found its symptoms in historical figures such as Saint Paul—remember the flash of light that beset him on the road to Damascus?—Muhammad, Joan of Arc . . ."

"And Dostoyevsky?"

"He certainly had it as well. In fact, the illness is named for him because in his novel *The Idiot* he describes its symptoms with extraordinary precision. He attributes them to one of the protagonists, Prince Myshkin. All the characteristics of this kind of epilepsy are laid out in detail—"

Jennifer interrupted. "So you're saying you wouldn't know what course of treatment to follow if you had a patient with those symptoms?"

"To be honest, I wouldn't."

"Do you know if it's hereditary?"

"Aha! There is no doubt about that, signorina. Although it is rarely diagnosed as a disease these days. In the past it was regarded as almost a divine gift. It is even said that Saint Teresa suffered from it, and it was this illness that led to her ecstatic communion with God."

Had she inherited this illness? And in that case, from whom? Her mother never suffered from it. Nor her father, who had been a cold, inflexible man till the day he died.

After leafing through some old family albums to jog her memory, Jennifer spent the rest of the day reviewing the last few years of her life. First there had been her inability to finish her studies at Georgetown University, then her recruitment for the Stargate project under the honorable cover of the Stanford Research Institute (SRI), and her eventful encounters in telepathy. From there, it had been a short trip to the little-known regions in the Defense Department.

All of it was coming back to her.

She also vividly recalled an exceptional man, a psychic named Ingo Swann, who had convinced her to accept the job. Swann could describe a faraway place simply by concentrating on predetermined coordinates. He also possessed the uncanny ability to change traffic light signals at will, and could disperse cumulus clouds whenever he wanted, simply by staring at them intently. He was a kind of mental athlete who insisted that his skills came from elsewhere, that they were powers he had inherited from his great-grandmother, a Sioux medicine woman who had transmitted them from the afterlife.

"And if in my case . . ."

A smile spread across her face. Her meeting with Swann, those old photographs—it had all made her feel like a young recruit again. The animated debates between the different remote vision teams inside INSCOM came vividly to mind. Everyone, without exception, was convinced that psychic behavior obeyed genetic configurations. In fact, they were certain that in sensitive families predisposed to astral voyages, prophetic dreams or telepathy, the psychic was always identifiable by his unstable, neurotic, or hysteric behavior. The paranormal was a weakness that skipped from one generation to the next.

Jennifer slammed the photo album shut. She needed to make a call to Phoenix, Arizona. A sudden inspiration had struck her. One of those impulses that Swann talked about so frequently.

A tired voice answered on the other end of the line.

"Mom?"

"Well, finally you call at night," her mother reproached. "At last you realize rates are much cheaper this time of day."

"Sure, Mom. I know. But I need to ask you something about the family."

"Again?"

"Don't worry," she said quietly. "It has nothing to do with Dad."

"Good."

"Do you know if anyone in our family ever suffered from epilepsy?"

"What kind of question is that, Jennifer! Epilepsy? Are you all right?"

"Just tell me yes or no."

The phone line was quiet.

"Well, when I was a child, my mother was very concerned about the attacks my grandmother suffered. But she died before I was ten years old, and I have no way of knowing what kind of attacks they were talking about."

"Your grandmother? My great-grandmother?"

"Yes, but all that is so long ago! It's too bad you never had the chance to get to know her. She must have been quite a character, like you. Her ancestors lived along the Rio Grande, in New Mexico, although later, during the Gold Rush, they emigrated south, to the other side of the border. They lived near Guadalupe."

"I know all that. But why didn't anyone ever tell me about my great-grandmother? Is it true she was named Ankti, like you?"

"Yes, and like your grandmother, too. But all these stories are ancient history. You young people have more important things to do than listen to old stories."

"What stories?"

"Well, the ones your grandmother Ankti was always telling. I'm very bad with that sort of thing, dear. And anyway, they were unbelievable. Stories about spiritual protectors, visits from the kachina gods, things like that. You would have been frightened!"

"You're impossible, Mom. I remember my grandmother's tales. Of the Indian Juan Diego, of the Virgin, and the flowers in the poncho."

"Yes."

"And you have no idea what tribe my great-grandmother came from?"

"That, no. Sorry. I know she was a kind of enchanter, and that the family emigrated because they had problems with the parish. But if you ask me, she never said much about this to her grandchildren."

"Does the name Cueloce bring anything to mind? Or la Gran Quivira?"

"No."

The voice on the other end of the line let out a deep sigh before continuing.

"Why this sudden interest in your great-grandmother Ankti?"

"No special reason."

"Hmm . . . You know"—her mother chuckled—"when you were born, the first thing she said was that you looked a lot like the 'witch.' "

"Great-Grandmother? Are you sure?"

"Of course. What's the matter? Don't tell me you're having premonitions in your dreams again? I thought you were through with that a long time ago!" The alarm was evident in her tone of voice.

"Calm down, Mom. It has nothing to do with that. I'm fine. The next time we see each other I'll explain it all."

"You promise?

"I promise, Mom."

Jennifer hung up the phone with a strange sensation. She had just discovered, almost without wanting to, that she had more in common with her friend Ingo Swann than she ever imagined. Both had an Indian past . . . and a great-grandmother who was a witch! But did that explain her peculiar dreams? And the diagnosis of Dostoyevsky's epilepsy?

What would Dr. Meyers think of it?

TWENTY-ONE

GRAN QUIVIRA

"Father! Say something! Can you hear me?"

Sakmo had grasped his father by the shoulders and was shaking him. He was slowly coming around.

The great Walpi was dazed. His cramped muscles refused to respond. He had no idea how much time had elapsed since the apparition had left him in the Canyon of the Serpent. But as he began to hear his son's voice urgently calling him, he remembered everything that had taken place. The ritual of invocation had been a success.

Little by little, the old warrior was recovering mobility in his arms. After he got to his feet, he at last saw the round face of his son.

"Sakmo . . . Did you see her?"

He leaned on his son's shoulders, trying to camouflage his confusion.

"Yes, I saw her again, Father. I have been here every night that the men have been in the kiva. All the watchmen have seen her moving from place to place."

"And she spoke to you?"

"She called me and I went, Father. I no longer fear her. She promised that she would return to teach us a new religion."

"I know as much," he said just above a whisper. "She left me this."

Sakmo took the object that the visitor had thrown to the ground for his father. It was a wooden cross, crudely tied together. It meant nothing to him.

"What is happening, Father?"

The warrior gathered the last of his strength in order to stand fully erect. Once he was on both feet, he leaned on his son's shoulder and looked into his eyes, then lowered his gaze to the rose-shaped mark that appeared on Sakmo's forearm.

"Do you see that sign?"

Sakmo nodded.

"I had one as well, in the same place as yours, from the day I was born. But now, my son, it is no longer there."

"What do you mean?"

The old warrior rolled up his sleeve so that his son could see his left arm. There were no marks there. It was as if it had never borne the image of the rose that now shone on his son's arm.

"Sakmo, the lady is saying that you will soon occupy my place in the tribe. My mission is coming to an end."

"But you cannot leave us. Not now, Father."

The old warrior remained calm.

"She also said," he went on, "that tomorrow at dawn, without fail, you and a group of Jumano warriors will go out from the village to meet the men bearing the new god. You will travel in a southerly direction, day and night if necessary, and before the full moon illuminates the plains again, you will pay your respects to these men. Whoever they may be."

"But how will I recognize them? I cannot do this."

"Carry this cross. It will help you."

"But Father . . ."

"There is no other way, my son. Our world has already ended. Is it possible you are blind and cannot see that?"

TWENTY-TWO

ÁGREDA

Carlos followed the nun's instructions to the letter, while Txema came up a step behind him, his pace slightly more hesitant. Txema was asking himself if the day's events were not, after all, slightly miraculous. In the final analysis, he was a man of faith. Discreet about it, of course, but still a man of faith.

They entered a small common room, and at one end there was a passageway that was blocked by a grating. Peering past it, they could make out a second room adjoining it in the interior of the cloister. The walls of the room where they stood were crowded with old canvases. On one of them appeared the fading image of a nun wielding a pen in her right hand, her left hand resting on an open book; on another, a Madonna of the sort that Bartolomé Murillo churned out by the dozens in the seventeenth century, while next to it hung a peculiar tapestry depicting the revelation of the Virgin of Guadalupe to the Indian Juan Diego in Mexico a hundred years earlier. But what really caught their eye was a modern canvas, in vivid colors and naive technique, which depicted a nun dressed in blue, surrounded by American Natives and domestic animals.

"Do you think . . . ?" Txema said under his breath.

"What else could it be?"

"Looks like a recent effort," Txema said, as if making an apology for the painting.

"And so it is!" a woman's voice piped up behind them. The iron grille separating the rooms had swung open; Carlos and Txema found themselves face-to-face with two nuns in white habits.

"It was painted by a sister from New Mexico who lived with us for two years," said the nun standing closer to the two men.

The two nuns introduced themselves as Sister Ana María and Sister María Margarita. They seemed as though they had just descended from another world, or at least another era, greeting their unexpected guests with large smiles while their hands remained hidden inside the sleeves of their billowing garments.

"And how can we help you?" one of the two interjected, after inviting the journalists to sit down.

"We want to learn about María Jesús de Ágreda."

"Ah! The Venerable María!"

Sister María Margarita's face shone with a generous smile, but it was the other nun who, from the outset, had taken the reins of the conversation.

Sister Ana María moved slowly, possessed of a serene demeanor, but she kept her eyes peeled like a mother watching her children from a park bench. Her indulgent expression and elegant deportment were the first things the men noticed. María Margarita was, based on first impressions, entirely different. Small in stature, with vivacious eyes and a chipper, biting voice, she looked every bit the young troublemaker, ready for an adventure at the drop of a hat.

The two nuns regarded their visitors with a mixture of curiosity and tenderness.

"And what exactly is it that you are interested in knowing about Mother Ágreda?" Sister Ana María asked them, after they had introduced themselves.

"Well," Carlos began, and then hesitated. "Actually, we'd like to know if Mother Ágreda was really in America, as some legends say."

The nun retained her equanimity as she stared directly at him.

"Those are not legends, my son. Our sister and founder had the gift of bilocation. She could be in two places at once, traveling to America without leaving her cell or ignoring her obligations here at the monastery."

"She bilocated?"

Like a good student, the photographer turned to face the painting that depicted the nun surrounded by Indians. The two nuns watched as he did so, finding him amusing.

"Of course! And many times! That was one of her first mystical demonstrations given outside the monastery, and she did it when she was very young, just after taking her vows here in this very monastery," Sister María Margarita blurted out, while pointing at the canvas that Txema was examining. "You should know that her case was closely watched in her time, and even entailed having Mother Ágreda successfully defend herself before the Inquisition."

"Is that so?" Carlos was still having difficulty accepting that without intending to he had stumbled into the house where "his" nun had lived.

"Absolutely."

"And how was it done? I mean, the other times, where did Mother Ágreda appear?"

"Well, as we told you, she in fact bilocated." Sister Ana María liked to be as precise as possible. "We believe that she revealed herself in New Mexico, where she visited the various tribes that lived along the Rio Grande. A report published in 1630 collected various facts about the incidents."

Carlos gave the nun a questioning look. She continued speaking.

"It was assembled by a Franciscan named Friar Alonso de Benavides, who spread the word of Christ in those lands in the seventeenth century. He was surprised to find that many of the natives he encountered in that region had already learned the catechism from a mysterious woman who had revealed herself to them."

"How did she reveal herself?" Txema repeated, astonished.

"Just picture it yourself!" María Margarita answered him in an imperious tone. "A woman all on her own, surrounded by natives, to whom she brought the teachings of Our Lord!"

Her passionate outburst made everyone smile. When the enthusiasm subsided, Sister Ana María sweetly turned the conversation around.

"What Friar Benavides wrote was that on many evenings a woman dressed in a blue habit appeared before the natives; she spoke to them about the Son of God who died on the cross, promising eternal life to those who believed in him. They had never been baptized, had never laid eyes on a white man. And the woman went so far as to tell them that representatives of the Savior would soon arrive in their lands in order to give them the good news."

"Did you say that this report was published?"

"It was indeed. It was printed in 1630 in Madrid, at Philip the Fourth's Royal Printing House. It is rumored that the king himself took a great interest in the book."

"Sister!" Txema, who was cradling his camera bag in his lap while he warmed up by the stove, suddenly jumped to his feet. "Just a minute ago you said that the bilocations were only the first external indication of Mother Ágreda's gifts."

"The first demonstration of her gifts," she corrected him, and then went on. "In fact, in her prayers Mother Ágreda asked God to free her from such phenomena. You must not think that the life of a mystic is pleasant. The events peculiar to the contemplative life always make things more difficult. Because of her, there were rumors running wild all over the province, with crowds of people turning up, curiosity seekers who wanted to gawk at her as she fell into an ecstatic state."

"Ah! So she also fell into trances?" For Carlos, it was one surprise after another.

"Naturally. And you would be wrong if you believed they stopped happening after her bilocations came to an end. Many years later, Our Lady appeared to Mother Ágreda in a trance in order to dictate the story of her life, about which we knew nothing from the Gospels. The Venerable wrote the story of her life by hand, in eight thick volumes that we still possess in our library, and that later were published under the title *The Mystical City of God.*"

Carlos was writing down everything as fast as he could.

Sister Ana María continued, "In that book she reveals that Our Lady is, in fact, in the city where the Heavenly Father himself resides. The subject is as great a mystery as the Trinity."

"But . . ." Carlos looked up from his notebook with a very intense expression on his face. "Forgive me, Sister, but something here makes no sense to me. When I tried to obtain information on your founder, I consulted several databases and rare-book catalogs, simply to see if I could locate any of her works, and frankly, I came up empty-handed. Unless perhaps I made a dumb mistake or had the wrong information."

The nun smiled.

"You are very lucky. The book I'm speaking of has just been published in a new edition, although I feel sure you will be more interested in one of the original editions, in which the story of our sister's life is recounted. Am I right?"

"If it were possible . . ."

"Of course!" The nun smiled yet again. "Don't worry. We will look for this volume and will send you a photocopy of it wherever you tell us to."

Carlos was grateful for the offer and after writing down his address on a piece of paper, he asked one final, innocent question.

"Maybe you could clear up another matter that I cannot figure out. I don't remember having seen her name in any of the Calendars or Lives of the Saints. When was Sister María Jesús beatified?"

He had hit a sore spot.

The faces of his conversational partners suddenly clouded over and, as if threatening clouds from the Cameros had discharged their wrath across the valley, the two nuns lowered their heads, slipped their hands inside their sleeves once again, and let an interminable moment of silence pass before responding.

Finally, María Margarita spoke.

"See here," she said as she cleared her throat. "In her book, Mother Ágreda revealed that the Virgin conceived Our Savior without sin, and as you know, this was a topic of great discussion among the theologians of the time. It was even a heretical idea. Our sister went even further, taking up certain political issues with Philip the Fourth, writing to him with great regularity and becoming his true spiritual adviser."

"And so . . . ? " Carlos was intrigued.

"Well, these matters did not sit well with Rome. The Vatican delayed the process of her beatification for three centuries. The only success we achieved was when Pope Clement the Tenth allowed private religious devotions to Madre Ágreda, awarding her the rank of Venerable a few years after she died. It was, if I remember correctly," she said, leafing through the pamphlet in her hands, "the twenty-eighth of January 1673. And since then, nothing. Not a single ecclesiastical recognition."

"This has something to do with Rome?"

"With the Vatican."

"And nothing can be done to correct this error?"

"Indeed." This time it was a more animated Sister Ana María who responded. "There is a priest in Bilbao, Father Amadeo Tejada, who is handling the paperwork for the Venerable's rehabilitation and the process of beatification."

"So all is not lost."

"No, no. Father Tejada is blessed with a great deal of willpower, thank God. He is a virtuous man, intelligent, and has worked on the new editions of our Mother's works. He, too, is a holy man."

Carlos's eyes shone. "An expert!" he thought. Txema could hardly contain his laughter as he watched his friend make his request, his voice shaking.

"Do you think I could possibly interview Father Tejada?"

"Of course. He lives in a residence run by the Passionist fathers in Bilbao, which is located next to a primary school, although he's a professor at the university," María Margarita clarified in her dulcet voice.

"If you were to visit him, please send our best wishes, and encourage him to continue," her companion requested. "Campaigns on behalf of saints are difficult undertakings God uses to put man's patience to the test."

"I'll be sure to tell him, don't worry."

"May God bless you," whispered the nun while crossing herself.

TWENTY-THREE

SAN ANTONIO MISSION, NEW MEXICO
SUMMER 1629

A scorching wind struck the Camino Real leading out of Santa Fe, bringing with it a dense cloud of sand and dust. It was midday. As the first gusts of the sandstorm tore through the juniper trees that lined the edge of the road, two lizards scurried for shelter under a rock. Friar Esteban de Perea, well acquainted with the desert, knew how to read the signs. Pausing for a second to look around, and before the unmistakable odor of dust reached his nostrils, he gave the order.

"Cover yourselves! Hurry!"

The ten friars of the Franciscan order followed as one, unfolding their sleeves and sheltering their heads as he had taught them. They wore heavy woolen habits with hoods, a rope belt, and leather sandals, garments that by all accounts offered little resistance to the gusts of fine-grained silica, as fatal as a downpour of steel knives.

"Stay where you are!" he exhorted them in the same voice, as the air around them plunged into darkness.

The storm, as black as a plague of locusts, pounced upon the friars for a few short minutes. But suddenly, one of the friars, standing toward the end of the caravan, called out.

"Holy Jesus! I hear music! I hear music!"

"So do I!" another voice joined in.

"And I!"

"Who said that?" Friar Esteban, his eyes mere slits, tried to locate where the shouts were coming from. The roaring noise of the storm made them seem far away, at the other end of the world.

"I did! Friar Bartolomé! Can you not hear it, Friar Esteban? It is sacred music!"

The Inquisitor in charge of the group concentrated again, trying to make out the silhouette of Bartolomé's figure.

"Where is it coming from, Brother?" he shouted.

"From the south! It's coming from the south!"

Although they could barely hear his words, all the friars without exception were listening intently.

"You still cannot hear it? Come here, at the end of the line!" Friar Bartolomé insisted at the top of his voice.

The melody was at last heard by all the missionaries. It was the faintest wisp of a song, almost imperceptible, as if it were coming from a small, fragile music box. If they had been somewhere else than in the middle of the desert, some five days on foot from Santa Fe, they would have taken it to be a choir intoning the Alleluia. But that was impossible.

The phenomenon vanished as quickly as it had come.

Before they could distinguish an intelligible phrase of music in that commotion of gusting wind, sand, and snatches of singing, the storm changed direction, taking everything along with it. A heavy silence then descended upon the caravan of friars.

Friar Bartolomé lifted up his deeply tanned face and let his shoulders relax.

"Is it not a sign?"

Disturbed by the interruption, Friar Esteban de Perea preferred to ignore the subject. The friars decided not to tempt the Devil, or their leader, for that matter, into ridiculing them. They cautiously poked their heads out of their hoods as if they had just seen a mirage, then threw their personal possessions over their shoulders and resumed walking.

They were headed for the mission at San Antonio de Padua, one of the oldest religious centers in the region, where they planned to stay for several days. Friar Esteban needed to learn about a perplexing phenomenon that had come to his attention while he was in

Mexico: in just this one settlement, over the course of the last twenty years, according to trustworthy accounts confirmed by the Archbishop, close to eighty thousand Indians had been baptized. In other words, nearly all the inhabitants.

It was a unique case in America. Neither in Mexico nor in the royal territory of Peru nor in Brazil had there been such a rapid, bloodless conversion to Christianity. No mundane rationale could explain the Indians' receptiveness. Quite the opposite, in fact: along with the great numbers of the converted came the persistent rumor that a "supernatural force" had convinced the natives to put their faith in Jesus Christ.

Such stories gave Perea no pleasure whatsoever. His allegiance was to the Sant'Uffizio, the Holy Office of the Inquisition, and he cringed at any mention of the miraculous. Born in Villanueva del Fresno in a region of Spain near the Portuguese border, he had a frontier mentality wedded to dogma. To understand the world required a set of rules, and it was faith that supplied this consolation to the young child. Tall and thin, with a huge head propped upon a gangly body, his presence alone was enough to intimidate people. His father, a soldier of fortune, had prepared him for struggle, and the son proved equally strong and unyielding. His mother had pushed him toward faith early on. And like her, he detested any sort of trickery.

"Listen to me!" he shouted, keeping up the pace and waving a piece of goatskin parchment over his head. "If this map is right, we should be arriving at the San Antonio mission shortly."

The men broke into shouts of joy and relief.

"From this moment on, I want you all to be very attentive to anything you hear the natives say, no matter how strange it may seem to you. I want to find out why they became Christians, if anyone forced them or told them to do it, or if they saw anything extraordinary that led them to convert to our faith."

"What do you mean by extraordinary, Friar Esteban?"

The question was posed by Friar Tomás de San Diego, a brilliant student of theology at the University of Salamanca. The other friars were relieved to hear him speak. The Inquisitor did not hesitate in his reply.

"I would just as soon not explain it, Friar Tomás. During my visit to the archbishopric of Mexico, I heard many absurd things. The men working for the Archbishop were fond of saying that the spirits of the deserts had encouraged the Indian tribes to ask us to baptize them . . ."

"What sort of spirits?"

"Man of God!" Friar Esteban was displeased with this young friar's persistence. "You ought to know that the savages who abound in these parts have not received even the slightest education. They will explain to you in the barest language what they saw, but it will be you who interprets it."

"I understand. When they speak to us of spirits, we are to explain to them that what they saw were our angels. Is that not so?"

The young friar's tone greatly irritated the Inquisitor.

"Tell me, Brother Tomás, what would you say just happened here?"

Friar Tomás de San Diego looked as if he had shrunk several sizes when Esteban de Perea laid his powerful arms on him.

"Here?" he vacillated. "Are you referring to the singing that we heard?"

The Inquisitor nodded his head, waiting for a response.

"Celestial music? A gift from the Virgin to help us persevere in our mission and to strengthen our faith?"

Friar Esteban took a deep breath. He shook Brother Tomás's bony shoulders and shouted so that everyone could hear him.

"No! No, my brothers!"

Every last one of the friars looked fearful.

"You are passing through the desert! In the very same place where Satan tempted Christ for forty days and forty nights! Beware of vain excitements, of mirages and strange shadows! Show the Indians whom we encounter the light! That is why we are here!"

TWENTY-FOUR

ROME

Stanislaw Zsidiv walked over to the windows that dominated his office and, his back turned to Giuseppe Baldi, began to relate a remarkable story.

Earlier that evening, Luigi Corso had informed Zsidiv that for the past forty years the Vatican had collaborated with American intelligence services through the offices of a highly placed organization inside the CIA known as "the Committee." Or, to be more precise, the American Committee for a United Europe (ACUE). According to Corso, this organization was founded in 1949 in the United States and directed by officials from the old Office of Strategic Services (OSS), precursor to the CIA, with the intention of consolidating a United States of Europe after the war.

At first, Zsidiv said, the Committee tried to keep a close watch on those left-leaning priests surreptitiously undertaking pro-Soviet activities in the Old World. Nevertheless, in the last several years, the organization had gained the Supreme Pontiff's confidence by uncovering a pair of high-level assassination attempts planned against him.

Baldi looked startled.

"And what does this have to do with Saint Matthew?"

"A great deal," Zsidiv said. "In those years the Committee did not limit itself simply to political activities. It also took an interest in our research programs, especially Chronovision. They informed us that one of their organizations, INSCOM, had years ago created a division whose goal was to train people with highly developed extrasensory abilities, whose minds were able to cross the barriers of space and time. They intended to integrate them into a unit they called 'psychic espionage.' Somehow they found out that we were working toward a similar goal with the help of sacred music and your studies in pre-polyphony. So they sent a man to work with us, a representative with whom we could exchange points of interest about our mutual findings."

"One of their men. A spy."

"Call him whatever you like. In any case, they sent him to the head of our team in Rome so that he could work hand in hand with Saint Matthew, whom we knew as Father Corso. Little more than a month ago both sides unearthed the file on the Lady in Blue. They believed they had come across something important."

"The Lady in Blue?"

Baldi had never heard the name before.

"That's right, you haven't heard that story yet."

Monsignor Zsidiv turned around, a benevolent look on his face directed at Father Baldi, his hands folded on his chest over his burnished gold cross. He walked back to his desk.

"Let me give you the full explanation, Giuseppe. In the archives of the Holy Office, Father Luigi Corso and the American discovered several written accounts that spoke of a Spanish nun who had undergone bilocation experiences of a spectacular nature."

"What kind of written accounts?"

"They are known as Benavides's *Memorial*. They refer to certain incidents that took place in 1629 in New Mexico, which were recorded by a Franciscan of the same name. He states, among other things, that this woman had succeeded in transporting herself physically from one part of the world to another, with God's mysterious assistance. In his report, Father Benavides attributed to her the evangelization of various American Indian tribes in what is now the southwestern United States. She was known as 'the Lady in Blue' when she appeared in that part of the world. That was what interested the Americans."

"Since when did the CIA take any interest in its country's history?"

"They weren't interested in history." A malicious smile played across Zsidiv's gaunt face. "In my opinion, Langley cannot tell the difference between 1629 and 1929. All of that is out of their league."

"And so?"

"What awakened their inquisitiveness was the possibility of being able to send men instantaneously to any part of the world, by proceeding down the road opened by that nun. Just imagine it. With a technique like that at their disposal, the military would have access to state secrets, be able to steal compromising documents, eliminate potential enemies, or move things from one place to another, without leaving any evidence of their presence. In short, if they could successfully reproduce what Benavides had set out in his report, they would have the perfect weapon in their hands. Discreet and undetectable."

"They wanted to militarize a divine gift?"

Baldi was perplexed.

"Yes, with the help of the music that provoked the ecstasies and bilocations of that blue lady. Isn't that what you spent so much time studying, Giuseppe?"

"But no known acoustical frequency exists that will allow for anything like that!" Baldi protested.

"That is exactly what the other two evangelists said. In fact, none of the documents relating to the nun provide convincing proof that she was in fact the party responsible for the visits to those Indians."

"What then?"

"Perhaps what the Indians saw was something far more important."

"What are you trying to say?"

"That perhaps the Lady in Blue was something other than a nun in a cloister with a gift for bilocation, that perhaps we find ourselves facing something greater, and far more sublime: a manifestation of the Holy Mother, for example. A manifestation of the Virgin. The Pope takes this possibility seriously, and he believes that no one other than she would have been able to appear in such glory and majesty before those Indians, setting the stage for the evangelization of America."

"A manifestation . . ." The idea sent Baldi into a long train of thought.

"Nevertheless, Saint Matthew and his American assistant never agreed with the Marian hypothesis, and they stuck to their guns, compiling every scrap of information they could find in an attempt to be certain."

"Do you believe this obsession had something to do with Father Corso's death?"

"I'm certain of it . . . beyond any doubt after the disappearance of his files. It is as if someone had taken possession of his research and had gone to the trouble of erasing every file from the map. Maybe he had discovered something. Something that brought about his death."

"And Father Corso's assistant? The American representative has yet to provide the police with any solid leads?"

Monsignor Zsidiv was sliding a silver letter opener between his fingers.

"No. And that, too, fails to surprise me. Look, Giuseppe, this man is hardly above suspicion. I believe INSCOM inserted him in our project simply to get wind of any advances the First Evangelist might make. Although I have to say that he made contributions to Chronovision as well."

"Meaning?"

"Well, you know better than anyone exactly how delicate this project is. Science on the one hand, faith on the other. Which is where our conflicts originate. From a certain point of view, one can only accept Chronovision if one is also willing to believe in prophets and the great men of the past upon whom God bestowed the gift of defying the laws of time. Which is why we are building a machine powerful enough to overcome that dimension, a machine that arbitrarily stimulates visionary states similar to those of the ancient patriarchs, converting normal persons, men and women of flesh and blood, into prophets. Or, it attempts to do so for short periods of time . . ."

"You can dispense with the long introductions, Your Eminence."

"Very well, Giuseppe." Zsidiv's smile was indulgent. "It was you who gave the evangelists the idea, and you were quite right, that certain notes in sacred music allowed our mystics to overcome the barriers of time. Do you recall? You also insinuated that the key to opening that inner region of the mind was sound. You compared it to Ali Baba's 'Open sesame.' "

"Everything is contained in the word. Sound is merely its acoustic manifestation."

"Very well," Zsidiv said, rubbing his hands. "This American was acquainted with a system even more efficient than yours, but of the same ilk."

Father Baldi removed his glasses and, trying to mask his surprise, began cleaning them with a little piece of cotton cloth. Had someone in the United States developed a system to provoke altered states of consciousness using musical frequencies?

"What sort of system is this, Your Eminence?" he asked after a long period of silence.

"It went like this: when this new partner in our project arrived, we entered all the material he brought with him into our files, and copied it as well. In the notebooks he kept on the job he mentioned the innovations of one Robert Monroe, a North American businessman who owned and developed radio stations, and who pioneered a method by which he could teach people to 'fly' outside their bodies to whatever destination they chose."

"Should I take this seriously?" asked Baldi, unnerved by everything he was hearing.

"We were surprised, too. At first we thought this was another charade, one of those New Age gurus. But as soon as we took a closer look, we realized our error."

"Robert Monroe? I never heard of him."

"It seems that in the years after the Second World War this man suffered various involuntary out-of-body experiences, and instead of turning them into an interesting story, as had so many before him, he wanted to understand the inner workings of the experience. Those notebooks explained how Monroe discovered that his 'voyages' were directly related to particular wavelengths inside of which the human brain functioned. In fact, his notes detail how similar wavelengths could be artificially induced through the use of hypnosis, or even better, by introducing certain synthetic sounds into the ears."

"This is nothing new for us."

"No, it's not, in theory. We later learned that this individual was so convinced of his hypothesis that, in the 1970s, he set up the Monroe Institute in Virginia, whose goal was to provoke 'astral voyages' at will. He developed a revolutionary technology of sound that he christened Hemi-Sync. And it was a success!"

"Hemi-Sync?"

"Short for hemisphere synchronization. It seems that his method consisted of equalizing the frequency in which the two sides of the human brain function, by augmenting or reducing their vibrations to a unison, elevating the subject to the furthest threshold of perception when he hears particular sounds."

"Not without reason, Your Eminence. We know that sound, rhythm, and vibration penetrate directly into the brain."

"From what we understand, Monroe even developed a system of acoustic charts that mapped exactly where you will go based on different frequencies."

"How did these charts work?"

Monsignor Zsidiv went through his papers. In a matter of seconds he found the material he was looking for.

"Here they are," he said. "Monroe discovered that if a patient was listening through earphones to a vibration of one hundred hertz (or cycles per second) in one ear, and a vibration of one hundred twenty-five hertz in the other, the sound the brain 'understood' turns out to be the mathematical difference between the two. To put it another way, the whole brain 'hears' a nonexistent sound of twenty-five hertz."

"Amazing."

"This spectral sound ends up dominating both hemispheres, neutralizing any sounds from outside. Monroe christened it 'binaural' and insisted that only such frequencies were capable of successfully generating altered states of consciousness. In the final analysis, it was a vibration created by the brain, a vibration that he believed aided the free movement of the astral body."

"How did his findings change our project?"

"Think about it! We have gone from training sensitive people to see things far off in time and space, to giving serious consideration to the possibility of projecting them out of their bodies." Zsidiv was smiling.

"Something like what the Lady in Blue did, no?"

"Exactly! And that is what Father Corso and his assistant believed. Which is why I think they persisted. Perhaps they thought that if they investigated every bit of information in the Blue Lady dossier, they would uncover new clues that would enable them to project people into the past. And not just the soul but the body as well."

"And at that moment, Saint Matthew dies."

The Cardinal lowered his eyes.

"Father Corso was a good friend to both of us."

"I understand, Your Eminence. I know I've bungled things recently, but perhaps now I have the opportunity to atone for my errors. If you deem it advisable," he said, addressing the Cardinal formally. "You could put me in charge of the First Evangelist's laboratories, where I could try to get a handle on his assistant, to see if he knows more than he's letting on."

Zsidiv cleared his throat and spoke in a less formal tone.

"That is exactly what I wanted to propose to you. Take charge of Saint Matthew's investigations. That way you will continue as part of the team, at least until the Holy Office decides to intervene on some other occasion. And that way I can keep an eye on you."

"Regarding my reintegration into the team, what happens with tomorrow's hearing?"

"Don't worry. I will see to it that it is canceled. If you keep your mouth closed, they will never miss your appearance. The Holy Father will understand."

"Thank you, Your Eminence. I will do as I am bidden."

"Take care, Giuseppe," Zsidiv warned. He was already standing in the doorway to his office. "We still don't know whether Father Corso actually killed himself."

"Where do you think I should begin to look?"

"Go tomorrow to Saint Matthew's studio at Vatican Radio. That's where he did all his work this past year. Have you already arranged for a place to stay while you're in Rome?"

Baldi shook his head. He had not planned on staying more than a day.

"Near the Colosseum, on the Via Bixio, there's a residence for pilgrims run by the Conceptionist sisters. Ask for Sister Micaela. She'll give you a room for a few days. And the first thing tomorrow morning go to Vatican Radio. Ask for Father Corso's assistant."

"What is his name?" Baldi asked, grateful for his friend's help.

"Doctor Alberto. His real name, however, is Albert Ferrell. Special Agent Albert Ferrell."

TWENTY-FIVE

SAN ANTONIO MISSION, NEW MEXICO
SUMMER 1629

Less than an hour on foot from Friar Perea's expedition, within a building that stood beneath two imposing towers of whitewashed adobe, Friar Juan de Salas was listening raptly to what the Indian Pentiwa had to say to him. A solitary missionary well along in years but with a sharp intellect, Friar Juan was known as *el adelantado* or "the advanced one," for having established his presence in those lands without the customary recourse to conquest. Pentiwa, "he who makes masks," was a venerated figure in the settlement. Famed as a witch doctor, he had, since Salas's arrival at that remote mission some sixteen years before, endeavored to ingratiate himself with Salas, inviting him to share power over the Indians. To you belongs the cleansing of souls, he would say to the curate; to me, the cleansing of bodies. Pentiwa was a shaman, a medicine man.

Friar Juan had received him in his modest sacristy. It was the intention of the Indian to bring the friar up to date on a matter of "great urgency."

"I had a dream last night."

The Indian, seated cross-legged on the ground, was laconic as usual. He had learned the Spanish language quickly, and was able to express himself with admirable fluency.

"And so?"

"I woke up after midnight last night, and remembered what I had heard from my grandfather; what he had heard from his grandfather many years ago. Then I realized that I must tell you as soon as possible."

The shaman augmented his words with lofty gestures for emphasis.

"My ancestors told me that, one day, in the time before the arrival of the Spaniards, the inhabitants of Tenochtitlán were visited by a man the likes of whom they had never seen before."

"Are you going to tell me another of your stories, Pentiwa?"

The shaman barely paused. He acted as if he had not heard Friar Salas, and went on.

"He had an enormous red beard and a long, sad face. He wore clothes from head to foot and when he had an audience with the powerful, he told them he was sent by a 'Child of the great Sun.' He announced that their kingdom was at an end, that another would arrive from far away, and that their bloodthirsty gods would disappear . . ."

"And where is this leading, Pentiwa?"

The friar's grave expression, heightened by a deeply lined face that conveyed the wisdom he had achieved, encouraged the Indian to get to the point.

"Very well, Friar. This prophecy was also given to my people."

"What do you mean?"

"It is something that no man in my tribe will ever tell you explicitly. And not out of fear. But I give you my word that we, too, were visited by a 'Daughter of the Sun.' She was as beautiful as the moon and knew how to make herself understood by everyone she encountered."

"Here? In Isleta?" Friar Salas, who had baptized Pentiwa with his own hands, was astonished.

"This seems strange to you? This land belongs to the spirits of our ancestors; they watch over it and protect it until the day that we inherit it. That sacred order was changed by the arrival of the Spaniards who placed us in settlements, and we lost the one thing that we possessed."

"Why are you telling me this now, Pentiwa?"

"It is not hard to understand, Father. My people have always enjoyed the protection of our spirits. Beings the same blue as the heavens, who watch over our well-being, and who can still be seen in the plains, or in our dreams; who protect us from any ruin that may come."

Friar Salas stroked his beard as he took the measure of the Indian's words.

"You are telling me about your guardian angels, son," he said after a long delay. "They, like the one who appeared to Mary before she conceived Jesus, reveal themselves to men in order to tell them what is to come. Would not that 'Daughter of the Sun' be a guardian angel?"

The shaman fixed his eyes on the Spaniard.

"Friar," he said. "I have seen her again."

"The 'Daughter of the Sun'?"

Pentiwa nodded.

"And she told me that men like you were coming. They will arrive soon. Men wearing long clothes such as those who visited Tenochtitlán, men with long beards like yourself."

"Have you seen anyone besides her?"

"You do not have to believe me, but listen to what she says," he said pointedly to the Spaniard. "Men are coming who will try to force us to tell the secrets of those visitations. Although, I warn you, they will not be successful."

"You dreamed all this?"

"Yes."

"And your dreams always come true?"

The Indian nodded a second time.

"And to what do you attribute this cowering before the arrival of new missionaries? You should be happy that—"

"Our life has already changed more than enough since you arrived. You understand that, do you not? We have seen how you punish anyone accused of being a witch or who believes in the old gods. You have burned the masks of our kachinas. Others among your brothers have even tortured women and grandfathers in Santa Fe and the lands to the south. All in the name of your new religion."

A flash of anger flickered in Pentiwa's eyes and the friar was moved by it.

"I can hear the hatred in your words. And I truly regret it. But I have never treated you in that manner."

"And for that I am grateful. That is why I want you to know that when these men arrive, our people will not open their mouths. They will not be exposed to the danger that awaits those who do not believe in the white god."

"If they arrive . . . ," Salas added pensively.

"They will, Friar. And soon."

TWENTY-SIX

VENICE BEACH

Jennifer fell asleep that evening with a picture of her great-grandmother in her arms. Ankti had written the year in the corner: 1920. It was an intriguing picture: Ankti, sunny and still a teenager, with dark eyes that seemed as if they were intent on leaping out of the picture, stood with her arms extended toward the photographer. She was wearing a pretty flower-print dress, her hair gathered into two long braids.

It was difficult to say where it had been taken. It looked like an Indian mission, perhaps in New Mexico. The white adobe building in the background seemed vaguely familiar. Nevertheless, something on the inside of her left forearm had caught Jennifer's attention. Judging from appearances, it was a hematoma or bruise, except that it had the shape of a rose. It looked exactly the same as the birthmark that Jennifer had on her own arm.

"You have it, too," she heard her grandmother's voice say, a brief flash in her memory. "You are one of us."

Shortly after midnight, with the vague intention of searching for answers to all that was on her mind, Jennifer stopped fighting the urge to fall asleep a second time. She flopped down on the big sofa on the back porch of her house, and there, caressed by the warm breeze wafting in from the beach, she let herself drift off to sleep. She wanted to travel to the land of her ancestors.

TWENTY-SEVEN

SAN ANTONIO MISSION

Never had the realization of an omen seemed to Friar Salas as threatening as this one. Not long after Pentiwa had left the sacristy, a group of young children burst into the room. Excited, they surrounded the friar and dragged him outside by his robes.

"We have visitors, we have visitors!" they shouted, dancing with joy.

The friar patted a few of the children on the head while trying to keep his balance. A good number of them were his students. He had taught them to read Spanish, and watched with satisfaction as they slowly crossed the frontiers of their new faith.

"A visitor? Who has come to visit us?" He was intrigued.

"There are many of them! And they are asking for you!" the oldest in the group responded.

Before he could formulate another question, Friar Salas was dragged out of the mission doorway. The strong contrast in light disoriented him. When his eyes at last adapted to the midday sun, he was frozen in his tracks. Lined up in front of the door to his church was a group of eleven Franciscan friars, their hair and beards whitened with desert sand. They stood in place, not saying a word, as if they had just arrived from the other side of the grave.

"Friar Salas?"

He did not reply. His voice, cracked with age, refused to emerge.

"My name is Friar Esteban de Perea." So said the man who stood at the head of the group. "I am the future custodian general of these lands and, it follows, successor to Friar Alonso de Benavides. I want to ask . . ." Here he hesitated for a moment. "I ask you to lodge us in this, your house of God."

Friar Juan, still in mute astonishment, looked him over from head to foot.

"Is anything wrong, Friar?"

"No, it's nothing," Salas said at last. "Only that I never expected to see so many friars at one time. It has been years since anyone visited me . . ."

"We realize that." The Inquisitor smiled.

Shaking his head with incredulity, Friar Salas was at last able to get a word out.

"But what are Your Reverences doing here?"

"Three months ago I arrived at Sante Fe accompanied by twenty-nine Franciscan friars," Friar Esteban confirmed with some pride. "King Philip the Fourth sent us personally. He is impressed by your good work and wants to continue the conversion of the indigenous people of New Mexico."

His host watched the speaker closely.

"And why did no one tell me of your visit ahead of time?"

"Because it is not a question of a pastoral visit, Father. I have yet to assume my duties, and will not do so for some time."

"Very well." Salas was relieved. "Your Reverence and the friars who accompany you may stay in this mission as long as you wish. I can offer you few comforts, but your presence will be a source of happiness for the Christians in this village."

"Are there many of you?"

"Many indeed. So many that I believe His Majesty will be wasting time and money if he desires to convert more Indians to the Christian faith. All are devoted to Our Lord Jesus Christ."

"All of them?"

"Yes." Friar Salas nodded, still uncertain as to the purpose of their visit. "But come in and refresh yourselves after such a long trip."

Esteban de Perea and his friars followed behind Friar Salas, passing first into the enormous church that the Indians had constructed years before and then entering a small passageway next to the main altar. Friar Juan de Salas pointed out small rooms that had been used for grain storage during times of war, because the building was, in addition to a house of God, a functioning fortress. Its windowless walls were three meters thick, and its nave could shelter as many as five hundred people. As they were proceeding across a small patio that led to the church's five private rooms, de Salas warned the friars to watch their steps, for beneath the spaced wooden boards underfoot was the village's one source of potable water.

"The Indians prefer to take water directly from the river, but when they are restricted to the church, they can draw water from below, which enables them to resist an attack or siege."

The second mention of the mission's defensive character induced the friars to take an interest in the stability of the region.

"Do they attack here often, Father?" one of the friars in line asked him.

"You have no need to worry about that!" The old friar brusquely dismissed the subject, lifting his arms up toward heaven. "Can you not see what goodness the Lord has lavished upon me, here, all by myself?"

The friars smiled.

"It has been many years since the Apaches attacked us. Droughts have forced them to seek game and silos of grain farther west."

"But they could return at any moment, couldn't they?" interjected Friar Esteban, who was paying close attention to the structure of the fortress.

"Of course. Which is why the village maintains the church in a perfect state. It is our assurance against such hazards."

Friar Salas pointed them toward the area where they could shake off the dust from their travels, and set a time for all to meet up later, when they would celebrate the evening prayers. He ceased his explanations, bowed, and left the church.

Salas needed time to reflect. How had Pentiwa done it? How could he have seen events beforehand? Had someone alerted him to Father Perea's arrival? And would his fear, which he had communicated to the priest, that the new arrivals intended to extract the secret of the unaccountable Daughter of the Sun's visits, be borne out?

Friar Juan meandered beneath the shady boughs of the junipers for a long while. There, on the riverbank, it was his habit to rest during the stifling afternoons. He sometimes brought the New Testament with him to read, and at other times he finished writing his letters or his pastoral reports while taking in the fresh air. But this afternoon was different.

"Friar Juan! Are you here?"

The old man, deep in thought, ignored the Inquisitor, who was strolling around the mission grounds shouting his name.

"I like to come here to speak to God, Father Esteban. A tranquil place, a good place to resolve problems." Friar Juan's voice sounded beleaguered.

"Problems? Has our arrival proved inconvenient for you?"

"No, not at all. Please, it has been nothing of the sort. Would you like to take a walk?"

Esteban de Perea accepted. And the two men, passing beneath the shade fed by the waters of the Rio Grande, observed each other slyly as each one contemplated how best to open the discussion.

"I am only fulfilling the instructions of our Archbishop, Friar. Every day I ask Our Lady to let me discharge my responsibilities before winter comes."

"So tell me," the old friar went on in his sibylline voice, "are you staying at this mission for any special reason?"

The Inquisitor hesitated.

"You might say so, yes."

"Is that so?"

"I had no plans to talk to you about it, but given that you are the only Christian of long standing who can help me here, I have no other choice. Archbishop Manso y Zúñiga charged me in Mexico with a task that I cannot begin to explain . . ."

"I will hear you out."

Esteban de Perea assumed a confident air. As they walked along the banks of the river, he explained to Salas that, as regards the subject at hand, even the friars who traveled with him had been left largely in the dark.

"Before leaving," he went on, "the Archbishop informed me about certain rumors making the rounds, rumors concerning the multitudes of Indians in this region who have converted to the faith. He explained to me that behind these outbursts of faith there seem to be hidden supernatural forces. Powers that have convinced the natives to let us guard their souls. Is that true?"

"And you, Friar, why are you interested in what are mere tales?"

"As you well know, in the Holy Office we closely watch any references to the supernatural. In Mexico City alone, His Excellency has had to take extreme precautions after the flood tide of Indians who were certain the Virgin of Guadalupe had appeared to them again."

"And do you believe them?"

"I neither accept nor reject what they say, Friar."

"Do you think that the same thing has happened here?"

"I cannot be sure. Although you will understand that this type of affirmation, on the lips of recent converts, is open to suspicion. My obligation is to investigate them."

Friar Juan de Salas paused before responding.

"Life in the desert is hard and leaves little room for fantasies. I cannot tell you that I have seen any phenomenon of a supernatural nature, because I would be lying, but you must understand that I may be the last one among all the people living in Isleta to witness them."

"What do you mean, Friar?"

"Just that, thanks to God, I already enjoy the gift of faith. But to the Indians this is something new. And so, if they saw or heard anything that moved them to ask to be baptized, blessed be the Holy of Holies! I limit myself to harvesting their souls, not to uncovering the reasons for their conversion. Do you understand me?"

The veteran friar paused for a moment to point out something to his guest. From the riverbank where they stood they enjoyed a fine view of the mission. A hundred or so adobe houses were spread out before them. Each one was crowned with small wooden crosses in imitation of the two iron crucifixes atop the towers of the church. To Friar Salas's way of thinking, their presence was proof of just how Christian the people felt.

"All of that is very well, Friar Juan," the Inquisitor said quietly. "But my objective is to determine the causes of such large-scale conversions. Please understand that this question has made a profound impression in Mexico City."

"Naturally."

Pentiwa was right, and his judgment sent a discomforting chill up Friar Salas's spine. Should he mention what the medicine man had called the "Blue Flash of Lightning"? Then he thought better of it. Why should he, if, when the time came, none of the Indians would corroborate his story? No. It was more prudent to stay quiet.

"Very well," Friar Esteban said forcefully. "Tell me about the rates of conversion in this area. Are they are high as people say?"

"I couldn't state them precisely. I have not had sufficient time to bring the baptism books up-to-date. Approximately eight thousand souls converted in 1608, and since then, almost eighty thousand baptized." Friar Salas moderated his tone. "Consider that in the last year the Archbishop of Mexico himself agreed to administer our region as part of the territories in the Protectorate of the Conversion of Saint Paul, so that we can better attend to the great number of new Christians."

Esteban de Perea was familiar with the fact. He had heard about it due to the widespread and growing belief that the Rio Grande conversions, like that of Saint Paul himself, had been produced through some miraculous intervention.

"Indeed." The Inquisitor nodded. "But the results you have achieved here, do they not strike you as exaggerated, given there was so little Christian labor involved?"

His cynical comment sounded almost mocking.

"Exaggerated? In no way, Friar Esteban! Something marvelous, something divine, is taking place here, even if I am ignorant of its causes. Who is conversant with God's design? Ever since we built the mission and the news of our arrival spread, I have hardly had to expend any effort to spread the Gospel to these people; it was they who came to me, begging to learn the catechism. Look around you at the result!"

"So tell me, Friar Salas, to what do you attribute the Indian's interest in our faith, while only a few hundred leagues to the west, other natives have threatened and even killed our brothers?"

If Esteban de Perea was trying to provoke him, he succeeded. The old man's face grew red, and he took two deep breaths before answering.

"At first I thought the Indians came to the settlement in search of security. Right here, in the time before our arrival, sedentary tribes like the Tiwas and the Tompiros were decimated by the Apaches, which is why I believed, erroneously as it turned out, that if I let them live close to the church, they would feel safe. From time to time the passing caravans would leave us two or three soldiers with weapons to protect us."

"Erroneously, you say?"

"Yes, it was a lamentable error. I was so busy instructing the first avalanche of Indians, I had no time to pay attention to their stories. They spoke of voices resounding in the canyons and lights on the banks of the rivers that ordered them to abandon their villages. Of miracles, Friar."

"Voices? No more than that?" Friar Esteban tried to camouflage his interest.

"I told you before that I considered their stories of little importance."

"And do you think that I could interrogate anyone who has heard these voices? It would help relieve us of our doubts."

The old friar once again thought of what Pentiwa had told him.

"No, Friar. I don't believe so."

Friar Esteban was surprised by his answer.

"The Indians maintain great discretion when speaking about their beliefs. They fear we will pull them out by the roots, all in the name of Jesus Christ. At this juncture," Friar Juan concluded, "you may perhaps get the information out of them if you apply a small measure of your strategy. Proceed slowly. In these parts, they have never even heard of the Inquisition."

"I will do so, praise God."

TWENTY-EIGHT

MADRID

By Monday, April 15, 1991, Carlos had practically recovered from his trek through the Cameros Mountains and Ágreda. Leaving the monastery behind, he had returned to Madrid at full speed. There had been too many emotions and too many coincidences during the past twenty-four hours. He had hurriedly dropped off Txema in front of his house in Carabanchel and then made a beeline for his "soldier's barracks" near the Escorial, where he slept like a dormouse until well into the next morning.

Leaving Ágreda, he had been possessed by a strange and persistent feeling. Perhaps it was the complex image of Sister María Jesús that had so affected him. Before saying good-bye to Sister Ana María and Sister María Margarita, he had received a final, unexpected revelation. In the church, situated next to the main altar and only a few short steps from where their conversation had taken place, he discovered inside a glass case the uncorrupted body of the "voyaging nun." She had lain there for three centuries, her face covered by a thin film of wax and her mummified hands hidden beneath the sleeves of her habit. She still wore the blue cloak that had made her famous. Carlos was stunned. He never expected to find himself face-to-face with a witness to the seventeenth century. But there she was, right before him.

This was too much for him; he needed to put his ideas in order.

One maddening thought continued to nag at him: the certainty that Txema had been right when he used the word "destiny." What else had guided him through the hills from Cameros to Ágreda? What else had carried him to the entrance of the convent María Jesús de Ágreda had founded more than three hundred years before? Wasn't this all the result of a careful plan, made by the "Programmer"?

For the first time in his life, Carlos was on uncertain ground. He was seated with a friend at the bar at Paparazzi's, his favorite restaurant, which was decorated with old photos of Rome's dolce vita and located near the Real Madrid stadium.

"The truth is, my friend, I can't picture you hiding behind a nun's skirts!" José Luis Martín chuckled.

José Luis was the first person Carlos had met up with after the strange series of events in the province of Soria, and was the only person to whom he could tell such an absurd tale. His friend had studied psychology at the University of Navarra and then worked as a military chaplain for twenty years at the Cuatro Vientos barracks, until he hung up his habit for Marta, who became his wife. His new office was located in Division 12 of the Police Information Squad, on Tacona Street. Martín, the priest-turned-police-officer, was a meticulous, methodical man who worked for the police bureau as an expert in matters of religious crimes, sects, and esoteric movements with suspected ties to judges and politicians. A small detail that, let it be said in passing, did much to cement their friendship over the years. Carlos called him because he wanted to talk to him about his spiritual state.

"Have you perhaps given any thought to the idea that it was you who attracted the nun?"

José Luis decided to move in for the kill as soon as he had heard the story. He had yet to recover from the surprise of seeing his friend, the journalist and unbeliever, wrapped up in religious themes.

"That's exactly what I like about you, José Luis: your ideas are even stranger than mine." Carlos was pleasantly amused. "What are you insinuating?"

"It is very simple, Carlitos. You already know that conventional psychology holds no appeal for me. I'd rather read Jung than the behaviorists."

"Sure, sure. Which is why you work for the police instead of having a private practice."

"No laughing at an old priest! You know what? Jung calls what you went through 'synchronicity.' That you already know: it's a lovely way of saying chance does not exist and everything that happens to a person always has a hidden cause. He never used the word 'God'; he danced around the idea. In your case"—he paused to take a sip of beer before launching into the part with the most relevance for his friend—"Jung would argue that the article you published about teleportations, the one from a few months ago in which you mentioned the nun, as well as your obsession with the theme, predisposed you to live through a synchronicity."

Carlos didn't have a chance to respond.

"You know better than anyone that instances of extrasensory perception cannot be limited to ridiculous experiments in telepathy with Zener cards, with their waves, their crosses, and all the rest of it. Extrasensory perception is much more complex, and manifests itself with far greater force when emotions are involved. Didn't you ever dream of someone close to you and the next morning receive a letter from that person? Or hear the phone ring and when you answer it, it's the person you were just thinking about?"

Carlos nodded.

"Well, the emotions intervened in each of these phenomena. And according to Jung, they are the motor of psychic episodes."

"I follow, even though I don't understand a word you're saying," Carlos replied, smiling.

"It's actually very simple, Carlitos: when you made your wrong turn onto the highway that contained a road sign for Ágreda, you were most likely in a disassociated frame of mind. On the one hand, everything was running smoothly in your normal or everyday state of mind; on the other, you were in a critical state that you were completely unaware of, but which had to do with your obsession with teleportations. And it was precisely that state, that sort of other you, that, on its own account, noticed the existence of that geographic marker, and it carried you there, leading your normal state of mind to believe that everything was the fruit of an unusual series of events."

"That critical state later guided me to the monastery at Ágreda?"

"Exactly."

José Luis finished off his third beer with a satisfied look on his face. He was sure he'd hit the bull's-eye. The Swiss psychiatrist Carl Gustav Jung had never disappointed him. And yet his innate pragmatism would not be long in tumbling down.

Carlos was finally able to put what he wanted to say into words. "Let us accept your hypothesis for a moment and agree that the whole experience was the outcome of tremendous self-deception, that no such guided journey existed. In that case, whoever or whatever dropped several tons of snow onto the mountains of the Cameros, leaving only the road going to Ágreda open? Because I remind you that that is what happened. And another thing. Was it also my spiritual condition that led me, without asking anyone, to the monastery? And how could my 'other I' have known how to get around Ágreda if I had never even seen a map of the city?"

José Luis Martín had taken his empty glass and was rolling it back and forth between his hands. He looked up at the journalist.

"Listen to me, Carlos. Apart from everything about synchronicities, there was a time when I believed in miracles. You know that. And if what happened to you doesn't follow a series of Jungian chance occurrences, or have anything to do with extrasensory perception, then . . ."

"Then what?"

"Then it's a matter of higher causes. Look for other proof. Investigate."

"You talk just like my old mathematics professor! What kind of evidence am I supposed to look for?"

"I have no idea. It's different every time, trust me. If it fails to manifest itself, then take your case to heaven! In the police station I get an eyeful of shit every day. I take part in interrogations and evaluate the psychological profiles of the worst delinquents. And that, day after day, makes you lose faith in the transcendent, in someone being up there. . . . So, all right then, should you manage to prove that what happened to you in Ágreda was an incident arranged by some sort of superhuman intelligence, and that same intelligence can respond to your requests . . ."

"Then?"

"I'll give some thought to putting my robes back on. I'd love to recover my faith! And yours, too!"

"Is that the psychologist or the ex-priest talking?" Carlos asked maliciously.

"A man who once searched for God. Who spent twenty years among those he took to be His ministers, and never found Him. Which is why your work in this matter is important to me."

José Luis left the glass on the table, gave the journalist a hard look, and then continued the exchange with an uncomfortable question.

"You aren't a believer, are you?"

Carlos was too surprised to answer at first.

"You mean am I a practicing Catholic?"

José Luis nodded.

"No," Carlos stammered. "And I stopped being one a long time ago. God cheated me."

"So perhaps you can find the Truth without being blinded."

"The truth in capital letters?"

"Exactly. It is an overwhelming energy, always returning to its original brilliance, even when it takes centuries to do so. It comforts you and cleanses you when you find it. It has something"—he suddenly lowered his voice—"something to do with that God who forgot about you."

TWENTY-NINE

SAN ANTONIO MISSION

Esteban de Perea and his party stayed in Isleta another three days. Following the Inquisitor's instructions, the ten friars who had accompanied him left San Antonio's fortress mission at dawn on the second day to install themselves among Isleta's most humble families in an attempt to get the Indians to reveal any incident, no matter how insignificant, that would explain their peaceful conversion to Christianity.

Perea's suspicions were growing by the second.

In Spain, he had learned that no one renounces his faith willingly. In that faraway world on the other side of the ocean, the Jews who had converted to Christianity after the edict of expulsion in 1492 went on practicing their faith behind closed doors in their homes. Those who did were given the name "Marranos" and found themselves implacably pursued by the Holy Office. Similarly, no one trusted the Moors. Even when they were baptized, those "sons of Allah" still bowed down to Mecca five times a day in secret. Why should these Indians be any different?

Whether for supernatural reasons or not, Esteban de Perea needed to find out what had prompted them to supposedly change their beliefs.

But his strategy was only partially successful.

Not a single adult explained to the friars who or what had moved them to ask to be baptized. A few of the youngest children blurted out something about a powerful "blue spirit" who had visited them and had convinced their parents to leave their totems behind.

The Inquisitor carefully noted this "clue." He wrote it down in the white margins of his Bible, which was where he hid his personal account of the trip. Even so, regardless of his meticulous nature, none of the information they collected helped him to resolve the mystery. He would need a miracle, a sign, that would change the attitude of the adults in the Indian community; something that would let him inside their hearts.

And the prodigy arrived; or to be more precise, Esteban de Perea provoked it.

It occurred on his fourth day in Isleta, Sunday, the twenty-second of July 1692, just as the friars were making preparations to leave the mission. It was the feast of Mary Magdalene, and the friars who worked with Perea, accompanied by Friar Salas, called the congregation to a solemn Mass. Esteban intuited that the religious ceremonies would move some of the natives, and that that, seasoned with a strong sermon, might convince them to talk. In fact, he was giving thought to the idea of preaching about their children's fear of the "voices" in the desert, and so wrote a homily that went straight to their souls. It was his final recourse.

With the last peal of the church bells resounding in the adobe towers, the church was filled to overflowing. Twelve friars were going to officiate at a service usually conducted by only one.

"Do your utmost, Friar," Juan de Salas said in a whisper as he pulled the chasuble over the priest's head. "I have never seen so many people before at Mass."

"You needn't worry. Everything is ready."

The Indians marveled at the power the place held. Hardly had they heard the first chords of the Introit when the atmosphere inside changed. Without understanding the words of the Latin rite, they perceived better than anyone a certain almost-forgotten bittersweet sensation, from the time when their kivas occupied the place where the church now sat.

Father Esteban carried the ceremony. After the reading from the

Gospel, the Inquisitor began his sermon. He appeared to be transfigured. His expression, which had been tense and watchful, gave way to a look of kindness and even docility.

"On the third day after Jesus was crucified," he began, "two of his disciples, traveling on the road to Emmaus, were marveling at the strange disappearance of the body of their 'rabbi.' They spoke of how Mary Magdalene and the other women had discovered his empty tomb, and of their encounter with an angel who told them the Lord was still alive."

The Indians listened intently. Esteban de Perea knew how they enjoyed stories abounding in marvels.

"Suddenly," he went on, "a man joined them on the road, a stranger to them. He asked who it was they were speaking about, and they, chagrined that this man had never heard of Jesus, told him his story in detail. After he had heard them out, this unknown man upbraided them for their lack of faith, but nonetheless invited them to his table and set out dinner. Only when they saw him breaking the bread did they realize who he was. It was their Lord, come back to life! The one they had been speaking of for hours! And yet before they could ask him a single question, Jesus vanished from their sight."

A few Indians exchanged looks of surprise.

"Do you know why no one recognized him before?" Friar Esteban asked. "Because they trusted their eyes more than their hearts! Sometime later, the two disciples stated that, in the presence of the stranger, they felt their hearts quicken. In other words, deep inside they knew who he was, but they let themselves perceive through the physical senses and not those of the soul. Here is a lesson for all of us: if one day you meet someone who makes your heart quicken, do not doubt! He is a messenger from heaven!"

The Inquisitor, at the climax of his story, paused for an instant.

"And if you encounter such a person, would you not share the news with your neighbor?"

A murmuring began to grow in the back of the church.

It took the friars several moments before they realized that the sound was caused by the arrival of a contingent of painted men who were opening a passage through the congregants. They had entered in silence, threading their way among the parishioners discreetly, and now stood nearly at the center of the church.

Indifferent, Friar Esteban continued with his sermon.

"Our Lord makes himself felt in many different ways. One way, which he uses frequently, is sending us his emissaries. And then again, as happened on the road to Emmaus, he tests our ability to recognize with the heart. To identify him, it is enough to be attentive to the signs. Have you never felt this fire deep down inside? Have your children not felt it? I"—and here he paused melodramatically—"I know that you have."

No one moved a muscle.

The families of Tiwas, Chiyauwipkis, and Tompiros listened intently to the Franciscan's challenge. Meanwhile, the newly arrived members of the congregation looked around them as if the sermon being preached was not directed at them. They remained silent as the rest of the congregation chanted the Deo Gratias and Pater Noster following the homily. Packed closely together in the middle of the crowd, they stood waiting for the ceremony to come to a close.

Their presence, nevertheless, did not surprise anyone.

The Isleta natives were familiar with the new arrivals, who were a group of peaceful Jumanos, much like those who frequently visited the region to exchange turquoise and salt for animal skins and meat. A friendly tribe from far away, but one with whom they had good relations.

At the end of the Mass, the leader of the group, a young Indian with a shaved head and spirals painted on his chest, drew close to the altar and approached Friar Salas. He spoke urgently for almost a minute in a Tanoan dialect the old missionary half understood. But it was enough to change the look on his face.

"What is happening, Friar?"

The Inquisitor could sense that something unusual was happening.

"The man speaking to me is a Jumano Indian, Friar Esteban. From the south." Salas spoke in a soft voice as he wiped the silver chalice.

"He just finished telling me that he has been several days crossing through the desert, with fifty of his best men, and that he wants to speak to us."

"If what they need is food and water, let us help them."

"That isn't what they want, Friar. This Indian is certain that a sign, or something like it, has directed them here, where they would find God's messengers. Do you know what he is referring to?"

A mischievous smile played across the old man's face as he observed the Inquisitor's sudden interest in what was going on around him.

"A sign? What sort of sign?"

Indulging his curiosity, Esteban de Perea walked over and asked the Jumano for more details. The young leader, who stared at him defiantly, went along, gesturing as he spoke. Father Salas, who was adept in the language of signs, interpreted the movements as best he could.

"He is telling us that a woman descends from the heavens toward his village. He says that she has a white face like ours, that she is as radiant as the light in the sky. She is wearing a blue robe that covers her from head to foot and told them about the friars' arrival in Isleta."

"Did he use the word 'friars'?" Perea stammered.

"Yes."

"And he says that it is a woman?"

The old priest nodded.

"He also says that the Mother of the Corn has never spoken to them in that way before. And that is why they believe it is another goddess, and they ask you to tell them if you know who it is."

"A goddess?"

"Indeed, this young man goes even further: he says it was this woman who ordered them to come here to seek you out, so that he could ask you to accompany him to his village to speak to the people there about our God."

The Jumano was speaking very rapidly, as if he were running out of time. His hand was nervously cradling the rough cross, made out of pine bark, which hung around his neck.

"Have you seen this man before?"

Perea's question distracted the old man.

"Him, no. But his father, yes. He is called the great Walpi and is chieftain of his tribe."

"And this one? What is his name?"

"Sakmo, Friar."

"Ask Sakmo if he saw this Lady in Blue with his own eyes." Perea was giving orders now.

Through a series of guttural sounds, Friar Juan translated the question, and a few seconds later translated the Indian's response into Spanish.

"Yes. On several occasions, always after sunset."

"This is indeed fortunate."

Friar Juan would not let the Inquisitor be the one to end the conversation.

"So you see?" he exclaimed joyfully. "This is another sign!"

"Another sign?" Friar Esteban cringed.

"Could it be any clearer, Friar? Even if no one in my parish wants to tell you what brought them to accept Jesus Christ, these people do. This young Jumano knows nothing of tribunals, has no fear of the Holy Office, and appears never even to have seen a Spaniard before, but still he recounts the history of a woman dressed in blue, a woman who encouraged him to come here to meet you. And he arrives just at this moment!"

"Please calm yourself," ordered Friar Esteban. "If things are as they seem, let us act cautiously. And if not, let us put a stop to this sort of deception once and for all."

"So what is it, according to you? One of Our Lady's miracles? Another manifestation of Guadalupe?" Friar Juan let himself get carried away for a few moments. "Did not Juan Diego describe the Virgin of Guadalupe as a woman wearing a blue robe?"

The Inquisitor speared him with a glance.

"What do you think we ought to do?" Friar Salas countered.

"Tell Sakmo that we will study his case this very day, and we will decide whether or not we are going to send a delegation to preach in his village." Esteban de Perea glared at him. "Above all, make sure that he explains to you very clearly in what direction we must travel and how many days stand between Isleta and his settlement. And then call the community together in the refectory. Have you understood me?"

"Certainly, Father." The old friar smiled enigmatically at his guest. "Did you notice the cross he was wearing around his neck?"

THIRTY

VENICE BEACH

If Carlos had known what was taking place on the West Coast of the United States while he was seated at the bar in Paparazzi's with José Luis Martín, his Cartesian vision of the world would have been forever shattered. It was noon in Los Angeles, but in Jennifer Narody's small beach house the venetian blinds were still drawn. The sunlight that was blistering Venice Beach could not penetrate her bedroom.

It had taken Jennifer a long time to get to sleep the night before. She had a great deal on her mind after her last session with Dr. Meyers. "This kind of fantasy," the doctor had told her, "is sometimes due to physical causes. A small clot in the temporal lobe of the brain, or a tumor, can impair the mind and alter its perception of reality. We should have an MRI taken, to see if there's anything there."

Jennifer was claustrophobic, and the mere idea of spending half an hour inside a cold metal tube terrified her. For that reason, she put off coming to grips with her dream and decided instead to read, turning to the Bible. She had a Gideon in the house, a small, manageable volume she could not remember ever having looked at, and opened it randomly to the Gospel of Matthew. She began reading the story of Joseph's dream, in which he learned of his betrothed's pregnancy from an angel of the Lord. It was strange. All the peoples of the ancient world believed that dreams were a means through which the divinities communicated with men, that through them the gods revealed hidden things.

But what were these things? And what divinity would be interested in sending a tormented young woman a dream like the one that began to sketch itself in her mind?

THIRTY-ONE

SAN ANTONIO MISSION
JULY 22, 1629

Friar Esteban de Perea's voice reverberated off the walls of the mission. The urgency in his summons, that all gather to hear the Indian's petition, was a complete mystery to the other friars at first. But it quickly became clear. The haste was due to Sakmo's allusion to the mysterious woman who commanded them to cross the desert. Friar Esteban had a look of shock on his face, as if the ghosts themselves, the ones who forced the Archbishop of Mexico to put him in charge of the investigation into "supernatural activity" in the region, had all landed on his conscience.

"Is anything the matter, Friar?" Friar Bartolomé Romero, one of the brothers in the caravan, delicately asked the Inquisitor.

"No . . . nothing," Esteban answered as he took off his chasuble and folded it. "But think about it: if the Jumanos left their village in Gran Quivira four or five days ago, then the Lady in Blue sent them on their journey before I made the decision to stay here at the mission. Do you understand now, Friar Bartolemé?

"And what is so strange about that?" A third voice sounded from the back of the sacristy. "Are you saying that the future would not be known by God or the Virgin?"

The words stunned everyone within hearing range. Standing in the threshold of the sacristy with a bemused smile on his lips, Friar Juan de Salas glanced around the room. And if it was true, as everything seemed to indicate, that a mysterious woman had reached the Jumano territory before they did, it must not have been a woman of flesh and blood. Not only had she traveled into an inhospitable region but she also possessed the extraordinary ability to persuade the Indians to adopt a new faith and set off in search of white men.

"A Herculean task!" he added. "Your worships may think what you like, but it would not strike me as strange if the woman were Our Lady herself."

No one responded to the elderly friar, who spun around on his heels and soon disappeared outside. He still needed to speak with Sakmo to reassure him that his petition had been heard, and that a small band of friars would soon be traveling with him to Cueloce.

"He's an odd sort, wouldn't you say?" Friar Bartolomé muttered in Friar Esteban's ear while their host was taking his leave.

"The desert does strange things to people, Brother."

When Juan de Salas finished explaining to Sakmo what the newly arrived friars planned to do, the young warrior fell to his knees. Then, without a word of farewell, he set off to meet his men at their encampment outside the mission, at the foot of the adobe houses. They, too, were overjoyed at the news. And yet even Friar Juan did not realize that the source of Sakmo's happiness was not his diplomatic success. Rather, it was because the friars' decision confirmed what the Lady in Blue had told them days before, and thus reaffirmed their belief that they had encountered an authentic "woman of power." Just as she had predicted, he had arrived to find new friars at the Mission of San Antonio de Padua, and it looked as if some of the friars would be returning to the Kingdom of Gran Quivira with them.

Keeping to their strict schedule, the Franciscans met in an improvised refectory shortly after their noon prayers. The Tiwas had taken great care in clearing some space in a back room of the mission.

The large meal was to be traditional: peas steamed and seasoned with salt, ears of corn, and nuts for dessert. To accompany it, there was water to drink and a half dozen large loaves of rye bread just out of the oven.

Two minutes after the benediction was pronounced, the Inquisitor stood up to speak.

"As all the friars know, a band of Jumano, or painted Indians, arrived at the mission this morning. They have asked our help in bringing the Gospel to their village."

Friar Esteban coughed lightly.

"It is up to us to decide what to do. We can either stay here until our return to Santa Fe, or else we can begin to assign missionaries to other parts, such as that of the Jumanos." He added, "Our decision depends, of course, upon how interested we are in starting to preach the Gospel."

The friars stared at each other. The idea of splitting up the members of their expedition surprised them. And even though they knew that something like this was bound to happen sooner or later, they never thought it would happen so quickly.

"And so?" Esteban de Perea exhorted them.

Friar Francisco de Letrado, a rotund priest from Talavera de la Reina, was the first who asked to speak. He raised his voice solemnly and delivered an apocalyptic speech. All of these "Indian tales," as he put it, were nothing more than the work of the Devil, whose goal was to disperse the various preachers to remote regions where they had little hope of success, and even fewer chances of returning alive. "Divide and conquer," he bellowed.

Friar Bartolomé Romero, Esteban's faithful helper, and Friar Juan Ramirez, a level-headed monk from Valencia, were, for their part, more tolerant of the Jumanos' intentions and argued for a rapid evangelization of their lands. These two believed that Sakmo's allusions to a light from heaven lent his story authenticity, and that it was similar to other manifestations of Our Lady, which frequently were accompanied by extraordinary displays of unearthly light.

A mere handful, namely, Friars Roque de Figueredo, Agustín de Cuéllar, and Francisco de la Madre de Dios, did not even trouble to enter the debate. Theirs was an abstention of the easiest sort: they would do whatever the group decided.

"Very well then, Brothers," Esteban de Perea again took charge. "Seeing as such diversity of opinion exists, we would do well if all of us interrogated the Indian who claims to have seen the Lady. Perhaps that will help us clear up our doubts."

With soft-voiced assents and nodded heads, agreement made its way around the table.

"Friar Juan de Salas will be our translator, yes?"

"Naturally," he agreed, and stood up from the table to go in search of Sakmo.

A few minutes later, the youngest son of the great Walpi knelt down to kiss the fringe of Friar Esteban's robes.

"Pater," he intoned the Latin word in a deep voice.

His gesture stunned everyone present. Where had the savage learned such language?

"Is this the evidence we were looking for?" a voice boomed from the back of the refectory.

Sakmo lowered his head as if answering the question posed by that strong, ponderous voice. Friar Esteban stood up from the head of the table, looked the Indian over carefully, and from where he was standing began his interrogation in a loud voice, so that everyone could hear.

"What is your name?"

"Sakmo. The man of the green field," Friar Salas translated for him.

"Where are you from?"

"Gran Quivira, a land of open spaces—a quarter-moon of travel from here."

"Do you know why we have asked to speak to you?"

"I think so," he said, lowering his voice.

"They have told us that you saw the woman who sent you to us. Is all that correct?"

Sakmo looked at the Inquisitor as if he was seeking permission to speak. The old man nodded in his direction.

"Yes, it is true. I have seen her many times in the mouth of what we call the Canyon of the Serpent. She always spoke to us in a friendly manner."

"Always? When did these visitations begin?"

"They have been going on for many moons. I was only a child when I first heard stories about the warriors whom she had visited."

"In what language did she speak to you?"

"In Tanoan. But if I had to explain to you how, I would never be able. She never moved her mouth. It was always closed, while I and other members of our tribe listened, understanding perfectly what she was saying."

"In what way did she appear?"

"It was always the same: at nightfall, strange flashes of light would enter the canyon. Then we would hear a rustling in the air like the sound the rattlesnake makes or the fast, curving wind along the river. Then we saw a trail of light fall from the sky . . . and then, it was silent."

"A trail of light?"

"As if a path had opened in the darkness. The woman, who was neither a priestess nor a Mother of the Corn, lowered herself through the light. None of us knew her name."

"How did she look?"

"She was young and beautiful. She had white skin, as if she had never been in the sun."

"Did she bring anything with her?"

"Yes. In her right hand she sometimes carried a cross, but not like the ones that the fathers here wear around their necks. It was more beautiful than theirs, it was completely black and radiant. Sometimes she wore an amulet around her neck. It wasn't turquoise, bone, or wood, but the color of moonlight."

Friar Esteban was taking note of what Sakmo was saying. After the Indian had finished speaking, he proceeded with his questions.

"Tell me, my son: do you remember what she told you the first time you saw her?"

The Indian fixed the Franciscan in his gaze.

"She said she came from far away and that she brought good news. She told us of the arrival of a new time when our old gods would give way to one, a greater god, as great as the sun."

"She never said her name?"

"No."

"Nor that of the new god?"

"No."

"Did she say where she came from?"

"No."

"One thing more. Regarding this new god, did this woman tell you that he was her son, that he came from her womb?"

Sakmo's eyes opened in astonishment when he heard Friar Juan de Salas translate the Inquisitor's question.

"No."

A few of the friars shifted in their seats.

"Did you notice anything else about this woman?" Esteban continued.

"Yes. Around her waist she wore a cord like yours."

This greatly moved the friars. "A cord like the Franciscans wear! What kind of prodigy is this?"

Esteban de Perea called for silence.

"Did you go so far as to touch this woman?"

"Yes."

Friar Esteban looked astonished.

"And?"

"Her clothes gave off warmth, like our clothes do when our women take them out of the dyeing vats. But they were dry. She even let me touch her black crucifix and taught me a handful of magic words."

"Magic words? Would you be able to repeat them?"

"I think so," he said hesitatingly.

"Please."

Sakmo went back onto his knees, his hands together as the woman had taught him. He then began to intone a litany familiar in Latin. It sounded strange coming from the mouth of a pagan.

"*Pater noster qui es in caelis . . . sanctificetur nomen tuum . . . adveniat regnum tuum . . . fiat voluntas tua sicut in caelo . . .*"

"That is enough," Juan de Salas said as he broke into Sakmo's chant. "Explain to Father Perea where you learned this. Who taught you these words?"

"I told you before: it was the Lady in Blue."

THIRTY-TWO

MADRID

Carlos Albert would meet with his friend José Luis again in less than two days, under circumstances that neither one of them could have imagined as they sat in the restaurant. In the meantime, Carlos dedicated himself to searching for more information on María Jesús de Ágreda. His quest led him directly to Madrid's National Library, an establishment whose sheer amount of information always provoked a strange dizziness in him. How could he get his hands on what he was looking for if he had to wade through its collection of thirty thousand manuscripts, three thousand books from the dawn of the printing press, half a million books published before 1831, not to mention the more than six million monographs written on the most diverse subjects imaginable? The forest that lurked inside the temple of Spanish wisdom struck him as impossibly dense but nonetheless alluring.

His first search among the library's card catalogs lifted his spirits. Carlos found various carefully annotated references to Friar Alonso de Benavides, the man who in 1630 undertook the investigation into Mother Ágreda's alleged bilocations. Toward the back of the drawer was a reference to an unusual document that, according to the bibliographic information, was filled with references to a certain "Lady in Blue" who preached to the indigenous tribes of New Mexico before the arrival of the first Franciscans.

A day and a half of bureaucratic requests later, on the seventeenth of April, in the manuscript room of the National Library, after Carlos had signed innumerable forms and permission slips, the book he had been waiting for was finally in his hands. The room itself was an immense rectangle, three hundred feet from one end to the other, its rarely swept floor pitted with ruts and pockmarks. Fifty slanted writing desks, ancient and unwieldy, were spaced around the room, all of them under the watchful eye of a librarian whose demeanor indicated she had very few friends. Her work, which she discharged like a soldier on guard duty, consisted of walking over to the lifts when they brought the books up from the archives, and then checking to see if the volumes the readers had asked for had arrived.

"*Memorial* by Benavides." The librarian read the pink card while hovering over Carlos's shoulder.

"Yes, I requested it."

The librarian regarded the journalist with displeasure.

"Don't forget, we close at nine."

"I know that."

The librarian put the book down on the desk and walked away. Carlos was excited. Here was a book of some one hundred nine pages, its leather cover faded to black over the course of time, its paper yellowed and crumbling with each turn of the page. On its worn frontispiece, printed on top of a crude engraving of the Virgin crowned with stars, Carlos read: "Memoirs that Friar Juan de Santander, member of the Franciscan order, Commissioner General of the Indies, presents to His Majesty the Catholic King, Philip IV." And in a handwritten line that followed: "By Friar Alonso de Benavides, of the Holy Office, Custodian of the Provinces, with respect to the religious conversions in New Mexico."

Carlos smiled with satisfaction. And yet, despite his precautions in handling the book, the volume was crumbling in his hands like rotting wood.

Several pages were enough to give him an idea of its contents: the author was explaining to a very young Philip IV what the expedition of twelve Franciscan missionaries, headed by the same Benavides, had achieved as they proselytized in the territories of New Mexico between 1626 and 1630.

Employing the baroque style of the day, Friar Alonso outdid himself in praise of "the Lord our God and his Power" (Carlos jotted

MEMORIAL

QVE FRAY IVAN DE SANTANDER DE LA Orden de ſan Franciſco, Comiſſario General de Indias, preſenta a la Mageſtad Catolica del Rey don Felipe QVARTO nueſtro Señor.

HECHO POR EL PADRE FRAY ALONSO de Benauides Comiſſario del Santo Oficio, y Cuſtodio que ha ſido de las Prouincias, y conuerſiones del Nueuo-Mexico.

TRATASE EN EL DE LOS TESOROS ESpirituales, y temporales, que la diuina Mageſtad ha manifeſtado en aquellas conuerſiones, y nueuos deſcubrimientos, por medio de los Padres deſta ſerafica Religion.

CON LICENCIA

En Madrid en la Imprenta Real. Año M. DC. XXX.

Cover of the memoirs of Friar Alonso de Benavides, published in Madrid in 1630

down Benavides's exact words), to whom he attributed the discovery of mines, the rapid eradication of idolatry, the conversion of more than half a million souls in record time, and, above all, the unceasing work of building churches and monasteries. "In one district alone, within a space of one hundred leagues," the journalist copied into his notebook, "the Order has baptized more than eighty thousand souls and constructed more than fifty churches and convents."

Carlos immediately realized that the Benavides *Memorial* was a typical work of propaganda for its century. It was clear that its author was attempting to secure the king's economic assistance, to reinforce the positions taken by the Franciscans in America, as well as to finance voyages by new missionaries. The text exaggerated when it spoke of "inexhaustible mines" and associated their exploration with the conversion of the natives.

In any case, the writing disguised its intentions in elegant fashion. It reviewed in passing all the Indian tribes that Benavides's men had encountered: the Apaches, the Piros, the Senecas, the Conchas, and many others.

"Quite a document. Yes, indeed," Carlos said quietly to himself.

The journalist also discovered something he did not expect: the name María Jesús de Ágreda failed to appear on a single page, nor did she receive credit for a single conversion; the term "bilocation" appeared nowhere in the text. What is more, only the Virgin was spoken of for the assistance she had lent in the conversions, and how "Our Lady's favors" had driven the unstoppable advance of Christianity in New Mexico.

How was it possible? Had the nuns in Ágreda pointed him in the wrong direction? Or were they simply confused about the true nature of Benavides's text?

He was tempted to set the *Memorial* aside. Only the librarian's face, so like that of a guard dog, kept him from doing so. The face of someone from whom one could expect few concessions, it begged him to stretch out his time in the reading room and give the book a second, more attentive, reading. His "destiny"—the same force that had guided him through the Sierra de Cameros days before—led him directly to page 83 this time.

He sat there glued to the desk.

And with reason: right in front of him, beneath the suggestive subtitle, "Miraculous Conversion of the Jumano Nation," he read an uncanny story. It mentioned one Friar Juan de Salas who, finding himself in the land of the Tiwas at the head of the group of missionaries, was visited by members of the Jumano tribe, also known as the tribe from the salt mines. They fervently petitioned him to send a missionary to preach in their village. It seemed that this request had been made years before, with nothing having been done about it, owing to the lack of missionaries in New Mexico. All of this changed with the arrival of a new Guardian, a sort of "ad hoc bishop" for the unexplored territories, a man by the name of Esteban de Perea. This man, on orders from Benavides himself, arrived at de Salas's mission with a small retinue of friars, ready to preach the Gospel to those Indians so disposed.

"And before they left for the village," Carlos read, "they asked the Indians why it was they so fervently asked us to baptize them and have the friars teach them the doctrine. The Indians responded that a woman like the one whose portrait we carried (which was, in fact, a painting of Mother Luisa de Carrión) preached to everyone in their own language. She told them that they should call on the friars to instruct them and baptize them, and not to be slow about it."

A complete revelation.

Carlos scribbled the story into his notebook. This was the only passage in the "Benavides report" that could be attributed to a bilocated nun (although, in fact, it mentioned one unfamiliar to Carlos: Madre María Luisa de Carrión), but it left open a whole array of unanswered questions. Without going any further, how could he be sure that the *Memorial* referred to the presumed apparitions of Madre Ágreda? The nuns in the monastery in Soria had been absolutely vehement in attributing such prodigious feats to their founder, had they not?

But even if one admitted that Sister María Jesús de Ágreda had split herself in two, appearing "more than 2,600 leagues from Spain," where would that good lady have learned to communicate with the Indians in their own language? Was this yet another prodigy, known as xenoglossy or "the gift of foreign tongues" by those experts in Catholic miracles, in addition to that of bilocation? On the other hand, didn't Benavides's descriptions appear to be closer to a manifestation of the Virgin than something as unusual as a bilocation?

The subject, no doubt about it, became much more compelling to him that afternoon. What a shame it was that the ferocious librarian threw Carlos out three minutes before the room's antediluvian clock struck nine.

"You can return tomorrow, if you like," the librarian muttered. "I will set the book aside for you."

"Thank you, but that won't be necessary."

THIRTY-THREE

SAN ANTONIO MISSION

Friar Esteban gave the Indian a long, hard look, as if he were a prisoner about to climb the scaffold. It was a defiant stare, one that could turn an accused man to stone. But Sakmo, who had never seen an auto-da-fé, brazenly returned the Inquisitor's stony expression.

"And you never saw a friar before?" the latter asked, his tone more serious.

"No."

Esteban de Perea knew the Indian was not lying. The first Franciscans had set foot in New Mexico in 1598, thirty-one years earlier, and none of the friars had gone to live in Gran Quivira. Perea knew the history well. The conquistador Don Juan de Oñate concluded that it wasn't worth his time and effort to stay in lands so barren and unprofitable as those on either side of the Rio Grande. Furthermore, from what Perea could observe of this Indian, he had been born after Oñate's incursions. It was therefore impossible for him to have seen any of the eight friars who accompanied Oñate, nor his eighty-three wagons, nor even the stupefying train of Mexican Indians and half-breeds who followed behind. Friar Esteban himself remembered the figure of Friar Juan Claros, the brave man who had founded the settlement of San Antonio of Padua, where the mission was now located, and who had yet to convert a single Indian by the time he was relieved by Friar Juan de Salas.

It was only later, with the arrival of the "blue miracle," that the situation had changed.

While Sakmo awaited a new battery of questions, Friar García de San Francisco, a young man from Zamora who had just taken vows, cautiously approached the Inquisitor. The timid Franciscan with a sickly air seized the opportunity, amid the general confusion, to whisper something in Friar Esteban's ear. De Perea smiled.

"Good idea. Tell him, Friar. We have nothing to lose."

García, a slip of a friar who seemed to shrink in size next to the well-built Sakmo, crossed the space between himself and the Indian with four large steps. He pulled out of his habit a small scapular with a tiny image on it.

"This is Mother María Luisa," he said in a strident voice, so that everyone could hear. "I carry her with me at all times. She protects me from evil. In Palencia, many of us believe she is one of the few living saints among us."

Brother García dangled the tiny portrait in front of Sakmo's face. And the Inquisitor, who continued to pace as if making his final decision, boomed out from the other end of the refectory, "Tell us, Sakmo, is this the woman you saw?"

The Jumano stared at the miniature curiously, without saying a word.

"Speak. Is it she?" de Perea repeated impatiently.

"No."

"You are certain?"

Sakmo explained to Juan de Salas.

"Absolutely, Friar. The woman of the desert has a younger face. The clothes are similar, but hers"—he pointed to the scapular—"are the color of wood, not of the sky."

Friar Esteban took a deep breath.

Sakmo would never dispel his doubts, nor those of Friar Benavides, when he, Perea, submitted his explanations. Who could this resplendent young woman be? What virtuous woman would let an Indian such as this touch her clothes, as if she were a physical entity, tangible and real, and then teach him the Pater Noster? What young woman in her right mind would visit such remote regions on her own? And what species of woman, save the Virgin, was capable of descending from the heavens on a luminous pathway?

Hurrying through his last questions, Father Esteban dismissed Sakmo, ordering him to wait until he had made a decision in his case. Then he asked the friars to tell him what they thought. Only Friar Bartolomé Romero, the most erudite of the group, dared to put forth an opinion. He spoke briefly.

"I do not believe we ought to regard this episode as proof that the Indians have had a mystical experience."

"What are you insinuating, Friar Romero?"

The Inquisitor watched as Romero anxiously clasped and unclasped his hands.

"From my point of view, Friar, we are not faced here with a manifestation of Our Lady, as you have intimated in certain of your questions."

"And why are you so certain?"

"Because, as Your Excellency knows, the manifestations of the Virgin are ineffable experiences, which are impossible to recount. If it is difficult for a good Christian to describe this sort of divine suffering, how much more must it be for an untutored pagan."

"Then you are saying that—"

"What I am saying is, this Indian saw something earthly, not at all divine," Friar Bartolomé concluded.

Esteban de Perea crossed himself, to the amazement of the other friars. He feared offending God with his lack of confidence. But that is how he was. He had to look at a question from all sides before rendering judgment.

"That is, I think, enough for now," he said at last. "I must meditate on my decision."

He ended the meeting, but before leaving the room he asked Friar Salas to accompany him. There was something important on his mind.

As soon as the two Franciscans were alone, the elderly friar approached Esteban de Perea with an expression of deep concern.

"Have you decided what you are going to do, Father?" Friar Juan cautiously inquired.

"As you might guess, I am not certain what is the correct decision in this case. It is not the same as documenting one of Our

Lady's interventions, or investigating a fraud, a mirage, or some sort of trick."

"I do not understand."

"If the person who has appeared to these Indians is Our Lady, we have nothing to fear. The heavens then sent us a great benediction, and will protect us when we visit Gran Quivira. If, on the other hand, as Friar Bartolomé says, such a prodigy does not exist, we would be walking right into an ambush. Our expedition would be divided up, we would lose contact with one another, and we would fail in our task of baptizing the peoples of New Mexico."

"And why do you so heavily emphasize this second possibility?"

"Well, Sakmo himself told us, did he not? The woman was wearing a rope tied around her waist like ours. It may perhaps be a question of a soul initiated into the Order of Saint Francis. Or a woman with no sense of judgment, or someone in disguise. Or simply a trap."

"Or perhaps none of that. Does not a descent from the heavens and a glowing face seem to you more in keeping with the way the Virgin appears?"

"I am certain you are right, Friar. But in that respect the Lady in Blue lacks one of the characteristics of Marian visions. Our Lady generally appears before isolated individuals, not to entire tribes like the Jumanos. Remember the apostle James the Greater, who saw the Virgin while living alone in Zaragoza, or Juan Diego and the Virgin of Guadalupe? No matter how much he might have wanted to, the Archbishop of Mexico, then the Franciscan Juan de Zumárraga, was never able to accompany Juan Diego and see the Virgin with his own eyes."

"But Friar Esteban!" the old man protested. "Is that sufficient grounds to consider the Lady in Blue a mere mundane creation?"

"I have a good reason, believe me. But if I share it with you, you must keep the secret."

"You may count on it," Juan de Salas said, nodding his head.

"You see, in addition to telling me everything they knew about these supernatural conversions, Archbishop Manso and Friar Benavides showed me an extraordinary letter, written in Spain by a Franciscan brother, Sebastián Marcilla, who resides in Soria."

"Sebastián Marcilla? Do you know him?"

"No." Esteban de Perea shook his head. "In this letter he advised the Archbishop of Mexico, who was very knowledgeable about evidence of our faith among the Indians in the Gran Quivira region—"

"I do not understand. How could a friar in Spain—"

"I will get to that, Friar."

"In that letter," the Inquisitor went on, "Friar Marcilla pleaded with the Archbishop to make all possible effort to find the origin of these appearances, to determine if behind them there could be the manifestations of a Spanish nun famous for being a miracle worker . . ."

Friar Salas was perplexed.

"A Spanish nun?"

"Of course, the correct term would be projections, given that Marcilla deduced that this nun, who most certainly lived in a Franciscan monastery, enjoyed the gift of bilocation. That is to say, she let herself be seen here without leaving Spain."

"And who is this? Is it the Mother María Luisa in the portrait?"

"No. This whole story concerns a young nun in a monastery in Soria. Her name is María Jesús de Ágreda."

"So what are you waiting for?" Friar Salas leaped to his feet with enthusiasm. "If you already have these indications, why have you not sent a small commission to the Quivira in search of proof? Two friars would be enough . . ."

"Who?" Friar Esteban brusquely interrupted the old Franciscan.

"If you consider it opportune, I offer myself as a volunteer. I could take one of the initiates with me, Friar Diego for example. He's young and strong, and would make a fine companion for the trip. Together we would complete our mission in little more than a month."

"Let me consider it."

"I don't think you have a better option, Father," the elderly man said, burning with confidence. "I speak the Tanoan language, they have known me for years, and I know how to survive in the desert better than any of your men. For me it is no hardship to travel with them to their village and then return alone, sidestepping the routes most closely guarded by the Apaches."

The Inquisitor took a seat.

"I suppose there is no greater force than that of enthusiasm, is there?"

"And that of faith," Salas said.

"So be it. You will leave on the next full moon, in August. Inside of ten days. Go over the mission thoroughly with Friar Diego, and bring me news of this Lady in Blue as quickly as you can."

THIRTY-FOUR

MADRID

The streets were quiet in the immediate vicinity of the National Library. It was 4:40 AM, and none of the buses from Plaza de Colón to the airport were running yet. There were a few taxis making the rounds, their green lights on and their backseats empty.

A silver Ford Transit turned off from Serrano onto the narrow Calle de Villanueva, heading downhill along the metal railings that surround the National Museum of Archaeology and the National Library. A few hundred feet from the end of the street, where it flows into the Paseo del Prado, the driver turned off the engine and lights and let the car roll until it reached the Recoletos Apartments, where he parked.

No one noticed his presence.

A minute and a half later, two dark silhouettes got out of the car.

"Quickly! Right here!"

The two figures climbed the high gates smoothly. Their running jumps carried them up and their catlike movements adapted easily to the iron fence. Both were wearing tiny black knapsacks, and both had on shortwave earphones. The third person sat inside the van, where he had just intercepted the last message sent over the walkie-talkies by security at the library's main entrance, which confirmed that the zone was clear.

Inside the open space in front of the library the two shadows quickly moved into place behind the statues of San Isidro and Alfonso the Wise. Both statues' subjects were seated fifteen steps above street level, and seemed to have been observing the intruders' movements.

"Run for it!" the shadow in front ordered. In ten seconds, the two clandestine visitors were standing next to the outside wall to the left of the stairs, and five seconds later, one of the two dark silhouettes, the "locksmith," opened one of the building's glass doors.

"Pizza to base, do you hear me?"

The voice of the locksmith came through loud and clear in the silver van.

"Copy, Pizza Two."

"Do you see the guard near the entrance?"

"Negative. All clear. Walk right in."

Once they had gained entrance into the building, they stood under the vaulted ceiling in the main lobby. No one was around, and in the corners, the red lights of the volumetric sensors were disconnected.

"He must have gone to piss . . . ," the lead shadow whispered when he saw the way was clear.

"Two minutes, thirty seconds," the locksmith replied.

"Right on schedule. Let's get going!"

They skillfully ascended the thirty-five steps of the marble stairway leading to the entrance of the main reading room. The dozen newly installed computers that gave readers access to the library's database sat in their places. After doubling around to their right and crossing the darkened wing where the file cabinets were located, they approached the glass door in the back of the room.

"Hand me the diamond blade."

Tracing with surgical precision, the locksmith carved a perfect circle out of the corner of the window farthest to the right, Attaching two small suction cups to the surface, he lifted the glass out without a sound.

"Lean it against the wall for now," the other shadow said.

"Right."

"Three minutes, forty seconds."

"Let's go."

The window with the hole had separated the area of the card catalogs from the manuscript reading room. Only the feeble light on the emergency power boxes illuminated the room.

"Hold on!" The locksmith came to a quick stop. "Base, can you hear me?"

"Pizza Two, I hear you."

"I want you to tell me if the eyes in the oven's anteroom see anything."

"Give me a second."

The man in the Ford typed instructions into the computer connected to a tiny rotating antenna situated on the van's roof. With a slight buzzing noise, it faced the library as it sought a particular electronic signal. The liquid crystal lit up quickly and a floor plan for the main floor of the library appeared on the monitor.

"Fantastic!" the third man blurted out. "I'll know in a few seconds, Pizza Two."

"Keep it coming, Base."

The mouse diligently flew over the map of the manuscript room, which leaped out of the flat plane into a three-dimensional diagram. With the same arrow sliding over the surface, he clicked on one of the cameras over the door on the far right. An icon, with the word "scanning" on its lower half, indicated that the system was connected to the library's main security system and with the central transmitter that kept it in contact with the security company's main office.

"Let's go, let's go," the third man muttered impatiently.

"One moment, Pizza Two . . . There it is!"

"Yes?"

"You can keep going. Only the main oven is activated."

"Excellent."

The locksmith and his accomplice climbed through to the interior of the manuscript room, swerved to their left, and hurried through a doorway that swung open when they hit the "release" bar.

"By the stairs."

"The basement room?"

"Yes, hurry. We've been inside four minutes, fifty-nine seconds."

Forty seconds later, the two silhouettes arrived at the end of the stairs.

"We're on our own now," the locksmith advised his companion. "Down here we are out of range of the support team's signal. The room is encased in steel."

"I follow. This is the right door?"

The locksmith nodded.

A metal barrier with two rectangular sliding doors, both eight feet across, blocked their way. The code box for the door was built into the wall on the right. It opened with the swipe of a magnetic card, after a numeric code was entered onto a tiny keyboard.

"No problem," the locksmith said. "Only the gates of heaven are safe from thieves."

After he had taken off his ski mask and slid the small pack off his shoulders, he removed a sophisticated calculator out of his bag. Then he pulled out of his pocket an electric cable that ended in a plug. He inserted it just below where the cards are swiped.

"Let's see if this works," he whispered. "It seems their security program is based on the Fichet system. So if we enter the master digits . . ."

"You're talking to yourself . . . ? "

"Ssssh! Seven minutes, twenty seconds . . . Open sesame!"

A green light next to the security system's keypad and the clicking sound coming from the door handle on the large doors indicated that access to the "oven" had succumbed to the locksmith.

The second shadow did not make a movement in response. The kid's precision had never ceased to amaze his coworkers, but they had learned to disguise their euphoria.

"Nice work. Now it's my turn."

The second shadow walked into the steel-lined vault. Once inside, she felt around inside her bag for her night-vision goggles, pushing aside the chic red shoes she always kept handy, and grabbed the latest model Patriot light beam. It was her favorite toy. After pulling off her ski mask, the shadow adjusted the goggles. A short whistle indicating that the power was on and the batteries fully charged made her nerves tingle.

"Okay, beautiful, tell me where you are," she hummed.

She slowly started to run her infrared vision along the shelves, reading the designations for the various sections. First came the letters Mss., then Mss. *Facs.*, and finally Mss. *Res*.

"Aha. Here you are. 'Reserved Manuscripts.' "

THIRTY-FIVE

MADRID

"Damn! Can't they leave me alone?"

Nothing got on Carlos Albert's nerves more than being awakened by a ringing telephone. He had gone out and bought the best answering machine on the market, telling himself he was not going to pick up the telephone unless he knew who was calling. But if he was at home, he was incapable of keeping his word.

"Carlitos, are you there?"

"I'm here . . . José Luis?"

"Who else? Listen, I've got something to tell you."

The cop sounded like a bundle of nerves.

"Last night thieves broke into the National Library and stole one of its historical documents."

"Really? So then go ahead and call *El País* with the story," Carlos responded apathetically.

"Hold on a minute. They've assigned the case to my department. And you know why?" Martín's theatrical pause got Carlos's attention. "Because they suspect there could be a sect behind it."

"Really?"

"Really, Carlos. But that's not the most important thing. What surprised me most was that this particular stolen item relates to you."

"No kidding." Now it was the journalist's voice whose tone had changed.

"No doubt about it. That's why I called you. You were the last person in the manuscript room yesterday, correct?"

"I think so."

"And you asked for a volume. Let me see: the *Memorial* of Benavides. A book from 1630."

"They stole the *Memorial?*" Carlos was in a state of shock.

"No. The book that disappeared is an unpublished manuscript of this Benavides, which, as the librarians explained to me, is a later, never-published version of the book you asked for. It is dated four years after 'your' *Memorial*. And it is infinitely more valuable."

"And what does this have to do with me? Do you consider me a suspect?"

"Well, Carlitos, technically you are the one clue we have. Furthermore, it is undeniable that a strong relationship exists between the book you asked for and the missing material."

"Is this going to turn out to be another one of your 'synchronicities'?"

"I guess so." He sighed. "I thought of that, too, but no one on the police force reads Jung. In a case like this, synchronicities are known as evidence."

"All right, José Luis. Let's straighten this subject out as soon as possible. Where do we meet?"

"Jesus, I'm glad we agree on something."

"How does the Cafe Gijón sound to you? It's right next to the library. At noon?"

"Noon it is. See you there."

Carlos hung up the phone with a strange, bitter taste on his tongue.

Three hours later, sitting at one of the tables at the Gijón, José Luis flipped through a magazine while waiting for his friend. From his perch near the window, he tried to distinguish the journalist among the swirling mass of pedestrians crossing the Paseo de Recoletos at that hour.

Carlos arrived on time, accompanied by a man with a crew cut who looked as if he had thrown his clothes on at the last second. He was stocky and somewhat flabby, and had eyebrows that crossed his face in a single line.

"Let me introduce Txema Jiménez, the best photographer at the magazine. In fact"—he laughed—"the only one."

The look on José Luis's face indicated he needed an explanation.

"He was with me in Ágreda," Carlos added, "and is completely in my confidence."

"Pleased to meet you."

The cop offered his hand to Txema, who remained silent. Once they had settled in their seats, they ordered three espressos and lit their cigarettes.

Carlos took the lead. "Let's get started. What exactly is it they stole?"

José Luis pulled a small pile of notes out of his sports jacket and put on his glasses to look them over.

"As I told you, the manuscript in question is very valuable. It was written in 1634 by Friar Alonso de Benavides, someone you seem to know very well."

Carlos nodded.

"According to what the librarian told me this morning, the text was reelaborated with the intention of sending it to Pope Urban the Eighth as an expanded version of the report that Philip the Fourth printed in Madrid, which you asked for yesterday."

"And who would be interested in something like that?"

"That is exactly the problem: a whole lot of people. The manuscript that disappeared contained a large number of marginal notations in the king's own hand. And that makes it priceless."

"Priceless? How much would something like that go for?" Txema's tiny eyes flickered.

"Hard to say for sure, mainly because there are very few specialists in the field who can put a price on a one-of-a-kind work. A million dollars on the black market? Two, maybe?"

The photographer whistled.

"What I fail to understand," the photographer went on, "is why they assigned the case to you. Carlos told me you work on cases involving sects."

The photographer's tone made Martín cringe. The cop's face was a question mark aimed at Carlos.

"Have no fear José Luis," Carlos said. "I already told you that I completely trust Txema."

"Okay then," he said. "In addition to the clue that points in Carlos's direction, several weeks ago a certain Order of the Sacred Image offered the library thirty million pesetas for that very same manuscript."

"Thirty kilos!" Txema blurted out. "A small sum in comparison—"

"The library, of course, refused and had nothing more to do with this order. The problem is that in the Episcopal Conference's registry of the various fraternal and religious organizations, there is no record of an organization with such a name, and the same goes for Rome. Which is why my team suspects we may be dealing with some sort of fundamentalist sect."

"And a rich one, at that," the photographer interjected, this time with more enthusiasm.

"Do you know how they stole it?"

José Luis had been waiting for that question.

"This is the strangest part of the case. The manuscript was kept in the library's steel-lined storage room, protected by a complex security system, with guards patrolling the library at all hours of the night. So, consider this: no alarms went off, no one heard anything, and except for a portion of window lifted out of its frame, which the guards found at the entrance to the manuscript reading room, the robbery would have gone undetected."

"Then they found some clues—" Txema once again jumped into the conversation.

"Right. An out-of-place window and . . ."

José Luis hesitated, and then continued.

". . . and a call made from a phone on the ground floor of the library to Bilbao. At four fifty-nine in the morning."

"During the time of the robbery?" Carlos asked.

"Most likely. The number was logged into the main switchboard's memory, and we have already made the appropriate investigations. We're almost certain it's a false lead."

"Why?"

"Because the number belongs to the telephone of a school that was, naturally enough, closed at that hour. We're probably up against well-equipped professionals, who electronically falsified the number, the better to lead us down a blind alley."

"Or maybe not."

Carlos's cryptic comment nearly made José Luis spill his coffee.

"You have something to add?"

"Let's just say I have a hunch."

The journalist then opened his notebook to April 14, the day they interviewed the two nuns at the Conception of Ágreda Monastery. His finger moved down the page searching for the entry.

"Txema, do you remember the clue our two sisters in the monastery gave us?"

"They gave us more than a few, didn't they?"

"True." Carlos nodded while he kept looking. "I am referring to a special one, an obvious one."

"I have no idea," said Txema.

"Here it is! José Luis, do you have your cell phone on you?"

His friend the policeman nodded, a bemused look on his face.

"And the number of that school in Bilbao?" asked Carlos.

He nodded again, pointing to a seven-digit number on his notepad.

Carlos grabbed the cop's cell phone and quickly dialed the number, prefixed by the Bilbao area code. After a number of loud clicks, there was a clear connection and a phone began ringing on the other end.

"Passionists. May I help you?" the voice said forcefully.

A happy smile spread across Carlos's face while the officer and the photographer stared at him incredulously.

"Hello, can you direct me to Father Amadeo Tejada, please?"

"He's at the university, sir. Try again later this afternoon."

"Thanks very much. But he does live there, yes?"

"He does."

"Thank you."

"*Agur*," the voice on the other end said in Basque.

Carlos took his eyes off the phone, only to encounter two surprised people staring at him.

"I solved it for you, José Luis. Your man is Father Amadeo Tejada."

"But how the hell . . . ? "

"Really, it couldn't be easier: chalk it up to another 'synchronicity.' " He elbowed his friend and went on. "When we were in Ágreda, the nuns told us about an 'expert' who is advancing the cause for the beatification of Sister María Jesús de Ágreda in Rome. I noted the information in my notebook for some future visit, knowing I could find him in a religious residence next to a school in Bilbao."

"Good Lord!"

"Do you think the National Police will pay for a short trip to the Basque region?"

"You can count on it." José Luis could hardly get the words out. "Tomorrow morning." And then he added, "But I remind you that you remain on my list of suspects."

THIRTY-SIX

LOS ANGELES

"Everything is fine, Jennifer. There's no tumor."

Dr. Meyers looked over the results of the MRI that Jennifer Narody had had the day before at Cedars-Sinai Medical Center. The razor-thin images revealed a well-formed skull and a spinal medulla with no irregularities. The temporal lobes were healthy and there were no white spots to denote the presence of foreign bodies inside the cranium.

"You don't look very pleased, Doctor."

"No, Jennifer, I'm happy. It is just that . . ."

"What?"

"I have yet to find a single cause to explain your dreams. You still have them?"

"Every night, Doctor. Do you know what? At times I have the impression that they're dictating something to me, as if my mind were an enormous movie screen that someone is projecting a documentary onto. They do it a little bit at a time. And every so often they let me see scenes that really affect me."

"Such as the scene of the Indian who has the same birthmark on his arm as you do."

"Exactly."

"Or the presence of a character who has a name that runs in your family, such as"—Meyers looked back at her clinical papers—"Ankti."

Jennifer nodded in agreement.

"Let me ask you a question," the doctor said. "How are you affected by all of this? What I mean is, do the dreams make you feel bad, do they give you a feeling of revulsion? Or is it completely the opposite: do they give you some sense of satisfaction?"

Her patient thought about it for a second. There was no easy way to answer the question. In fact, far from being an obstacle, her dreams were intriguing her a bit more every night.

"The truth, Doctor," she said at last, "is that I have progressed from being troubled by the dreams to being curious about them."

"In which case, we should perhaps change the course of our therapy. You tell me what you dreamed last night, and I will tell you about the benefits of a technique called regression therapy. Are you ready?"

Jennifer's face took on an enthusiastic expression.

"Are you?"

THIRTY-SEVEN

BETWEEN ISLETA AND LA GRAN QUIVIRA
AUGUST 1629

Six days after they left the mission at San Antonio, exhaustion had overtaken Sakmo and the rest of the party. Forward progress had been reduced to a minimum, while provisions began to be in short supply. Of the twelve miles covered on a daily basis on previous journeys, they were now lucky to reach six.

The increase in security measures also played a part. Three men would go ahead, marking rocks and the bark of trees to indicate whether the route was passable or not. At the same time another group kept watch on the friars from a half-mile behind.

They traveled on a continuous southeast course, gaining a few minutes of light with each sunrise while crossing the old Apache hunting grounds. They knew the tribe had emigrated to other latitudes but their old territory still filled the pilgrims with a superstitious dread.

Nothing came to pass. No sign of Apaches.

Friar Juan made use of the days of slow progress to learn as much about the desert as he could, but he was surpassed by Friar Diego López, a strapping youth from the north of Spain. Built like a spreading oak tree, he was as curious as a child and interested in everything. Most of all he wanted to learn the Indians' languages quickly in order to preach the Word of God to them.

During this part of the journey, the Franciscans' eyes were opened to "the flatlands to the south," as the Jumanos called them. What was only a wasteland at first glance turned out to be, in fact, abundant with life. The Jumanos taught the Spaniards to tell the difference between the dangerous insects and the harmless ones. They told them about the harvest ants, whose venom is more poisonous than the sting of a wasp. They showed them how to split open a cactus to drink the water inside, and they instructed them during the brief summer nights that they need not be afraid should they roll over and find a horned lizard lying next to them. The lizards, they said, protected humans from scorpions and other venom-bearing reptiles, and they made a good breakfast the next morning.

On the ninth day, shortly before nightfall, an event took place that changed their plans. All day long there had been heat lightning, and even when there were no clouds directly overhead, the Indians' spirits soared. They saw portents in each of nature's phenomena.

"Perhaps tonight we will see the Lady in Blue," Friar Diego whispered to old Friar Salas, when the leader of the group stopped to pitch camp. "The Jumanos seem very jumpy, as if they were waiting for something."

"May God hear what you say, Brother."

"My body feels a bit strange, too. What about you, Friar?"

"It is only the storm," the old friar replied.

Two paces behind them, the Jumanos followed Sakmo's order to drop what they were carrying and prepare camp by clearing the brush from a wide circle of earth. Great Walpi's son knew there would be no rain that evening, and therefore he decided to sleep in the open. By doing so, they would have an ample view of the horizon.

They made camp with the same precision as in the previous days, jamming sharp-pointed poles into the ground at the four cardinal points and then tying a strong rope, studded with metal bells, between all of them. That way, should an intruder above a certain size enter the camp, the bells would ring, alerting the sentries. They had to be careful. If their attention lapsed, anyone could mistakenly set off the alarm. After nightfall, the men took turns on watch and tending the campfire in three-hour shifts.

While the Franciscans were preparing their straw mats, the Indians' sudden excitement drew their attention. The sentries had spotted the shifting outline of a band of men on foot, in the lowest part of the valley, making their way toward them. They were carrying torches, and they had seen the travelers.

"Are those Apaches?"

Friar Juan raced over to Sakmo to hear the news.

"I doubt it," Sakmo replied. "The Apaches rarely attack once night starts to fall. They fear the darkness just as much as we do. . . . And they never light torches before an attack."

"And so?"

"Let's stay on guard. They may be a delegation of traders."

Ten minutes later, when the plains were wrapped in the dark mantle of night, the torches arrived at the encampment. There were twelve torches, each raised high in the air by a painted Indian. At the head of the troupe was a man with wrinkled skin who walked up to Sakmo and kissed him on the right cheek.

The new arrivals drew close to the fire, ignoring the presence of the white men, and threw their torches into the bonfire where the flames were leaping highest.

"Look at that!" Friar Diego whispered to Father Salas. "Every one of them is old."

Juan de Salas did not answer. These Indians had weathered faces, with long manes of silvery gray hair. They were about his age, but their skin by no means looked as soft or flabby as his did.

"Huiksi!"

One of the visitors walked up to the Franciscans. It took some effort for Friar Juan to decipher what he was saying. The venerable Jumano was telling them, in a mixture of Tanoan and Hopi dialects, that he prayed for the "breath of life" to always be with them.

The friars bowed their heads in a sign of gratitude.

"We come from Sakmo's village and the village of his father, the great Walpi, two days' journey from here. None of our warriors has seen you yet, but we the elders knew you were near. That is why we came out to receive you."

Friar Juan was translating the long string of phrases to Friar Diego. The elder who had broken the silence looked directly into Friar Salas's eyes without moving.

"We brought corn and turquoise to welcome you," he went on, offering a basket laden with objects whose shiny surfaces flickered, reflecting the flames of the fire. "We are grateful for your visit. We want you to speak in our village about this Lord-of-all-Lords, and to initiate us into the secrets of your religion."

The Franciscans turned pale.

"And how did you know that we were coming at precisely this time?" Friar Juan inquired in the Tanoan dialect.

The eldest of the Indians took the lead.

"You know the answer: the Woman of the Desert descended among us in the shape of a blue streak of lightning, and told us of your arrival. This happened two nights ago, in the same place where she has appeared for many moons."

"Then she is here?" The Franciscans' hearts were racing. "What is she like?"

"She is nothing like our women. Her skin is as white as the milk of the cactus; her voice is the air when it whispers between the mountains, and her presence brings peace like a lake in winter."

The beauty of what the eldest Jumano said impressed the Franciscans.

"You are not afraid of her?"

"No! Never afraid. She won the confidence of the village when she cured our neighbors who carried a sickness."

"Cured them? How?"

The Indian gave Friar Salas a severe look. His eyes flickered like sparks from the fire.

"Didn't Sakmo tell you? A group of our warriors led us to the Canyon of the Serpent to see the woman. It was just before the son of great Walpi left the village to look for you. In the sky there was a full moon. The whole field was illuminated. When we came to the place sacred to our ancestors, we could see that the blue spirit was sad. She told us why. She spoke directly to me, chastising me for not telling her my granddaughter was ill."

"What happened to your granddaughter?"

"A serpent bit her. There was a great swelling on her thigh. I defended myself, saying that none of our gods were capable of curing a wound like that, but she asked me to bring the child to her."

"And you brought her, surely."

"Yes. The blue lady took her between her arms and wrapped her in a powerful light. Afterward, the shining ceased, she lowered her back to the ground, and the little one, on her own two feet, ran into my arms, completely cured."

"You saw only light?"

"That is so."

"And she never threatened you or asked you for something in exchange for cures like this?"

"Never."

"Did she ever come into the village?"

One of the other old men, bald and almost toothless, stood up and started speaking to the friars.

"The lady in blue gave this to us as proof that she was among us, and as a sign of her relationship to you."

The old man straightened up. He was only a short distance from the friars when he started to make a series of gestures. He did so very cautiously, as if he did not want to make an error. He raised his right hand to his forehead and then lowered it to his chest.

"He is crossing himself!" Friar Diego exclaimed. "What kind of marvel is this?"

The night held several more surprises.

Seated around the fire, the visitors related the woman's first teachings. From everything they said, what struck the friars was that each of them had some personal, private experience with her. They swore they had seen her descend in a blinding light, and that everything in Gran Quivira, even the tiniest field mice, became still and watchful when she appeared. To the Indians, she was flesh and bone, not a ghost or a mirage. They felt she was closer and more real than those spirits called forth by the shamans when they ingested the sacred mushrooms. In fact, such was the coherence of what they related that the friars began to wonder if they were not confronting an impostor who secretly made her way from Europe and hid in the desert for the better part of six years.

Nevertheless, the idea was almost immediately discarded.

THIRTY-EIGHT

ROME

Giuseppe Baldi headed toward the Vatican Radio studios from Saint Peter's, making his way down the Via della Conciliazione and turning left past the monument to Saint Catherine of Siena in the Piazza Pio, with its sweeping views of the Castel Sant'Angelo. There, at number 3, in an enormous old palace from the eighteenth century, was a double doorway clearly marked with the radio station's name.

The institution, which is the "official" organ of the Pope, covers his public appearances and his many overseas trips, and coordinates the work of foreign journalists who have an interest in rebroadcasting papal events of special relevance. In short, it has a direct line to the Holy Father. Perhaps for that reason, between the times of Paul VI and the long pontificate of John Paul II, its masthead became exponentially more complex. Four hundred people work at putting more than seventy programs a day on the air, all under the direction of a Jesuit-run board of directors. The station broadcasts in thirty different languages, including Latin, Japanese, Chinese, Arabic, Armenian, Lithuanian, and Vietnamese.

Vatican Radio displays an impressive technical ability to broadcast its radio waves to the five continents. Its technology is so multidimensional that some observers insinuate that the station is using equipment far in excess of its real needs, an assertion that can neither be proven nor refuted.

One thing, however, is certain: when Father Baldi arrived at the station's offices he was ignorant of all these facts. The high-level politics of telecommunications were as close to his heart as a scientific base camp in Antarctica. He had had time to have a cappuccino next door to Ufficio Stampa in Saint Peter's Square, and then distract himself for a minute in front of the display windows of the nearby bookstores.

After passing through the Vatican Radio doorway and climbing the marble stairs leading to an information desk, the Third Evangelist asked for the studios of Father Corso.

"Second basement. Once you exit the elevator, continue down the hallway in front of you until you arrive at office 2S-22," the clerk said to him while entering the number on father Baldi's ID card into the visitor's log. "We were expecting you."

The elevator, an old Thyssen with metal gratings, left him facing a corridor punctuated with white doors whose handles had been replaced with large metal wheels. Although at first glance they looked like the portholes on a submarine, he quickly realized that they were in fact large doorways that sealed off the recording studios from any extraneous sound. Over each doorway there were two indicator lights, one red and the other green, installed so that people like Baldi would know whether or not they could enter.

Room 2S-22 was a short distance from the elevator, and was almost indistinguishable from the others, save for a slight difference in its electronic lock. Without thinking about it beforehand, Father Baldi spun the wheel on the door ninety degrees, giving it a forceful turn. The door had been left unlocked, and it gave way. The Benedictine found himself in a circular room with a domed ceiling; its large floor, some seven hundred square feet, was partitioned into various smaller spaces by gray room dividers. Sitting in the center, with space surrounding it, was a black leather anatomical table with medical apparatuses on rolling stands arranged around it.

The studio was dimly lit, and Baldi could just make out the shapes of the various pieces of furniture in the different parts of the room created by the room dividers. There were three: one contained a complete system of oscillators, equalizers, and a table with mixers designed to synthesize various sounds; the second was crowded with boxes jammed with magnaphonic tape and clinical reports;

and the last had several office desks, each equipped with current-generation IBM computers, as well as two tall metal file cabinets above which hung an unopened calendar from the Barcelona Olympic Games.

"Look at that! You found it all by yourself," an animated voice thundered behind the Benedictine in American-accented Italian. "You must be the Venetian priest coming to replace Father Corso, or am I wrong?"

A man in a lab coat walked over, his hand outstretched. "I'm Albert Ferrell, but everybody here calls me *il dottore* Alberto. I don't mind."

"The doctor" gave Baldi a wink. He was a short individual, with a well-trimmed goatee and a rosy face, who tried to hide his incipient baldness by combing his side hair over the top. Vain. A slick seducer. While Baldi took his measure, the American with the transparent blue eyes tried to gain his visitor's confidence.

"So you like the equipment?"

Baldi reserved judgment.

"We based our design for the room on the 'dream laboratory' built by the National Security Agency at Fort Meade in the United States a few years ago. The most difficult part was the domed ceiling, as you can probably guess. The work we do with ambient sound makes it necessary to have perfect acoustics."

Baldi reached for his wire-rimmed glasses so he wouldn't miss a detail.

"The apparatuses you see behind the anatomical table serve to monitor the subject's vital signs. And the sounds we experiment with are controlled from the sound board on your right. We direct them to the subjects through stereo headphones, while we measure the balance at the computer. Do you follow?"

Dr. Alberto made every attempt to be friendly. It was obvious that this was his private realm. He was comfortable here, and proud of the equipment that he had installed with funds provided by the U.S. Congress.

"All of our sessions are recorded on video," he went on. "We keep a record of any changes in the subject's reactions during the course of the experiment with a special software that lets us compare the data with our previous experiments."

"Tell me something, *dottore* Alberto." There was a certain disdain in Baldi's tone when he pronounced the American's nickname.

"Yes?"

"What exactly was the work that you did for Father Corso?"

"Let's say that I handled the technical elements of his project. The technology developed by you, the 'Four Evangelists,' for Chronovision was rather primitive."

Baldi could have crucified the insolent man. He spoke of the "saints" as if their work applied only to the Vatican and not to a layperson such as himself.

"I understand," Baldi said, holding himself in check. "And what do you know about the Four Evangelists?"

"Not much, to tell you the truth. Only that there were many other highly placed groups trying, by more-or-less unorthodox and sometimes almost paranormal techniques, to overcome the barriers of time."

"Well then, you already know more than many people at Saint Peter's."

"I'll take that as a compliment, Father Baldi. As a matter of fact," he added with particular emphasis, "just before you arrived, I received a call from Cardinal Zsidiv announcing your visit."

The priest gathered that the American had more to say on the subject.

"And so?" Baldi encouraged him.

"I received the written report on Father Corso's autopsy. Cardinal Zsidiv asked me to share its conclusions with you. He believed you would be interested to know the details as soon as possible."

Giuseppe Baldi nodded.

"Luigi Corso died from a fracture of the neck, after his fall from the fourth floor. He fell headfirst. The first cervical vertebra was pushed through the occipital opening into the cranial cavity, and he died. But preliminary analysis has discovered something more. Father Corso suffered an ulcer from stress. His stomach revealed the striations pertaining to this painful condition."

"And what does that mean?"

"It's simple, really. Father Corso suffered an elevated level of stress before dying. The doctor performing the autopsy was almost certain that his anxiety was what led him to throw himself out the window. But he wants to find out if Corso's adrenaline levels were abnormal before taking his plunge. That will require a little time."

"And what could have caused this anxiety?"

Like a good soldier, Albert Ferrell was accustomed to questions like that. He had already had to answer several of them when the team of detectives from the carabinieri visited him two hours earlier. They were the ones who had told him what he now was going to reveal to Father Baldi, who, for his part, bravely resisted its implications.

"It seems, from what the doorman at the Santa Gemma residence says, that Corso received a visitor a short time before his death. A woman."

"A woman?"

Ferrell smiled.

"And quite good-looking, judging from what the doorman saw of her. He described her as tall and elegant, with long black hair and green eyes. What caught his attention were the expensive red shoes she was wearing. Brand name, very pricey. It seems this woman visited Father Corso for some forty minutes, leaving a quarter of an hour before he threw himself out the window."

"Well," Father Baldi whispered. "That tells us who took his computer files."

"You don't say," Ferrell jested. "You wouldn't happen to know this lady, would you, Father?"

THIRTY-NINE

BETWEEN ISLETA AND GRAN QUIVIRA

Dawn was chilly and damp the next morning along the eastern slopes of the Manzano range. The encampment of the Indians and the two friars lay nearly eight leagues to the southeast of the mountain ridges. With the first rays of light, the Indians had already gathered their possessions and were covering the embers from the night before.

While the Indians were pulling out the last of the wooden stakes, the Franciscans withdrew to give thanks to God for the harvest of souls he had brought to them. They were well aware that it had not always been so easy, and that the progress the Church made in the New World had been paid for in blood. Soon elderly Jumanos crept up to join them in their prayers, falling down on their knees beside the Franciscans and leaning over to kiss the crosses hanging around the latters' necks. They carried themselves like Old Believers. It was merely the latest surprise for the Franciscans, repeated evidence that this could not be the fruit of a misunderstanding, but of a divine plan. As soon as the prayers came to an end, the expedition once again set out for Gran Quivira.

The landscape around them changed dramatically as the daylight increased. They traveled from salt marshes to the sloping hills of the south, which were dotted with cactuses that drew the Indian's attention. These stubby plants had fleshy spikes that they carefully broke off in order, as the Franciscans later learned, to ingest them in their kivas. Everything that grows in the desert has a use, whether sacred or profane.

Friar Juan wanted to learn a little more about their final destination. Over the course of their trek, he walked close to the old man who was farthest behind, asking him many questions.

"Friar," the old man said, "ours is the only village built out of stone. The first time we saw the Castillas was when I was very young. They were astonished when they saw how we lived."

"The Castillas?"

"That is right. They told us that that was their country's name, and that they had come in search of the seven cities of gold, which we had never seen. They only stayed with us a little while. . . . We were not what they were looking for," he said with a laugh.

"That must have been Vázquez de Coronado."

"I do not remember his name, Friar. But my ancestors, who came long before me and were wiser, too, told me about his arrogance and his terrifying army. They were dressed in brilliant colors, but were more venomous than scorpions."

"We are not like that."

"We shall see, Friar."

On the eleventh day of the march, the second day after the Franciscans had encountered the welcoming party, Sakmo's party felt confident that they would soon reach their destination. All were in good spirits, no longer anticipating misfortune. When at last they saw the outline of their houses carved into the rock and, behind that, the barely visible cleft leading into the Canyon of the Serpents, their hearts were overjoyed.

Something, however, caught the friars by surprise.

Directly before them and awaiting their arrival stood some five hundred or more people. A great number of them were young women accompanied by their children, standing together at the entrance to the village. In front of the crowd were two elderly women carrying a large cross made out of wood and hemp, and wreathed with flowers. The cross, as tall as a pine tree, was tilting back and forth in their arms. It reminded the Franciscans of a procession during Holy Week.

Sakmo left his position at the head of the travelers and, walking back to the Franciscans, said to them quietly, "They must be Owaqtl women, from the Falling Stones clan. Some of them have seen the Lady in Blue near their village."

Friar Juan looked at him doubtfully, but the Indian, ignoring his look, went on speaking.

"Ever since the Woman of the Desert came to us, many women have spoken with her. And even though they are not allowed to ingest the sacred mushrooms that enable one to speak with the spirits, they talk to her easily."

"The women? Who do you mean?"

"Look closely, Friar. Can you see the two women who are carrying the cross?"

"Of course."

"When they encountered the Woman of the Desert for the first time, they called her Saquasohuh, which means Kachina of the Blue Star. Later, when they began to anticipate her arrivals beforehand, they believed that she was a Corn Mother, a spirit. Now nobody is exactly sure what they think."

"You mean they know when she's about to appear?"

"Yes. It is one of women's gifts to see into the future. You are unaware of this?" Sakmo paused, and then added, "If they are here, it is because the woman has sent them. Let's wait and see."

When the two guides from the Falling Stones clan saw the two white men dressed exactly as the Lady in Blue had described, they broke out in enthusiasm. They lifted the cross above their shoulders and approached the friars. And then, before the astonished eyes of the Franciscans, they crossed themselves. One of the old women asked Friar Diego to show them "the book."

"The book?"

"The Bible, Brother!" Friar Salas said excitedly.

"But Friar Juan . . ."

"Do it! Give it to her!"

The Indian took the Bible in her hands, kissed it softly, and then shouted something incomprehensible, which increased the fervor of the women around her.

The old woman's long white hair was tied in two braids. She never wavered. Holding the Bible between her arms, she passed among the crowd, letting the people touch the book. There were sick people who kissed the dark leather covers of the Scriptures as if they expected to be cured by it. Others even threw themselves to the ground, begging the book to bless them. Still others merely let the tips of their fingers brush the surface of its pages.

"This is no doubt the work of God."

The friars stood there, amazed.

"No one will believe us when we tell them!"

"They will, Brother. These people's faith will make us strong."

FORTY

ROME

Il dottore Alberto was satisfied with Giuseppe Baldi's explanations. The Benedictine had absolutely no idea who Father Corso's mysterious visitor could be. And as they both knew, there would be no easy way to find her. Corso had also taught at a high school and frequently received visits from students of both sexes. If none of the female students wore red shoes or formal dress such as the doorman described to the police, the description might just as well fit one of the women who worked at the school. Or one of his coworkers from Vatican Radio.

"Listen closely, Albert. Before he died, Father Corso wrote to me, bringing me up to date on the project. He said you had synthesized the sound frequencies that would enable a person to observe the past. Is that true?"

"It is." He nodded. "All of our results were erased from his hard drive. Although I have to tell you that we achieved something grander than observing the past."

"What are you referring to?"

"You'll see, Father. Chronovision's principal objective was to capture images and sounds from the past. The Vatican simply proposed that we take a glance at history. We, on the other hand, discovered that we could intervene in it. And to pass from being mere spectators to actors changed the project into something much more important than anyone had imagined."

The Third Evangelist glared at Albert Ferrell incredulously.

"Intervening in it? Are you saying that you can manipulate history at will? To rewrite it?"

"Something like that. Father Corso was very conscious of what that could mean, and in the last weeks of his life he became taciturn, and even cold."

"Give me a fuller explanation, please."

"Look at it this way: our method of projecting the human mind into the past by means of certain harmonic vibrations allowed us, in principal, to pry into other epochs. But that was it. It was like watching a movie. The 'traveler' was unable to touch anyone, pick up the salt shaker, or play an instrument. He was a species of ghost who looked briefly into the past. And that was all."

"Harmonic vibrations!" Baldi blurted out. "That was my theory."

Albert Ferrell scratched his goatee and smiled.

"It was indeed. But we improved it. Are you familiar with Robert Monroe's research?"

"Vaguely. Cardinal Zsidiv told me about him."

"Perhaps you know that this recording engineer developed a kind of acoustics that, if correctly applied, permitted what is called 'astral projection.' "

"Yes, I understood that. . . . The Church knows nothing of 'astral bodies.' Those are vulgar terms, from the New Age. Fuzzy."

"Technically, you're right," Ferrell conceded. "But it's important that we avoid letting ourselves be blinded by terminology. Although Monroe spoke of 'astral bodies,' Catholics also use a term to refer to the existence of that invisible element that resides in every human being: the soul. Or do you not believe in its existence?"

"A far better word," Baldi said just above a whisper. "It is not, in my opinion, the soul that appears in two places at—"

"All well and good, Father. I'm not trying to discuss theology with you. It all depends on what sort of soul we're talking about." Corso's helper threw his arms up into the air. "I studied this subject before I came here. Recall that Saint Thomas Aquinas allowed for the existence of three kinds of souls, with three distinct functions: the sensitive; that which gives movement or life to things; and that which creates intelligence."

This time Baldi made no attempt to reply. He simply questioned Ferrell with his eyes. The man made him nauseous, and yet at the same time he was surprised that here was someone trained by the military who used Thomist concepts to justify his activities. Ferrell guessed at what he was thinking.

"And why not, Father?" His tone was insulting. "Even Tertullian believed in the corporality of the soul, which is, in the final analysis, the same idea that Monroe proposed."

"Corporality of the soul? The soul weighs nothing at all; it has no shape, no smell. It is not a physical object!"

"Saint Thomas was very concerned with the sensitive soul, which is the one that connects us to the material world, and which is, at the same time, the one easiest to 'awaken' with sound. I myself would not be so certain that this species of soul could not go so far as to take physical shape. In fact, Father Corso told me that you, with your investigations into sacred music, and Monroe, with his sonic frequencies in the laboratory, were trying to achieve similar ends. Only that Monroe was further along than you, Father, because he had managed to achieve 'soul separation' at will."

Albert Ferrell turned his back to Baldi as he walked over to the window to lower the venetian blinds. He then turned on the lights in the studio. The priest, from the other side of the room, changed the conversation.

"You said this room was constructed in the image of another, in the United States. Is that right?"

"Yes. The dream chamber at Fort Meade."

"Why would they build something like that on a military base?"

"Ah, Father, I did not take you to be so naive. Over the course of the cold war we learned that the Russians, in addition to developing conventional and nuclear weapons, were in the process of opening a new battlefield, one of the mind. They trained their best men, so that in a state of 'astral separation' they would be able to spy on secret North American military installations or locate the positions of Allied missile silos in Europe—without leaving Siberia."

"And you call me naive? Your country believed that and took countermeasures."

"True enough." Ferrell appreciated Father Baldi's ironic tone. "Our mission was, first of all, to protect our country from offensives of this type, and immediately afterward to investigate the phenomenon with the help of Monroe's techniques. A number of our agents attended his courses, perfected his methods, and went on to build the first dream chamber in 1972. I was a mere sergeant back then, far from having any real ideas about what kind of 'weapon' they were designing inside that room. By the time I entered Fort Meade, I knew that Monroe had achieved a twenty-five percent success rate with his astral 'takeoffs.' Those of us in the military working on the project had the same level of success thanks to a tough psychological training program. Which is why we recruited people with the most developed sensory abilities in the country."

Baldi stared at Ferrell. He was somewhere between incredulous and stupefied. This man, openly a charlatan, really believed what he was saying. It was a shame that his patriotic sentiments, as revealed by his military dress, had turned out to be so ridiculous.

"And how did you use the room, your 'dream chamber'?"

"The same way Father Corso and I used the one here. Obviously, this model is much more developed than the one from 1972," he said, gesturing to the anatomical table that dominated the room. "It allows us to obtain more information with each experiment. But the standard procedure is essentially the same."

"Standard procedure? I had no idea one existed."

"Of course it does." Albert Ferrell cut Baldi off before he could continue. "First we choose a 'sensitive,' a 'dreamer,' and then we bombard him with sound on a gradually increasing scale. That is how we attempt to induce the mental state conducive to his 'soul' detaching from the body and flying freely wherever he wishes."

"And you call them 'dreamers'?"

"The idea came from one of our last sensitives. She told us that her family gave her that name. We liked it."

Baldi disregarded Ferrell's remark.

"Could you give me a better explanation of the sounds you use?" The priest sat down in front of one of the IBMs and started to take notes in a black moleskin agenda book he took from his robes. Albert Ferrell's eyes remained fixed on him.

"Well, it's relatively simple. Monroe believed that the different frequencies of sound he synthesized were something like the essence of every one of our habitual states of consciousness: from the normal waking state to lucid dreaming, to stress and even mystic ecstasy. He was convinced that if he managed to synthesize these 'essences' and deliver them to a subject through headphones, his or her brain would harmonize with the frequency and, eventually, submerge the patient in the mental state desired. Can you imagine the possibilities of something like that? He could achieve any kind of change in mood or in attitude simply by making us listen to a particular sound vibration!"

"And he pulled it off? He managed to synthesize the sounds?"

"Definitely! For that alone they should give him a Nobel Prize," Ferrell said as he leaned toward Baldi with a flyer he had pulled out of a nearby box. "He called each of these acoustic 'samples' or essences a Focus and assigned them each a number that indicated the level of intensity with which they affected the human brain."

"An ascending scale."

"Exactly. A scale," Ferrell repeated. "For example, while employing what he called Focus 10, he discovered that he could access a curious state of relaxation, one in which the subject's mind was completely awake while the body slept. That essence was a sort of whistling sound, designed to achieve the first synchronization of the two cerebral hemispheres and to prepare the subject to receive more intense frequencies. The synchronization in question is achieved over the course of three to five minutes, and is generally accompanied by strange yet ultimately inoffensive bodily sensations. Phenomena like partial paralysis, itching, or uncontrollable trembling."

"Do all the sessions in the dream chamber start like that?"

"Pretty much. Little by little, the patient passes to Focus 12, which tends to stimulate states of expanded consciousness. The person achieves 'remote vision' of objects, places, or persons; their ability to control that was, in the beginning, the thing that most interested us, as it could be applied to military espionage."

"And they did so?"

"With relative success. But the best part was when we discovered the utility of other, more powerful Focuses."

"There were others?"

"Indeed, Father. Monroe also synthesized Focus 15 sounds, which gave their subjects the experience of being in a 'state outside of time'; they designed a tool that allowed them to open their subjects to information originating so deep in the subconscious that they appeared to be from another class of superior intelligence."

Albert Ferrell tried to gauge his visitor's reaction.

"Have you ever heard of 'channeling'?"

"Of course." The priest grimaced. "Yet another product of the New Age movement. Pseudomystical garbage. I am surprised you would give credit to such notions."

"In reality, Father, the channeling experiences are the modern version of the mystics' dialogues with God or the Virgin, or of the voices that Saint Joan of Arc is said to have heard. In antiquity they attributed these voices to the angels. The reality is that frequencies of the Focus 15 type, involuntarily camouflaged in spiritual chants, could have stimulated these kinds of states in the past. Which is why I took an interest in Chronovision and its research."

"And, naturally, I should suppose that there are further Focuses . . ."

"Naturally, Father. Now comes the interesting part."

Ferrell took a seat across from Father Baldi, as if what he was going to say required the priest to give it his utmost attention.

"Of all the Focuses discovered by Monroe in his experiments, those that interested us, as well as Father Corso, were those Monroe designated 21 and 27. The first facilitated astral separation and the second allowed the subject to utilize those psychic 'doublings' at will. Even so, he intuited that there existed a higher Focus, which he called X, which could materialize a doubled soul in the place it was traveling to, creating something almost supernatural: a person could be physically in two places at once."

"He wanted to provoke a bilocation artificially?"

Baldi stopped taking notes and backed his question with an icy look.

"Well, neither Monroe nor we had this 'essential sound.' But Corso wanted to simulate it in another way. In the Vatican Archives he discovered the file on a seventeenth-century woman who, it seems, managed to project herself across thousands of miles. And Corso hit upon the idea of sending one of our 'dreamers' to that exact date in order to 'steal' the sound."

"And what date was that?"

"Sixteen twenty-nine. In New Mexico. And do you know why?"

"The Lady in Blue!" A stroke of lightning flashed in Baldi's mind.

"Very good, Father!" said a pleased Ferrell with a smile. "I see that Cardinal Zsidiv has informed you well."

FORTY-ONE

LOS ANGELES

"As insane as it sounds, he exists! Your troublesome little friar exists, Jennifer!"

Linda Meyers was excited. Jennifer had never seen her like this. In her hand she held notes written in an almost indecipherable handwriting, and triumph was written across her face. Jennifer had rushed over to her therapist's office for a session at noon after receiving her phone call. The psychiatrist had discovered something important, but had roundly refused to say anything over the phone.

"Let me explain," Dr. Meyers said. She took a deep breath and invited her patient to take a seat. "This morning, early, I had the occasion to practice a bit of Spanish."

"Practice Spanish?" It sounded absurd.

"I was mulling over your dreams. Over how incredibly detailed they are, and the quantity of precise dates they contain. I took the liberty of making a few calls to Spain to see if anyone there could shed light on the subject you've been telling me about."

Jennifer remained silent. Her psychiatrist was checking to see if her dreams had a historical basis?

"First I telephoned the Royal Academy of History, and they gave me the number of the U.S. embassy in Madrid. My Spanish classes were paying off at last!"

"And what did they tell you?"

"Well, the people at the embassy didn't know much, but they recommended that I call the National Library. And when I told the library that I was calling on behalf of the embassy, they were very accommodating and gave me the director's private line."

"You said on behalf of the embassy?"

Linda Meyers's smile brightened the office.

"Don't look at me like that, Jennifer! It was an international call! I didn't have all day. I needed an answer quickly! The director finally spoke with me and was very helpful."

"You got to talk with the director of the National Library?"

"Sure. But when I mentioned the Lady in Blue he became a little reserved, even suspicious. As if I were asking about a taboo subject."

Jennifer nodded.

"That surprised me. Then he quickly confessed that they'd had funding problems in maintaining documents relevant to this subject. But he told me that he clearly remembered having seen the name of Friar Esteban de Perea in those papers. Can you imagine my surprise? He established the fact that Perea was a Catholic in the Order of Saint Francis and one of the religious governors of New Mexico. It was the proof I was looking for. Your man, the friar who appears in your dreams, did indeed exist!"

"So then . . . then . . ." Jennifer took a deep breath.

"So what you're dreaming about is not just a product of your imagination! The dates are accurate! The director of the library did not even hesitate: he told me that Friar Esteban de Perea arrived in New Mexico in 1629 in order to investigate the apparitions of a sort of blue lady. Of the Virgin or the like."

"And that's all he said, nothing else?"

"It was hardly so easy. We talked for almost forty minutes. He was very surprised that I had called him with an interest in precisely this material. He even asked me if I knew of a book called the *Memorial* written by Benavides."

"Benavides?" Jennifer was startled. "The same Benavides who turns up so often in my dreams?"

"So it seems, Jennifer. Have you heard anything about this book?"

Her patient shrugged her shoulders.

"I said the same thing. That I had never heard a word about him before. The thing that struck me most was how the director seemed to know about everything I was explaining to him."

"Really?"

"She must be a very well known subject in Spain, this Lady in Blue. That definitely surprised me!"

"And did he tell you anything else? Something that might turn out to be useful to my therapy?"

"No, but I gave him my number and address so that he can call or write me if he finds anything." And then, lowering her voice, she said, "Me, who thought the Spaniards were careless about their heritage!"

Jennifer stared at Linda Meyers, a serious look on her face.

"What now, Doctor?"

"I've been thinking a lot about this. Lacking physiological explanations, and with no psychic disturbances, only one route of exploration still remains open to us if we want to know what's happening to you: regressive hypnosis."

The face of Dr. Meyers's patient quickly passed behind a dark cloud. She stood up and shook her head from side to side, uttering a series of adamant refusals.

"No, no. Nothing of the sort. Absolutely not hypnosis!"

"What's wrong?"

"I won't have anything to do with hypnosis, Doctor," Jennifer insisted. "I have thought about it."

"Hypnosis is a harmless treatment. It won't cause you any pain, and it's the only thing that will let us delve into your subconscious so that we can find the cause of your visions. It's very likely that the roots of your dreams lie in—"

"I already know what hypnosis is, Doctor!" her patient protested. "I just don't want to submit to any sort of treatment that agitates my mind."

"I'm sorry, but your mind is already agitated. What I'm trying to do is to bring some order to it, and thereby bring these dreams to an end. Don't you realize? The dreams you're experiencing have some kind of historical basis, perhaps a question of genetic memory. Genetic memory!" she repeated, as if she herself had to hear it twice.

"It's not something accepted by traditional psychology, but it could perhaps apply to your case."

"That's enough, Doctor! I have no intention of being hypnotized."

"It's all right, Jennifer. Calm down."

Meyers walked over to her patient and gently led her to the leather couch next to her office window.

"Of course, we won't undertake any treatment against your wishes," she promised. "But let me ask you something: this phobia about hypnosis, does it have something to do with the work you told me about, for the Department of Defense?"

Jennifer nodded as she poured herself a glass of water. That whole period made her uncomfortable, and not just the hypnosis related to her work in Italy, but her dreams. She wanted them to disappear.

"It's national security, Doctor Meyers," she said after emptying the glass. "As you know, I'm not permitted to tell you about that. It's classified material."

The one concrete thing Dr. Meyers extracted from her patient that noon session was the story of her new dream. Paradoxically, Friar Esteban de Perea did not appear in this one; two other friars did. They were the men chosen by the Inquisitor, sent to the large settlement at Cueloce to investigate the strange interest the Jumano tribe had taken in the religion of the people from far away.

FORTY-TWO

GRAN QUIVIRA
AUGUST 1629

The young warrior Masipa and the beautiful Ankti found the August nights very much to their liking. For two weeks Sakmo's daughter had been slipping outdoors secretly, climbing to the roof at midnight, and stretching out beside her young *kéketl* to gaze at the stars.

Masipa was fearless. His father had been the shepherd of one of the nine families in the village and the meadows had trained him to confront darkness, its wolves and its spirits. Ankti was different. No one had taught her those things. For Sakmo, his twelve-year-old daughter was a treasure he had to protect from the brutal tales of the plains. Which is why Masipa left her in the dark, only revealing a few things at a time.

"Where are you taking me tonight?" she asked.

"To watch Hotomkam set," he answered. "It will be going away in a while, and the autumn stars will take its place. I want us to wish him farewell together."

"How do you know when Hotomkan is leaving?"

"Because Ponóchona the star disappeared two nights ago behind the horizon," he said with all the certainty of an astronomer, referring to the descent of the constellation Sirius. The two young fugitives had abandoned the village. When they had come close to the Canyon of the Serpent, they felt an indescribable freedom and power at that hour as they looked once again toward the sky.

And yet that night they would not find sufficient time to become accustomed to the darkness. Something unexpected and subtle electrified the body of the young warrior, making him more alert.

"What happened?"

Ankti could see that her companion was standing very still.

"Don't move!" he whispered. "I saw something . . ."

"An animal?"

"No, can you feel how the wind has come to a stop?"

"Yes . . . ," she agreed, and held on to his arm.

"It must be the Woman of the Desert."

"The Lady in Blue?"

"It always happens when she is nearby."

Masipa's confidence imparted a touch of serenity to the terrified Ankti. The young falcon listened intently to the silence.

"But there is no light . . . ," she whispered.

"No. Not yet."

"Should we go and tell the elders?"

"And how do we explain what we are doing here?"

The young woman was quiet. The evening was silent only for another second before a strange humming noise moved toward them from the south, advancing slowly. The whole desert quivered with its vibrations. It was as if a plague of locusts were flying nervously in and out of the branches of a juniper, waiting for the best moment to descend upon them.

"Don't move now. She is over there."

Hidden in the darkness, the two adolescents moved cautiously closer to the source of the sound.

"How strange," Masipa whispered. "It is utterly dark."

"Maybe . . ."

Ankti did not finish the sentence. When the two of them were a mere ten steps away from the tree, a torrent of light fell on it, paralyzing them with surprise. The humming noise instantly stopped, and the fiery cascade of light came to life, tracing short circles around the edges of the bush, as if it were looking for something, or someone.

Holding their breath, the two young people took in the scene. It all took place in seconds. The light, which seemed like a living thing, finished its descent from the sky. It withdrew into itself but as it lost strength and size, its last flames took on a human dimension. At first there was the outline of a head, and then out of the final sparks of light came the shape of arms, the waist, a long tunic, and finally legs and feet. The fugitives fell on their knees, astonished, as if the prodigy deserved a great act of veneration.

Then they heard her voice.

"May you both be welcome."

It was the Lady.

Her voice sounded just as the warriors had described it: the strange combination of thunder, birdsong, and the breath of the wind.

Neither Masipa nor Ankti was able to respond.

"I have come to you because I know that the warriors have already arrived with the men I asked for."

The young Jumano lifted his eyes to the woman of light and tried to say something. But he could not.

"The plan is close to fulfillment," she went on. "The lords of heaven, those who tell me about what you do, and who bring me here each time, have said that your hearts are now ready to house the seed of the Truth."

The seed of the Truth? The men in the sky? What sort of code was that? The woman's odd diction was adjusting to the rhythm of the Jumanos' language little by little, like water finding its way to a riverbed.

"I am the herald of a new time." She now spoke with greater fluidity. "They sent me to tell you about the arrival of a different world. The lords who have sent me have been watching you for a long time. They have the ability to live among you, because they look like humans, although their essence is immortal. They are angels. Men of flesh and blood who broke bread with Abraham, who fought with Jacob, who spoke with Moses."

Ankti and Masipa shrugged their shoulders. They had no idea what this woman was talking about. But then they remembered the stories their grandparents had told them about the creation of the world, stories that in turn had been inherited from the Anasazi (the ancients) and the Hopi (the peaceful ones). Ankti and Masipa knew that humanity was born in the time of the First World, a time that ended in a great catastrophe of fire, and that gave way to two other worlds. Their grandparents told them that there was a "third world," in Kasskara, when the gods warred among themselves for control of the human race. The Kachinas, beings who look like humans but who came from beyond the stars, fought one on one. Afterward, they rarely let themselves be seen, and when they did, they were always disguised as men and women of flesh and blood. And they swore they would return only at the end of the Fourth World, or at the beginning of the Fifth, to warn men of the crisis that was drawing near.

Was the woman of the desert one of them? Did she come to warn them about the end of the world?

"Listen to me," the woman said. "I want to give you something for the white men you will encounter. It will be proof of my visit. Tell them that the Mother of the Sky is with them, and that she commands them to spread the water of eternal life among you."

"Why among us?" Ankti managed to ask.

"Remember: the water of eternal life."

"But why us?" Ankti repeated.

"Because your heart is pure, Ankti."

The visitor lifted her hands, brought them together at chest level, and disappeared in the middle of a sudden, whirling dust storm. The humming ceased, and darkness returned to rule over the plain. The sparks of fire that had imparted a human shape to the woman had been extinguished, leaving no trace behind.

Ankti and Masipa embraced, frightened. An object unlike anything they had ever seen before glittered at their feet. The lady had left it there for them.

FORTY-THREE

ROME

It was nine o'clock at night in Rome and noon in Los Angeles when Albert Ferrell handed Father Baldi the records on the "dreamer" Luigi Corso sent to the New Mexico of 1629. The file mentioned one Jennifer Narody, a North American, thirty-four years old, lieutenant in the U.S. Army, resident of Washington, D.C., whose mental flights, fed by the sounds of Focus 27, ended in several alterations to her personality. "She is the one her family calls the 'Great Dreamer.' Weird, isn't it?" Ferrell said quietly.

The report contained one final, laconic annotation, written by hand in red ink, which deeply disturbed Giuseppe Baldi. "Abandoned the project Friday, March 29, 1991. Suffered severe anxiety attacks, along with sleep deprivation. Returned to the United States April 2 on the express recommendation of the Ospedale Generale di Zona 'Cristo Re' in Rome."

FORTY-FOUR

MADRID

"Did you warn Father Tejada about our visit?"

José Luis Martín was driving fast, his eyes fixed on the highway. It was eight o'clock, and at that hour of the morning very little traffic was heading out of Madrid. Although he was still groggy, Carlos was enjoying the spring landscape that was opening up before them. Somosierra, the mountain north of Madrid, loomed ahead, wearing its last coat of snow for the year.

"Father Tejada?" the journalist mumbled, in need of some strong coffee. "No, I never spoke with him. I left a message telling him that we would arrive in Bilbao this afternoon."

"You told him that this was a police interrogation?"

"Good Lord, no! The police are your business."

"Good, Carlitos. It's much better that way."

Carlos shifted his legs under the glove compartment of José Luis's Renault-19, making himself as comfortable as possible.

"José Luis," he said, beginning to awaken. "I've given a lot of thought to that phone call from the National Library."

"So have I."

"So you must have the same doubts I do."

"Such as?"

"Okay, there's something I just can't fathom: if whoever pulled off this heist are professionals, which seems certain, why did they make that call from the library? To give themselves away?"

Martín's hand was cupping the stick shift like a professional.

"I don't know," he replied. "It's entirely possible that the number was falsely inserted into the system by a computer."

"Okay, but then why is it that the number belongs to the one person implicated in the Ágreda case?"

"Mere chance."

"But you don't believe in that," Carlos protested.

"True."

The laconic cop lifted a cigarette to his lips and depressed the lighter in its socket.

"Do you know how long the conversation lasted?"

"Less than forty seconds."

"Not very long, right?"

"More than enough time to tell someone the operation was a success."

"I thought something like that myself."

"I would definitely prefer that when we speak to Father Tejado, we don't tell him we're investigating a robbery."

Carlos gave his friend a look of surprise but didn't say a word.

"Let's act as if we don't know anything. I expect that, if he's involved, he'll end up revealing it himself."

"You give the orders on this trip. I'm just along for the ride."

FORTY-FIVE

GRAN QUIVIRA

The next day, Ankti and Masipa doubted whether they ought to carry out their strange task. They knew that if they brought the lady's gift to the elders, they would have a great amount of explaining to do. For that reason, they preferred to wait for the most discreet moment to complete their mission. Just before midday, as Friar Juan de Salas left the house of the warriors in order to perform his necessities in camp, the two youngsters raced out to meet him.

They caught up with him in front of the oak cross that the Owaqtl women had jammed in the ground the day of his arrival in Gran Quivira.

"Father . . . ," Ankti said as she pushed her hair away from her face, "can you talk to us for a moment?"

Friar Juan spun around and looked at them. The two young Jumanos were offering him something wrapped in dried leaves of corn. They seemed indecisive, even perhaps afraid.

"What do you need, my children?" he said with a smile.

"Well, Father . . . last night, near the Canyon of the Serpent, we saw something."

"What was that?"

"The Woman of the Desert."

Friar Juan suddenly forgot his prior urgency.

"The Woman of the Desert? The Lady in Blue?"

The two nodded in unison.

"And only you saw her?"

"Yes."

"Did she say anything to you?"

"Well"—Masipa hesitated for a second—"that is why we wanted to see you, Father. She said that you and the other man who accompanied you were to spread the water of eternal life among us."

Friar Salas's legs grew weak.

"The water of eternal life?" He looked at the two closely. "Do you know what that means?"

Out of confusion, Ankti and Masipa took a step back.

"No."

"Of course not. How could you?"

"Father," the young *kéketl* interrupted. "The woman also gave us this for you. She wanted you to take it to remind you of the Blue Woman's visitations."

Friar Juan was trembling as his eyes regarded the small bundle of corn leaves that Masipa was holding out to him. He took it and opened it quickly.

"But . . . Good Lord!" he blurted out in Spanish. "Where did you get this?"

Masipa and Ankti looked fearful.

"As we told you, Father. The Woman of the Desert gave it to us last night. For you."

Friar Juan fell to his knees, submerged in a strange state of hysteria, laughing and crying at the same time. The Franciscan felt among the corn leaves and grasped the object inside. There was no doubt about it: here was a rosary with black beads, all of them perfectly round and glistening, from which dangled a delicate silver cross. An object such as belonged to old Christians, possessing a rare beauty.

"Most Holy Virgin!" de Salas thundered.

Who but the Virgin could be behind these visits?

Friar Juan remembered the story he had heard during his religious training in Toledo, and which at the time had seemed outrageous to him. It was said that Saint Dominic de Guzmán, founder of the Dominicans, had instituted the saying of the rosary in the thirteenth century after the Virgin herself had given him one. Was not this a similar prodigy?

FORTY-SIX

BILBAO, SPAIN

Tucked away in a remote corner of the city, far from the estuary, the Plaza de San Felicísimo turns out to be a simple traffic circle of stone and mortar around which the Passionist Fathers have taken up their principal residence. The two main buildings on the plaza belong today to the order—founded in 1720 by the Italian missionary Paul of the Cross, now sainted—which answers to the high-sounding Congregation for the Barefoot Clergy of the Most Holy Cross and Passion of Our Lord Jesus Christ. And yet its most striking peculiarity is not its name but the rule that obliges its members to take a fourth vow before their entrance into the order. To poverty, chastity, and obedience, the order adds: an initiate must agree to propagate the cult of the passion and death of the Nazarene.

When they showed up at the foot of the stairs leading to the Passionist residence, José Luis and Carlos were ignorant of that historical detail. Instead, they carried with them a thin folder with a few bits of information pertinent to their objective. To wit: Amadeo Tejada had entered the order in 1950, pursuing studies in psychology and the history of religion, and had occupied, since 1983, a seat as professor of theology at the University of Deusto in Bilbao. He was furthermore considered to be an authentic expert on angelology.

"Father Tejada? One moment, please."

A Passionist, whose hair was rapidly receding and whose simple black robes had a cloth heart stitched onto the chest, asked them to take a seat in the cramped waiting room.

Three minutes after they sat down, a burly giant flung open the glass door and entered the room. Father Tejada must have been about seventy. His clerical robes accentuated his height and his white hair and long beard, along with his tone of voice, conferred on him the beatific aspect that had so impressed the nuns in Ágreda.

"So you've come to ask me about Mother Ágreda," Father Tejada said with a smile, after offering his hand to the two visitors.

"Well, we had no choice after speaking with the nuns. They assured us that you are very learned on the subject."

"Oh, come now! I'm only fulfilling my obligation. Ever since I began studying Mother María Jesús's life, they've held me in the highest esteem." He smiled pleasantly. "The feeling is mutual. In fact, that monastery was the site of the most extraordinary case of bilocation I have ever encountered. And that is why I have dedicated so many hours to it and spent such long periods of time there."

"Forgive my diving right in, Father, but we don't want to take too much of your time. Have you arrived at any conclusions about the authenticity of her bilocations?"

Tejada pulled on the lobe of his left ear before answering.

"I don't know if you are aware that actually there are various types of bilocations," he said to Carlos, with one eye on José Luis. "The most simple can basically be distinguished as mere clairvoyance. In that case, the bilocated subject sees things that are occurring far from where she is, even if it is not her eyes that enable her to do so. It is her psyche. Here we are speaking of a very basic and not so interesting sort of bilocation."

"Please continue," Carlos urged their host.

"On the other hand, the most complex kind of bilocation, and the one that interests me, is one in which the subject physically doubles and is capable of interacting with others in the two different places she inhabits. She lets herself be seen by witnesses to whom the prodigy can impart faith, as well as touch objects and leave traces of herself behind. That class of bilocation is, on its own merits, the only sort we can call miraculous."

Father Tejada stopped speaking long enough to let his guests make notes on the various categories of bilocation. When they were finished, he went on.

"I believe that between the one and the other there exists a wide range of states in which the subjects materialize to a greater or lesser extent in the places where they appear. Of course, the most interesting cases are those of 'total materialization.' The others could be mere cerebral experiences."

"And Mother Ágreda fits in the second category?" Carlos asked with all the tact of which he was capable.

"Not always."

"How so?"

"Perhaps her bilocations did not always pertain to that second category," the Passionist reiterated patiently. "You ought to know that when this nun was interrogated by the Inquisition in 1650, she confessed that she had visited the New World on more than five hundred occasions, although not always in the same manner. She didn't always fully materialize. At times she had the impression that she was an angel who disguised herself as a nun and revealed herself to the Indians; on other occasions, a second angel accompanied her while she flew through the heavens at terrific speed; but on the majority of occasions, everything took place after she had fallen into a trance and was being cared for by her companions in the monastery."

"An angel?"

"Well, you shouldn't be too puzzled by that. The Bible speaks of them frequently and says they much resemble ourselves. Even other, more recent mystics, such as Ana Caterina Emmerich in the eighteenth century, said her bilocations were provoked by angels, in whose company she 'crossed the oceans faster than the mind can imagine.' A lovely expression, no?"

Father Tejada smiled briefly before continuing.

"Don't make it seem stranger than it is," he said in a jocular manner. "What is there to prevent angels from making a woman appear in America? If we accept what is said about them in the Scriptures, they could be seated here with us and you would never notice it at all."

Tejada winked at them complicitly, a gesture Carlos did his best to avoid noticing.

"Would you consider them a species of . . . infiltrators?" he asked.

"Let's say they are a 'fifth column' who control certain aspects of human evolution from inside. Do you understand the comparison?"

"A 'fifth column'? Of course." The journalist snapped to attention. "The term was used during the Spanish Civil War to refer to a group of resistance fighters working secretly inside a city or a country."

"Precisely what I refer to, young man."

"Well then . . . since you're an expert in angelology, you must know what you're talking about."

José Luis's barbed comment struck home.

"Don't make a joke out of it," Tejada snapped back. "If you want to get to the bottom of the mystery of the Lady in Blue and her connection to Mother Ágreda, you're going to have to take angels very seriously."

The police officer remained unfazed and Carlos continued with his questions.

"Getting back to specifics, Father: do you believe that the nun in Ágreda at any time transported herself physically to America?"

"It's difficult to say. But in truth, nothing prevents me from believing it. Many others have lived through the same experience and have left us sufficient evidence of their instantaneous 'voyages,' in soul and body."

José Luis shifted in his seat. None of these circumlocutions gave them the slightest clue as to the whereabouts of the manuscript. Summoning more tact than he usually employed, he sought to bring the conversation around to his concerns.

"Excuse our ignorance, Father, but does there exist, or did there exist, any documents or chronicles from that period which offer details about these voyages?"

Father Tejada regarded the policeman with affable condescension.

"There you are! A practical man. I like that."

José Luis accepted the compliment.

"The answer is yes. A Franciscan by the name of Friar Alonso de Benavides wrote the first report in 1630, in which he collected clues to what today can be interpreted as bilocations by Madre Ágreda."

"Clues? Is that all there is?" he inquired.

"Not only. Four years later, the same friar wrote a second, expanded version of his report. Sadly, I have never been able to examine it. It was never published, although it is rumored that Philip the Fourth himself was so fascinated by the document, it became one of his favorite books."

"Do we know why?"

"Indeed"—he hesitated for a second—"what I am going to tell you is by no means official, but it seems that in the margins of his text, Benavides appended the formulas that Madre Ágreda utilized in order to bilocate. And those notations entranced him."

"Fantastic!" Carlos blurted out. "An instruction manual!"

"Something like that."

"And do we know if anyone made use of it after the king?"

"From what I heard, the later report never left the hands of the royal family, although in the Vatican they possess a written copy. Friar Martín de Porres, a Peruvian of mixed blood and a Dominican, also experienced numerous bilocations around the same time as the nun in Ágreda."

"Are you insinuating that this friar read . . . ? "

"Absolutely not. Friar Martín died in 1639, before news of this could have reached him in Lima, and by the time of his death he had achieved the status of a saint. They called him 'Friar Broom.' Did you know that? His 'double' was seen preaching in Japan sometime before the *Memorial* was written in 1634."

Father Tejada suddenly lowered his voice.

"He even at times went so far as to leave flowers on the altar at Santo Domingo, flowers not from Peru but Japan."

"Do you believe things like that?" José Luis asked with a certain distaste.

"It is not only a question of faith, although that influences it. Have you ever heard about Father Pio?"

Of the two, only Carlos nodded.

The journalist knew that Padre Pio, whose real name was Francesco Forgione, was an extremely famous Italian Capuchin who had lived in Pietrelcina during the middle of the twentieth century. There he played a leading role in a great number of mystical prodigies, from the physical appearance of Christ's stigmata on his body to displaying the gift of prophecy, and after his death continued to inspire great popular fervor throughout Italy.

"Indeed, a number of celebrated bilocations are attributed to Padre Pio," Tejada went on. "The best known was witnessed by Cardinal Barbieri, who was at the time Archbishop of Montevideo. He saw Pio in Uruguay on several occasions, although he only identified him later, when he visited Italy. And Pio recognized Barbieri despite the fact that he had never been physically present on the other side of the world."

"Do you suppose Father Pio controlled his bilocations?" Carlos was fascinated.

"Not only him. Madre Ágreda did as well, although I'm only acquainted with two or three other instances throughout history. What sets them apart from the others is their great gift of controlling the distance of their bilocations."

"What do you mean by the 'distance'?"

"Exactly that. Both Father Pio and María Ágreda were the active agents in bilocations over distances both short and long. In local manifestations, they traveled outside the walls of their respective monasteries or to nearby homes. But they also traveled over great distances, letting themselves be seen on other continents."

José Luis shifted anxiously in his chair. He did not seem disposed to lose much more time talking about famous mystics. If he had decided to come to Bilbao, it was to solve a robbery and not to take a class in miracles of the faith.

"Pardon my clumsiness, Father," he said as he sat up in his chair. "But what do you know about this second *Memorial* of Benavides that was in Philip the Fourth's possession?"

Tejada came to a sudden stop. He had not mentioned the title of the second document.

"What exactly is your interest in that document, gentlemen?"

José Luis straightened up still further in his chair. He wanted to be on the giant's eye level if he could. He felt around in his coat and pulled out his badge. Showing it to Tejada seemed not to have the desired effect, so he delivered an ultimatum. "I am sorry to have to give a slight twist to this conversation, Father, but you need to answer a few more questions for me. The robbery we are investigating is a significant one."

"So you say." Father Tejada stared at José Luis grimly. Even Carlos felt his contempt, and he thought to himself, nothing will come of this.

"Did you receive a telephone call yesterday just before five AM?"

"Yes."

"And?"

"There is not a great deal to tell. It was very unusual. Someone called the switchboard and they transferred the call to my room, which woke me. I answered the phone, but nothing. There was no one on the line."

"No one?"

"No one. I hung up."

Tejada's answers gave the policeman enough to go on. He had at least proved that someone had called Tejada from the National Library.

"Any other questions?"

"One more." José Luis paused as he looked through his notes. "Do you know anything about a certain Order of the Sacred Image?"

"No. Should I?"

"No."

"Now I have a question for you," said a very serious Tejada. "May I know why the police are interested in the calls I receive?"

Carlos was unable to hold back. Since his friend was hesitating, he answered for him.

"We already told you, Father, that we're investigating a robbery. Yesterday morning a manuscript was stolen from the National Library in Madrid. It was Philip the Fourth's copy of the *Memorial* as revised by Benavides . . . the second, complete version."

Father Tejada nearly exploded.

"Yesterday at four fifty-nine AM someone used the phone in the National Library to make a call. It could only have been the thieves."

"Good Lord! I had no idea."

"Now you do, Father," Carlos said in a soothing voice. "But it's important that if you remember anything, no matter what, or if they contact you again by phone, call us."

"Do you know anyone in the National Library?"

José Luis's question sounded almost like an accusation.

"Enrique Valiente, the director, is a good friend. He was a student of mine at the school here."

"Fine, Father. If we need something, we'll call you."

Father Tejada was no longer smiling. News of the robbery had gotten to him.

"I'll walk you out," he told them.

The Passionist grabbed Carlos by the arm as they stood at the entrance to the building. José Luis had gone ahead to the car, to make a call to his office on his cell phone. Tejada, meanwhile, whispered something to Carlos that disconcerted him.

"You aren't a cop, are you?"

"N-no . . . ," Carlos stammered.

"So why are you interested in Madre Ágreda?"

The giant held such a firm grip on Carlos's biceps, he felt compelled to be honest.

"It's a long story, Father. To tell you the truth, I have the feeling that someone has somehow dragged me into this."

"Someone?" The giant leaned in closer. "Who?"

"I have no idea. That is what I want to find out."

Tejada smoothed the creases in his robes, and began to act like a confessor.

"You know what, young man? Many of us have come to Madre Ágreda thanks to a dream, a vision, or after a long accumulation of chance events that, all of a sudden, deposit us against our will at her feet."

The journalist's stomach tightened.

"I know people who dreamed of Madre Ágreda without knowing that it was her," he went on. "She appears, bathed in a blue light, and takes you where she wishes."

Carlos swallowed hard. He could still feel the muscle on his arm being squeezed.

"The Lady in Blue is a powerful archetype," Tejada said. "A symbol of transformation. To the Indians she announced the arrival of a new era, politically and historically; to the friars she revealed wonders that overwhelmed them. And now, suddenly, it seems she wants to emerge from the mist of time once again."

The priest suppressed a cough before going on.

"Remember that, whatever the task, she always has the help of angels. They organize everything. Everything. Even if her actions are concealed beneath layers of coincidences. Why are you here, if you don't believe?"

"Exactly, why am I?" Carlos asked himself. He shook hands with the giant, relieved to be able to make his escape, and hurried toward the Renault-19, which was already pulling into the plaza below.

FORTY-SEVEN

"And so?" José Luis's tone was exultant. "A strange fellow, that Tejeda. Did he tell you anything else?"

Carlos shook his head, trying to camouflage his uneasiness about what the priest had said.

"Well, I have news. Big news." José Luis was clearly delighted.

"What happened?"

"This morning, while you and I were en route to Bilbao, the director of the National Library, none other than Father Tejada's friend, received a phone call from the United States. And what were they asking about? Benavides's *Memorial.*"

"Impossible."

"It struck him as very odd that anyone should be interested in the contents of that book, so he took the call himself. Then he contacted the police. They just gave me all the details. Enrique Valiente is his name, correct?" Martín said as he browsed through his notes.

Carlos stifled a look of admiration. That was the name that Father Tejada had just given them.

"The synchronicities are following us, my friend. We are getting close. Very close. Care to join me tomorrow when I pay a visit to the director?"

The journalist nodded. His uneasiness had now turned into a troubling preoccupation.

FORTY-EIGHT

VENICE BEACH

At 5:25 PM Pacific Standard Time, a U.S. postal truck pulled up in front of Jennifer Narody's small white house, situated in a small alley running parallel to Venice's celebrated Ocean Front Walk. The mailman made his way to her front door carrying a heavy envelope bearing the postmark of the Eternal City.

"Rome!" she murmured as she examined it. "Today of all days."

She hurried to open it.

There was something unusual about the package: there was no indication of the sender. Jennifer could only make out the city of origin. And yet what was in the package was stranger still: a handful of parchment pages, stitched together along the border, emerged from it without even so much as a note accompanying them.

Jennifer had no idea who had sent her the package. Moreover, the text on the pages was in Spanish, in a devilishly difficult handwriting that made it hard to decipher a single word. "Perhaps Doctor Meyers can lend a hand with this tomorrow," she said to herself, remembering the calls her therapist had made to Spain.

Deciding to try to forget about the contents of the envelope, she placed it in a drawer for safekeeping and spent the rest of the afternoon watching television. Outside the sky grew dark and soon unleashed a torrent along the coast.

"Damn this weather," she groaned.

Jennifer remained sleeping until 7:54 the next morning. Her dreams, of course, continued as usual.

FORTY-NINE

ISLETA
END OF SUMMER, 1629

"Look! Take a good look, Father!"

Friar Diego López brushed the sand off Friar Salas with a heavy cloth. Their hours marching through the desert had had their effect on him. Only the rosary that Masipa and Ankti presented to him before he left gave him the spirit necessary to keep from dying.

"Do you see it?" the friar asked again.

"But if that is . . ."

"Yes, Father, it is. Isleta! We made it!"

The old man's face became animated.

"May God be praised!" he cried out.

Almost lost in the horizon and still farther away than the tall junipers that marked the course of the Rio Grande, the towers of the Mission of San Antonio de Padua rose proudly in the distance.

Friar Juan smiled for an instant. Squinting, he noticed something unusual surrounding the mission.

"Do you see it, too, Brother Diego?" His voice was trembling.

"See? What is there to see, Father?"

"The shadows around the church. They look a bit like the caravan of autumn, the one that journeys from the City of Mexico."

Diego concentrated, trying to make out the shapes resting near the bottom of the towers.

"That caravan comes through here only twice a year. It takes the route between Santa Fe and the City of Mexico with an armed escort, and it is the great event of the season. But it is still very early for it to be here."

Friar Diego was still trying to make out the caravan. "Do you remember Friar Esteban telling us that the Father Custodian, Friar Alonso de Benavides, would leave his position in Sante Fe in September? Perhaps that is his caravan, returning to Mexico."

Salas ended up agreeing with his young disciple's argument. No other explanation made sense: the mission was surrounded by the military convoy of the new viceroy, the Marquis of Cerralbo, and among those traveling in the caravan should be counted Friar Alonso de Benavides. Who else could it be?

Their conjectures came to an end once they were closer to Isleta. Approached from the east, the mission resembled a small Andalusian town holding its annual fair. There were as many as eighty large wagons, some with four wheels and some with two, scattered around the tent-bearing stakes. Protected by patrols of soldiers, the land beyond the walls of the mission overflowed with Indians, mestizos, and Spaniards.

If only Isleta were always like this!

Wading through the middle of the crowd, the two friars found it easy to enter Isleta without calling undue attention to themselves. They entered the settlement and headed toward the front of the church. There, as they rested at the foot of the adobe towers, they felt the satisfaction of having fulfilled their duty.

"We should look for Esteban de Perea."

"Certainly, Brother Diego, certainly." The old man nodded.

"Have you come to a decision about the Lady in Blue yet, Father? As you well know, Esteban de Perea is very demanding, and he will ask me to confirm your account word for word."

"You needn't worry about that, Diego. I intend to make such a powerful impression, they will have no energy to interrogate you."

Friar Diego laughed.

The two men squeezed through the passage leading toward the large white tent raised at the foot of the eastern wall of the church. A soldier in drab cloth pants, a sheepskin jacket, and a cuirass stood guard at the doorway, his lance at the ready.

"What do you want?"

Gripping the lance in his left hand, the soldier's arm prevented them from going any further.

"Is this where Friar Esteban de Perea keeps store?" Salas inquired.

"This is where Friar Alonso de Benavides, the territorial custodian, works," he said curtly. "Friar Perea can be found inside."

The friars shared a complicit smile.

"We are Juan de Salas and Diego López," the former said by way of introduction. "For more than a month we have been in the Jumano territories, and we bring him news."

The soldier remained at attention. Without the slightest change in his martial bearing, he made a half turn and walked into the tent. Several seconds went by. The silence that reigned under the canvas was broken by the unmistakable voice of the Inquisitor.

"Brothers!" He thundered from somewhere inside. "Come in. Please come in!"

The two travelers let themselves be guided by Esteban de Perea's shouts. Four men were sitting around a long table at the back of the tent: Perea, two of the Franciscans who had accompanied him to the mission, and a fourth, a priest whom they could not at first identify. He was a severe-looking man with thick white brows, a wrinkled forehead, and a large flat nose, with every hair perfectly in place. He was already past fifty, but the years, far from weighing him down, had conferred a solemn, majestic bearing upon him. He was none other than the Portuguese friar Alonso de Benavides, in charge of the Holy Office of the Inquisition in New Mexico, the Church's highest authority in the desert.

Benavides fixed his attention on the two men while leaving it to Esteban de Perea to handle matters. "Has everything gone well?"

Friar Esteban seemed excited.

"Divine Providence has watched over us as always," Friar Juan answered.

"And the Lady, what have you learned about her?"

Benavides raised his eyes toward the two men at mention of the Lady in Blue.

"She came very close to us, Friar. One Indian even saw her near the village the day before we entered Cueloce."

"Indeed?"

Friar Juan became very serious.

"Those are not just words, Father," he said. "We have brought with us concrete proof of what we are saying. A gift from heaven."

Father Salas searched in his sack as Friars Esteban and Alonso de Benavides exchanged perplexed looks. Father Salas reminded Benavides of another humble man, although one without religious instruction, who had presented a gift from the Virgin to a handful of disbelieving clerics so that he might convince them of her apparition. This man existed one hundred years before, toward the end of Christmas 1531, in the hills of Tepeyac, near Mexico City. His name was Juan Diego and his Virgin was known as Guadalupe. Yet Pope Urban VIII had given specific orders that her religious cult be suspended. So why then should Benavides accept the gift that Friar Juan de Salas brought for them from the very same Virgin?

The old Franciscan held up his offering at last.

"This rosary," he said solemnly as he held the perfectly preserved necklace out to them, "was the gift of the Lady in Blue to two Indians in Cueloce."

A spark of avarice flickered in Friar Esteban's eyes. He took the black beads in his hands, and kissed the cross. He then handed the rosary to Alonso de Benavides so that he could examine it. The latter gave it a brief look and placed it in his robes for safekeeping.

"Tell me," Friar Benavides said at last in his thick Portuguese accent, "how did this . . . gift . . . come into your hands?"

"The Lady in Blue entrusted it to a pair of Jumanos. It is clear that Our Lady wanted to give us a proof of her apparitions."

"Leave the theology to me," the Custodian snapped. "Now tell me: why did this Lady not present it directly to you, Friar?"

"Your Eminence," the young Diego López broke in, "you well know that God keeps his reasons to himself alone. Nevertheless, you will permit me to say a few words? The Virgin only appears to those with innocent hearts, those who have most need of her. Or perhaps is it not to children and shepherds that she has always revealed herself?"

"Do you believe that as well?" the Custodian drily asked the elderly Father Salas.

"I do, Your Eminence."

"You therefore believe that the Lady is a manifestation of Our Holy Mother?"

"She is, Father, an original manifestation of the Virgin. We are certain of it."

The Portuguese friar turned bright red. His hand gently grasped the pocket where he had placed the rosary, while he let his fingers caress the individual beads. And then, suddenly, his other hand pounded on the long table. Everyone was staring at him.

"That is not possible!" he exploded.

"Friar Alonso, please . . ." Esteban de Perea did his best to calm him, bringing him cool water in a clay cup. "We already discussed this subject once before."

"It simply is not possible!" he reiterated. "We have in our possession another report that contradicts your conclusion. That invalidates your hypothesis! That sheds some light on this deception!"

Benavides would not be placated.

"Have you not read Friar Francisco de Porras's declaration? It is all there!"

"Friar Francisco de Porras?"

Esteban de Perea stood up.

"There is no way for them to be aware of such a document, Friar Benavides. It only arrived here after their departure for Gran Quivira."

"What document are you talking about?" Juan de Salas was livid.

The Inquisitor walked over to Friar Salas, his face full of compassion. He felt such an overwhelming respect for the old man, who had spent his life preaching the Word in a part of the world that was so barren and harsh, that he almost regretted having to contradict him.

"You see, Father, after you had set out with the Jumanos," Friar

Esteban said in a conciliatory fashion, "Friar Benavides sent a second expedition of friars to the northern part of the territories."

"But this Porras?" Father Salas insisted. He had heard about him.

"Friar Francisco de Porras was in fact the leader of the group. We are talking about a small expedition of four friars, with two armed men for protection. They arrived in Awatovi, the largest Moqui settlement, on the feast of Saint Bernard, and founded a mission there bearing his name. That was where they gathered news of the various incidents, which we want to pass on to you, Father Salas."

"Incidents among the Moquis?"

"You have no doubt heard of them under a different name. The Indians also call themselves Hopis or Hopitus, which means the Peaceful Ones. They live quite a distance from here."

Friar Alonso stared at everyone, his face still flush with anger. It was unacceptable to him that the Most Holy Virgin would waste time instructing the unbelievers. And yet there must doubtless be a more rational solution to this quandary. And Benavides, his Spanish laden with its curious Portuguese accent, was ready to supply it.

"The expedition to the Moqui lands returned yesterday," he announced. "They have given us their report of their first contacts with the inhabitants of Awatovi."

"And what did they say?"

"Father Porras's expedition reached its destination on the twentieth of August. There they encountered a welcoming population, but one reticent about our faith. Their tribal leaders moved quickly to put the new arrivals to the test, as a means of discrediting them."

"Put them to the test? How?"

"The witch doctors are very powerful in those parts and keep the population in fear with their tales of kachinas and the spirits of their ancestors. Our friars attempted to combat this by preaching about the All Powerful Creator to the Indians, only to have the witch doctors, who were acting most unjustly, present them with a blind child, whom they asked the friars to cure in the name of our God."

"The Moquis have not seen the Lady in Blue?"

"Be patient, Friar," Esteban de Perea begged him. "What happened there was very different."

"How is that?"

"Do you remember when, a little more than a month ago, we interrogated Sakmo, the Jumano?"

"As if it were yesterday, Friar Esteban."

"And do you remember when Friar García de San Francisco, our brother from Zamora, showed the Indian the portrait of Mother María Luisa de Carrión?"

"Of course I remember! The warrior said the Lady in Blue that he had seen bore a certain resemblance to her, but that the Woman of the Desert was younger."

"Very well, Friar, the governor has good reason to believe that this nun, Mother María Luisa, is currently intervening in our lands in a miraculous manner."

"And why would she do that?" he asked incredulously, almost as if he were irritated. He directed his question to the vigilant Benavides.

"Do not overreact, I beg you," Perea said. "The friars who visited the Moquis were devotees of Madre María Luisa. And when the Indian chiefs brought the young child to them, they placed a small, inscribed wooden cross, blessed by this nun in Spain, over his eyes. It was through her grace, and after many prayers with the crucifix resting on the child, that he was cured."

Benavides, who had calmed down somewhat, added, "Do you understand now, Fathers? The child was cured through the agency of Mother Carrión's cross. She is the one who is intervening here!"

"And where does Your Eminence see the hand of the Lady in Blue in this episode?" Brother Diego protested energetically. "That a child is cured by a blessed cross does not prove . . ."

"The connection is quite clear, Brother," Benavides interjected. "If an object blessed by Madre Luisa cures someone, then why not admit that she has the power to bilocate as well, to send a second body to these lands, thereby discreetly helping us in our task? Is she not a Franciscan like ourselves? Would she not quietly watch out for our success, if it were in her hands to do so?"

"But . . ."

"Of course, this prodigy will be studied by my successor, Friar Perea," he announced. "He is the one who will determine whether or not a relationship exists between the two occurrences. Nevertheless, before I return to Spain, there is something I want to agree upon with all of you."

Juan de Salas craned his neck and Brother Diego took two steps closer to the long table in order to get a good look at what Benavides wished to show them. He placed Ankti's rosary and Madre Carrión's cross directly in front of the two friars. He fumbled among the beads until he found the silver cross that was the centerpiece of the rosary. He then placed it next to the cross that the friars had brought back from the territory of the Moquis.

"Do you see? Exactly alike!"

Friar Salas took both crosses in his hands, lifting them close to his face. They were in fact the same size, with the same borders in relief. He scrutinized them slowly, and hefted them in his deeply wrinkled fingers to calculate their respective weights.

"With all due respect, Friar Benavides," he said after a long silence. "All crosses look alike."

Brother Diego vigorously seconded him.

"It proves nothing."

FIFTY

MADRID

Paseo de Recoletos 20 was bustling with activity at nine in the morning. Seen from the sidewalk in front of the Colón Apartments, that fabulous neoclassical edifice gave the impression of being a gigantic anthill: ordered and precise. Overflowing with life.

José Luis Martín and Carlos Albert strode energetically toward the National Library's sentry box. Their names were listed among the visitors with appointments, so it turned out not to be difficult for them to gain access to the restricted area of the library and be accompanied to the director's office. The anthill was very quickly transformed into a sumptuous palace, its marble corridors adorned with valuable works of art that peered at the visitors from every imaginable angle. At the center of this labyrinth was Enrique Valiente, who received them in his spacious wood-lined office while seated behind a mahogany desk that was over two hundred years old.

"Pleased to meet you," he said as he offered his hand to his visitors. "Have you learned anything about the Benavides manuscript?"

José Luis shook his head.

"As of yet, no," he confessed. "But don't worry, we'll recover it."

Valiente was not so sure, and his face showed it. He invited his guests to sit down.

Enrique Valiente had a rather quixotic air about him. Thin, with a well-trimmed beard and a smooth brow, he had a manner both alert and honest. If not for his impeccable wool suit and blue tie, his two visitors would have thought they were meeting Don Alonso Quijano in his library overflowing with books on chivalry. As the courteous introductions were coming to a close, Enrique started nervously fishing through the sea of notes, Post-its, oversized cards, official bulletins, and press digests that swamped his desk.

"I hope you get your hands on the manuscript before they tear it to pieces and sell it as individual pages," he groaned as his hand retrieved an agenda from the pile. "It's hard to believe the unlucky streak we're having with those manuscripts right now."

"Streak?" The police officer was intrigued. "What are you referring to?"

"Aha! So no one told you when you came to investigate the theft? A week ago we suffered a separate attack on our historical records. And curiously enough, an attack on a text intimately related to the missing manuscript."

Carlos and José Luis exchanged looks of surprise.

"It was at the end of March," Valiente continued. "An Italian citizen, a woman, came to our reading room and requested a copy of a book printed in 1692, written by a Jesuit from Cádiz named Hernando Castrillo. It is certainly a strange book," he said as he searched the top of his desk. "Its title is *History and Natural Magic, or the Science of Occult Philosophy*. A sort of popular encyclopedia of the period."

"And why do you say it's intimately related to . . . ? "

"Hold on. I'll get to that."

Enrique Valiente reached for a copy of that same volume, pulling it from a table that sat behind his desk.

"Here it is! This is the book in question."

The volume he held up to them was a solid, leather-bound tome whose well-stitched spine bore the author's name.

"The woman was in the process of tearing out one of the chapters," he said as he flipped through the pages. "The one entitled 'Has the Faith Been Carried to the Farthest Reaches of America?' "

Carlos was startled, and blurted out, "A work on the evangelization of America! The same as the *Memorial* of Benavides!"

"And what happened with this Italian woman?" José Luis, somewhat more practical than his friend, brought the subject back to the attempted theft.

"This is the strange part. The librarian surprised the woman in the act of trying to cut the pages out of that chapter. Naturally, she prevented the woman from doing so and asked her to stay where she was, seated at one of the raised desks in the reading room, until a security guard arrived."

"And?"

"And she vanished!"

"How?"

The head of the library looked straight at José Luis. His hands rested on top of the shifting chaos of paper as he leaned over his desk toward his visitors; his expression was utterly serious.

"Exactly as I just said, Officer. She vanished. Vaporized. Disappeared. As if she were a ghost."

"You're not going to tell me the library has ghosts, too, like Linares Palace?"

Carlos relished the chance to refresh the director's memory about that little incident. A few city blocks away, at Paseo de Recoletos 2, a deserted old mansion had become a hot topic when rumors spread that it was infested with ghosts. It was a little over a year ago. The press had gone to town with the story, and several magazines even went so far as to give away cassette tapes that purported to be voices of the spirits trapped inside the house.

"What I am telling you is deadly serious," the director said, his eyes still fixed on Carlos. "The woman was real. She registered at the entrance. She took out her library card. She filled out the form requesting Castrillo's book, and then she evaporated."

"Like a ghost," José Luis said with finality, remaining skeptical.

"Could I take a look at the book?" Carlos asked.

The journalist's request did not surprise the head of the library, who handed it to him.

"Go ahead, my friend!"

Carlos opened the book to the "injured" chapter. José Luis leaned closer, trying to identify the source of so much interest. The pages were stitched to the spine, although a strip of gray fabric tape covered the cut inflicted by the "ghost." The wound was deep.

"So what does it say, Carlos?"

"Look at this. The author asks if anyone successfully proselytized in the New World before Columbus arrived."

"You must be joking."

Enrique Valiente observed them closely.

"It states in no uncertain terms that the Lady in Blue was not the first. It says that the first Jesuits to reach South America already discovered that other Christians had preached there centuries before."

"This is a curious book indeed," the director broke in. "It asserts that Columbus himself realized that the Indians of the Antilles worshiped adulterated forms of the Holy Trinity. And it refers to Paraguay, where at that time they still remembered the visit of one Pay Zumé, who, with a cross on his shoulder, preached the good news of the resurrection two hundred years before the Spaniards arrived."

"And this book takes that for a fact?"

"Catholic missionaries in America before Columbus?" José Luis looked as if he was listening to undiluted nonsense.

"Well," Director Enrique said in a doubtful tone, "what the Jesuits said at that point, in order to avoid, I imagine, going against the interests of the Spanish crown, is that the prodigy must have been the work of Saint Thomas. Which is ironic: he was the Apostle known as Doubting Thomas!"

"So why choose him?"

"They believed that the 'Pay Zumé' of the Indians was a corruption of the name 'Santo Tomé' or 'Saint Thomas.' Although the most curious thing of all is that there exists archaeological evidence that suggests that, in fact, missionaries did visit the Americas before 1492."

"Really?"

"For example, at the Tiahuanco ruins near Lake Titicaca. At that site high up in the Bolivian plateau, there is a stone monolith, six and a half feet tall, that depicts a bearded man. As you probably know, the Indians at those latitudes have no facial hair. Even today you can view the statue in a large semienclosed space, known as Kalasasaya, something like the kivas of the North American natives. It is thought to represent a preacher." He paused and then added, "And very nearby there are other statues that the Indians call 'monks,' which could well represent the first Christian evangelists, who came well before Columbus or Pizarro."

José Luis shrugged his shoulders.

"But why would anybody want to rob this chapter?"

"I asked myself the same thing. The woman could have requested a microfilm. But it seems she was interested in something else: she wanted to make that chapter disappear. This kind of thing happens sometimes; people do this because they don't want anyone else to have access to certain information."

That caught the police officer's ear. "Was there anything else about that visitor that struck the librarian's attention?"

"Now that you ask, yes. After filling out her request slip, she said that she had just come back from Brazil."

"Brazil?"

"Yes. She said that she had gone there, to Bahia de Todos os Santos, the capital of the State of Bahia, to see a rock on which the imprint of human footprints can still be seen. The Indians say that they are Pay Zumé's footprints. She also said that more footprints like those existed elsewhere in Brazil: in Itapuã, in Cabo Frio, and in Paraíba. The librarian who took care of her coincidentally happens to be a Brazilian, and she had never heard anything about this before."

"I see."

José Luis stared at the man on the other side of the desk.

"What can you tell me about the call you received from the United States yesterday?"

"The one that asked about Benavides's *Memorial*?" Valiente asked incredulously. "That one even caught me by surprise!"

"Tell us about it."

"Well, just imagine: it's hardly normal for a manuscript by a seventeenth-century Franciscan to be stolen, and then a few hours later for me to receive a call from a psychiatrist in the United States, asking me about a friar who is cited in the stolen book."

"There's no such thing as normal. Don't you agree, José Luis?" Carlos added ironically.

Enrique Valiente continued.

"The relevant thing here is that I took her address and telephone number so I could inform her if I managed to learn anything about this friar she was so interested in. She told me one of her patients was having strange visions that took place during that period."

"Did she mention the Lady in Blue?"

The head of the library nodded.

"In fact, yes. All of this is very strange, wouldn't you agree?"

"Do you think you could share her contact information with us?"

The director searched through his pile of notes, and handed the policeman a piece of paper.

"We'll do what we can," José Luis said as he accepted the note. "Although it is outside of our jurisdiction, thanks to Interpol, the FBI generally collaborates on this sort of case. Especially when it is related to national patrimony."

"Is there anything stopping us from going to the United States ourselves?"

If José Luis hadn't covered his mouth, he would have laughed out loud.

"Us? It was hard enough for me to get the Federal Police to pay the expenses for our jaunt to Bilbao, so imagine what they'd say about a flight to"—he looked down at the note in his hands—"to Los Angeles."

The journalist had an idea. Maybe it was nothing more than a crazy idea, but what did he have to lose by trying it?

"Maybe the police won't pay for your trip to Los Angeles," he said, "but my magazine might make the effort for me. If you get me a pass and hook me up with a contact at Interpol, I could learn a few things. And whatever I come up with, I will, of course, share with you before we go to press."

"And why not?" Enrique Valiente leaped in enthusiastically. "It would restore the library's prestige to know where exactly this book has ended up."

José Luis rubbed his chin as he thought it over.

"We can give it a try. Perhaps the director can give me a solid lead so I can stay on the case here in Madrid, while we send Carlos off to the United States."

José Luis's words did not go down well with the director of the library. In reality, the policeman wasn't asking anything, but just searching for an excuse to end the conversation on a friendly note. And yet this pressure inspired Valiente to come up with something unexpected.

"How would you like another detail about the Italian who tried to steal the pages from the Castrillo book?"

The question caught José Luis off guard.

"Just a detail about how the woman was dressed," he said, downplaying its importance. "The librarian told me that the woman was wearing the most eye-catching red shoes she had ever seen in her life."

"What?"

"The woman, who was dressed impeccably in black, was wearing red shoes that completely clashed with the rest of her outfit."

Something inside José Luis reacted at that moment. He would have bet his badge that this was a good lead.

FIFTY-ONE

ROME

"The man is a bloody eccentric," Baldi thought to himself, but would later regret the thought.

Giuseppe Baldi reluctantly walked through the gate designed by the architect Filarete in 1433, which opened onto the Loggia della Benedizione, the portico of blessing, and into the most famous basilica in Christendom, headed toward the area where tourists were lining up to ascend to the dome of Saint Peter's.

After a quick glance at the confessionals along the south wall, he sought out number nineteen. The identifying Roman numerals near the top of the tall wooden booths were barely legible, but looking closely a keen observer could discern what were once resplendent numerals hand-painted in gold, with the designation "Heavenly Listening Room" in the upper-right corner. Number nineteen was the easternmost booth, closest to Adrian VI's extravagant tomb. Visible at its entrance was a plaque, laden with years of grime, which announced, CONFESSIONS WILL BE HEARD IN POLISH BY THE DESIGNATED PRIEST, FATHER CZESTOCOWA.

Baldi felt like a fool. Just thinking about it embarrassed him. It must have been more than a hundred years since members of the clergy used the confessionals for clandestine meetings, much less in these times when the Vatican had entire auditoriums equipped to counter illegal listening devices. Still it was unlikely that the sophisticated listening devices the Holy Office's secret service and other foreign agencies liked to plant in the offices of the cardinals had been installed here.

The Benedictine had no choice. The message in the mailbox at the residence where he was lodging had made it perfectly clear.

Thus, obediently, Baldi entered booth nineteen on the right-hand side and knelt down. As he might have guessed, there were no Polish Catholics in line at that hour to receive absolution. The Holy Father's countrymen tended to use that time of day to sleep or watch television.

"Hail Mary, full of grace," he whispered.

"Conceived without sin, Father Baldi."

The voice on the other side of the screen confirmed that he had made the right choice. The "evangelist" tried to camouflage his enthusiasm.

"Monsignor?"

"I am glad you have come, Giuseppe," he said. "I have important news for you, and I have good reason to believe that even my office is no longer secure."

Stanislaw Zsidiv's unmistakably nasal voice bore a certain funereal air that disturbed the "penitent." His heart began to beat faster.

"Have you learned anything new about the death of Father Corso?"

"Analysis of the adrenaline content of his blood indicates that our beloved Saint Matthew had some sort of grave crisis before he died. Something that so overwhelmed him, he made the decision to take his own life."

"What could it be, Your Eminence?"

"I have no idea, my son, but doubtless something terrible. Now, as Doctor Ferrell will tell you, we must make every effort to find out who was the last person to see Corso alive, and what his or her influence was on Corso's decision, if any."

"I understand."

"But I did not make you come here for that, my son."

"No?"

"Do you remember when we spoke of Benavides's *Memorial* in my office?"

"If I remember correctly, it was a report assembled by a Portuguese Franciscan in the seventeenth century concerning the apparitions of the Lady in Blue in the southwestern United States."

"Exactly." His Eminence nodded with satisfaction. "That document, as I already told you, fascinated Corso at the very end of his life, because he believed that he had discovered in it a description of how a cloistered nun was physically carried from Spain to the New World in order to preach to the Indians in 1629!"

"I see."

"What you may not know is that Corso was in the process of requesting an unpublished manuscript by the same Friar Benavides, in which he identified the Lady in Blue as a nun by the name of María Jesús de Ágreda, and that he had learned the method she used to transport herself, through bilocation, to America."

"The formula for bilocation . . . ?"

"Just so."

"And he discovered it? Is it in the manuscript?"

"This is where things get murky, my son. We are talking about a text to which no one has paid the slightest attention until now. Corso searched for it in the Pontiff's archives the very day before his death, without success. Nevertheless, someone entered the National Library in Madrid and stole a manuscript belonging to King Philip the Fourth."

The Cardinal took a deep breath and continued before the Benedictine had a chance to react.

"Yes, Giuseppe. It was the very same *Memorial* that Saint Matthew was looking for."

The Venetian monk struggled desperately to find some sort of logical connection between the disparate events.

"According to what we learned this morning," Zsidiv went on, "the Spanish police have not as yet detained any suspects, but everything points to the robbery being the work of professionals. Perhaps the same criminals who stole Father Corso's files."

"What makes you suspect that, Your Eminence?"

"It is my impression that someone wants to make all information relating to the Lady in Blue disappear. Someone on the inside who wants to block the development of our Chronovision, and who does not seem inclined to settle for half measures in order to succeed."

"But why go to so much trouble?"

"The only thing that makes sense to me," Zsidiv whispered, "is that this someone has developed an investigation parallel to ours, has obtained promising results, and is currently erasing each and every clue that led them to their accomplishment."

Baldi protested.

"But that is nothing more than conjecture."

"Which is why I asked you to come here today. I don't feel safe in Saint Peter's, my son. The walls have ears. The Holy Office has called a meeting to review the latest developments on the project. A meeting at the very highest level."

"Do you think the enemy resides in the very heart of the Church, Your Eminence?"

"And what alternative would you propose, Giuseppe?"

"None. Perhaps if we knew the contents of that purloined document, we would know where to start looking."

Zsidiv made an effort to stretch his legs inside the sort of vertical coffin that is a confessional, then added laconically, "But we know what is in it."

"Really?"

"Certainly, my son. Benavides wrote his *Memorial* of New Mexico here, in Rome. He made two copies of the document: one for Urban the Eighth and a second for Philip the Fourth. The second is the copy that was stolen."

"Which means, we still have it!"

"Yes and no . . . ," he clarified. "You see, Friar Alonso de Benavides was Father Custodian of the Province of New Mexico until 1629. After interrogating the missionaries who had collected data on the Lady in Blue, he went off to Mexico, whence his superior, the Basque archbishop Manso y Zúñiga, sent him to Spain to bring a certain investigation to a close."

"Which investigation was that, Your Eminence?"

On the other side of the screen, Saint John, the coordinator of the Chronovision project, let out a short laugh. "Benavides left New Mexico convinced that the Lady in Blue was a nun famous in Europe as a miracle worker, a woman by the name of María Luisa de Carrión. The only problem with that theory was that the Indians described a woman who was young and attractive, and at that point Carrión was well over sixty years old. However, that still was not enough to convince Benavides. So instead of believing that the Lady in Blue could be a new apparition of the Virgin of Guadalupe, he preferred to believe that this 'voyage through the air' had somehow rejuvenated Carrión."

"Ridiculous!"

"It was the seventeenth century, my son. Nobody knew what might happen to someone who could fly through the air."

"Of course, but . . ."

"And another thing," the Monsignor cut in. "Something I learned this morning in the Secret Archive."

Giuseppe Baldi's ears pricked up.

"In Mexico City, the Archbishop showed Benavides a letter from a certain Franciscan friar by the name of Sebastián Marcilla, in which he spoke of another nun, younger, with mystical powers, who suffered all sorts of supernatural ecstasies."

"She was able to bilocate?"

"That was, in fact, one of her graces. Her name was María Jesús de Ágreda. Manso y Zúñiga, unnerved by the letter, sent the very same Benavides to Spain to investigate. The latter crossed the Atlantic at the beginning of 1630, disembarking at Seville, and from there traveled to Madrid and then Ágreda to investigate. He personally interrogated the alleged Lady in Blue, and afterward took up residence in Rome, where he wrote his *Memorial*."

"Then why did you say that the copy of *Memorial* he made for the Pope is of no use to us?"

"Because the copy in the king of Spain's possession and the one in the Pope's library are not identical. To begin with, the copy given to the Pope was incorrectly dated 1630, and it is still listed under that date in the archive, which is why Corso never found it. Second, in the copy that Benavides sent to the king, the Portuguese friar added notes in the margins, specifying how he believed the nun was able to transport herself physically, taking with her liturgical objects that she gave to the Indians."

"Liturgical objects?"

"Rosaries, chalices . . . The Franciscans found them when they arrived in New Mexico. The Indians had preserved them, regarding them as gifts from the Lady in Blue. Benavides obtained one and asked to be buried with it."

"And how could this lady—"

"It seems, my son, that at the same time that the nun in the monastery in Ágreda plunged into a trance that left her in a sleeplike state, her essence materialized in a different location. It became flesh."

"Exactly like Ferrell's 'dreamers'!"

"What's that?"

Baldi imagined Cardinal Zsidiv's surprised expression on the other side of the screen.

"I thought you already knew about that, Your Eminence."

"Knew what?"

"That the final experiment undertaken by Corso, in conjunction with the doctor, was an attempt to project a woman whom they called 'the dreamer' back to the time of the Lady in Blue. They hoped she would discover the secret of those voyages, which they would then present on a silver platter to INSCOM, an organization within the CIA."

"And did they succeed?"

"Well, they dropped the woman from the experiment. They said she became distraught and broke off all connection with them. She returned to the United States, but I have not as yet been able to verify her whereabouts."

"Find her!" Zsidiv ordered solemnly. "She has the key! I am sure of it."

"But how will I do it?"

The Cardinal leaned in so closely to the partition that Baldi could feel the man's breath on his face.

"Let yourself be led by the signs," the Cardinal said.

FIFTY-TWO

VENICE BEACH, CALIFORNIA

From the severity of the New Mexico desert to the suffocating heat of the Castilian plain: Jennifer Narody leaped over the barriers of time and place with a facility only dreams permit. But were they only dreams and nothing more? And why were they linked together as if in logical sequences? Perhaps she was "channeling" memories from another time, from an age to which she was connected for some mysterious reason.

Was Dr. Meyers right when she mentioned "genetic memory"? And if so, did her visions of her Indian ancestors, all of them from the remotest past, share a common source?

Jennifer shifted in bed, seeking the most comfortable position to go on dreaming.

If it was true that all her dreams were part of a real history, she wanted to know about it. She was beginning to believe that during her sessions in the "dream chamber" at Fort Meade, or perhaps during the time she spent in Italy, they had injected her mind with images that were now flowering in her oneiric world. She felt unclean, as if they had desecrated her intimate life. But at the same time she was intrigued, wanting to know where her visions would take her. Thus, dream after dream, Jennifer found herself faced with scenes that became increasingly distant and exotic.

Spain, for example.

She had never been there. The history of the Hapsburgs, Spain's ruling imperial dynasty, and its capital, Madrid, had never interested her. Nevertheless, the clear image of a fortified building, its balconies with their iron railings and its spacious rooms sunk deep in shade, permeated her retinas. And now Jennifer knew the era and the location of the building.

She went from one surprise to another.

FIFTY-THREE

THE ALCÁZAR, MADRID
SEPTEMBER 1630

"You have made a deep impression on His Majesty, Friar Alonso."

"That was my intention, Father."

"The king receives dozens of memoirs every few months on the most varied subjects, but only yours has merited the honor of being printed at the Royal Printing House."

Friar Alonso de Benavides took his time passing through the Tower of France, enthralled by the paintings by Titian, Rubens, and Velázquez that Philip IV had displayed there. As opposed to his austere predecessors, the young king had sought to enliven the dark corridors of the Alcázar with majestic works of art.

Friar Bernardino de Siena, commissary general of the Franciscan Order, accompanied Friar Benavides. The former was an old acquaintance of the king's, and one for whom he expressed a genuine sympathy.

Bernardino de Siena was a man skilled in diplomatic relations, and was envied for it by heads of other orders, none of whom were the recipients of such royal favor. And Bernardino was the one man responsible for the rumor that had made the rounds at court, that a miracle was the force behind the Franciscan conversions in the New World.

In short, a genius when it came to palace strategy.

"Your audience with His Majesty will take place in the library, which is a rare occurrence," he confided to Friar Benavides as the king's black-clad steward escorted them down the corridor.

"Is that so?"

"Indeed. The usual practice is to be received in the king's salon, but it pleases His Majesty to overlook protocol depending on the matter at hand."

"Is that a good sign?"

"An excellent one. As I told you, your account made a great impression on him. He wants to hear, from your own lips, other details relating to your expedition. And most especially, everything you remember on the subject of the Lady in Blue."

"Then it is true that he has read my report?"

"From the first word to the last," the commissary said with a smile of satisfaction. "That is why, Father, if we manage to interest him, we will be guaranteed control over the future diocese of Santa Fe. The fate of the order rests in your hands today."

The steward came to a halt in front of an unadorned oak door. He spun around to face his guests, asking them to wait. Without a pause and employing great ceremony, he walked into a precariously lit room, making an exaggerated bow.

Standing on the threshold, Benavides could see that it was a large room that ended in balconies with iron railings. A red carpet covered part of the floor and an enormous copper globe of the world cast its shadow from one of the corners.

"Your Majesty," the steward said in a booming voice, "your visitors have arrived."

"Show them in."

It was a strong, serious voice. Friar Bernardino, familiar with court protocol, took the lead, letting Friar Benavides trail behind him. The certainty of being in the palace, a few feet away from the most powerful monarch in the world, produced a slight chill in Friar Benavides.

At the far side of the room, which was filled with books and tapestries, seated on a silk-upholstered chair with leather armrests, Philip IV silently contemplated the new arrivals. Standing behind him was the chief steward. As soon as he saw them enter, his voice loudly announced the visitor's names.

"Your Majesty, the commissary general of the Order of Our Seraphic Father Saint Francis, Friar Bernardino de Siena, and the last governor of its dominions in New Mexico, Friar Alonso de Benavides, beg your attention."

"Very well. Bring them to me." With an informal gesture, the king silenced his steward.

The king was a fine-looking man. Despite the languid, fatigued face he had inherited from his grandfather Philip II, he had a rosy glow in his cheeks. The rumors concerning his health were unfounded. His blue eyes had more luster than his blond hair, and his body seemed reasonably strong. Leaving aside protocol, the young monarch rose from his throne and walked over to Friar Bernardino to kiss his hand.

"Father, I have wanted to see you for some time."

"And I you, Your Majesty."

"Life at court is monotonous. The latest developments in my overseas dominions are the only things that distract me from my worries."

A mere twenty-five years old, Philip already spoke like a seasoned king. He had just left behind an adolescence spiced with excess and a life controlled by his guardian, the Duke of Olivares.

"I have brought Friar Benavides, the author of the document you found so interesting, along with me. He landed in Seville on the first of August."

Friar Alonso gave a short bow as a sign of respect for the king.

"Well, well, Friar Benavides. So you are the man who states that Mother María Luisa has herself appeared in the Province of New Mexico, converting several tribes to our faith."

"Yes, Your Majesty, but for the moment this is only a hypothesis."

"And perhaps Your Grace knows that Sister Luisa of the Ascension, better known by her popular name as the nun from Carrión, is an old friend of the royal house?"

Friar Benavides's eyes opened wide.

"No, Your Majesty. I was completely ignorant of this."

"Nevertheless, your report has left me confused on one point. According to what you have written, the woman who appeared before the northern Indians was young and beautiful."

"Yes, that is so. This also confused us, Your Majesty."

"And how could it be, if Mother María Luisa is already old and infirm?"

"My king"—Friar Bernardino interrupted the monarch as soon as he saw the custodian of New Mexico wavering—"although the description that the Indians gave to Friar Benavides does not agree with how she actually looks, Mother Luisa's ability to bilocate is more than proven. It would not therefore be strange if—"

"I already know this, Father."

The king's eyes, lit by a spark of playfulness, bored into the commissary's; he then proceeded to address his subsequent questions directly to him.

"Perhaps you do not recall, Friar Bernardino, that my father exchanged letters with the nun from Carrión over the course of many years, or that my queen does so to this day? You yourself questioned her about her bilocations several years ago. It was you who determined that this nun went so far as to miraculously transport herself to Rome, where she shattered a glass filled with poisoned wine before Pope Gregory the Fifteenth could drink from it."

"May he rest in peace," murmured the commissary.

"And you also confirmed that Mother Luisa was, by the grace of God, present at my father's deathbed, accompanying him until the moment when he ascended to heaven."

"Yes, Your Majesty. My memory is fragile and I lament it. Nevertheless, I remember how Madre María Luisa spoke to me of an angel who transported her from her monastery to this court, and how it was she who convinced His Majesty Philip the Third to die wearing the Franciscan habit."

"That did indeed happen." The king became uncomfortable when speaking about his father, and he turned to look at Benavides once again. "Nevertheless your report does not match Mother María Luisa's current physical description."

"We are at present making inquiries in other avenues."

"Other avenues? To what do you refer?"

"We believe . . . ," and here Benavides's voice was shaky, "we believe that we may be faced with the bilocations of a nun from another cloister."

"How is that?"

Philip crossed his hands just beneath his chin and stared at the friar.

"You see, Your Majesty," Benavides said and took a deep breath. "When Friar Bernardino was investigating the prodigies of Sister Luisa, he visited a monastery in Soria where he questioned another nun, a young woman who was suffering from strange enchantments and ecstasy."

"Father Bernardino! You never spoke to me about this."

"No, Your Majesty," the commissary apologized. "I did not believe the case would be an important one, and I abandoned the subject."

"Tell me now about this nun," the king said, with rising interest.

The commissary general's weathered face assumed a certain air of solemnity as he took charge of the discussion and began to explain, while his hands traced small circles in the air.

"Shortly after questioning Sister Luisa in her monastery at Carrión de los Condes, I received a letter from Friar Sebastián Marcilla, who is now the provincial of our order in Burgos."

"I know him. Go on."

"Father Marcilla was at that time confessor for the Monastery of the Conception in Ágreda and he observed that one of the nuns, a woman by the name of María de Jesús, suffered strange bouts of hysteria. When in a trance state she became light as a feather, and even the look on her face changed dramatically, becoming beatific and pleasing to behold."

"And why did they ask you to visit her?"

"That much is easy to explain, Your Majesty. It was known within the order that I was very interested in proving the truth of Mother María Luisa's bilocations, so as a result, since that young woman also took part in several incidents in which it seemed she had been in two places at once, I presented myself at the monastery to question her."

"I understand," said the king, lowering his tone of voice. "I suppose this nun is a Franciscan as well?"

"God so rewards our order. I remind you that Saint Francis also received the stigmata of Christ."

"And could not this whole matter perhaps be a question of some other sort of phenomenon?"

Philip, already accustomed to disputes over information depending on the particular interests of one or another party, wanted to show his guests that he no longer was the guileless lad of yesteryear.

"I do not follow, Your Majesty."

"Indeed, my dear Father. Have you not considered that perhaps the woman who brought the Gospel to the Indians was someone other than a nun? She could be the Virgin, or a devil!"

The two friars crossed themselves.

"But Your Majesty," Friar Alonso answered, "a devil would never teach the Gospel to souls he has already won over to the fiery depths."

"And the Virgin?"

"This was a theme much discussed in New Mexico, and the truth is we did not find the proofs necessary to affirm it. We have no evidence that confirms her presence, such as occurred with the miraculous image of Our Lady that the little Indian at Guadalupe delivered to Bishop Zumárraga in Mexico."

"Aha! The famous Virgin of Guadalupe!" the king exclaimed. "I would like to see that image some day."

"Many painters have copied it by now, Your Majesty. It shows a beautiful young woman, her face unearthly and sweet, wearing a blue garment sprinkled with stars, which covered her from head to foot."

"A blue lady, is that correct?"

"Yes," the friar said hesitantly, "but she appeared almost a hundred years ago, in 1531. And in a populated region like Mexico. Why would the Virgin appear in a desert region like the Rio Grande?"

"Very well," the king conceded. "Tell me, what will be your next steps with regard to this subject, Fathers?"

Friar Bernardino stepped forward.

"Two, with your indulgence, Your Majesty. The first, to send friars to New Mexico, as reinforcement in converting your new subjects to the Christian faith. And second, to send Friar Benavides to Ágreda to interview Sister María Jesús."

"I would like to be kept up to date on these matters."

"Certainly, Your Majesty."

"As for now," the king announced with solemnity, "Friar Benavides's *Memorial* will be printed in our workshop during the coming week. That is correct, Gutiérrez?"

The steward sprang to life for the first time during the meeting. He walked over to the ebony desk next to the bookshelves, and after searching through its drawers, filled out a routine document confirming the king's wishes.

"Four hundred copies will be printed, of which ten will be sent to Rome for review by His Holiness Urban the Eighth," the steward intoned gravely.

"Excellent," Friar Bernardino said with evident pleasure. "Your Majesty is a good king and a better Christian."

Philip smiled.

FIFTY-FOUR

ROME

Three quick blasts resounded inside Saint Peter's, echoing in the confessional where Zsidiv and Baldi had been talking. The two men sat there frozen. What was happening? It sounded as if the colossal statue of Saint Longinus, Bernini's masterpiece, had tumbled from its pedestal and its entire fifteen-foot length had shattered on the floor. Had it been destroyed? The blasts sounded as if they came from close by. Baldi instinctively shifted position in the booth, leaning away from the screen in an attempt to determine their origin. The bursts of noise emanated from the gigantic statue of Saint Veronica. From where he sat in the confessional, all he could make out was a cloud of billowing smoke rising toward the roof of the nave.

"An attack!" he muttered fearfully.

"What did you say?" Zsidiv was paralyzed.

"It looks as if someone tried to destroy the statue of Veronica," Baldi enunciated loudly.

"Impossible. Saint Veronica?"

There was no time to react. Two seconds later, a woman with an athletic build, swathed in black, emerged from the cloud of smoke and dust. Moving like a cat, she eluded the crowd watching the unfolding events and ran straight toward Father Baldi and the door leading to the dome.

"One minute, thirty seconds," she said, panting.

The Benedictine lost his balance and stumbled backwards, while the fugitive seized the moment—and took a deep breath—before delivering a cryptic message.

"Ask the second, Giuseppe. Pay attention to the sign."

Baldi nearly lost his balance again. Did she say his name? And what was that about a sign? Zsidiv had just said the same thing.

"The second?" Baldi quickly went to the heart of the message. As he turned around to look in the direction of the fugitive, he raised his voice and shouted, "Were you speaking to me? Listen! Was that for me?"

"The second," she repeated.

It was the last he saw of her.

A burly German tourist, wearing an ugly jogging suit and armed with a silver Canon, began taking one photo after another while standing alongside one of the tombs near the confession booths. The overwhelming glare from the camera's flash disconcerted the Benedictine.

"Santa Madonna!" he groaned aloud, his eyes still irritated by the flash.

The woman in black had quickly disappeared, leaving both men with their mouths hanging open. The German tourist was inspecting the front of his camera.

"Did you see where she went?" Baldi shouted at him.

"Nein, nein."

The Swiss Guards were the next to arrive. They raced to the scene at full speed without losing the solemn composure expected of the Pope's personal guard.

"Father, we are searching for a woman who fled in this direction," said the guard at the head of the first group of *sampietrini* to arrive. He was a redhead, a robust young man whose face was pitted with acne. "Do you know if she fled to the terrace?"

"A fugitive?"

"A terrorist," emphasized the impeccably dressed Swiss Guard.

"She passed right in front of me . . . She flew by . . . But I swear to you I have no idea what became of her. The man over there, the tourist, he photographed her!" Baldi stammered.

"Thank you, Father. Please remain inside the basilica."

The patrol took care of business skillfully: they pulled the German aside and took possession of the film in his camera. They then returned to Father Baldi, wrote down his name and temporary address at Via Bixio, as well as the telephone number at Vatican Radio, and asked him not to leave Rome for two days. Two other guards raced up into the dome overhead. Baldi somehow suspected they would return empty-handed.

"Can you tell me what is happening here?"

Baldi sensed the guard's disappointment.

"It was a fanatic, Father. We get plenty of them each week, but we usually intercept them in time."

"I can see that."

"She tried to blow a hole in the marble base supporting the statue of Saint Veronica. All that just so she could jam a note in it!"

Baldi was perplexed. He prudently remained silent about what the terrorist had whispered to him.

"A note? And what did it say, if I may ask?"

"Here, take a look, Father." The youthful redhead smiled as he held the piece of paper in question out to him. "Can you make that out? 'Property of Ordo Sanctae Imaginis, Order of the Sacred Image.' Does that make any sense to you?"

"No, to tell you the truth."

"The majority of these people are only trying to scare you. Crazy people, believers in the Apocalypse. Deranged people who would put an atom bomb under the Pope's chair if they could get away with it."

"It is . . . shocking."

"If we catch her, Father, we'll call you. We need you to identify her, although perhaps this may be of help."

The Swiss Guard held the roll of film in his hand with a sense of satisfaction before slipping it into a small breast pocket of his uniform. A moment later, he then took his leave, bowing slightly to Baldi as he did so. At the same time the two guards returned from the dome at full speed. They came back covered with sweat and shrugging their shoulders.

"She vaporized!" Baldi heard them say.

Baldi, who could hardly think straight at the moment, walked back to Confessional 19 in search of answers. But the Cardinal had disappeared as well. He must have taken advantage of the confusion to slip out without being seen.

The Benedictine was overcome by an odd feeling of isolation.

"I don't understand," he repeated several times just above a whisper, as if he were imploring someone to help him. "I don't understand anything."

The priest stood there, lost in his thoughts, for several more minutes. What was the meaning of everything that had happened? Was it mere chance that "Saint John" and the mysterious woman both told him, in a matter of seconds, to pay attention to the signs? The clouds of smoke, the fugitive who suddenly disappeared, the tourist who nearly blinded him, and the phrase "Ask the second" directed at him ("Who could it be?" Baldi thought); he turned all of it over and over again in his mind like an outstanding play repeated on television during a sporting event.

"What sign?"

Sunk deep in thought, he retraced the sixty-odd feet that separated him from the five-sided column where the explosives had gone off. He still had time to take a quick look at the damage caused by the attack before the Swiss Guards finished cordoning off the area. There was nothing to show for the three blasts: the marble plinth at the base of the statue suffered no damage; the inscription that Pope Urban VIII had had engraved at the statue's feet appeared to be slightly blackened, but that was all.

"How curious," Baldi mused to himself. "Was not Urban the Eighth the Pope to whom Benavides sent his *Memorial*? Is that the sign?"

Not convinced in the slightest, the evangelist wandered through the adjacent part of the basilica until he arrived at Bernini's spectacular canopy above the pulpit. An astonishing work. He had heard it said that the sculptor designed it when he was barely twenty-five. He must have been one of those who are touched by the hand of God,

Baldi thought. And there, overwhelmed by so much beauty, the priest raised his eyes to the dome and begged that same God to let him see the blessed sign.

Baldi had no way of knowing his gesture was going to resolve his confusion.

The priest was hardly concentrating when he lowered his gaze toward the base of that celestial section. His eyes lingered on the curvilinear triangles immediately beneath the dome itself. The spectacle of Michelangelo's work of genius was unique: its size—137 feet in diameter and 446 in height—made it the largest vault in all Christendom. Within it stood the four evangelists, who had written the four most important texts of the New Testament. Matthew wielded a pen five feet in length: as colossal as the mystery surrounding the death of Baldi's "Matthew," Luigi Corso.

"Domine Noster!" he blurted out when he realized. "It really is right in front of my nose!"

The likenesses of all four Apostles seemed to be laughing at him from inside the huge, round bas-reliefs, each of them twenty-six feet tall.

"It was obvious the whole time. I was an idiot to miss it! The Second Evangelist is the sign I was looking for."

FIFTY-FIVE

MADRID

The interview with the king left Friar Bernardino with an uneasy feeling. The short, combative commissary had watched as his interests passed through a moment of danger, and he made certain Friar Alonso knew it as they exited the royal palace.

"What made His Majesty think the Lady in Blue was the Virgin?" he demanded, raising his voice.

"He has a point, Father. You yourself said that the Lady was covered by a blue cloak, as was the Virgin of Guadalupe; she was wearing a white habit, as did Guadalupe. She even descended from heaven like her. I, too, was tempted to defend that idea. Nevertheless, following your instructions and those of the Archbishop of Mexico, I defended the hypothesis of the Franciscan who bilocates."

"And continue to do so! If the king, the Jesuits, or the Dominicans were able to turn this subject around and lead everyone to believe it was the Virgin who appeared, we can say good-bye to the Franciscan claims of authority! Do you understand me?"

"I would prefer that you explain to me."

"It's very simple really," said Friar Bernardino in a whisper. "If we don't manage to convince His Majesty that it has been a Franciscan Conceptionist nun, aided by Divine Providence, who was responsible for the conversions in New Mexico, he could confer the evangelization of our overseas territories to another order tomorrow. You know how capricious the will of kings can be. And if the idea spreads that these conversions have been the work of Our Lady of Guadalupe, you can be sure that in less than a week the Dominicans will be asking the king to intervene. And then the Jesuits will arrive. That could put an end to our primacy in America! Now do you understand?"

"Of course, Father. The Virgin belongs to everybody—not so, a Conceptionist nun. Please rest assured, the message is clear to me."

After crossing the patios, the two friars were led to the palace gates. From there, they walked through the streets and alleys of the capital on their way to the convent of Saint Francis.

"As soon as we have the first copies of your *Memorial* in our hands, I want you to travel to Ágreda to interrogate Sister María de Jesús."

The commissary's harsh tone was even more inflexible than usual.

"I will pave the way for you by writing the orders for her to speak to you, and will bring you up to date with information about her so that you go fully warned."

"Warned?"

"Sister María de Jesús is a woman of strong character. Before reaching the minimum age required, she had already obtained the permission to become abbess, and she enjoys a good reputation in the province. It will not be easy for you to convince her to promote our interests."

"Well," Friar Alonso interjected as they walked toward the Plaza Mayor, "perhaps that may not be necessary. Perhaps she is the person truly responsible for the bilocations."

"Indeed. But we cannot run any risks. When I met her, she was much younger, and I discovered that she inherited her mystic abilities. She would never, and permit me the choice of words, deliberately lie. Now you understand me."

Friar Alonso shook his head.

"What do you mean that 'she inherited her mystic abilities'?"

"Clearly you do not know her family history. Sister María is the daughter of a wealthy family that later came down in station, and that some years ago decided to relinquish the family holdings in an unusual manner. Her father, Francisco Coronel, entered the monastery of Saint Julian of Ágreda, while the mother converted the family's residence into a cloistered monastery, obtaining the permissions to do so in an unexpectedly short time."

"Interesting . . ."

"The fact is that, years earlier, the bishop of Tarazona, Monsignor Diego Yepes, had already confirmed María Jesús at the young age of four."

"Monsignor Yepes?" Benavides marveled. "The biographer of Saint Teresa of Ávila, the great mystic?"

"Just imagine. Yepes saw very early on that the young girl had mystical leanings, and that is not surprising, either."

"No?"

At that midday hour, the center of Madrid was crowded with people. Friar Alonso and the commissary crossed the Plaza Mayor, making their way past vendors hawking breads, fruits, and fabrics as they continued their conversation.

"Her mother, Catalina de Arana, was a woman with great ecstatic gifts: she heard the voice of Our Lord. In fact it was she, following the instructions of that voice, who pushed her husband toward life in a monastery. Later on came her trances, visions of extraordinary lights in her cell, angels. . . . These things are beyond me!"

"Angels?"

"Yes. Not angels with wings, but flesh-and-blood people with extraordinary powers. When I visited Ágreda for the first time, Sister Catalina herself told me how, from the time when work began on the monastery in 1618, a pair of young men came around who, almost without eating or drinking, and without being paid, worked from sunrise to sunset on building the monastery."

"And what does that have to do with angels?"

"Well, for example, they saved a number of workers from falls and from wounds caused by sudden accidents. And what is more, they managed to become good friends with Sister María de Jesús, exactly during the period from 1620 to 1623, when she was undergoing her fiercest mystical attacks."

"That is certainly curious."

"Curious? What seems curious about it to you, Friar Alonso?"

"Well, I remember what the two friars from New Mexico who investigated the Lady in Blue's apparitions among the Jumanos told us. In their report they stated that the woman spoke to them about several 'lords of the sky' who are able to move among us, who can invoke all kinds of extraordinary phenomena."

"What kinds of phenomena?"

"All sorts, Father. She even explained that it was those angels who carried her through the air."

"Good Lord, Friar Alonso. Find out whatever you can on this subject. Angels who can camouflage themselves while living among us and who can carry people through the air make me very agitated. And the Holy Inquisition, too, believe me."

FIFTY-SIX

EN ROUTE TO LOS ANGELES

Carlos couldn't get the image of Txema Jiménez, his bulky silhouette standing beside the road sign to Ágreda a few days before, out of his mind. As he settled into seat 33C on American Airlines Flight 767, which would take him to Los Angeles, he did some serious thinking about the bizarre series of events, subtle connections, discoveries, and fortuitous encounters that had brought him to the present moment.

"I'm convinced that we all have our own destiny," the ghost in his mind repeated in the photographer's boastful voice, "and that sometimes the force of that destiny pushes us violently, like a hurricane."

The previous afternoon, after leaving Enrique Valiente's office, Carlos had called the *Mysteries* editor in chief. José Campos, already accustomed to his best writer's sudden enthusiasms, had given in and agreed to pay for Carlos's unexpected flight to the United States. "But you better bring back a good story," he threatened unconvincingly. "Or two."

This time Carlos was not afraid of failure. The succession of synchronicities was pushing him into the realm of confidence, toward a belief in his own star. And from there to faith was only a short step.

He had been so involved in his own thoughts that he hadn't noticed the plane was almost empty. It was a Wednesday, in an unlikely month for anyone in Spain to take a vacation.

From his first visit to Ágreda, and then to Bilbao, and now onto the plane, everything had happened so rapidly. It seemed almost as if those events, including the theft at the National Library, had been determined long before and he was merely playing a part according to a preestablished script. "What I wouldn't give to know the librettist of this opera!" he mused. The feeling reminded him of when he was a young child copying wild, meaningless phrases written in someone else's hand, imitating the letters that appeared in a workbook.

For example, what explanation did he have for the fact that the editor of the magazine approved his trip to the other end of the ocean without asking for an explanation? None whatsoever.

That everything had come together so easily disturbed him. Even Interpol had failed to raise objections about assisting him. In his carry-on luggage he had the fax from Mike Sheridan, the head of the Los Angeles office of the FBI's Cultural Patrimony Department, confirming their meeting in less than twenty-four hours. And yet, far from comforting him, all of that made him nervous, as if he were being manipulated. The question was, by whom? And for what reason?

What higher force was dragging him to the United States in search of a woman whose only crime had been to ask about a stolen document at the wrong time? Most likely that clue was a mere illusion. Even so, with his editor's approval and the plane ticket in hand, he could hardly turn back.

"Violently, like a hurricane."

Carlos whispered the phrase again. And without opening his eyes he closed his notebook and after that the book he was reading. It was written by a Princeton psychologist, one Julian Jaynes, and it attempted to explain in a scientific manner some of the most outstanding mystic phenomena of history.

"Mystics . . . crazies!" Carlos grumbled.

His plane, with its Pratt & Whitney engines, flew like a breeze across the Atlantic, cruising at an altitude of thirty-six thousand feet when the pilot announced to the passengers that they were leaving the Azores to the south.

"In the next ten hours we will cover almost five thousand miles, before we land at the Dallas–Fort Worth Airport in Texas," the pilot said over the public address system. "And then another thousand miles until we reach our final destination in Los Angeles. I hope you have a pleasant flight."

Carlos sat distractedly in his coach seat, trying to make sense of the information: five thousand miles, more or less, represented the same distance that Mother Ágreda had to travel in a bilocated state. Which is to say, a woman from three centuries before overcame ten thousand miles, almost halfway around the world, during the time the ecstasy lasted. To travel the same distance, he needed nine hours and an astonishing amount of technology.

"Simply impossible," he said to himself.

He took a deep breath before he gave in to an enveloping drowsiness. As soon as things settle down, he thought, I should sleep at least until we fly over Florida. He unlaced his shoes, unbuttoned the collar of his shirt, and, tilting his seat back slightly, drew a blanket over himself and tried to sleep.

He was in this pleasant state when, seconds later, he became aware that someone was sitting next to him. "With all the empty seats on the plane, someone has to come and sit next to me," he thought. He was about to shift position, turning his back on his unexpected fellow traveler, when a woman's soft voice, with a strong Italian accent, stopped him cold.

"Nothing is 'impossible,' Carlos. That word does not exist in God's vocabulary."

His eyes snapped opened. He quickly sat up and looked directly at the woman speaking to him.

"Do we . . . Do we know each other?" he said doubtfully.

The woman who had taken the seat next to him had a hypnotic quality about her. Her skin was dark brown, and her long, straight hair was gathered in a ponytail, accentuating the beauty of a sweet, moonlike face. Her flashing green eyes studied him curiously. She was wearing a fitted black wool sweater. If he had had to guess where she was from, Carlos would have said she was Neapolitan.

"Know each other, you and I? No, not directly. But it hardly matters."

What was so unique about this woman? Carlos's metabolism reacted out of all proportion to her presence: his heart rate sped up to

120 beats per minute and a rush of adrenaline was making him shake. At 36,000 feet above sea level, with an outside temperature of eighty degrees below zero, her voice alone was enough to lift Carlos to the outer limits of his heart's ability to function. All that in a second!

"Have you heard about the Programmer?" she asked.

"The Programmer?"

Carlos knew about him. Definitely. His old professor of mathematics, whom he had visited several weeks before, had been the last person to mention that word to Carlos. And yet, with a shake of his head, he denied it. The woman smiled, as if she could read his thoughts.

"He is the one who wrote this play. You were the person who wanted to get to know him, weren't you?"

The journalist swallowed.

"But how . . . ? "

"How do I know?" The young woman whistled enigmatically as she adjusted her seat. "I also know what you are going to do in Los Angeles. And that you are following us."

"I'm following you?"

"Yes. Don't you remember? A few days ago you made the decision to 'hunt for the Programmer.' Everything started with the tiny medal you're wearing around your neck, the one you found just outside the doorway to the magazine."

Carlos's fingers felt for the medal, while she took the opportunity to mention another detail.

"That medal is mine, Carlos."

He turned pale.

"I put it there in order to draw you toward where you are today. I thought you were ready for it."

"But who are you?"

"They call me many different things, but to make it easy for you, I will just say that I am an angel."

Carlos grabbed hold of the medal with the Holy Face in order to be certain that he was awake. The gold chain was still hanging around his neck. The book he had just closed, *The Origin of Consciousness in the Breakdown of the Bicameral Mind*, was an audacious essay that tried to explain, as precisely as possible, the origin of "voices in the head" and the religious visions that have taken place throughout history. Carlos had just finished reading that the great biblical prophets, Muhammad, the Sumerian hero Gilgamesh, and hundreds of Christian saints had visions in which they confused reality and hallucinations as a result of a common neurological problem. Julian Jaynes maintained that until the year 1250 BC, the minds of such men were split into two sealed-off compartments that occasionally talked to each other, giving rise to the "myth" of divine voices. The prophets, first and foremost, were men with a primitive brain mass. Therefore, when the right and left hemispheres of the human brain evolved sufficiently to be able to interconnect, the voices disappeared completely . . . and with them the ancient gods.

And him?

What had happened to him?

"You're an angel. Fine." Carlos tried to calm his heart, which was still beating furiously against his chest.

"Does that surprise you?"

The woman placed her hand on his neck, letting him feel her soft, warm skin. She delicately lifted the medal from around Carlos's neck, looking at it affectionately.

"Veronica's veil," she said. "One of my favorite images."

"Let's say that I believe you," the journalist interrupted her. "That you put this medal in my path to attract me toward everything that is happening to me now. So, what role are you playing in all this? Why are you suddenly revealing yourself to me?"

"My job is to protect an old secret. A secret that until now only one man had obtained from us accidentally."

"You don't say."

"His name was Alonso de Benavides. And his secret is what I am trying to protect from falling into the wrong hands, which is why I am revealing myself in this manner." She hesitated for a moment. "I know you find it hard to believe."

"Let me try. If I believe that you are an angel, I can accept just about anything."

"Although I can touch you, although you see me here, in reality I am a projection," she said. "A double. A bilocated image."

"You don't say!"

"I knew you wouldn't believe me. At this moment, another part of me is in Rome, getting ready to go to the Leonardo da Vinci Airport to catch a plane to Spain."

"Sure."

The woman was not affected by Carlos's disbelief.

"Very soon you will be convinced of our existence. It's just a question of time."

" 'Our existence'?"

"Come on, Carlos!" The woman's green eyes sparkled. "Do you think I work alone? You never read anything about angels? We were the ones who warned Joseph in his dreams what Herod was planning against his wife and his child. We very subtly planted ourselves in his psyche. But Jacob wrestled with one of us and his leg was broken, as it states in the Bible. Abraham gave us food to eat. In Sodom they even tried to use us for their own ends because we looked so beautiful to them. Flesh and bone, and lovely to look at. You've never read the Scriptures?"

Carlos was astonished.

"Why are you telling me this?"

"First, so that you know we exist. Now you see me. Although I am bilocated, I am as real as you." She smiled and once again put her fingers on his neck. "And second, because we believe that you are going to help us with our secret."

The journalist shifted in his seat.

"What makes you think that?"

"Everything fits, my friend. You touched on our secret in Italy, when you interviewed Giuseppe Baldi. That is where we first met."

"Chronovision?"

She nodded. A torrent of images flooded his mind. His visit to the island of San Giorgio Maggiore. Txema bombarding Baldi with photographs, while he himself tried to lead the man he was interviewing toward a subject he had spent nearly twenty years trying not to say a word about. And then, his report. The great applause he had received from his readers. His obsession to know more . . .

"After your encounter with Baldi, we realized that you are a peculiar type. Disbelieving on the outside, Carlos, but inside, in your heart, you have a tremendous desire to believe. So we channeled your search for transcendence toward our own interests."

"You channeled?"

"For example, why do you think I called Father Tejada in Bilbao the night we entered the National Library, if not to leave a clue for you to follow?"

Carlos felt a sudden shiver.

"There's no reason to feel bad. We have been doing this for centuries."

"Really?"

"Of course." She looked at him again with those emerald eyes. "The voices that Constantine, George Washington, Winston Churchill, and so many other people listened to during decisive moments in history were ours. Read their biographies and you will find references to their inspirations. And we were the ones who guided Moses out of Egypt, who carried Elijah and Ezekiel through the air, and we even darkened Jerusalem when Jesus died on the cross.

"And the synchronicities? The can't-be-real chance occurrences?"

"Our specialty! We love doing them, Carlitos!"

The journalist once again felt that odd current running up and down his spine. Only José Luis called him that, and he was the first man to speak to him about synchronicities and Jung. Did she know him as well?

"But I thought angels were incorporeal—"

"A very common error."

"Why have you come to see me?"

"The word 'angel,' my friend, comes from the Greek *angelos*, for 'messenger.' And so, of course, I have come to deliver a message to you."

"What kind of message?"

"In your briefcase you are carrying information on Linda Meyers, a Los Angeles doctor who forty-eight hours ago telephoned the National Library asking about a stolen manuscript."

Carlos decided to let himself be led.

"Very well. You should know that she is not your final goal. I have come to save you a bit of time."

"Meyers is not the person I am looking for?"

"No. Take note of the name you are looking for. She will be the one, and not the doctor, who will help you resolve this case. Her name is Jennifer Narody. We have spent some time implanting ourselves in her dreams, preparing everything for your arrival."

The angel spelled out the name letter by letter while Carlos wrote it down.

"She has the secret, without knowing it."

"And how is that possible?" His heart was still racing. His accelerated pulse made him scribble the woman's name in the worst handwriting he could remember. He carefully entered it in his cork-covered notebook, as if that were the last thing he would do that day.

"You ask how is that possible? Let's say that I put it in her hands specifically so that it will end in yours. Does that seem strange to you?"

The young woman did not say another word, but stood up from her seat, taking the medal the journalist had been wearing and putting it in the pocket of her black dress, and with the excuse of returning to her own seat, walked off down the aisle in the direction of business class.

That was when he saw it.

And it was as if his chest felt once again the jolt of a whip.

The woman, so impeccably dressed in dark colors, was wearing red shoes.

FIFTY-SEVEN

VENICE BEACH

Differences in time zones are difficult to calculate when one is crossing imaginary terrestrial meridians at some four hundred and fifty miles per hour. Every one of the fictitious lines, drawn at intervals of fifteen degrees on the map of the world, marks roughly an hour of difference from the previous zone. So that it could well be said that at five meridians of distance, from American Airlines Flight 767 to the beach in Venice, California, Jennifer Narody received a new piece of the puzzle of which she still did not know she formed a part.

This time, her psyche flew in the opposite direction of Carlos. It was on course to Spain.

FIFTY-EIGHT

ÁGREDA, SORIA
APRIL 30, 1631

Benavides had been detained more than six months in the Madrid of the Hapsburgs, attending to his ever more voluminous correspondence and the tasks born in the shadow of the *Memorial*'s success. In the hallways of the palace, no one could remember a similar state of anticipation. The good friar had amassed a mountain of letters, congratulations, and unexpected commitments, which obliged him to become even more involved in the matter before the Court.

The bureaucracy in the capital set aside his investigation into the "case of the Lady in Blue" until a later date, which saddened him considerably. Nevertheless, the palace intrigues, above all those of the Dominicans attempting to convince the king to investigate the number of conversions in New Mexico, forced him to stay alert. Luckily for Benavides, he was able to preserve the spirit necessary to struggle on behalf of his interests. How well he knew that the "hounds of the Lord," the *domini canes*, were trying to send their own missionaries to the Rio Grande in order to keep Benavides from carrying off all the glory for the conversions.

Their plans failed.

Documentation and necessary permissions fortunately arrived in April 1631, making it possible for Friar Alonso to abandon Madrid and continue his task. The results of his work would paralyze the Dominicans' ambitions forever. He was authorized to visit the

Monastery of the Conception at Ágreda to question the prioress and ordered to write a report of his findings.

All of which gave the Portuguese friar a newfound energy.

On the morning of April 30, Benavides's horse-drawn carriage, an unassuming coach of laminated wood adorned with copper filigree and cast-iron trimmings, advanced at a gallop across the temperate Soria countryside, in the direction of the foothills of Moncayo. In its interior, the former custodian of the Holy Inquisition in the Province of New Mexico completed his preparations.

"So you were Mother Ágreda's confessor before she became prioress . . ."

The movement of the carriage was tossing Father Sebastián Marcilla about as well. His stomach was bouncing from side to side, in time to the driver's caprices. Father Marcilla had had experience putting a good face on disagreeable activities, so it was not difficult for him to maintain the composure necessary to respond.

"Indeed, Friar Alonso. In fact, it was I who wrote to the Archbishop of Mexico, making him aware of what would come to pass if the regions to the north were explored."

" 'What would come to pass'? To what do you refer?"

"This you already know: that they would discover new kingdoms such as those of the Tidán, the Chillescas, the Carbucos, and the Jumanes."

"Ah, so it was you?"

Father Marcilla's oval face glowed with satisfaction.

"I advised His Eminence Manso y Zúñiga of the existence of those regions, and if Your Reverence read my letter, then no doubt you did not miss my invitation to confirm the existence of vestiges of our faith in those lands."

"And naturally," Benavides deduced, "that information was transmitted to you by Mother Ágreda."

"Of course."

"And how did you dare to violate a secret of the confessional?"

"In fact, it was nothing of the sort. The confessions were exercises in mea culpa, by a young woman who had recently taken vows and who did not understand what was happening to her, and were in no way the source of such precise details. Rest assured, I never absolved her of her 'sins' of geography."

"I see." Friar Alonso nodded his head as if in agreement. "I do have to tell you that of all those kingdoms I am only familiar with that of the Jumanos—not 'Jumanes,' by the way, which is located to the northeast of the Rio Grande. As regards the others, no Franciscan or soldier of His Majesty has any knowledge to this day."

"None?" Father Marcilla's tone was incredulous.

"Not so much as a rumor."

"Perhaps it is not so strange. We will have time to clear up these points with the Prioress of Ágreda herself, who will give us a full account of whatever we ask her."

Friar Alonso de Benavides and the Franciscan provincial of Burgos, Sebastián Marcilla, were soon fast friends. Marcilla had joined the veteran custodian of New Mexico in his carriage when it stopped at the city of Soria, and from there the two men shared several hours that served to allow them to agree upon the questions they intended to ask Mother Ágreda, as well as to establish the limits of their rivalry.

So lengthy and intense was their discussion that neither of the men took note of the abrupt changes in the landscape, the profiles of the towns they passed, or even of their rapid arrival at their destination.

At first glance, Ágreda appeared to be a serene corner in the highlands of Castile, an obligatory stopping point between the kingdoms of Navarra and Aragón, a crossroads for sheepherders and farmers. As in any village perched on the border, the few noble families in the locality and the religious orders were the only points of lasting reference. And the Monastery of the Conception was one of those.

In that recently erected cloister, all had been prepared for the visit. The nuns had placed a long red carpet between the road to Vozmediano and the front door of the church, and had even set up tables with pastries, water, and a strong wine to slake the thirst of their illustrious visitors.

Thanks to the authorizations arranged by Father Marcilla, the entire population of religious stood outside the cloister awaiting the arrival of the delegation. They prayed and sang throughout the morning, reciting the stations of the cross alongside the exterior walls; they were joined by a growing number of the faithful, who knew in advance the importance of the awaited delegation.

For that reason, when Benavides's coach pulled up in front of the red carpet, a superstitious silence took hold of the crowd.

The view from the carriage could not have been more revelatory: the nuns were standing impatiently in two lines, one headed by a Franciscan friar, the other by a sister who the travelers promptly decided must be Mother Ágreda. Following the rules laid down by Saint Beatriz de Silva in 1489, each nun was wearing a white habit, a silver scapular bearing the image of the Virgin, a black veil over her head, and that impressive blue cape.

"May the Lord be with us!"

Friar Benavides's unexpected exclamation surprised his traveling partner. He let it slip out between his teeth no sooner than his feet were on the ground and he took a quick look at his surroundings. Marcilla was startled.

"Are you all right, Brother?"

"Absolutely. It is simply that this level ground and these valleys abounding in chants and those white habits seem a reflection of the lands I left behind on the other side of the sea. I feel as if I have been here before!"

"*Omnia possibilia sunt credenti*," Marcilla enunciated. "For the believer all is possible."

Their reception was shorter than planned. After descending from the coach, between the Te Deum and the genuflections of the nuns, the Franciscan who accompanied the initiates was introduced as Friar Andrés de la Torre, Mother María Jesús's confessor since 1623, who resided at the nearby Monastery of Saint Julian. At first glance, he seemed an affable fellow, large-boned, with a flat nose and oversized ears that made him slightly resemble a rabbit. As for Mother Ágreda, she looked quite the opposite: her skin was milky; her long, slender face was tinged with pink; and her large dark-brown eyes gave her a look that was mild and yet forceful at the same time.

Benavides was impressed.

"May Your Worships be welcome here," she said. And with barely a pause, she added, "Where do you wish to question me?"

The tone of the alleged Lady in Blue was dry, as if she were displeased at having to render an account of her intimate life to a stranger.

"I believe the church will be convenient," Marcilla said just above a whisper, as he thought back over his time as a priest in this enclave. "It is agreeably located, without the necessity of entering the cloister, and we can have a writing desk placed there, with candles, ink, and any other necessary articles. Furthermore, we will have Our Lord as a witness."

Benavides accepted the suggestion willingly, and let the prioress take care of the details.

"In that case, Your Worships will have everything at your disposal tomorrow morning at eight o'clock sharp."

"Will you be present at that hour?"

"Yes, if that is the will of the commissary general and my confessor. I wish to stand before Your Worships as soon as possible, in order to dispel those doubts you have brought with you."

"I trust that it will turn out to be less painful than you imagine, Sister," the Portuguese friar interjected.

"Our Lord's crucifixion was painful as well, but no less necessary for the salvation of humanity, Father."

The sudden upsurge of the sisters chanting the Gloria in Excelsis Deo on the path to the cloister spared Benavides from responding to Sister María Jesús's comment.

"And now, if you will excuse us," Mother Ágreda said, "we must gather to attend our evening prayers. Help yourself to the banquet we have prepared for you. Friar Andrés has arranged for you to be put up at the Monastery of Saint Julian."

And with that, she disappeared into the cloister.

"A woman of strong character."

"No doubt, Father Benavides. No doubt."

FIFTY-NINE

EN ROUTE TO LOS ANGELES

Carlos needed several minutes to catch his breath. He did not know how to put it into words, but the proximity of that woman had changed him profoundly. An angel? What difference did it make? She seemed to know everything about him, while he in turn was utterly ignorant of everything about her.

If, as he suspected, the Italian woman who tried to make the pages of Castrillo's book disappear and the angel were the same person, perhaps she knew something about the *Memorial*. It all seemed strangely related!

He left seat 33C and, taking several long strides, stood in business class. She was not there.

"An Italian woman, dressed in black, with red shoes?"

The skeptical flight attendant shook her head.

"I'm sorry, sir. We have only thirty passengers on board, and none in business class. I can assure you that no one matching that description has passed through here."

"An angel?"

Carlos remained awake for the rest of the flight, wondering who in the world he could tell about all of this.

SIXTY

ROME

Before making his way to Leonardo da Vinci International Airport, Father Giuseppe Baldi made a detour to the headquarters of the Swiss Guards. He had already deciphered the sign that would lead him to his next step, although for the moment he preferred to remain silent about it. Nevertheless, he wished to resolve a small detail before taking leave of Vatican City. Once there, he had no difficulty locating the office of Captain Ugo Lotti, the redheaded man with the ruddy face who had assisted him in the basilica the day before.

Captain Lotti offered to resolve any doubts he might have. Unfortunately, in the twenty-four hours that had elapsed since the incident, he had been unable to shed any light on the circumstances surrounding the attack. The Swiss Guards remained utterly in the dark concerning what might have prompted such an assault against the statue of Saint Veronica.

"A truly strange case," the official admitted, gesturing toward some folders that were lying on his desk. "The devices were placed close together, at the three weak spots in the pedestal of the statue, with a skill that allows us to conclude it was the work of a professional. And yet, at the same time, everything unfolded as if whoever did it did not in fact want to cause any damage to the monument."

"Are you trying to say that it was this woman's intent not to destroy anything, but only to call attention to or to distract us from something?"

"So it seems."

"I'm not convinced."

"Well, Father, every year there are five or six violent attempts on several of the three hundred ninety-five statues in Saint Peter's. The *Pietà* is the most vulnerable. This was the very first attack on the Saint Veronica, a minor work of Francesco Mochi, without any particular relevance . . ."

"If they did not intend to destroy the statue, perhaps it was a symbolic act. Have you considered that?"

Captain Lotti shifted in his chair and, leaning toward his visitor, took on a mockingly complicit tone.

"Would you happen to know something I should be aware of?"

"Unfortunately, no," Baldi responded. He had not been expecting that question, and he wavered.

"Now I am the one who is not too convinced, Father."

"I studied the history of the piece, and came up with nothing," the priest said in his defense. "As you know, it was designed by Bramante, but when Julius the Second put Michelangelo in charge of the construction of the dome, the latter modified that particular work, expanding the pedestal underneath the statue. It was at that time that the 'openings' for placing treasures were designed."

"You are referring to relics when you say 'treasures'?" the Swiss Guard said, looking at the priest with a smile.

"Well, Veronica's actual cloth was kept in the pedestal that suffered the attack. This is the cloth on which it is believed Christ dried his sweat on the road to Calvary. Some even believe they see the profile of the Messiah in the stains on the fabric."

"And what do you know about this Order of the Sacred Image?"

"Not a single thing."

"So why have you come to see me?"

Giuseppe Baldi sat up straight.

"For two reasons. First, to inform you that I am leaving Rome today, but that you can find me through the secretary of state. They will know where I am at any moment. Second"—and here Baldi hesitated—"so that you can tell me, to whatever extent you are able, whether or not the roll of film the guards confiscated in the basilica has provided any clues."

"Ah! That is another fine mystery. Yesterday, naturally, we developed the film in our laboratories, and when we took a look at the last photo, something very unusual turned up . . ."

The Swiss Guard searched among the folders for the image.

"Aha, here it is. Do you see?"

Baldi took the photograph in his hands. It was a five-by-seven print on matte paper. He looked at it carefully for several seconds. The low-quality print seemed to have a filter of some sort across it. The basilica's marble floor was visible on the lower part of the photograph, and near the back, he could just make out a pair of expensive red shoes. Nevertheless, the object that most called attention to itself was not on the floor, but occupied the center left section of the photograph.

"What do you think that could be?"

"I have no idea, Captain. I already told you when we were in the basilica that the camera's flash blinded me and prevented me from seeing where the woman made her escape. What I did not remember," he said, with the trace of a smile, "was that she was wearing such outrageous shoes."

"But how can such a ridiculous little camera blind you, Father?" the guard protested.

"Well, even its owner was astonished by the flash of light. And if this detail is only present in this one photograph, everything becomes complicated, don't you think?"

Baldi pointed out a series of strange luminous marks that lay like the tails of a comet across the photograph. He asked the guard for his impression. The captain hesitated.

"They are perhaps the flames of the numerous tall candles in the basilica, which in this exposure . . ."

"But Captain," Baldi objected, "you yourself have said that it was a ridiculous little camera, the kind that comes with a pop-up flash and that does not allow you to set a longer or shorter exposure."

"Well, perhaps it malfunctioned."

"But then those marks would appear in all the photographs."

"That's true," he conceded. "Those marks do not appear in any of the other photographs. And there's no way to explain them. Yesterday afternoon, Lieutenant Malanga enlarged this section of the image with the help of a computer, but he couldn't find anything behind the streaks of light. That is all they are: streaks."

"Rays invisible to the human eye, Captain." The Benedictine pushed his glasses back up before resuming. "Although it may seem ridiculous, do you know the impression they give me?"

"Tell me."

Giuseppe Baldi smiled curiously, as if he were about to pull the captain's leg.

"They look like the wings of an angel, Captain."

"An angel?"

"As you already know, a being of light. One of those personages who, according to the Scriptures, always appears in order to deliver a message from on high. A sign."

"Yes, of course," Ugo Lotti replied unenthusiastically. "And yet an angel in Saint Peter's . . ."

"May I keep it?"

"The photograph? Why not? We have the negative."

SIXTY-ONE

ÁGREDA

The life of the Lady in Blue had been subject to an unbending routine for the last ten years. The end of that day's labor would not be an exception.

Once the sun had set, around eight o'clock in the evening, and having barely touched any food, Sister María Jesús retired to her cell to undertake the daily examination of her conscience. It was always done in silence, far from the individual activities of her sisters, in a state of deep concentration that never ceased to seem painful and pitiful to all others.

The initiate prayed until nine-thirty, stretched out on the floor of her room, her face against the tile. She then washed with cold water and lay down to sleep on a hard wooden bench, trying not to think about the lacerating pain that soon took possession of her back.

Around eleven at night, when the rest of the sisters were closed in their cells, Sister María Jesús submitted herself, as was her custom, to the "exercise of the cross." It was a terrible practice. Over the course of an hour and a half, she berated herself with thoughts of the passion and death of Our Lord Jesus Christ; she then placed an iron cross weighing some one hundred pounds on her shoulder while she walked on her knees until she was exhausted. Finally, after a pause to gather strength, she hooked the cross on the wall of her cell and hung from it for an additional thirty minutes.

Sister Prudencia awakened her every morning around two to go downstairs and preside over matins, which usually lasted until four in the morning. She always attended, no matter whether she was taken with a fever, was sick, or in pain. But that day and only that day, she preferred to stay on the floor above. She wanted to hide the distress of knowing that, in a few hours, a commission of friars would interrogate her.

Some two hundred yards away, in the Monastery of Saint Julian, the last night of April passed in a more tranquil manner. By seven in the evening, Fathers Marcilla and Benavides had already completed their prayers and ingested a frugal meal consisting of bread and fruit. They had had sufficient time to prepare the necessary sheets of parchment where Mother Ágreda's answers would be recorded.

"Mercy, Mother of God, Mercy."

Sister María Jesús's anguish drifted under her door and to the floor below.

"You know that I am faithful and that I discreetly keep the marvelous things you teach me to myself. You know that I have never betrayed our dialogues. Succor me in this difficult encounter."

None of the sisters heard her. Nor did anyone answer her pleas. Bewildered by the silence, the prioress fell down on the hard wooden bench that served as her bed. But sleep did not come to her aid.

Thirty-five minutes later, the Monastery of Saint Julian opened its doors for Friar Andrés de la Torre and the secretary charged with transcribing the interrogation. After formal greetings and examinations to verify that everything was in order, the four walked across Ágreda toward the Conceptionist cloister. And there, as the prioress promised them, they found a writing desk and five chairs arranged around it, as well as two large candelabra at the head of the table.

Nothing more could be asked. The church was clean and quiet, set apart, a place where their work would be more comfortable. And it would also permit one of the sisters in the congregation to observe the inquiry from the choir loft as it unfolded.

The prioress arrived punctually. She was dressed in the same habit as the previous afternoon, and her young face gave evidence of exhaustion; she had already undergone too many years of sleeping two hours daily.

Sister María Jesús greeted the four priests who were waiting for her. After bowing before the tabernacle of the main altar, she took her seat and waited while they completed the initial formalities. Her eyes were glistening. She had passed the night weeping.

"On the first of May, of the year of Our Lord 1631, in the main church of the Monastery of the Conception of Ágreda, we proceed with the questioning of Sister María Jesús Coronel y Arana, a native of the village of Ágreda and prioress of this holy house."

Sister María listened in silence as the scribe read aloud her full family name. When he was finished, he raised his eyes from the nearly empty page and directed a question to the nun.

"You are Sister María Jesús?"

"Yes, I am."

"Do you know, Sister, why you have been called before this tribunal today?"

"Yes. To render account of my appearances outside the monastery and of the events in which Our Lord wanted me to play a role."

"In that case, respond under oath to everything that you are asked. For the purpose of this tribunal, the privileged nature of confession has been lifted and you must answer all its questions with Christian humility. Do you accept?"

She assented. The nun looked Friar Alonso de Benavides in the eyes. His severe manner and large nose reminded her of the figure of Saint Peter hanging over the altar of that very church. He was a man of authority. Benavides was seated directly in front of her, behind a mound of papers covered with indecipherable annotations, and a copy of the Bible. When he sensed the prioress observing him, he took the initiative.

"The reports we have received state that you have experienced instances of rapture, or ecstasy. Could you explain to this tribunal when they began?"

"Approximately eleven years ago, Father, in 1620, when I had just turned eighteen. It was then that Our Father desired that I be assaulted by trances during religious services, and that several of the sisters saw me floating above the ground."

Benavides watched her closely.

"It was not a gift I solicited, Father, but rather one I was granted as was my mother, Catalina. She, too, fell into trances, and such was her faith that, when she was well on in years, she decided to live as a nun in this order."

"You levitated?"

"So they tell me, Father. I was never conscious of it."

"And how do you explain your ecstasy carrying you beyond the walls of the cloister?"

"My first confessor, Friar Juan de Torrecilla, was not an expert in such matters."

"What do you mean by that?"

"Only that, carried away with his enthusiasm, he spread word of those events outside the bounds of the convent. The news stirred interest throughout the region, and many of the faithful came to see me."

"Were you aware of this?"

"At that time, no. Although it struck me as strange when I awoke to find the church surrounded by devotees. But as always when I came out of that state, my heart was overflowing with love, and I did not pay much attention to them, nor did I inquire regarding their attitude."

"Do you recall when the first ecstasy took place?"

"Perfectly. The Saturday after Pentecost in the year 1620. The second came over me on the feast of Saint Mary Magdalene."

Friar Alonso leaned across the desk in order to give emphasis to his next words.

"I know that what I am going to ask you is a subject matter for confession, but we have heard that you enjoy the gift of being in two places at the same time."

The nun assented.

"Are you conscious of this gift, Sister?"

"Only at times, Father. My mind is suddenly in another place, although I have no idea how to explain my arrival there nor the method used. At first they were voyages of no importance, to the outside walls of the monastery. I saw the bricklayers and their assistants at work there, and even gave them instructions to change the work they were doing in this or that way."

"They saw you, Sister?"

"Yes, Father."

"And later on?"

"Later on, I watched as I was taken to strange places, places where I had never been and where I found myself with people who did not even speak our language. I know that I preached the faith of Jesus Christ to them, since those peoples, of what race I do not know, were utterly ignorant of it. Nevertheless, the thing that most stirred me was listening to the voice inside of me that urged me to instruct them. To teach them that God created us as imperfect beings and sent Jesus Christ to redeem us."

"A voice? What kind of voice?"

"A voice that gave me greater and greater confidence. I believe that it was the Holy Spirit who spoke to me, as it had done to the Apostles at Pentecost."

"How did these voyages begin?"

Friar Alonso watched out of the corner of his eye to be certain that the scribe was taking note of everything that was said.

"I am not sure. From when I was a child I was consumed by the knowledge that in the regions newly discovered by our Crown, there were thousands, perhaps millions, of souls who had no knowledge of Jesus Christ and who were in close proximity to eternal damnation. I grew ill merely thinking about it. But on one of those days when I was sick, my mother called two bricklayers over, men who had a certain fame as healers. She asked them to carefully examine me and treat me in such a way as to eradicate the humors that had left me prostrate in my bed."

"Go on."

"Those bricklayers shut themselves in my cell. They spoke to me of things I barely remember, but they made it clear to me that I had an important mission to fulfill."

"They were not bricklayers, is that what you are saying?"

Friar Alonso called to mind the warning that the commissioner general had given him when he was in Madrid.

"No. They admitted that they were angels and their mission was to travel from place to place. They said they were of the same blood as myself and my family. And they explained to me that they had lived among men for several years, in order to see which of us was fit to serve God. It was then that they spoke to me of the souls in New Mexico and of the great sufferings our missionaries underwent in order to reach the very remote regions."

"How long were you with them?"

"For nearly the entire day the first time."

"Did they return?"

"Oh, yes. I remember that that same night they came back to me; they came into my room and took me away without waking anyone. It all happened so quickly. I suddenly found myself sitting on a throne on top of a white cloud, flying through the air. I could make out the monastery, the fields where we grow our food, the river, the mountains of Moncayo, and I began to rise higher and higher until everything faded away and I saw the round face of the earth, half in shadow, half in light."

"You saw all this?"

"Yes, Father. It was terrible . . . I was very afraid, above all when they carried me over the oceans toward a place I had never seen before. I clearly felt the wind in that latitude as it blew against my face, and I saw the bricklayers, transformed into radiant creatures, controlling the movements of the cloud, very ably guiding it now to the right and now to the left."

Friar Alonso's expression changed when he heard her description. That account tallied with the heretical assertions, investigated sometime before, from the mouth of the Bishop of Cuenca, Nicholas de Biedma, as well as the celebrated Dr. Torralba, who between the end of the fifteenth century and the beginning of the sixteenth had both claimed that they had risen up on clouds of that sort, had flown to Rome on them, and, what was even worse, had been guided by evil spirits.

"How can you be so sure that those men were angels of God?"

The nun crossed herself.

"*Ave María!* What other creatures could they be, if not that?"

"I do not know. Tell me yourself, Sister."

"Very well." She hesitated. "At first, like Your Worship, I asked myself if I was being tricked by the Evil One, but later, when shortly after undertaking that flight they ordered me to descend in order to preach the word of God, my fears disappeared."

"They ordered you to descend, you say?"

"Yes. They laid down a kind of carpet of light below my feet and invited me to take a message to a group of persons who were waiting there. I knew they weren't Christians, but neither were they Muslims, or enemies of our faith. They wore animal skins, and drew close to me, fascinated by the light that descended from the cloud."

"Mother, I must insist: are you certain they were angels?"

"What else might they be?" The prioress was adamant. "They did not flee from my words, they accepted in good spirit my faith in God, and they regarded it with respect and devotion. The Devil would not have put up with so much praise of Our Heavenly Father."

"Indeed. And what happened afterward?"

"I did all that they asked. That night I visited two other places, and spoke to different Indians. And although they spoke other languages, they seemed to understand me."

"Can you describe them?"

"I was much struck by the light brown color of their skin, and by the fact that nearly all of them had their torsos, their arms and legs, and their faces painted. They lived in houses of stone, as in our villages, but they entered them by the roofs, and when they assembled for their ceremonies it was in a sort of well, to which only those men authorized by their witch doctors entered."

Friar Alonso hesitated. He himself, with his own eyes, had seen all of that in New Mexico. But how could she . . . ?

"You spoke to the Indians of the arrival of the Franciscans?" he continued.

"Oh, yes! The angels made certain that I did. They even allowed me to see places where friars in our seraphic order were laboring. In one of them, I saw how an Indian whose name was Sakmo implored one of our members, an old preacher, to send the Word of God to the people where he came from. This Sakmo, a dark-skinned man with big, broad shoulders, prayed that they would assign missionaries that I myself had told them to demand."

"Isleta!"

"I would not know how to tell you the name of the place, for no one told me what it was. Instead, I found myself devastated that the friar denied him help for lack of men. Did you know that I myself spoke with this Sakmo a short time before, and I showed him where he ought to travel in order to come in contact with our missionaries?"

"How many times do you believe you were there?"

"It is difficult to be precise, because I have the conviction that on many occasions I was not conscious of it. I dreamed daily of those lands, but I could not say if I did so because I was there in body or because Our Lord wanted me to relive certain scenes from my preaching."

"Try to estimate. It is important."

"Perhaps some . . . five hundred times."

Friar Alonso's eyes opened all the way. His voice quavered slightly.

"Five hundred times, from 1620 until today?"

"No, no. Only between 1620 and 1623. Later, after I pleaded with Our Lord God and his intercessors with all my strength, my exterior manifestations ceased. Little by little. And those angels who had accompanied me daily began to extend the time between their visits. First once a week, and then once a month. And finally, they came no more."

"I understand. Did someone tell you how to put an end to your 'exterior manifestations'?"

"No. I mortified my body in order to make them cease. I stopped eating meat, milk, and cheese, and began a vegetable diet. Furthermore, three days a week I maintained a strict fast of bread and water. Shortly thereafter, it all ended."

"Forever?"

"Who can know this except God?"

"Nevertheless, a woman of your appearance continues to be seen in those far-off lands," Benavides said in a lowered voice.

"Perhaps what could be happening, Father, is that those angels are borrowing my form and they continue to show it to the Indians without my knowledge. Or perhaps they have asked the help of some other sister."

Friar Alonso scribbled something on a sheet of paper and folded it over.

"Very well, Sister María Jesús. That is all for today. We must think about what you have stated to this tribunal."

"As you wish."

The nun's obedience disarmed the Portuguese friar, and reassured Father Marcilla, who noted with pleasure that the expectations of the former guardian of New Mexico were not disappointed. Benavides already had no doubt: this nun was the Lady in Blue he was looking for. Now all his efforts would center on forcing her to divulge the secret of her flights to the New World.

He would not leave there without it.

SIXTY-TWO

ROME

Two hours later, as he was checking in his luggage at the Alitalia counter, the Benedictine still wore an ironic smile. The airport was quiet, and there were no traces of other passengers at the departure gates in his terminal.

Baldi passed swiftly through security without noticing that a young woman dressed in black, with red shoes, was close behind him. The Benedictine had other things on his mind. He felt rejuvenated by the endorsement he had received the day before from His Holiness's personal secretary, Monsignor Stanislaw Zsidiv, after his flight from the confession booth. Baldi had been granted a *speciale modo* authorization allowing him to meet face-to-face with the Second Evangelist. That was the sign! And although he would once again violate the rules of Chronovision, this time he was doing so with a safe-conduct pass from Saint John. John had told him to trust the signs, which obligated him to back his envoy.

"Return with news before the internal assembly on Sunday," John had instructed him. "Your priority is to find the woman who worked with Corso. May Mark, the Second Evangelist, guide you."

Thus, Giuseppe Baldi flew to El Prat Airport outside of Barcelona, where he made a connection to one of Aviaco's veteran Fokker F27 Friendships, whose destination was the always-tricky runways of San Sebastian, in the north of Spain. There, using the credit card that Zsidiv himself had put in his hands, he rented a white Renault Clio three-door and took Highway A-8 to his destination, the Basque capital of Bilbao.

Forty-five minutes later, near the outskirts of the city, he parked the car. Preferring not to drive into an unfamiliar city, he hailed a taxi, giving the driver a piece of paper bearing the address of his final destination. While the Third Evangelist was busy reflecting how rapidly one could cross Europe in the late twentieth century, the cabdriver, unnerved by the mannerisms of the nervous priest in his backseat, increased his speed as he headed toward the University of Deusto. He was there in less than ten minutes. On the second floor of the neoclassical building where the Theology Department was located, "Saint Mark," or Father Amadeo María Tejada as he was otherwise known, had his office. A directory posted at the entrance gave the office number and location.

Baldi took the marble steps two at a time, and once he stood in front of the door leading to the vestibule, he rang the doorbell. A second later, he announced his presence by rapping with his knuckles.

"How may I help you?"

The gigantic Amadeo Tejada peered down at the person standing at his door as he racked his brains trying to figure out what had brought a man well on in years into that swirling mass of students in the middle of exams. His visitor was wearing the long habit of the Benedictines, and he regarded Tejada with a look of astonishment.

"Saint Mark?" he stammered in Italian.

The giant's face lit up. He understood everything in a flash.

"*Domine Deus!* You received permission to come here?"

Baldi nodded. The perfect Italian accent of the man standing across from him encouraged Baldi to continue the conversation in his native tongue.

"I am 'Saint Luke,' Brother."

"The musician!" Tejada said, arms lifted to the sky as if in thanks. "Please! Come in, sit down. You don't know how long I have waited for such a visit!"

Tejada was beaming like a young student. He did not have the faintest idea what had brought one of the leaders of the Chronovision team to his office, but he sensed it must be something important, since the primary rule protecting the security of the project was being transgressed for the first time in almost fifty years.

"Monsignor Zsidiv authorized this visit, Father Tejada. You already know him." Baldi winked. "Saint John."

"I take it, therefore, that the matter is serious."

"Of the greatest importance, Brother." Saint Luke began to explain, but could not at first find the right words. "Of course, I imagine you have already heard about the First Evangelist's suicide, no?"

"I heard the news a few days ago. I'm in shock."

Baldi nodded.

"What you perhaps do not know is that, after his death, documents related to his research disappeared from his computer. And we have no idea where to begin to look for them."

"I don't understand. Why are you bringing this to me? I am not a policeman."

"Well, Divine Providence guided me here. Let's say"—he hesitated for a second—"that I have let myself be carried by the signs."

"All well and good, Father," Tejada said approvingly. "It's only been a few times in my life that I've seen a cleric carry his faith to its ultimate conclusions!"

"Furthermore, you are an expert in angels. Isn't that so? You have studied their behavior more closely than anyone. Since as you already know, they plant seeds here and there, you are the best person to interpret their designs."

Tejada shrugged. It was obvious that someone in Rome had provided his visitor with his curriculum vitae.

"I take that as a compliment," he said.

"What I want to say to you, Brother, is that . . . Better that you should see it yourself."

Saint Luke riffled around in his bag in search of the photograph that Captain Lotti gave him. He withdrew it from a brown envelope, and carefully placed it on Professor Tejada's desk.

"It was taken yesterday, in Vatican City, after the woman who should be in the picture had set off three small explosives at the base of the pedestal supporting the statue of Veronica."

"Those are the woman's red shoes?"

Baldi nodded.

"Incredible. That news did not get this far. Was there any damage?"

"It was an unimportant incident that did not even merit two lines in today's *Osservatore Romano*. But look closely. The shoes that you see a little behind the red ones, at the same spot where those lines cross the image, are mine. I was there and witnessed the attack."

Father Tejada took a magnifying glass out of his desk and examined the image carefully. Once he had viewed it at thirty times its normal size, he looked up at Father Baldi and scratched his beard.

"Do you know what sort of camera was used to take this?"

"A pocket-sized Canon. The shot was taken by a tourist in the basilica."

"I understand. And you didn't see anything, correct?"

"Nothing . . . The burst of light from the flash overpowered everything in the vicinity and even startled the camera's owner. It blinded me."

"Hmm," Tejada rumbled. "Most certainly the disorienting light was not from the flash, Father."

Baldi looked surprised but said nothing.

"Perhaps," Tejada continued, "the flash of light passed through our supposed terrorist."

"Passed through?"

"Do you know anything about physics, Father? Have you read any scientific publications on the subject?"

"No, my area of expertise is the history of music."

"In that case, I will try to explain it in the simplest manner possible. Perhaps what you saw was a side effect that has been studied in numerous experiments in particle physics, especially those in which a photon is capable of splitting in two, projecting an exact replica of itself to any other location in the universe. That phenomenon of doubling is called the teleportation of particles, although if they chose their words wisely, they would call it bilocation."

Baldi shifted slightly. Bilocation?

"During that process of the duplication of materials," Tejada went on, "it is possible to prove that the original photon discharges an enormous quantity of luminous energy, a strong radiation that is perceptible to scientific instruments and that can easily leave traces of itself on a photographic negative."

"But you are talking about elemental particles, not humans who somehow show up in two places at once!"

The tremendous implications of this theory were just beginning to dawn on the Venetian. If what Tejada was saying was true, Baldi had been a few meters away from a person capable of bilocating in the same manner as Sister María Jesús de Ágreda.

"And who told you that no technology exists that can transfer what photons do to physical bodies onto the human scale?"

"Lord! Has someone done that?"

Saint Luke's volubility was becoming a source of amusement to Father Tejada.

"It will seem strange to you, but this is not the first time that I have seen these types of streaks in photographs. Sometimes, in cases where it is believed that supernatural entities have intervened, such as in the apparitions of the Virgin of Medjugorje, in Yugoslavia, similar images have been obtained."

"Really?"

"We are face-to-face with some type of energetic manifestation that surrounds certain individuals, which is invisible to the human eye. It is something like the halos that artists give the saints, except in this case we are talking about something with a physical basis."

"Are you saying that the Virgin—"

"Absolutely. In order to prove this we would have to pull together an extraordinary series of proofs. On the other hand, to be frank, I believe that the woman who is not visible in the photograph can only be an 'infiltrator,' an angel, someone capable of controlling her disappearance from the scene as if she were a photon, and who took advantage of the flash on the tourist's camera, disguising her escape, and vanishing in the middle of a burst of light."

"But those are speculations."

"No doubt. But we already know that so much of the Christian tradition as well as other, older, more ancient ones, speak to us of angels as beings of flesh and blood, who frequently take on human shapes and forms, and who watch us from inside our society, as if they were a fifth column. . . . You don't follow? Just like photons, which are both particle and wave, angels are corporeal and immaterial at the same time."

"You surprise me, Brother."

"Furthermore," Tejada added, waving the photo, "for some reason that we do not understand, photographic cameras, more sensitive than the human eye to different frequencies of light, do not capture the physical aspects our eyes see but a different one altogether."

By this point in the conversation Baldi was convinced he had come to the right person. He had paid attention to the signs, and they were guiding him well. Trusting in the designs of a Divine Providence, the Benedictine adjusted his wire-rimmed glasses and, without taking his eyes off Tejada, said, "I have yet to tell you the second part of this adventure, Brother. As you will understand, if I have taken the trouble to come here from Rome, it was not simply to show you a photograph, even if you are a respected specialist in the field."

"Flattered to hear it, Father Baldi. I'm all ears."

"Before I ever saw this photograph, the 'terrorist,' or angel, or whatever you want to call her, whispered something when she was standing next to me. She said something to the effect that I should be attentive to the signs, and that I should ask the 'second.' I came to the conclusion that I had to speak to you, the 'Second Evangelist.' You could call it an inspiration."

The professor loomed over Friar Baldi.

"It is well-established that angels take on physical form in order to reveal signs to us. But what does all this have to do with me?"

"While that camera was taking pictures, I was busy trying to come up with an answer to the disappearance of Saint Matthew's files. That was my mission and, believe me, I had no idea what to do. So, Saint John, Zsidiv, told me that I should let the signs show me the way, And a sign arrived with this image. Do you understand now? You have something to tell me."

"Then let's find out what it is!" Tejada exclaimed good-humoredly.

"I am convinced that information you have will help me find the whereabouts of the information stolen from Saint Matthew. That was why they sent me the sign, and why I have come here. Isn't it obvious?"

"In which case, Father, *credo quia absurdum*."

The Latin phrase, "I believe it because it is impossible to believe," perfectly summed up Tejada's situation. The good-natured giant endeavored to help out without quite understanding how to do so. Such is Providence.

"Tell me, Father Baldi, what sort of information disappeared after Matthew's suicide?"

"It is difficult to say precisely."

"Give it a try."

"All right then. Before he died, Luigi Corso became obsessed by a very curious subject: he studied the remarkable ability of a Spanish nun who was able to travel back and forth between the Old World and the New during the seventeenth century. It seems that her visits to America earned her the name 'The Lady in Blue' among the Indians of the southwestern United States."

Tejada stood stock still.

"The Lady in Blue! Are you certain?"

"Yes, of course. Why do you ask?"

"That's your Providence right there, Father!" Tejada said as he broke out laughing. "Marvelous, isn't it?"

"I'm happy to hear you are familiar with the subject."

"And how could I not be?" the giant said in booming voice, with a theatrical flourish. "How could I not be, if I am the man responsible for the process of her beatification?"

What Amadeo Tejada told Father Baldi next left him perplexed. Despite the enormous prodigies attributed to her during her lifetime, Mother Ágreda was never declared a saint by the Church in Rome. Something had happened. None of the Popes who opened the case for sainthood lived long enough to see her arrive at the altar. Both Clement XIV and Leo XIII closed their inquiries with "decrees of silence." No other woman in the church had ever received such harsh treatment. In 1987, Tejada was able to have both decrees lifted, and he successfully reopened the investigation of the Lady in Blue. Amadeo Tejada was doubtlessly the most well-versed man in the world when it came to the nun who bilocated to America. And by a caprice of destiny, Baldi had him right in front of him.

"Listen to me well, Father," said the Passionist, who was as astonished as Baldi himself. "Just a few days ago, the police paid me a visit in order to ask me about a manuscript from the seventeenth century belonging to Philip the Fourth. In it, the complete history of the Lady in Blue is recorded for the first time."

Baldi was incredulous.

"It seems," Tejada continued, "the text detailed the method used to bilocate."

Zsidiv had spoken to him about that text. Baldi knew perfectly well that someone had taken it from Madrid, but he didn't let on.

"Why are the police interested in this manuscript?" he asked Tejada.

"Very simple: it must have been stolen from the National Library . . ."

"Incredible. And do you know what else this manuscript contained?"

"Naturally. In 1630, when the Franciscans suspected that perhaps the woman who had been seen in New Mexico could be a nun of their order and not an apparition of the Virgin of Guadalupe, they sent the former father custodian in Santa Fe to Ágreda. They asked him to interrogate her and, if the case merited, to unmask the 'suspect.' His questions extended over a full two weeks, after which, the custodian . . ."

"Benavides?"

"Exactly. The custodian wrote a report where he stated his conclusions."

"Do you know what they were?"

"Only in part. It seems that Benavides came to the conclusion that each instance of the nun successfully being in two places at once (or bilocating, if you prefer) came after listening to hymns that drew her into a profound trance. In fact, I spoke about this subject several times in the past with Matthew's assistant."

"Doctor Albert. I am familiar with him," said Baldi.

"The very person."

"And what did he tell you?" Baldi asked as he tried to put the pieces of the puzzle together. If Tejada had spoken with *il dottore* about the Lady in Blue, why did Ferrell never mention Luigi Corso's special interest in the matter? And why had none of them, not even "Saint John," mentioned the existence of the nun?

Tejada, who had no idea what Baldi was thinking, went on.

"Albert Ferrell took great interest in this 'clue.' And to some degree, that was logical, since your studies on pre-polyphony had already circulated among the Evangelists. The studies in which you concluded that certain frequencies in sacred music could aid in provoking altered states of consciousness that were favorable to bilocation."

"So they took my work seriously. . . ." Baldi smiled.

"Of course! I remember one of the reports you sent to Father Corso, in which you spoke of Aristotle. You said the philosopher made detailed studies of the effect of music upon the will."

"And not only him!" Baldi interjected. "For their part, the Pythagoreans discovered that the Phrygian mode roused their warriors' fury, while the Lydian mode achieved the opposite effect, relaxing the mind of the person listening to it; the Mixolydian mode provoked bouts of melancholy. . . . And they used this on the battlefield, to lift their army's spirits or depress those of their enemy."

"So listen, Father: Luigi Corso's assistant assured me that they had discovered that every thing or situation existing in nature possessed an exclusive vibration, and that if one's mind managed to position itself inside that vibration, it would have access not only to its essence but to its time and place as well."

"This Ferrell said that to you?"

Father Tejada was so excited his eyes had stopped blinking.

"Of course! Don't you understand? The little I knew of Benavides's interrogations of Mother María Jesús was that she explained to him by gestures and in minute detail at what moments she generally entered into a trance and took flight to America. She bilocated listening to the Alleluias during the Mass. And their vibrations catapulted her a distance of more than six thousand miles."

"During the Alleluias? Are you certain of that?" Baldi straightened his glasses.

"And what is so strange about that, Father? Saint Augustine

made it very clear in his writings: Alleluias facilitate the mystical union with God."

"Are you aware, Brother, whether Corso managed to reproduce one of those trances with anyone?"

Baldi was playing with marked cards for the second time during the conversation. He knew that the answer to that questions was yes. But did Tejada know anything else? Something that Albert Ferrell was not aware of, despite working so closely with Corso?

"Now that you mention it, yes," the Passionist replied, choosing his words. "I remember Corso telling me that in the musical compositions for the medieval masses he found acoustic elements that functioned in that way. And he played them for several subjects."

The Benedictine was beaming with expectation, but preferred to make a small detour before posing the most important question.

"Do you know what sounds in particular they employed?" he asked.

"Let me think . . . From the sixteenth century the Introit from the Mass in the key of do. The Kyrie Eleison, or Lord, Have Mercy, and the Gloria in Excelsis Deo, or the latter part of Glory to God in the Highest, in the key of re. And the key of mi that was employed between the readings of the Bible and the Consecration with the Alleluias."

"Of course!" the Venetian interjected. "The traditional Mass embraces a full octave, from the beginning to the end! It is clear that the liturgy was designed, among other things, to provoke mystical states that catapult the most sensitive listeners outside of their body. My thesis exactly!"

"And yet, Father Baldi, why is it that this 'catapulting effect' was only experienced by Mother Ágreda and not by the other nuns in the monastery?"

"Well . . ." Baldi hesitated. "There must be a neurological explanation for that."

The Benedictine rose from his seat and began pacing in small circles. The moment had arrived.

"I was told that Corso utilized these frequencies with other people. Only yesterday, in Rome, Ferrell indicated to me that they played those sounds to a woman they named 'the Great Dreamer.' However, in the middle of the experiments, she decided to leave and return home."

"A woman? Italian?"

"No, a North American. Did he say anything about this to you?"

Tejada stood staring at Baldi while an enormous smile spread across his face. It was a look somewhere between mocking and affectionate, a look that was hiding something. A game, perhaps.

"Now I know the information that destiny intends to put in your hands, Father Baldi."

Tejada's confidence impressed Baldi.

"Today, a friend of mine, the director of the National Library, told me that the police had identified a woman who has been dreaming of the Lady in Blue for some time. She lives in Los Angeles and worked for a short time in Rome, at Vatican Radio. The police are already on their way to her. She is the person you are searching for, isn't that right?"

SIXTY-THREE

LOS ANGELES

"Good Lord!"

Linda Meyers's face reflected her indignation. She had spent the last hour in the FBI interrogation room on the third floor of 1100 Wilshire Boulevard. Two FBI agents, and a third person, a foreigner, were hoping she could help them straighten out the situation they had on their hands.

"I've already told you: I have no clue who robbed this valuable manuscript from the library in Madrid. And I know even less about some friar, whom I asked the director of the National Library about, and who is cited in the document. Why don't you believe me?"

Mike Sheridan's face had disbelief written all over it. He was not about to swallow a single word of her story. Dr. Meyers could see that in his body language. The foreigner, for his part, seemed more willing to listen.

"What could I know about Spanish history?" she said, directing her question at him.

"In fact, it isn't Spanish history but American," said the young man, who seemed more like a university student than a special agent. He spoke with a strong Spanish accent. "The missing document is part of the history of New Mexico."

"Who said I committed the crime? Was it Mister . . . ? "

"Valiente, Enrique Valiente."

"Did Mister Valiente accuse me of stealing the book?"

"No. We are merely investigating one of the case's loose ends:

you." He then added, "By the way, my name is Carlos Albert. I came over from Spain to investigate."

Meyers continued to direct her attention to him.

"Are you here because of my phone call to the library?"

"That's right."

"What we want to know, Doctor Meyers," Sheridan said, reentering the conversation, "is where you got the name of Friar Esteban de Perea."

The beauty of the doctor's African features now concealed a simmering rage, something that intimidated Carlos and the second agent in the room, who stood motionlessly by the door. Carlos watched the scene unfolding in front of him as if it were taking place in a Hollywood film. Police stations in Spain were never so spacious as this federal building, and the agents there were never so impeccably dressed as Sheridan.

"Well, then?" he insisted. "Aren't you going to tell us who spoke to you about this friar?"

"It is a private matter between doctor and patient."

"How can that be a private matter! I am only asking you for a name. A source we can check out," he insisted. "If you don't give it to us, we will have to consider you a suspect in the robbery."

"You are joking, right? I made a single phone call!"

"Look, Doctor," Carlos interjected. "I spoke with Enrique Valiente in Madrid yesterday. And as he recalled the conversation he had with you, he said something that struck my attention."

Dr. Meyers waited for the Spaniard to finish speaking.

"He told me," Carlos went on, "that the information on Friar Esteban de Perea had been given to you by one of your patients, a woman who had remarkable visions of a certain Lady in Blue. Is that true?"

The doctor did not respond.

"Is that true, Doctor Meyers?" Agent Sheridan prodded her.

Carlos looked back at the federal agent. He found it strange that an officer of the law was chewing gum in order to avoid smoking. In Madrid all the cops smoked.

"Couldn't you give us the name and phone number of this patient?" The journalist was insistent, but his tone of voice was much softer.

After a second of silence, Linda Meyers answered their questions just as they had feared.

"I'm sorry. It is a matter of doctor-patient privilege. I cannot give you any personal information on this person. And if you are going to continue to question me, I will have the pleasure of calling my lawyer."

"And if we already had that information?" Carlos looked at her defiantly. "Would you confirm it for us?"

"You have that information?" Dr. Meyers said incredulously. "I never gave that to the director of the library."

The visitor from Spain pulled out his cork-covered notebook, and looked for his last entry. Finding the note, he sat down next to the suspect and with an enigmatic smile said, "Does the name Jennifer Narody mean anything to you?"

The doctor froze.

"How . . . How the devil did you get that name?"

"It had nothing to do with the Devil, Doctor Meyers. An angel gave it to me," he said, laughing.

SIXTY-FOUR

BILBAO, SPAIN

"Watchman to Base, do you copy?"

"I copy you five by five, Watchman."

"The bird has left the nest. Do I let him fly?"

"No. If he gets too far away, clip his wings. The cage will be ready in a few seconds."

"Signing off."

When Giuseppe Baldi left Tejada's office at the university and saw the magnificent spring day all around him, he decided to walk to the center of town. Bilbao had just passed through a week of heavy rains, which left it clean and abounding in the scent of new life.

Everything around him was peaceful. That is, except for a Ford Transit with Barcelona plates and tinted windows, whose engine revved up as soon as the Third Evangelist appeared in the doorway of the university building.

"The bird is ready to fly."

A man with rippling muscles sat at the wheel of the van, lighting a cigarette as he followed Father Baldi with his eyes.

"When he enters the crosswalk, grab him. Did you read me, Watchman?"

There was a burst of static at the end of their conversation. The man with the cigarette threw the walkie-talkie on the seat, adjusted his sunglasses, and moved the vehicle closer to the Benedictine. Baldi was strolling with an air of confidence.

"Now?"

Watchman's voice thundered over the walkie-talkie as he demanded instructions.

"Go ahead."

That was all he needed.

"Watchman" was ruggedly built, from the Piedmont region of northern Italy. He stashed the walkie-talkie in the pocket of his bomber jacket and walked briskly toward his objective. In a few seconds he was there, coming to a stop at the red light. He made certain that no one else was in the immediate vicinity of the evangelist. A perfect opportunity. And so, standing shoulder to shoulder with the priest, the Watchman took the liberty of addressing the stranger in perfect Italian.

"A beautiful day, isn't it?"

Baldi was surprised. He nodded his head, smiling indifferently, while he tried to ignore the stranger, whose eyes were fixed on the other side of the street. It was the last thing he did before the man with the shaved head, impeccably dressed in Armani, pulled out a short pistol equipped with a silencer from his jacket and stuck it in Baldi's ribs.

"If you move, I'll fire right here," he whispered.

The evangelist was outraged. He hadn't even seen the pistol, but he could visualize the barrel of the gun pressing against his guts. He had never had a gun pointed at him and found himself paralyzed by a cold, irrational terror.

"You are . . . You are mistaken," he whispered in an awkward Spanish. "I have no money."

"I don't want your money, Father."

"But . . . But if I have no—"

"You are Father Giuseppe Baldi, aren't you?"

"Yes," the Third Evangelist stammered.

"Then there's no mistake to talk about."

Even before Watchman had finished speaking, the van had pulled up to the traffic light. One hard shove and the priest fell forward into the van. Then two strong arms dragged him all the way in and pushed him to the back of the vehicle.

"And now I hope you behave yourself. We don't want to hurt you."

"Who are you? What do you want with me?"

Baldi babbled the two phrases in Italian. His pulse was racing, and his forearms were slightly bruised. He was beginning to understand that he had been taken hostage.

"Someone wants to see you."

The man who had stuck the pistol in his gut was now sitting next to the driver and staring at the priest through the rearview mirror.

"Don't try anything stupid, Father. We have several hours to go before we arrive at our destination."

"Several hours? Where are we going?"

"To a place where we can talk, my dear Saint Luke."

Baldi feared for his life.

Those men had not taken him hostage by mistake: they knew who he was. And what was worse: in order to know where he was, they must have followed him from Rome. The question was why.

One poke in the arm, and he lost consciousness. They had injected him with ten milligrams of Valium, the dosage indicated to keep someone asleep for the next five hours.

With darkness falling, the Ford Transit had already left the highway around Bilbao, turning onto Route A-68 in the direction of Burgos, and from there onto Route 1 heading to Santo Tomé del Puerto, climbing into the mountains toward Somosierra. There they picked up Route 110, which took them to Segovia, where the kidnappers purchased gas at a service station next to the Roman aqueduct and then continued on the secondary road to Zamarramala, turning off before they arrived.

The clock on the dashboard read seven minutes past ten when the car pulled up next to a stone cross, a mere twenty feet away from one of Spain's most unusual medieval churches. The driver cut the engine. Two long strokes of light from the car's high beams advised the building's occupants that the guest for whom they had been waiting had just arrived.

SIXTY-FIVE

VENICE BEACH

Jennifer Narody answered the door on the third ring. She had a hard time imagining who could be looking for her so insistently at seven o'clock on a Sunday morning. She threw on her white silk robe, smoothed back her hair, and hurriedly threaded her way across her disorganized living room. Glancing through her front door peephole, she saw a thin young man, some thirty years old, wearing wire-rimmed glasses and standing impatiently on the other side of the door. She had never seen him before.

"Miss Narody?" Her visitor formulated his question the second he could feel her eyes watching him.

"Yes. What do you want?"

"I'm not sure how to explain . . ." Upon hearing the annoyance in her voice, he hesitated for a second. "My name is Carlos Albert, and I am working with the FBI on an investigation in which you could possibly be of some assistance."

"The FBI?"

"I know it sounds absurd, but does the name 'The Lady in Blue' mean anything to you?"

Jennifer did not move.

"What did you just say?"

"I came here to ask you about the Lady in Blue, Miss Narody. And about something that has come into your possession, and which I believe you ought to put in my hands."

Carlos had decided to play all his cards, including whatever tricks the angel in the red shoes might have provided him with. He had actually gotten permission from the FBI officers to let him interview Jennifer alone. That took some doing, but he had finally convinced them that it would be in their interest for him to do so. It would be far less obvious in her eyes, and less threatening, for a foreign journalist to be seeking any relevant information to recover a manuscript actually stolen in Madrid than for the FBI to be grilling her.

Jennifer looked at him suspiciously.

"Who gave you my address? It's not in the phone book," she added.

"Look, Miss Narody, I need to talk to you about something important. I came here all the way from Spain for one reason only: to see this manuscript. Your psychiatrist called the National Library a few days ago asking about the Lady in Blue, which is what led me to you. May I come in?"

Jennifer opened the door.

The woman who let him enter her house was an unconventional beauty. Despite the fact that she had just gotten out of bed and had circles under her eyes, she was someone who radiated harmony. She had dark features, with a tan that lent her a bronze cast; she had a fine figure and a friendly face, with thick lips and prominent cheekbones. Her living room was full of souvenirs from Italy—a shiny, metallic Leaning Tower of Pisa paperweight; a collection of albums by Italian singers scattered on the floor in front of the stereo; and a huge aerial photo of the Coliseum covering the largest wall in the room. The various objects brought back memories for Carlos.

"Are you familiar with Italy, Ms. Narody?"

Jennifer smiled for the first time. Her visitor was examining a tiny bronze Venetian gondola that was sitting on top of the television.

"Absolutely. I lived in Rome for a time."

"Really?"

"It's a marvelous city. Do you know it?"

Carlos nodded. For the next few minutes they exchanged impressions regarding the warmth of character of the Italians, the ease with which any tourist can adjust to the chaos of the Roman traffic and the hurried pace of life there, and how much one could miss the food. The coincidence—yes, once again—of their knowing the same little restaurant near the Pantheon, called La Sagrestia, where they prepared the best pasta dishes in the city ("exclusively for Romans," they joked). It turned out that this simple point of contact was enough to settle their conversation into a much more relaxed vein. Soon Jennifer had more or less forgotten Carlos's reference to the FBI's interest in the Lady in Blue. She invited him to have a seat.

"So," she said, "would you care for some refreshment? A glass of water? A soda?"

Carlos shook his head. He was already contemplating how best to begin the battery of questions he had prepared for her, when Jennifer suddenly took charge of the conversation.

"Actually, while I have you here, perhaps you can help me to clear up a mystery."

"What kind of mystery?" He turned to face her from the sofa.

"You're Spanish, aren't you?"

"That's right."

"Well, look: yesterday I received an envelope containing a very old manuscript written in your native tongue. I thought you could help me to translate it."

His heart skipped a beat.

"A manuscript?"

"That's right." Jennifer lit a cigarette before she began to look for the envelope. "It should be around here somewhere. I thought about showing it to Doctor Meyers tomorrow, since she speaks some Spanish. But you're a native and will understand it even better. You've fallen out of the sky!"

Carlos smiled to himself. "You could, in fact, say that." When she walked over to him with a handful of old manuscript pages tied together by a thick piece of twine, the journalist knew right away that this was it. Saints in heaven! He had covered more than six thousand miles just to hold those pages in his hands. The angel in the red shoes was right: the woman sitting next to him held the secret in her hands without knowing it.

"Incredible!" He whistled. "Do you have any idea what this is?"

"Obviously not, which is why I'm asking you."

The awestruck journalist took the bundle in his hands. It required some effort at first to get used to the baroque script, full of arabesques, but soon he was reading effortlessly: "Memorial Dedicated to His Holiness Pope Urban the Eighth, Relating the Conversions in New Mexico That Transpired During the Most Felicitous Period of His Administration and Pontificate, and Presented to His Holiness by Father Friar Alonso de Benavides of the Order of Our Father Saint Francis, Guardian of Said Conversions, the 12th of February 1634." Attached to the document on a thin strip of onion paper was a more recent inscription in red ink: "Mss. Res. 5062."

"This document," Carlos said when he had finished, "was removed from the steel-lined vault at the National Library in Madrid a few days ago. It is because of this document that I am working with the FBI, to recover it and return it to where it belongs."

Jennifer Narody tried to contain her surprise.

"I didn't steal it!" she said in her defense. "If I had, would I have shown it to you so quickly?"

Carlos shrugged his shoulders.

"All well and good. The only thing I know is that, given that the body of evidence is right here in your house, it is going to be difficult to justify the possession of a rare book stolen from a library in Madrid."

"A stolen item? But—"

"The Criminal Activities Division of the Spanish Police and the Anti-Sect Squad notified Interpol when they became afraid that this text"—and here he slapped the manuscript with his palm—"had been taken illegally from my country. And here it is in plain sight, so they knew what they were talking about."

Jennifer became alarmed.

"And why is an Anti-Sect Squad investigating such an old document?"

"They suspected a group of fanatics were involved. Sometimes this type of group takes an interest in a book or a work of art for the strangest reasons. In fact, the person who entered the library took only this document, and whoever it was could have taken many other, much more valuable works."

"Hold on a minute!" she cut in. "I deserve an explanation, Mister . . ."

". . . Albert. Carlos Albert."

"Mister Albert: you asked me about the Lady in Blue. What does she have to do with this book?"

"Everything!" Carlos smiled. "This document explains what happened to the Lady in Blue, and how Sister María Jesús de Ágreda was able to be in two places at once, appearing as far away as New Mexico, at the beginning of the seventeenth century."

"Sister María Jesús de Ágreda!"

Jennifer did not pronounce the woman's difficult name as well as the Spaniard sitting across from her, but she instantly knew who the woman was.

"You know about her?"

"Of course! Her, and Friar Alonso de Benavides, and Philip the Fourth . . . I have watched them. I've spent days watching them."

"Watching them?"

Jennifer understood her visitor's perplexity.

"Mister Albert," she said, "although it may be difficult for you to believe, the knowledge that I have of Benavides and of what transpired in New Mexico has come to me through my dreams."

"At this point, Miss Narody, nothing is too difficult for me to believe," Carlos replied.

"I swear to you, I never heard of Benavides before this, nor did I ever read a book that mentioned him. I had no interest in the history of my country, nor that of the Native Americans. But I believe that my genes predisposed me to it. My psychiatrist believes it is a 'genetic memory.' "

"Right. But she has no idea why you have those dreams. She didn't want to talk to me about it, and I had the sense that she was pretty lost."

"Well . . . There are a few things I never told her. Mostly having to do with how those dreams related to my last job."

"Where did you work?"

Jennifer frowned.

"What makes you think I'll tell you what I wouldn't tell Doctor Meyers?"

"Perhaps if I explain how I arrived here, what I lived through before I met her, that will encourage you to tell me. Do you believe in random occurrences?"

That morning, while Jennifer prepared two cups of coffee and toast with blueberry jam, her visitor told her everything: from the snowstorm that led him to Ágreda to the powerful impression he had when looking at Sister María Jesús's face inside a glass display case where her body was miraculously preserved at the monastery that she herself had founded. When he told Jennifer how a tiny medal with Veronica's image of the "Holy Face" had led him onto a road rich with surprises, and then how that chain had been returned to its legitimate owner on the plane that carried him to Los Angeles, Jennifer was struck by something. A small detail which, in that context, could not be mere chance: while she was in Rome, she had seen a similar medal.

It was when she was in the "dream chamber" at Vatican Radio. Her first day on the job there, after being transferred from Fort Meade by an agent of INSCOM working out of Rome, she remembered having seen the chain, during her inaugural session, hanging around the neck of her instructor, Albert Ferrell. And it was—it had to be—identical to the one the Spaniard had held in his hands.

"Do you know something?" she said at last. "I don't believe in random occurrences either."

Carlos was beaming. He knew that, once again, something—or someone—had made the road ahead smoother. Jennifer Narody, comfortably situated on her favorite sofa, recounted the last part of a history in which both of them, in some extraordinary manner, had already played a part.

"Until a short time ago I held the rank of lieutenant in the United States Army. I worked in the Intelligence Division," she said. "My work was associated with the area known as 'psychic espionage,' which was limited to people with specific extrasensory abilities. As you can imagine, our activities were highly secret."

Carlos nodded.

"During the last two years I worked out of Rome to participate in a project whose goal was to explore the borderline powers of the human mind. Psychic abilities, such as the transmission of thought or remote vision by means of people trained in clairvoyance. Do you know what I'm talking about?"

"Perfectly."

Carlos was still astonished. He had heard about this type of project on various occasions. He had even read in *Mysteries* about a certain "Psychic War" between the old Soviet Union and the United States. But he never thought he would meet someone involved in such a program.

"During the Reagan administration," Jennifer went on, "my team attempted to emulate the achievements of the Russians, who were able to spy on far-flung military installations with the help of persons with psychic abilities. They formed an army of astral travelers who could fly toward their objectives. But, unfortunately, the greater part of these experiments failed. Simply put, they could not control the experiments at will. Our commanding officer was discharged."

"And when did you enter the scene?"

"In the mideighties. The psychic espionage project was never completely shut down because, after the fall of the Berlin Wall, we knew that the Russians would continue their experiments. They secretly continued working with those borderline powers. What is more, the Russians had sold some of their psychic discoveries to other governments."

"I see."

"To top it all off, we had a limited budget, so that the institute where I worked, INSCOM, decided to go into business with a discreet ally who was interested in the same subjects."

"An ally?"

"Yes, the Vatican."

Carlos shook his head.

"Don't be surprised. The Vatican has been investigating questions for centuries that we've only taken an interest in during the last few decades. Consider, for example, that they were the ones who coined the term 'bilocation' to refer to astral voyages. Church records are full of such cases. The Curia was interested to know the psychic mechanisms that provoked such out-of-body experiences, and we came to an acceptable agreement: they'd provide the historical documentation, and we'd provide the technology that would allow them to reproduce such states."

"What kind of technology?"

Jennifer paused for a moment to finish her last piece of toast. She felt as though she was being liberated from a great weight, as if this conversation were the therapy she had needed ever since she left Italy. Carlos continued to watch her closely, observing her every gesture.

"The institute I worked for," she continued, "sent one of our men to Rome, to Vatican Radio. He was a sound engineer who had worked in Virginia. Before my arrival he was already aware of the fact that certain types of sacred music aided the psychic doubling of the body. He definitely wore one of the medals that you were talking about."

"And only by means of music could they . . ."

"Music wasn't the important thing. The crucial element was the vibratory frequency of a particular sound. That was what provoked the brain to act in a determined manner, making intense psychic experiences possible."

"And you? Why did you go to Italy?"

"They sent me to Rome to work with the leader of a weird group that called him the 'First Evangelist.' "

"The 'First Evangelist'?"

"It was of course a code name. Once I had settled into work, in a room identical to the one we had at Fort Meade, they used me like a guinea pig. The evangelist was attempting to project me to another era in time with the new sounds that they had synthesized."

"To the past?"

"Yes, but nothing came of it. I submitted to fifty-minute sessions in which they exposed me to nerve-racking sounds. If nothing positive happened in the lab, at night it would be even worse: I would have nightmares full of geometric figures dancing in my head until I grew dizzy. Colors and voices overwhelmed me and I was having a hard time sleeping. I was losing weight from the trauma. I was like a television station with a defective antenna: I couldn't pick up a good signal."

"And they didn't tell you why they wanted to send you to the past?"

"They did. I didn't understand it at the time, but now it makes sense."

"What do you mean?"

"They wanted to decipher the contents of a lost document containing instructions for the physical projection of persons through sound."

"Physical projections? In flesh and blood?"

Jennifer's eyes confirmed the importance of that detail.

"It seems a woman pulled it off in the seventeenth century."

"The Lady in Blue."

"Exactly. But neither the Vatican nor our government could figure out how. And that document evidently contained the keys to doing it. It was written by a Franciscan, for the king of Spain."

"And the document," Carlos said in a whisper, "is right here."

"Yes. It's incredible, isn't it?"

"Did you dream of it?"

"Yes, I dreamed of the man writing it. I suppose that in Los Angeles, far from the laboratories, my brain tried to 'adjust the signal' on its own and finally managed to do it once I was outside the fixed deadlines of the experts in Rome."

"And why have they sent you a document you cannot even read?"

"You'd know that better than I. Or the woman in the red shoes you met on the airplane. She sent you here to recover it, didn't she?"

SIXTY-SIX

SEGOVIA, SPAIN

The Sanctuary of Vera Cruz, its silhouette plunged in darkness, stood out against the distant mosaic of Segovia's streetlights. Even the Alcázar, the impregnable fortress that looms over the city, could not detract from the mystery of that rare dodecagonal building. The sanctuary is distinct from all the buildings surrounding it, and different from almost every other European church: no other edifice in the Old World was constructed with a perimeter of twelve walls arranged in exactly the same fashion as that of the Church of the Holy Sepulchre in Jerusalem.

In the utter darkness surrounding the building, only a thin thread of light slipping out from its western door hinted at the presence of anyone inside.

"Let's get a move on, Watchman. We're running late."

A pair of bulky shadows carried the inert body of the evangelist into the church. Feeling their way, they walked past the nearly invisible medieval frescos with their portraits of Knights Templar and Crusaders, and sought out the steep stairway that led to the church's holiest enclosure. It was an edicule, a small room concealed inside the enormous column that was the building's main support. The Sanctuary of Vera Cruz hardly resembles a church: it is, in fact, a martyrium, a chapel designed to evoke the death and resurrection of Christ. And the inner room is the sanctum sanctorum of Vera Cruz.

The two gorillas lay Giuseppe Baldi down on the flagstones, careful to avoid hitting his head against the altar that dominated the room. An eccentric couple stood by, waiting for him: a man in a white tunic and a woman dressed in black, wearing red shoes.

"You're late," the man said.

His reproach bounced off the bare walls and mocked the darkness. The shadow smoking a cigarette offered an excuse.

"The bird took longer than we had counted on."

"Well, you got him. That's all that matters. Now leave us alone."

The van driver bowed as he withdrew. Seconds later, the sound of metal scraping against metal in the back of the church announced the bolting of Vera Cruz's main door. The man wearing the white hood leaned over the prone Baldi and attempted to awaken him.

The Third Evangelist came around slowly.

The first thing he felt was a current running from his head downward. Then his heart sped up and, with the surge of blood to his head, his temples began to pound. Finally, the priest was able to open his eyes. Everything looked fuzzy and indistinct. Everything, that is, except the red shoes he had seen once before, somewhere else.

A second later, Baldi was sitting up.

"Where am I?" he asked shakily.

"In Segovia."

The hooded man's voice was firm, in contrast to his own. Even so, Baldi could detect a certain familiarity of tone.

"Who are you? What do you want from me?" he demanded.

"To hold on to you for a while, Father. Nothing more. Time enough for the plan to be executed without interference."

"What plan?"

"You have already found out too much in too short a time. And should you achieve your goal too soon, you would spoil our mission."

"Your mission? Who the hell are you?"

"Don't get worked up, Father. You know me. And I'm not going to do you any harm."

The man wearing the white tunic pushed back the hood covering his face, revealing the unmistakable face of Albert Ferrell.

"*Dottore Alberto!*" Baldi almost fell over he was so surprised.

"I believe you also had occasion to cross paths in Rome with my companion, isn't that so?" Ferrell said, laughing. He gazed at the beautiful woman who stood next to him.

"In Saint Peter's! That's right!" Giuseppe Baldi blurted out. "You are the woman in the photo, the one who told me to pay attention to the signs. The woman wearing the red shoes!"

Staring at her with a look on his face that suggested he was having a hard time believing what he was seeing, he added, "I know what sort of being you are."

"So much the better," she said in a soft Neapolitan accent. "Then you'll understand what we have done."

"And what is that?" Saint Luke asked. He had calmed down a little and was staring at Ferrell now. "From what I understand, you were sent to Rome by the American government in order to develop the technical aspect of Chronovision. In which capacity you . . ."

"You're confusing two different things, Father. She and I, and the men who brought you here, work together. There are many of us. Hundreds. But we have no bosses in either the Pentagon or the Vatican."

"I don't understand."

"You will shortly," he promised. "We work very closely with a very ancient group that calls itself the Ordo Sanctae Imaginis. The Order of the Sacred Image. We are the legitimate custodians of churches such as this all over Europe, which have guarded important relics of Christ. You are now in our domain. But let me explain that over the course of centuries we have also kept a secret with terrible implications for Christianity. A secret that, had it been revealed in the past, at the wrong moment, would have destroyed the entire Church. Nevertheless, it is now time for it to emerge."

The woman took the initiative.

"You, Father, with your work on Chronovision, were very close to discovering it, which is why we brought you here. So that we could be certain you will not reveal it without our controlling when and how you do so."

"The Order of the Sacred Image?" Baldi's brain, and his pulse, were accelerating by the minute. "You were the ones who placed the explosives in the column supporting Veronica's statue!"

"Come on! Do you think there is any reason for someone of our nature to go around planting bombs?"

"Of your nature?" Baldi still felt traces of the sedative, but he was beginning to understand. His eyes were still blurry as he directed his attention to Ferrell, and asked, "Are you trying to tell me that you two are angels?"

Even he thought the question was odd. Despite his strict theological training and all his preparations to face transcendental reality directly, Baldi resisted the idea that someone as mundane as Albert Ferrell could have so sublime an origin. That was not what he had learned from Father Tejada in Bilbao.

"My name is María Coronel, Father. Thirty years ago I became an angel."

The second part of her statement slipped right past the Benedictine. He preferred to go on the attack.

"And you placed the bombs in Saint Peter's."

"No, Father," she replied, without losing her cool. "The bombs were the work of our enemies, persons inside the Church who desired to strike a blow at our most sacred symbol, with the sole intention of leading us into a trap, and capturing us."

"They wanted to capture you?"

"There's something I should tell you, Father: Veronica herself holds the key to this matter. Are you familiar with this medal?"

From one of the pockets in her dress María removed a necklace, whose pendant bore the face of Jesus engraved on a cloth. Veronica's veil. A representation of a relic whose name, The Veronica, is in itself a cryptogram, for Veronica was not originally a woman's name, but derives from the Latin *vera icon*, or true image. Baldi gave it his full attention.

"You have studied history," María Coronel continued. "You know that the pillar of Saint Veronica was built by orders of the Pope in order to shelter the relic of the Holy Face. The other three pillars supporting the dome of Saint Peter's contain Saint Andrew's skull, a piece of the Holy Cross, and the lance that pierced Our Savior's side. All of them false relics. And yet the Holy Face is indeed the portrait of Christ, mysteriously imprinted on a piece of cloth."

"Everyone knows that story."

"The Templars who built this church," Ferrell interjected, "were in on the secret and protected it as well."

"What secret?"

"That is what I wanted to explain to you, Father." María's beauty was radiant, and perhaps that was why Baldi felt short of breath. "Clement the Seventh, in the sixteenth century, was the first to realize that the Veronica was imprinted in the same miraculous manner as the cloak worn by the Indian Juan Diego in Mexico in 1531. At that time no one knew anything about light waves, and they decided to call the two relics *αχειροποίητος* (acheiropoiétos), a Greek term that refers to images not made by human hand."

"You mean that you are protecting the secret of how these images are formed?"

"Let me finish," María said calmly. "The Holy Shroud of Turin, the 'Holy Face,' and the Cloak of Guadalupe all have the same source. They were created by the radiation waves emitted by a very particular class of 'infiltrators,' beings who are half human and half divine. Jesus was one of them. Those of us who belong to this lineage continue to journey over the face of the earth. The energy invested in those objects, which we ourselves emit, is the same energy that altered the photograph you recovered this morning in the Swiss Guard's office."

"How do you know that . . ."

"The walls have ears, Father."

"And what does this have to do with me?"

"Quite a lot."

"So who planned the attack against the pedestal of Saint Veronica?" the Third Evangelist asked nervously. "And why?"

"Our enemies wanted to force us to make an appearance, the better to take us out of circulation. But they failed."

"And who are they?"

"The same ones you work for, the very ones who are trying to take Chronovision out of your hands. Have you already forgotten why you were called to Rome?" María directed a cold stare in the priest's direction. "Our enemies are yours as well, Father Baldi. The same who for centuries have pursued people like Ferrell and myself, while they attempt to exploit our energy."

The Benedictine did not respond.

María Coronel then began to unfold an amazing tale for Giuseppe Baldi. It was the tale of her family and her origins. A fable that retold the very book of Genesis where it was explained how God's angels slept with the daughters of men, who then gave birth to creatures with dual natures, children half-human and half-divine. Humanity, as she explained it to him, was born from this mixture, and since then, little by little, certain families engendered creatures with extraordinary powers, closer to angels than to their biological mothers. Many of them discovered only later that the energy they radiated was capable of changing life around them; that they emitted a certain type of energy powerful enough to kill, an invisible force that was at the same time capable of transforming them into pure energy and which led them to undergo experiences as prodigious as bilocation, the gift of predicting the future, or even the ability to enter the psyche of normal humans and alter it.

"My family, Father," María clarified, "belongs to one of those. Sister María Jesús de Ágreda was in fact named María Coronel, the same name as mine. That was what society called her before she changed her name upon taking religious vows. She died consumed by her own energy. And there were others like her: in the fourteenth century, yet another woman named María Coronel suffered the same raptures. Her body has remained uncorrupted in the Royal Convent of San Inés in Seville, after she was hounded to death by the Castilian king Peter the Cruel."

"You said that persons like yourself are pursued . . ."

"Yes. The Church of Rome very quickly discovered our caste's potential, and they decided to exploit it to their own advantage."

"How?"

"Take, for example, the case of Sister María Luisa de la Ascensión, better known as the 'Nun of Carrión,' who experienced bilocations to many different parts of the world. She, too, was the daughter of angels. She went to Assisi to visit the tomb of Saint Francis; to Madrid to be present at the death of Philip the Third; in Japan she comforted the Franciscan martyr Friar Juan de Santamaría in battles against the pagans; she visited the Spanish ships returning from America, when they feared assault from the British pirates; and she was even seen spreading the Gospel in the midst of more than one tribe in the western lands of New Mexico. All of that without ever leaving the province of Palencia."

"And how could anyone exploit a gift such as this, María?"

"By chance, during a number of her 'leaps,' Sister María Luisa was mistaken for an apparition of Our Lady. When the Holy Office discovered the effect she had on the pagan population, they instructed her so that she might pass for the Virgin. Her work was of great assistance in establishing the Catholic religion in many parts of the new territories."

"Impossible!" Baldi objected, each time with less conviction.

"No, Father. It is possible. And this is where you come into the game."

It was Albert Ferrell's turn to speak.

"There were persons like ourselves who, over time, learned to master the ability to be in two places at once. They discovered that bilocation was associated with certain classes of musical vibration, and they decided to prevent the Church from being able to control the secret. So we devised a plan: by letting this secret knowledge circulate freely, we would prevent Rome from using us for its ends. We would put an end to its persecution and its centuries-old fraud."

"And did you get that far?"

Ferrell chose not to respond.

"Our first move was to place this technique in Robert Monroe's hands. He is the sound engineer I spoke to you about in Rome. He possessed a certain natural propensity for astral voyages and for 'channeling,' so we decided to help him. We thought that if Monroe developed the technique of astral voyages, which is one of our 'angelic' skills, perhaps he would come to the conclusion that humanity had been tricked over the course of centuries by false apparitions, and he would release us from this servitude."

"Why did you choose him and not someone else?"

"The right temporal lobe in his brain was very sensitive. That lobe is the 'antenna' of our brain, and his was extremely receptive. It was easy for us to enter his dreams and lead him where we wanted him to go. We were looking for a man of the twentieth century who could systematize what Friar Alonso de Benavides, three centuries before, had scribbled in the margins of the *Memorial* that we stole from the National Library."

"And why did you steal that book?"

María Coronel walked over to Father Baldi and gave him a piercing glance.

"We offered to buy it, but we were turned down. So we decided to take it on loan. They never let anyone study the manuscript; for all intents and purposes it was being held hostage. What we needed was someone—not one of us—who could discover it and make its contents known. And yet the Church, through one of its many tentacles, always prevented its contents from coming to light. Luckily, they never managed to have the book sent to Rome."

"I still don't understand what you were trying to do," Baldi said. He was short of breath. "Why did you want to go public with what was in the book?"

"Actually," Ferrell continued, "we stole the book so that what was in it could be revealed, along with the existence of Chronovision, and INSCOM's attempts to create a division of 'astral spies.' What we were trying to do was to have one person pull the whole story together and then explain that the Virgin never visited New Mexico. That what the Indians saw were nuns, of an angelic nature, members of our species, using precise techniques. That they were the ones who really appeared, and that everything else was part of a conspiracy to maintain a primitive faith based on manipulation."

"What person could do this?"

"First we tried to convince Luigi Corso. In addition to being Saint Matthew on your project, and being well versed in the technical advances in sound as applied to bilocations, he was a writer."

"But he refused," María clarified.

"And so you killed him."

"Not so, Father," María responded testily. "I was with Corso before he died. I spent several hours trying to convince him, without success. Distraught, he decided that very morning to shelve the Chronovision project. He let me copy his archives and, extremely agitated, he reformatted his hard drive while I stood there watching."

"And then?"

"And then I left him there alone, making up his mind whether he was going to work with us or continue to serve the enormous lie to which he had consecrated his life. And he decided to end his life."

Baldi looked away, grief-stricken.

"How can I be certain you didn't kill him?"

"At least, we had no desire to do so," Ferrell interjected.

"And what does that mean?"

"You have perhaps already noticed that our presence can change a person's normal cardiac rhythm, yes?"

Baldi was shaken, and surprised. It was true: his heart was still pounding against his chest. And if he gave it a little thought, the same thing had occurred the last time he had met Ferrell.

"Well, then," Ferrell went on, "the autopsy revealed that Corso suffered from a moderate cardiac irregularity. Let me put it another way. Perhaps, after being around María for too long, Corso's irregular heartbeat turned into a heart attack, which caused severe pain. And when the pain led him to his window to call out for help, he fell out, having already died."

Baldi's face was a picture of horror.

"That," he stammered, "is that merely a hypothesis?"

"No, it's a certainty. Corso's heart was no longer beating when he fell to the ground from his apartment at the Santa Gemma. The final autopsy stated that fact; I simply forgot to mention it." He smiled.

"And so, tell me," Baldi said as he got control of himself, "have you already chosen a substitute to replace Corso?"

"We have. At this moment," María said, looking at her watch, "he is a little over six thousand miles from here, and he is just about to discover his mission."

SIXTY-SEVEN

VENICE BEACH

Carlos took more than two hours to read the version of the manuscript Benavides wrote for the king. He devoured not only the principal text—not so very different from the *Memorial* printed in 1630 for Philip IV—but also the notes in the margin, the ones specifying the sacred melodies that encouraged "mystical flight," as well as the interventions certain angels carried out in María Jesús's brain, which enabled her to converse with them.

The journalist was aware that the world's mystical literature abounded in these types of stories. In fact, María Jesús de Ágreda was not the only religious figure of that era who interacted with angels of flesh and blood. Saint Teresa of Ávila, the greatest mystic of Spain's Golden Age, also suffered from these "interventions." "In his hands I saw an enormous golden spear, and on its iron tip there seemed to be a point of fire," she wrote. "I felt as if he plunged this into my heart several times, and that it penetrated to my entrails. When he drew it out, he seemed to draw them out with it, and left me aflame with a great love of God."

Benavides's *Memorial* included another sort of commentary as well. There existed—the text confirmed it—a formula based on acoustic vibrations that made bilocation possible. A formula given to Christianity by a class of "infiltrators" who had descended to earth during the Dark Ages. The text further stated that the Holy Office of the Inquisition had identified the whereabouts of their descendants, and had wrested the formula from them.

"Jennifer . . . ," Carlos said in a whisper after a long period of silence.

"Yes?"

"You saw the Lady in Blue in your dreams, didn't you?"

"Yes."

"What did she look like?"

"Well . . . I saw her descend from heaven in the middle of a cone of light. She was glowing so brightly it was very hard to see her clearly . . . although I'd bet that she was the same woman I dreamed of later on. The one they called María Jesús de Ágreda."

"It was always the same woman?"

"I believe so."

"And she was always alone when you saw her?"

"Yes, why do you ask?"

"Because according to this document," Carlos said, holding the pages in his hand, "there were a number of different ladies in blue who flew to America during this time period. It says that at least three nuns were sent to spread the Gospel in the same area. And that they were all later identified by the natives as the Virgin. Do you know anything about that?"

"No, no one in the project told me about any other ladies in blue."

Carlos stared at Jennifer, who was anxiously waiting for him to finish translating the text.

"You have absolutely avoided telling me the name given to the Vatican and INSCOM's joint project."

"I haven't told you, no. I have no idea if it's important, or whether it's a state secret. It's all the same. Do you know what I mean?"

Jennifer leaned closer to him on the sofa and whispered something that left him unable to move.

"It was called Chronovision. Have you ever heard of it before?"

The journalist avoided Jennifer's gaze.

"Yes . . . some time ago."

Jennifer let the subject drop.

Carlos by then had unequivocally embraced a faith in synchronicity. A pattern of events minutely designed by the Programmer. And it was no longer important whether one day he hunted down the Programmer or not; now Carlos knew that he was real.

And that was more than enough.

SIXTY-EIGHT

ROME

Five sleek black Fiats, small curtains drawn across the windows in the rear seats, passed through the entrance to the one building that stands apart from the others on the Piazza del Sant'Uffizio: number 11, a short distance from the esplanade leading from Saint Peter's Square to the basilica. Their joint entrance was not a good sign. The Prefect of the Council for the Laity, the Cardinal in charge of the Holy Congregation for the Causes of the Saints, the director general of the Institute for External Affairs (IEA), the Pope's personal secretary, and the Prefect of the Holy Congregation for the Doctrine of the Faith had all been ordered to attend the meeting on the highest authority. Their gathering was to be held in the master salon belonging to the latter organization, in the Holy Office, at 9:30 PM sharp.

The five men climbed to the third floor, escorted by their secretaries. As they took their seats, three Benedictines served them tea and cookies on small plates embossed with Saint Peter's keys in low relief, while various functionaries of the Holy Office handed them thick files documenting the matters under debate.

The Prefect of the Sant'Uffizio, a man with the reputation for having few friends, waited while his guests settled in. He then announced the beginning of the session with a formal gesture in keeping with his character: he rang his little bronze bell.

"Your Eminences, Holy Mother the Church has been torpedoed from within, and it is the desire of His Holiness that we alleviate the effects of the attack before it is too late."

The Cardinals looked at one another with expressions of surprise. None of them had heard so much as a word about sabotage, conspiracies, or intrigues inside the Vatican for months. On the contrary, in the aftermath of the attack that the Pope had suffered at the hands of a fanatical Turk in Saint Peter's Square, a certain calm had descended on Rome. Only Monsignor Ricardo Torres, head of the Congregation for the Causes of the Saints, raised his voice above the others and demanded an explanation.

Joseph Cormack, Prefect of the Holy Office, was of slender build. Infamous by reason of his unbending nature, he had enjoyed great stature ever since 1979, when the Pope had put him in charge of neutralizing liberation theology. He waited for the whispering to taper off and observed the Cardinals with the demeanor of someone about to deliver news of an irreparable disgrace.

"We have yet to receive any news of Father Giuseppe Baldi, who was taken hostage this week in Spain."

He paused. The prelates began whispering among themselves again.

"His disappearance has not only left the Chronovision project up in the air, it has also forced our secret services to investigate, taking the lid off a great deal of information I believe you must come to grips with immediately."

Cormack glanced around the room, and called for silence.

"In the folders that you have just received," he went on, "you will find documents that I ask you to examine carefully. They have been reproduced for the first and only time for this meeting. They were being kept in the sealed chamber of the Vatican's secret archives, and I trust that you will watch over them with utmost caution."

The file folders to which Monsignor Cormack referred, whose plastic covers bore the Vatican's white-and-yellow flag, were opened with great curiosity by everyone present.

"Pay careful attention, please, to the first document," their host continued. "There you will see a chronological table enumerating a number of the Virgin's earliest apparitions. If you study it closely, you will see that before the eleventh century, the only documented apparition is the visit Our Lady made to the Apostle James the Greater on the banks of the Ebro in Spain, in the year forty AD."

"Your Eminence . . ."

Monsignor Sebastian Balducci, Prefect of the Council for the Laity and the oldest cardinal in attendance at the meeting, rose to his feet, waving the files in a threatening manner.

"I hope that you haven't called for an urgent meeting merely to discuss old apparitions of the Virgin."

"Sit down, Your Eminence!" Cormack protested, his eyes flashing red. "You all know of His Holiness's great regard for devotion to the Mother of God, and how much energy he has expended in its consolidation."

No one said a word.

"Well, then, someone wishes to reveal the methods we have used in promoting this cult, and to bring dishonor upon our institution."

"The situation is disconcerting, Your Eminences," said Stanislaw Zsidiv, the Pope's secretary and the last man to see Baldi in Rome, as he regarded everyone present with a fixed stare. "Somehow the technique we have used to provoke particular apparitions of Our Lady has filtered out beyond the walls of the Vatican."

"Methods? Techniques? Is it permissible to know what you are talking about?" The elderly Balducci once again rose to speak, and he was even more noticeably irritated than before.

"Monsignor Balducci, you are the only one in this room who is ignorant of the object of tonight's discussion," Cormack said, interrupting Balducci a second time. "Even so, you are going to play a fundamental role in trying to control the storm that is breaking over our heads."

"What storm? Speak so that someone can understand you, please."

"If you look at the chronology again, I will explain something to you, something our institution has kept secret for many centuries."

Despite his thirty years in Rome, Joseph Cormack had never successfully refined his manners, which were those of a priest from an embattled Catholic neighborhood. He waited patiently for Balducci to finish studying the docket of papers at the top of the pile.

"What you are reading, Father, is the history of the Virgin's first appearance. To put it briefly: it is believed that Mary, preoccupied by the meager advances of the Gospel in what was then Hispania, revealed herself body and soul to James the Greater on the banks of the Ebro, in the city of Caesar Augustus."

"This is the legend that gave rise to the construction of the Basilica of Pilar, in Zaragoza," stated Monsignor Torres, the only Spaniard at the meeting and a declared devotee of Our Lady of Pilar.

"The fact of the matter is, Your Eminences, that this 'visit' took place during the life of the Virgin, before her assumption to Heaven. In addition, it served to establish a physical memory of her visitation in Zaragoza: a stone column that is venerated to this day."

Balducci looked at Cormack out of the corner of his eye and muttered something.

"Tall tales!" he said defiantly. "The Apostle James never visited Spain. It's nothing more than a medieval myth."

"Perhaps James was not in Spain, Father, but the Virgin was. In fact, there was great discussion of that prodigy in the first years of our institution, and it was concluded that this was a miracle of bilocation. By the grace of God, Our Lady appeared on the banks of the Ebro, bringing with her a stone from the Holy Land, which remains there to this day."

"And so?"

Cormack was undeterred.

"If you continue down the list, the historical apparitions that follow date from the eleventh century. A thousand years later!"

Monsignor Balducci was unimpressed. He regarded that enumeration of names, dates, and places incredulously, oblivious to where the Prefect was headed.

"After the year 1000, fresh visions of the Virgin spread like an epidemic throughout Europe. No one knew what was happening, the Church even less so, until Pope Innocent the Third headed a thorough investigation, which uncovered something surprising. Something which, given its historic consequences, he decided to keep secret."

"Go on, Father Cormack."

"Very well," he said, taking a deep breath. "Maybe you don't remember, but Europe was close to collapse in the year 999. Everybody, including the Pope, thought the world would end on December 31, but nothing happened. As a result, churchgoers redoubled their faith in salvation, and the monastic orders saw recruitment grow to levels unthinkable in the past. Many of these new divinity students and religious people suddenly found themselves encouraged to explore their supernatural abilities, and mystics began to proliferate everywhere, generally women, who suffered intense ecstasies in which they radiated light, levitated, or underwent severe epileptic attacks. Pope Innocent's commission established a clear parallel between the apparitions of the Virgin and the mystical phenomena lived by numerous monks and nuns."

"And why was all that hidden?"

The men at the meeting smiled at Balducci's naïveté.

"Man of God! The uncertainty stirred up between bilocated nuns and the Virgin was not prejudicial to us. The growing medieval faith in Our Lady had the effect of burying many of the religions in existence before Christianity, especially the pagan goddesses, and it justified the construction of cathedrals and monasteries all across Europe. Where the faith was endangered, a Marian shrine was 'invented.' Nevertheless, it wasn't until sometime later that the phenomenon of certain female mystics who could be in two places at once was brought under control, and appearances of the Virgin were created at will. We began to place the female mystics under ironclad control."

"At will?" Balducci still did not believe what he was hearing. "What are you trying to say? That the Church made the Virgin appear when it wanted to?"

"Yes, Your Eminence. The church discovered that when these women underwent exposure to particular musical frequencies, it would increase the likelihood of an ecstasy that later led to bilocations. It was a dangerous game. The women would rapidly grow old, their mental health deteriorated in a few years time, and they were almost of no help in any new undertakings."

Monsignor Balducci cast a glance at the inventory of names included on the dossier that the secretary of the Holy Office had provided. On it were the names of religious figures, from the eleventh century to the nineteenth, who participated in the program. It was a scandal. Nuns like the Cistercian Aleydis de Schaerbeck, who became widely known around 1250: her cell overflowed with a pulsating light at the same time her body 'appeared' in Toulouse and other parts of southwestern France; the Santa Clara reformer Colette de Corbie, later sainted, who until her death in 1447 was seen on the outskirts of Lyon, inspiring the creation of various shrines to Our Lady of the Light, due to the intensity with which her image was seen in those farms and villages; Sister Catalina de Cristo, in Spain in 1590; Sister Magdalena de San José in Paris a century later; María Magdalena de Pazzi in 1607 in Italy . . . and so on down the list of more than one hundred nuns.

"But this would require an organization that coordinated an enormous number of people," Balducci argued. His astonishment grew with each new name.

"Such an organization existed: it was a small subdivision inside the Holy Office," Giancarlo Orlandi replied amiably. The director of the IEA had been silent up until that moment.

"And it acted with impunity over the course of so many centuries, without being discovered?"

"More or less with impunity, Father." Cormack stepped in to clarify things for Balducci; his voice was tinged with a certain regret. "That was precisely the motivation for this meeting. In fact, in another part of the dossier you will find the details surrounding the one grave indiscretion that the project committed in its eight centuries of existence. It took place in 1631, after the Holy Office had successfully completed a program of long-distance evangelization, projecting a nun from a Spanish monastery to the province of New Mexico.

"The Lady in Blue?"

Balducci's answer took the other men at the meeting by surprise.

"So, you are aware of that case?"

"And who isn't? Even rats in Rome have heard that historical documents relative to this incident have disappeared from libraries and public archives over the course of the last few months."

"That is our subject, Father."

Cormack cocked his head, allowing Monsignor Torres to speak further on the matter.

"The issue of the disappeared documents remains a mystery. They've been stolen from the National Library in Madrid and even from the Secret Archives here at the Vatican. The thieves selected only those texts that highlighted the existence of this program of Marian 'apparitions,' and they have tried to leak them to the public."

"Which means the thieves know everything," Zsidiv said quietly.

"That's not the problem. There's no doubt that a very powerful organization has infiltrated itself among us, and they are seeking our ruin. There exists a fifth column that is trying to pull down the labor of centuries."

"Father! You aren't accusing anyone at this table, are you?" exclaimed Giancarlo Orlandi.

"Don't get carried away. The column of which I speak operates behind the back of Holy Mother the Church. It has at present been able to take possession of a document that all of us considered under control and even forgotten, in which the techniques used to create false apparitions of the Virgin and other prodigies such as the voice of God are explained through the use of acoustical vibrations."

"Good Lord! Can that be possible?"

Balducci looked in horror at Father Cormack.

"It is indeed."

"And what would occur if the deception were uncovered?"

"We would fall into tremendous disrepute. Imagine it: we would appear to be the creators of apparitions by means of 'special effects.' Our followers would feel betrayed and would wander away from the protection of Holy Mother the Church . . ."

"Now I understand why they called me here," Balducci said just above a whisper. "They want me, as Prefect of the Council for the Laity, to convince Christianity of the authenticity of these apparitions. Is that not the case?"

"Not exactly. The damage is irreparable, and the hostile force that stole the documentation has already taken steps to expose the truth, as terrible as it is."

"So then?"

"Your mission will be to let that information out into the world in small doses so that it does not have so traumatic an effect when our enemies make it public, for we seriously fear that the matter is already out of our hands."

"And how will I do it?"

"That's what we must agree upon. But I have several ideas. For example, you can ask someone to write a novel, film a television series, shoot a movie . . . whatever! They could use a version of our propaganda. As is well known, when the truth is disguised as fiction, it for some reason ends up being less credible."

Monsignor Zsidiv stood up from his seat, beaming in triumph.

"I have a proposal. Baldi, before he disappeared, spoke with a journalist to whom he leaked certain details about Chronovision that were later published in Spain."

"We remember that," Cormack cut in.

"Why don't we simply invite this journalist to write the novel you propose? When all is said and done, he already possesses certain elements with which he can begin to weave the story. He could even title it something like *The Lady in Blue* . . .' "

The Prefect of the Holy Office was smiling broadly.

"A good point of departure. You think like an angel," Cormack said to Zsidiv, completely taking him by surprise.

Zsidiv smiled to himself. Indeed, it was the first time in history that an angel had come to occupy such a powerful position in the Vatican, and had even managed to impose his point of view. But neither Cormack nor the others at the meeting knew it. Zsidiv thought about the bitter confusion in which Baldi must have been floundering these past hours during his seclusion in Segovia. He regretted having to trick the man, sending him on a search for documents that he himself had had in his control for a long time, but he couldn't let others in the church take advantage of what he knew. He intended to free Baldi that very night, allowing him to return to his post in Venice. By this point Baldi would have already learned about Zsidiv's angelic lineage, so the Cardinal would now propose that the Venetian join their cause, putting his technical knowledge in the service of the truth.

As regards Carlos Albert, it gave Zsidiv pleasure to consider the many synchronicities that were going to assault him in the future. He was certain the journalist, who had caught the attention of the Ordo Sanctae Imaginis one day by asking uncomfortable questions about Chronovision, would return to believing—at least in angels. And something similar would happen to Jennifer Narody. But none of his joys was as great as that of knowing, from this day forward, that no one of his lineage would be used to deceive his fellow men.

"Like an angel, you say?" he whispered to Cormack in a mocking tone. "Make that a rebel angel."

THE END

POST SCRIPTUM

SOME HISTORICAL TIE-INS FOR BUSY READERS

The last word has yet to be written on the Lady in Blue. For three centuries, history textbooks have overlooked the ecstasies and bilocations of Sister María Jesús de Ágreda, as well as other religious figures of her time, such as Sister María Luisa de la Ascensión, also known as the nun of Carrión. Historians have preferred to stress Ágreda's other merits: the Lady in Blue's intense life, her dedication to literature, and her wide-ranging correspondence with the leading political personages of her time, among them King Philip IV of Spain.

Among all the writings of her maturity, one has become immortal: a voluminous work in eight volumes entitled *The Mystical City of God*, which she created, as she said at the time, at the express desire of the Virgin. In it she gave an account of the life of Our Lady with such a wealth of detail that it has even in our time inspired motion pictures such as Mel Gibson's *The Passion of the Christ*. Sister María Jesús devoted seven years of her life to the book, during which time she experienced nine visions and many encounters with angels of flesh and blood. Intrigued by the stories he heard, and shortly afterward by the interrogations carried out by Friar Benavides, Philip IV wrote to the nun for the first time. The date was October 1631.

The monarch, like his predecessors, decided to confide the secrets of his soul to a highly inspired woman, whose advice was of assistance to him even in important political matters. Sister María Jesús consoled the king on various occasions, offering herself as a kind of "medium" between him and his departed wife, Isabel de Borbón, and between the king and his dead son Prince Baltasar Carlos, "destined," according to the nun, to Purgatory.

Sister María Jesús burned the original manuscript of *The Mystical City of God* in 1643, and began rewriting it in 1655. Over the course of her life she burned many other writings, especially those written during the time of her bilocations in New Mexico, with the resultant loss of precious clues to the origin of her experiences for those of us engaged in historical research. Nevertheless, some were saved, such as the text preserved in the National Library in Madrid (Manuscript No. 9354), entitled "Treatise on the Roundness of the Earth," in which she gave an account of how our planet looked to her when she was airborne.

Of all the documents that allude to her adventure, the most important is, without a doubt, the *Memorial* of Benavides. The first one, printed in 1630, is of great value, for it is the first historical text to describe the territory of New Mexico, and it is currently a required text in the state's universities.

With regard to the other actual events depicted in this novel, I should say that the government of the United States did indeed set up a laboratory at Fort Meade whose purpose was to create "psychic spies," many of whom have for years related publicly and in the first person some of their experiences working for INSCOM. Their accounts have served in large part as a basis on which I built the essential parts of this novel's intrigue, as did the studies initiated by Robert Monroe, an engineer who died in 1995, who managed to bring us an illuminating vision of the phenomenon of astral travel in his books *Journey Out of the Body*, *Far Journeys*, and *Ultimate Journey*.

The Chronovision project was also quite real. In fact, at the beginning of the 1990s, I interviewed a Benedictine priest in Venice who had participated in certain experiments whose goal was to "see," and even to "photograph" the past. That exemplary monk, an expert in pre-polyphony, was named Pellegrino Ernetti. He died in 1994. In the brief interview that I held with him at the Venetian monastery of San Giorgio Maggiore, he limited himself to telling me that Pope Pius XII classified the experiments as *riservatissimas*. It seems that the Pope believed that widespread dissemination would have changed the course of history. And Ernetti, faithful to the Pope's wishes, carried his secret to the grave.

This novel is, then, the fruit of the many different narrative threads I stumbled upon while investigating the legend of the Lady in Blue, well known today in the southwestern United States but practically unknown in Spain. And also the fruit of my obsession with the enigma of space-time "leaps" and of synchronicities. Some threads, once properly connected, allowed me to reach at least one intimate certainty: that in this universe, nothing is due to chance. Not even, reader, the fact that this book has fallen into your hands.

ACKNOWLEDGMENTS

This book is a homage to those men who, in 1629, set out to explore the inhospitable territories of New Mexico, carrying with them the most important values of the Old World. That expedition was made up of twelve soldiers, nineteen priests, and twelve laymen. Led by Friar Esteban de Perea, those adventurers of the faith are not generally known to posterity. And I would like to change that. Therefore, I believe that the moment has arrived to remember Antonio de Arteaga, Francisco de Acebedo, Cristóbal de la Concepción, Agustín de Cuellar, Roque de Figueredo, Diego de la Fuente, Martínez González, Andrés Gutiérrez, Francisco de la Madre de Dios, Tomás Manso, Francisco Muñoz, Francisco de Porras, Juan Ramírez, Bartolomé Romero, Francisco de San Buenaventura, García de San Francisco, and Diego de San Lucas. Their names figure in disparate documents and histories that no one reads. May this work provide vindication for their memory.

Of course, the creator of this book is the Lady in Blue, into whose path I fell on April 14, 1991, in the middle of the heavy snowfall referred to in these pages. I know that she, in some way, is the one who has directed my book to the wise hands of Carolyn Reidy, Judith Curr, and those of my favorite editor, Johanna Castillo, at Atria Books, and who pushed me to write novels at a time when I could only look forward to editing newspaper reports.

There are many more people behind this work. For example, Tom and Elaine Colchie, my agents in the United States, who went carefully over every page of this work and proposed ingenious solutions to difficulties into which I alone had fallen. And my principal literary agent, Antonia Kerrigan, and her team, whose enthusiasm and efforts were even more charged by the "blue force" of these pages.

Thanks to the team that also worked on *The Secret Supper*: Michael Selleck, Sue Fleming, Karen Louis-Joyce, Christine Duplessis, Kathleen Schmidt, David Brown, Nancy Clements, Gary Urda, Dina d'Alessandro, Isolde Sauer, Nancy Inglis, Amy Tannenbaum, and David Gombau.

For still others, permit me, reader, to guard their anonymity. They have been like angels for me, and everyone knows that with angels you have to let them fly in peace.

DRAMATIS PERSONAE

Historical figures play crucial roles in this work of fiction. The following are succinct biographies of the novel's central characters, in the hope that they will stimulate the curiosity of those readers who have already intuited that *The Lady in Blue* is much more than a work of fiction.

Ágreda, Sister María Jesús de (1602–1665). Her secular name was María Coronel y Arana. From an early age she possessed a mysterious, introverted, and highly intelligent personality. To more than a few of her biographers, she seemed to enjoy what was called "inspired learning," which is another way of saying that she had knowledge of subjects she had never studied.

When she was only thirteen years old, her parents transformed the family home into a convent. Her mother encouraged her to become a nun, and at sixteen she accepted her destiny. Her mystical experiences began in 1625, when she was twenty-three years old. She bilocated, levitated in front of the other nuns, and participated in many kinds of "manifestations," or supernatural phenomena; this period coincides with her mysterious evangelization in America. Shortly thereafter, when she turned twenty-five, she was chosen prioress; granted a special dispensation by the Pope, she wrote a life of the Virgin, *The Mystical City of God*, and began an intense correspondence with Philip IV, the king of Spain. Although her story remains little known, she was doubtless one of the most compelling personalities of Spain's Golden Age.

Albert, Carlos. This character was created as a way of giving the reader some idea of the incredible events that took place when I was in the process of documenting *The Lady in Blue*. He is, in some ways, my alter ego. The haphazard manner with which Carlos stumbled upon María Jesús de Ágreda's village, as depicted early in the novel, was something I experienced firsthand, and which profoundly affected me.

Baldi, Giuseppe. Although the character is fictional, he is inspired by the Benedictine priest and exorcist Pellegrino Ernetti (1925–1994), a Venetian professor of pre-polyphony. In May 1972, Ernetti gave a polemical interview to the Italian newsmagazine *Domenica del Corriere* in which he confessed to having worked on the construction of a machine, known as the Chronovisor, capable of photographing the past. I was, in fact, able to interview him at the Monastery of San Giorgio Maggiore in Venice a year before his death. What I learned in that interview inspired major portions of this novel.

Benavides, Friar Alonso de (c. 1580–1636). Born on the island of San Miguel in the Azores, he was ordained as a priest in 1598 in Mexico. In October 1623, he was placed in charge of the New Mexico region, which was at that time known as the Guardianship of Saint Paul. By the time he was relieved by Friar Esteban de Perea, around 1629, eighty thousand Indians in that region had been successfully converted. After writing his celebrated *Memorial* for Philip IV, he visited Ágreda in order to interview María Jesús and clarify her involvement in the apparitions of the Lady in Blue in America. April 30, 1631, marked the beginning of a series of encounters between the two that stretched over the course of two weeks. Friar Alonso was later appointed auxiliary bishop of Goa in what was then the Portuguese Indies, but he died during the course of the voyage to his destination.

Philip IV, king of Spain (1605–1665). María Jesús de Ágreda's bilocations took place during his reign. In July 1643, Philip himself visited the convent at the foot of the Sierra del Moncayo in Soria, and met with the Lady in Blue for the first time. Six days later the two began a correspondence that lasted until 1665. While there is no definitive proof, it was probably through the mediation of the king that the Franciscans finally identified the Lady in Blue described by the Indians of New Mexico as the nun from Ágreda. It was also on his orders that the Friar Benavides *Memorial* was printed at the Royal Printing House in Madrid, in 1630. Philip IV had a great appreciation of Sister María Jesús de Ágreda, and his letters to her reveal more about the personality of the monarch than any other document of the time.

Manso y Zúñiga, Francisco (1587–1656). The Archbishop of Mexico between 1629 and 1634, and the man who put Esteban de Perea in charge of investigating the nature of the apparitions of the Lady in Blue in New Mexico.

Marcilla, Sebastián (c. 1570–c. 1640). Reader in theology at the Convent of Saint Francis in Pamplona and provincial administrator of the order in Burgos, he was the first member of a religious order to question María Jesús de Ágreda about her "supernatural voyages" to what is now the southwestern United States. Drawing on these conversations, he wrote a letter to the Archbishop of Mexico, sometime around 1627, to inform him of her visions.

Monroe, Robert (1915–1995). An audio engineer who began to take an interest in what was called out-of-body experiences (OBE), or extracorporeal experiences, when he himself underwent an "astral split" in 1958. After discounting the various possibilities that he was suffering from a cerebral tumor, hallucinations, or an early warning of the onset of imminent mental illness, he began to take a closer look at his situation. He came to the conclusion that the experience, and others that would come later, were produced when his brain "synthesized" a particular sound frequency. In 1974 he founded the Monroe Institute, in Virginia, in order to perform his first investigations under one roof and to develop the Hemy-Sync technology, which allowed him to stimulate the brain through sound in order to provoke "astral voyages" at will.

Perea, Friar Esteban de (c. 1585–1638). Franciscan monk born in Villanueva del Fresno (Badajoz), on the border with Portugal. The son of a distinguished family, he was afforded a rapid rise in the ecclesiastical hierarchy. At the beginning of the seventeenth century he was charged with establishing the Inquisition in New Mexico, the region where he served as custodian in 1629.

Porras, Friar Francisco de (?–1633). Franciscan missionary who in August 1629 founded the San Bernardino mission in Hopi territory. On that voyage he was accompanied by the friars Andrés Gutiérrez, Cristóbal de la Concepción, and Francisco de San Buenaventura. He died on June 28, 1633, poisoned by "medicine men" at the Awatovi mission.

Salas, Friar Juan de (?–c. 1650). Franciscan missionary from Salamanca, Spain. In 1622 he founded the San Antonio Mission, in the part of New Mexico today known as Isleta. He administered the mission until the June 1629 arrival of Friar Esteban de Perea, who ordered him to undertake a journey to La Gran Quivira in order to investigate the apparitions of the Lady in Blue.

Torre, Friar Andrés de la (?–1647). From Burgos, Spain. For twenty-four years, his "great labor," as he put it, was to be Sister María Jesús de Ágreda's first confessor. Philip IV intended to make him a bishop, but he refused the privilege in order to remain in close proximity to the nun. He spent his last years at the Monastery of Saint Julian de Ágreda.

***Benavides's* Memorial** (1630) In an excerpt from the *Memorial* written by Friar Alonso de Benavides for Philip IV and published by the Royal Printing House in 1630, an account is given of his interrogation of the Lady in Blue. It is the first historical document that recognizes the surprising involvement of an "attractive young woman" in the evangelization of the Province of New Mexico.

EXCERPT FROM THE TEXT OF THE MEMOIRS OF FRIAR ALONSO DE BENAVIDES.

BENAVIDES'S MEMORIAL (1630)

An excerpt, in old Spanish, from the Memorial written by Friar Alonso de Benavides for Philip IV and published by the Royal Printing House in 1630, in which an account is given of his interrogation of the Lady in Blue. It is the first historical document that recognizes the surprising involvement of an "attractive young woman" in the evangelization of New Mexico. A translation of the text appears on pages 338 to 339.

Conuersion milagrosa de la nacion Xumana.

DExando pues toda esta parte Occidental, y saliendo de la villa de Santa Fè, centro del nueuo Mexico, que està en 37. grados, atrauesando por la nacion Apache de los Vaqueros por mas de ciento y doze leguas al Oriente, se va a dar en la nació Xumana, que por ser su conuersion tan milagrosa, es justo dezir como fue. Años atras, andando vn Religioso llamado fray Iuan de Salas, ocupado en la conuersion de los Indios Tompiras y Salineros, adonde ay las mayores salinas del mundo, que confinan por aquella parte con estos Xumanas: huuo guerra entre ellos, y boluiendo el Padre fray Iuan de Salas por los Salineros, dixeron los Xumanas, Que gente que boluia por los pobres, era buena, y assi quedaron aficionados al Padre, y le rogauan fuesse a viuir entre ellos, y cada año le venian a buscar, y como estaua tambien ocupado con los Christianos, por ser lengua, y muy buen Ministro, y no tener Religiosos bastantes, fui entreteniendo a los Xumanas, que le pedian, hasta que Dios embiasse mas obreros, como los embiò el año passado de 29. inspirando a V. Magestad, mandasse al Virrey de la Nueua-España, q̃ nos embiasse treinta Religiosos, los quales lleuò, siẽdo su Custodio el P.F. Esteuã de Perea, y assi despachamos luego al dicho Padre cõ otro compañero, q̃ es el P.F. Diego Lopez, a los quales ivan guiando los mismos Indios; y antes que fuessen, preguntãdo a los Indios, que nos dixessen la causa por que con tanto afecto nos pediã el Bautismo, y Religiosos que los fuessen a dotrinar? ✱ Respondieron, que vna muger como aquella que alli teniamos pintada (que era vn retrato de la Madre Luisa de Carrion) les predicaua a cada vno dellos en su lengua, que viniessen a llamar a los Padres, para que los enseñassen y bautizassen, y que no fuessen pereçosos; y que la muger que les predicaua, estaua vestida, ni mas, ni menos, como la que alli estaua pintada, pero q̃ el rostro no era como aquel,

sino

ſino que era moça y hermoſa: y ſiempre q̄ venian Indios de nueuo de aquellas naciones, mirando el retrato, y confiriendolo entreſi, dezian, que el veſtido era el miſmo, pero que el roſtro no, porque el de la muger que les predicaua era de moça y hermoſa.

TRANSLATION OF "THE MEMORIAL OF FRAY ALONSO DE BENAVIDES, 1630"

TRANSLATED BY MRS. EDWARD E. AYER,
CHICAGO, PRIVATELY PRINTED 1916.

MIRACULOUS CONVERSION OF THE XUMANA NATION

Leaving, then, all this western part, and going forth from the town of Santa Fe, the center of New Mexico, which is in 37 degrees north latitude, traversing the Apache nation of the Vaqueros for more than a hundred and twelve leagues to the east, one comes to hit upon the Xumana nation; which since its conversion was so miraculous, it is just to tell how it was. Years back, when a religious named Fray Juan de Salas was traveling, occupied in the conversion of the Tompiras and Salineros indians –where are the greatest salines in the world, which on that side border upon these Xumanas–, there was a war between them. And when the Father Fray Juan de Salas went back for the poor were good people; and so they became fond of the Father, and begged him that he would go to live among them. And as he was likewise occupied with the Christminister, and not having enough Religious, I kept putting off the Xumanas, who were asking for him, until God should send more laborers. As He sent them in the past year of 1629; inspiring Your Majesty to order the Viceroy of New Spain that he send us thirty Religious. Whom the Father Fray Esteban de Perea, who was their Custodian, brought. And so we immediately dispatched the said Father Salas, with another, his companion, who is the Father Fray Diego López; whom the self-named Indians went with as guides.

And before they went, we asked the Indians to tell us the reason why they were with so much concern petitioning us for baptism, and for Religious to go to indoctrinate them. They replied that a woman like that on whom we had there painted –which was a picture of the Mother Luisa de Carrión– used to preach to each one of them in their own tongue, telling them that they should come to summon the Fathers to instruct and baptize them, and that they should not to be slothful about it. And that the woman who preached to them was dressed precisely like her who was painted there; but that the face was not like that one, but that she was young and beautiful. And always whenever Indians came newly from those nations, looking upon the picture and comparing it among themselves, they said that the clothing was the same but the face was not, because the face of the woman who preached to them was that of a young and beautiful girl.

BRIEF CHRONOLOGY OF ACTUAL EVENTS

April 2, 1602. María Coronel y Arana is born in the village of Ágreda. She will pass into history with the nickname "The Lady in Blue" thanks to the mysterious evangelization of the southwestern United States. She never physically traveled outside her native village.

July 22, 1629. A group of Jumano Indians arrive at the San Antonio Mission from the interior of New Mexico to ask the Franciscans to bring the Gospel to their village. While the expedition of twenty-nine Indians rests at San Antonio, they relate how a young, mysterious Lady in Blue foretold the arrival of priests to their region. The priests accede to their requests.

July 1629, a few days later. Friars Juan de Salas and Diego López set out in the company of a band of Jumano Indians in the direction of Cueloce, a Hopi village more than 180 miles from Isleta. There they preach the Gospel and baptize the first of the tribes visited by the Lady in Blue.

August 1630. Friar Alonso de Benavides arrives in Madrid, the seat of the Spanish government under Philip IV, in order to deliver an account of his assignment as father custodian of the province of New Mexico and of the miraculous conversions he has witnessed. That same summer he begins to write his celebrated *Memorial,* which will be published by the Royal Printing House.

April 1631. Friar Benavides meets face-to-face with Sister María Jesús de Ágreda. The encounter takes places in the nun's monastery in the Spanish village of Ágreda. He becomes convinced that this nun is in fact the Lady in Blue for whom he is searching. Sister María will go so far as to give him the garment she wore when she traveled to America.

May 1631. Friar Benavides writes a letter to the Franciscan missionaries working in New Mexico, revealing what he has discovered about the Lady in Blue. His message will ultimately be printed in Mexico City, in 1730, under the unwieldy title "Everything taken from the letter that the Reverend Father Friar Alonso de Benavides, at that time Custodian of New Mexico, sent to the monks of the Holy Mission of Saint Paul in that kingdom, from Madrid, in the year 1631."

February 12, 1634. Pope Urban VIII receives a version of Benavides's *Memorial* with amplifications by the Franciscan, in which he includes the outcome of his conversations with María Jesús de Ágreda and his conclusion that she was the only person responsible for the apparitions of the Lady in Blue in America.

April 2, 1634. Rome. At the Pope's express order, Friar Alonso de Benavides delivers a new report on the apparitions of the Lady in Blue in New Mexico to the Holy Congregation for the Propagation of the Faith, also known as the Inquisition.

April 15, 1635. The Inquisition begins its interrogations of Sister María Jesús de Ágreda. The material gathered will be placed in Vatican archives without a proceeding being undertaken against the nun.

January 18, 1650. The Inquisitors Antonio González del Moral and the notary Juan Rubio arrive at the Ágreda monastery to interrogate the Lady in Blue, who is by now its abbess. Over the course of several days, the nun cooperates with the Inquisition for the second time, describing many of the mystical phenomena she had experienced during her lifetime, among them her bilocations to America. She is never condemned.

May 24, 1665. María Jesús de Ágreda dies at age sixty-three in the monastery her family had founded. After her funeral rites, her notes, letters, and manuscripts are placed in a strongbox sealed with three locks in order to assure the proper use of her legacy. The notes concerning her visits to America are not among them. She herself burned them years before, when she tried to erase her "manifestations" from her memory. With their destruction, history loses materials of incalculable scientific and cultural value.

For more information, please visit the website
www.theladyinblue.net.